THE
SECRET
CHORD

KATHRYN GUARE

THE VIRTUOSIC SPY o BOOK 2

THE
SECRET
CHORD

Within a circle of safety...
a deception that could kill

KILTUMPER
CLOSE
PRESS

Published by

KILTUMPER
CLOSE
PRESS

PO Box 1175
Montpelier, VT 05601

Copyright © 2014 Kathryn Guare
ISBN-13: 978-0-9911893-0-4
LCCN: 2013921365

Cover Design by Andrew Brown
Print Design by Chenile Keogh

Dedication

For Eleanor and Tom
who inspired the setting
and graciously let me linger in it

The house was still far from empty. Apart from a few personal items sent to hired storage, it remained intact, the fate of its contents left for others to judge. He was grateful for the illusion of permanence the furnishings offered, helping sustain the pretense that he had something left to lose.

He considered it another small mercy—one he'd not always appreciated—that they'd never been the sort of family that collected things. His mother, with her abiding air of transience, had eschewed the decorative bric-a-brac colonizing every surface of the typical Irish household. She was singular in this respect among others. Brigid McBride was the ultimate, esoteric day-tripper, fluent in the geography of dimensions most never visited. She traveled light and gathered no souvenirs.

He remembered a particular period during his boyhood when her ways had seemed unbearably eccentric to him. Once, for a Christmas gift, he'd bought a cheap ceramic bird at a school jumble sale—a goldfinch, neck stretched in song, anatomy truncated by a clunky base encasing the area where its legs ought to have been.

He presented the bauble with the half-formed hope of tickling some dormant gene, to nudge her into becoming someone more conventional, someone more like the mothers of his friends.

She made much of the gaudy little ornament, and so much of him for his thoughtfulness that he'd felt sheepish, and almost relieved when it quickly disappeared from view. A few weeks later he caught sight of the thing on her bedside table, nestled into a tiny bower of dried sage and hawthorn twigs. It should have looked hopelessly cloying and twee, but it didn't. The painted eyes gleamed in the shadows, seeming to peer straight at him, and a heady energy had passed through him. Suddenly, he was everywhere and nowhere at once, like lying on his back and staring too hard at the sky. He sensed an unseen presence sizzling the air close around him and was frightened, then somehow knew he needn't be. It was the first time he'd experienced this pulsing aura but not the last, and it was the moment when he recognized how wrong it would be to try changing his mother.

So, it wasn't for any sentimental bits of rubbish Conor mourned, wandering back and forth through the house like a greedy ghost wanting to haunt all the rooms at once. It was for the aroma of its interior, every molecule saturated in decades of peat smoke, and for the ivy on its exterior walls rustling in tune with the ocean breeze, reflecting pieces of sunlight in its polished leaves. And for the land itself, arranged in parceled acres all around him. The unconditional love for a small patch of earth—and the desire to keep and hold it no matter how rocky, desolate or unforgiving—was the immutable obsession of his people. He'd thought to escape it at one time, but the land had captured him in the end.

In the growing darkness, Conor drifted into the kitchen and registered the ice-blue glimmer of computer light leaking from the adjacent pantry-turned-office. Bending around the door he found his farm manager, Phillip Ryan, where he'd left him hours earlier. Conor opened the door a little wider.

"Jaysus, awfully late, isn't it? I didn't know you were still here."

Phillip raised his eyes from the laptop, surveying him with the jaded stare that had grown habitual over the past week. "You look half-dead. Are you all right?"

"I'm okay. Just tired."

"I brought some lunch 'round hours ago. It's in the fridge—the only feckin' thing in the fridge, in fact. Eat before you fall over, for Christ's sake."

"I'll have something later. Thanks, though." Conor smiled. "Next you'll be telling me I need a good dose of Bovril."

"Bovril's your only man for puttin' the life back into you." Phillip glanced up as though he might play along, but then gave a dismissive shrug of his broad shoulders and dropped his eyes back to the keyboard. "But, go ahead and fall over, if you'd rather."

He'd turned up in the local pub more than five years earlier, a penitent émigré looking for re-entry, happy to absorb any insult to his Americanized accent if it led to a job. At the time, Conor was grappling with his brother's disappearance and the chaos left behind for someone else to fix. He wasn't sure he even wanted a farm manager, but two weeks later he wondered how he would have survived without one. They worked well together, and their camaraderie had grown stronger over the years, a fellowship that helped him overcome the bitterness and confused anguish of his brother's desertion.

For that and so much more, he owed Phillip Ryan a great deal. Certainly, he owed him a better ending than this. In selfish moments and in the face of his friend's new aloof distrust, Conor ached for confession but couldn't risk it. His secrets were not safe for sharing. Phillip couldn't understand—nor should he be expected to—so the sacrifice of a friendship became one more penance to absorb as he went about the business of ending things.

"That's it, then." Phillip shut the laptop and got to his feet, running a hand over his wiry, rust-colored hair. "Thanks for letting me have it. I wiped it clean. Your stuff is all on the flash drive. You're flying out in the morning?"

"I am."

"Should I tell her you'll be there tomorrow, then? She wants to know."

"Oh…ehm, not tomorrow, no. Can you say about a week?"

"A week? Where are you—ah jayz, forget it." Phillip scowled. "I suppose I can tell her that."

"Thanks. What about you? Have you got something lined up, yet?"

"Yeah, they had a place open up on the ferry run over at Dunquin. Keep me going through the summer, I guess."

"Right, so." Conor paused, before adding, "For what it's worth, Pip, I hate this, too."

"I know you do. I see that much, anyway." Phillip's face softened into something approaching its old affection and he offered a parting handshake. "Look after yourself, boss. And be careful, yeah? 'Be wide', like they say. Be dog wide."

An hour before dawn, he walked to the barn one last time and stood in its doorway, staring through the shadows at the floor's rucked up layers of sawdust, waiting to see if he would weep. A breeze rumbled against the tin on the roof, sending an echo like a rolling drum into the empty space below.

Like a final farewell.

It had been his decision, and he'd needed it to happen quickly, but watching his birthright stripped almost to bedrock within a few days had torn something from him he'd never get back.

Conor turned away and headed back across the pasture, dry-eyed.

He was too damned tired to cry.

1

Hartsboro Bend, Vermont

From the south-facing window of her attic studio, Kate Fitzpatrick surveyed a landscape that usually enchanted her and blew out a sigh. Yesterday, the first grass of spring had uncurled to stretch over the long rolling meadow below her house, but now only twenty-four hours later, the new blades lay stunned, smothered under a snowfall coating them like a layer of rock salt. She sensed their shock and disappointment as keenly as her own.

In the distance, the bowl-shaped surface of Lake Rembrandt was colorless, its thinning crust of blue ice again obscured by a winter that had long ago outworn its welcome.

Kate tossed her brush into a canning jar where it clattered against the others. A full complement of paint-free artist brushes. Stopping herself from sighing again, she gathered up the dark copper hair that fell around her face and let it drop behind her shoulders. A shadow caught the corner of her eye and she turned to the front window, which faced a dirt road that was falling short of even the lowest expectations for its Class 3 status. Already pot-holed by the sweep of winter plows, the road had thawed, rutted into impressively deep furrows ... and then had frozen again.

Jared Percy was on its opposite side, head down and slump-shouldered, lumbering up the steep driveway toward the barn.

After a full day's work on his own property the young farmer was on his way to milk her sixteen cows.

"I should go help him." Kate noted a habitual surge of guilt and indecision as soon as the words left her mouth. She tracked his weary progress to the top of the hill before turning back to her easel, but the room had grown cold and the blank canvas confronted her like an accusation. Surrendering, she crossed the floor at a trot, pulled the door shut on the ascetic chill of the artist's garret, and fled down to the more hospitable domain of the innkeeper.

The temperature rose as she descended to the first floor but Kate's mood remained low. The Rembrandt Inn was just starting the second month of its annual two-month closure, and an inn on hiatus projected a forlorn emptiness that didn't exist in one simply waiting for its next guests. She went looking for comfort in the kitchen and found while she'd been moping, her chef—with sleeves rolled up under a blue tartan jumper—had been making more productive use of the day.

Abigail Perini had transferred the entire contents of the spice cupboard to the stainless steel prep counter and was scouring the shelves as though they'd never been washed before. She turned at Kate's entrance, her plump face warm and red, and pushed aside the graying brown hair escaping from an improvised bun.

"You're in a mood," she observed and went back to her shelves, transparently confident in her analysis. "Have you been painting?"

"By which you mean 'not' painting. No, I didn't really try today. It isn't that. It's the weather."

Her chef responded with a guttural croak that conveyed a wealth of meaning, and Kate glared at her broad sturdy back. "A 'harrumph?' Why a 'harrumph?' You don't think I can be in an ugly mood about the weather?"

Abigail glanced back, offering a peacemaking smile. "Ugly

moods are few and far between where you're concerned, sweetie. I'd say you're entitled to one. Anyway, cheer up. Supposed to hit sixty tomorrow and then rain like hell later this week. Have you got a check ready for Jared? I just saw him on his way to the barn."

"I saw him, too. Maybe I should take over again for a few weeks."

"Take over the milking?" Abigail dropped the sponge on the shelf and turned, hands on hips. "You tend not to enjoy that Kate, and the cows know as much. Makes them nervous, and as I'm sure you recall—"

"Makes them want to kick me. Yes, I remember." Kate absently stroked her left forearm, fractured by one such kick six months earlier. "I feel guilty for not helping more. I could give Jared a break, at least. He'd probably appreciate some time off."

"I think what he appreciates is the extra money, and I think he likes helping you."

Kate slid on to a kitchen stool. "Sure. The lonely widow Fitzpatrick and her crazy hillside dairy farm. Everyone wants to help. It's like a Disney film."

"Lord, you *are* in a mood." Abigail rolled her eyes. "When is the Irish fellow going to turn up, anyway? He's supposed to be a farmer. Couldn't he—" She paused as Kate sprang up, grabbing the stool before it toppled to the floor. "What the hell's the matter now?"

"I'd forgotten about him, and I haven't looked at my email for days. What if I was supposed to pick him up somewhere?"

Hurrying to her office behind the registration desk, Kate sat at the computer and scanned her messages. Nothing. She sank against the chair, relief turning to annoyance. When *was* the Irish fellow going to turn up? It was a bit rude to keep her guessing. If he was coming at all.

The request had been odd enough, but the source of it—

her late husband's Irish cousin—had been the greater surprise. Her attitude about Phillip Ryan had always remained ambivalent. God knows she could never repay what he'd done for her, but gratitude had not come quickly or easily, and even now it was layered with a vague hesitation.

Her husband had died. A horrible accident and not Phillip's fault, but in her grief it had been easy to blame him, to hold him responsible for the worst day of her life. Upon receiving the first of his annual Christmas cards five years ago she'd thrown the envelope away unopened, unable to separate the man from the memories he evoked.

She'd come a long way since then. Now, she could prop his ubiquitous seasonal greeting on the mantelpiece without a second thought and send back one of her own, and remember him with a bittersweet gratitude. Still, when his name had appeared in her inbox, a twinge of reluctance made her hesitate before reading the message.

Kate began thumbing up the piles of clutter on her desk like a botanist searching under rocks, and eventually found the printed copy of Phillip's note and their follow-up communications. He'd seemed to anticipate her guarded reaction in his very first line:

Dear Kate,

I hope you're well. No doubt it strikes as something odd to hear from me outside of the Christmas season. The fact is I'm writing about a lodger I'd like to send your way. He'll be a paying one of course, but might be looking for an extended stay, if you allow such a thing.

His name is Conor McBride, and I've been working as his farm manager for a good few years. For various reasons—his mother's recent death and some personal issues—he's sold his land and is leaving Ireland for America.

In your last holiday card (thanks for that, by the way), you mentioned no end of trouble keeping managers engaged at your place. Conor's experience might be useful to you there. He's a good farmer, though he's maybe not fit for work straight away. He was nearly killed with pneumonia a month ago and he's still a bit shook. A dose of your mountain air would set him right, I'm thinking.

Kate, please will you let me know as soon as you can if you've the space, and the inclination, to board him for a while.

Kind Regards,
Phillip

Kate's eyes skimmed over her acceptance and request for arrival details, and Phillip's apologetic reply.

Sorry not to be able to give more exact information. He says he'll arrive in about a week.

That had been a week ago. Kate was still frowning impatiently at the print-out when she heard a heavy footstep on the porch, and then the doorbell.

"Come in out of the cold, Jared." She rooted around the clutter in a fresh search, this time for the check she'd written earlier. The front door opened a crack.

"Afternoon." Jared's low voice came through the opening. The lazy cadence of his Vermont drawl always made him sound like he was just up from a nap, but he was one of the hardest working young men she knew. "I'm okay out here, Kate. I'm pretty muddy and it ain't that cold, so—."

"Oh, who cares? I'll be washing all the floors down here, anyway. What's a little more mud?"

Kate came from her office, smiling at the disembodied bearded face peeking around the door. With a bashful grin, Jared's eyes dropped to the floor and he shuffled inside.

"We haven't seen you for breakfast, lately. Abigail misses cooking for you."

"I been missin' it, too." Jared sighed. "Been kinda crazy up the house, with Dad and all."

"Oh, his knee surgery! I'd forgotten." Again, guilt poked a

sharp finger into her chest. "How is he?"

"Doin' okay. Ornery as hell, so I guess that's good. He had fifty bucks on the ice-out contest. His last pick went by yesterday, so now he's pissed about that, too."

Kate laughed. "I only put down ten but I nearly cried myself when I saw the lake this morning."

"What date is your last pick?" Jared's eyes darted to her face and tailed away again.

"Today. Like, now."

"Shit."

They both laughed.

"Well, there you go." Jared summed up the injustice with equanimity. He swept a hand through his mop-headed tangle of brown curls. "I better get back."

Kate executed a quick maneuver to tuck the weekly check into his pocket. He was expecting it of course, but could acknowledge it only with a soft grunt and duck of his head. Holding the door as he left, her eye wandered to the corner of the hallway.

"Oh, wait a minute, Jared. Can you hang this back up for me on your way down?"

She lifted the wooden sign and gave it a final inspection. *Rembrandt Inn, Hartsboro Bend, Vermont.* Here at least, was an artistic project she'd finished without paralyzing seizures of self-doubt. She re-painted the sign every year and its installation ordinarily signaled they were accepting guests.

Jared's sleepy eyes widened. "You open already? Thought you stayed closed until May."

"We do, but I'm taking on a long-term guest, and it sounds ridiculous but I don't know when he's getting here, or how, or if he's still coming. I want to be sure he knows the place when he sees it. If he sees it. God almighty, why did I get myself involved in this? Just hang the sign. If he hasn't shown by the time the ice goes out, I'll take it down again."

"Unless the ice don't go out 'til May." Jared chuckled.

"Not even funny, Jared." Kate reproached him with a teasing scowl. Not the least bit funny."

2

Like a cobra striking at its prey, she stabbed the brush down into a glistening dot of color and then hesitated, the instrument rigid in her grasp. She'd layered the canvas with a fresh coat of gesso to seal the hairline cracks that had appeared since the last application, and Kate stood now with eyes closed, breathing in the soft oily smell from her palette, filled with the anticipation of beginning.

The problem was it could only be called "beginning" if something followed. In an all-too-familiar pattern, hesitation lengthened into paralysis, anticipation faded to anxiety, and "beginning" became inertia.

"Maybe I should try watercolors instead." Kate let the palette drop to the floor with an echoing slap.

Watercolors wouldn't work, either. The medium wasn't the problem. Once, she'd been able to move easily from oils to watercolor to ink sketches, and the connection between her mind and the hand holding the brush was like one long elastic synapse, tingling with precise obedience. She always knew where the next stroke would go, knew how it would look carrying the paint over the canvas. Her hand was as steady and reliable as her life, until a day almost six years ago when it wasn't anymore. Since then, the empty canvas had been a metaphor for everything she'd lost. Except for re-applications of primer she could never bring herself to make a mark on it, could hardly bear to rest the bristles of a perfectly dry brush against its blank surface.

Above her, the room's track lights flickered and the darkness beyond the windows abruptly stuttered with blue-white light. A roll of thunder followed and Kate's mood brightened. She loved a good thunderstorm.

She moved down the hall to the living room of her third-floor apartment. Its large picture window provided a view of the lake and the road on her left, as well as the trout brook running along the bottom of a gorge on the right, which served as the property's western border.

The fat drops pelting the window were already multiplying as she settled on the sofa, and a minute later the rain was beating down in wind-driven sheets, filling the potholes in the dirt road and adding greater volume to the seasonal flood of the brook.

Cozy and snug, Kate's eyes drooped as she gazed at the storm, but opened wider when a figure appeared on the road—a man, head tucked down against the downpour, carrying a large duffel bag in one hand and an oddly shaped case on his opposite shoulder. He turned up the driveway, briefly illuminated in the pool of light from the roadside sign, and she sat up, bemused and staring.

"Oh, come on. Are you kidding me?"

She hurried downstairs and as he reached the front steps Kate opened the door, leaving the chain lock secured. "Lousy night for a walk," she remarked through the opening.

He stopped short at the sound of her voice—and of the chain drawing tight against the wood—and darted a rueful glance down at his clothes. "I couldn't agree more, but it seemed a good idea at the time. I'm sorry to be getting here so late. Should I come back in the morning, maybe?"

"That's remarkably polite. If I said 'yes', where would you go?"

"Hmm. Good question."

With a laugh, she snapped on the porch light and swung the door open. "I think you'd better come inside. From the accent I assume you are the long-awaited Conor McBride."

"I am." He blinked at her in the sudden wash of light, looking startled.

"I'm Kate Fitzpatrick." Opening the door wider she tilted an eyebrow at him. "Welcome to the Rembrandt Inn?"

"Sorry." He stepped forward to take the hand she offered. "Pleasure to meet you, Kate." He swept his hair—jet-black and dripping wet—away from his forehead, revealing straight dark eyebrows and a pair of deep brown eyes. He examined the area around his feet. "I'm flooding the hallway, I'm afraid."

"Doesn't matter. The floor is still due to be washed. Procrastination is my specialty. I'd nearly given up on you. Phillip thought you'd get here three days ago. The ice went out at eight this morning but I decided to leave the sign up anyway."

"The ice ... *went out?*" Conor regarded her blankly.

"Local expression." She closed the door on a deafening crash of thunder. "Every year we have an 'ice out' contest. A concrete block is tied to a clock on the lake and people take bets on the date and time when it will fall through."

"Right. I see."

He didn't of course, but it seemed too complicated to explain why she'd come to connect him with the habits of ice on the lake.

"You must have flown into Burlington? How did you get here?"

"Ah, bit of a story, there," Conor said. "Poor planning. I'd no clue Vermont was so short on bus routes. I rode one from Burlington and got as far as Montpelier, then I ended up at the Coffee Corner having a cup of tea and a chat about what to do next. Somebody mentioned your state senator lives nearby, so they rang to find out was he in town, and please could he give this gack of an Irishman a lift."

"You got a ride from Bob Franklin?" Kate grinned. "I'll bet he talked your ear off."

"He did have some things on his mind. I've learned a lot my first day. He stopped at the village store down the road and I was a bit stir crazy, so I decided to walk the last few miles."

"And now, here you are."

His lips twitched into an ironic smile. "Right. Here I am."

Kate had grown mesmerized by the Irish brogue. His voice was deep and quietly resonant, but held a note of splintered hoarseness. When he ducked his head away to clear his throat she snapped back to attention.

"Now *I'm* talking your ear off and you're standing here soaked to the bone. Let's get you upstairs."

She'd decided to put him in one of the spare bedrooms on the third floor. Asking how long he intended to stay seemed inhospitable, but housing a long-term boarder in a regular guest room gave her less flexibility. The large attic room at the far end of her apartment was an emergency spare, with its own small hallway to provide enough privacy for both of them. The downpour continued pounding above their heads as she inserted the key, and once inside the room a muffled crash of water sounded outside the window. Conor threw her a quizzical glance.

"Do the lifeboats cost extra?"

Kate laughed. "A trout brook runs next to the house on this side and empties into the lake. It'll roar on for another week while the snowmelt comes off the hills. I'll give you the tour in the morning."

She placed the key on the bedside table and turned on the lamp. The bed was an antique four-poster, and on the opposite wall a marble mantle with brass sconces framed a fireplace. In front of it a matching set of armchairs and a low glass table sat on a braided rug, completing the picture of a comfortable attic hideaway.

Conor dropped his soggy duffel to the floor as though glad to be rid of the weight, but was gentler with the bag on his shoulder, which Kate realized was a soft-sided violin case. He set it down on the window seat next to the bed, and while he was stripping off his wet jacket and peering down at the brook she took the opportunity to examine him more closely.

He stood several inches taller than her—a little over six feet, she estimated. Although disheveled and in need of a bath and a shave, nothing could disguise the essential fact: the man was exceptionally good looking. Kate somehow hadn't expected that, but thought it a nice reward for her generosity toward Phillip Ryan.

He also appeared painfully thin and exhausted. In the midst of a yawn Conor turned and caught her staring at him. He closed his mouth, cleared his throat again and sat down on the window seat with a grunt.

"Sorry. Sort of a long day."

"Of course. My exit cue." Kate hesitated, concerned by his wan appearance. "Can I bring you something to eat? Or at least some hot tea? It sounds like your voice is going and I don't want you getting pneumonia again on the first night." A flush warmed her cheeks as Conor stiffened, his face sobering into watchfulness. "I apologize. I shouldn't make light of your illness."

"No, don't worry." He flashed a cautious smile. "I didn't know Phillip told you. I'm fine, though. My voice just always sounds like it's going." He pulled at the t-shirt under his V-necked sweater, revealing a scar below his Adam's apple, about the length of Kate's little finger. "Emergency surgery. Kept me from suffocating so I can't really complain, but the old vocal cords got a good scrape."

Fascinated, Kate tried not to stare. "Does it hurt?"

Conor inclined his head, appearing curious as well. "Funny how everyone asks that. No, it doesn't hurt." After a short silence he added, "I'm not hungry but I'd love a cup of tea, and I could do with a shower."

Kate gave him some time to shower and get settled before returning with the tea tray. She knocked on the door he'd left ajar, catching a whiff of shaving cream and sandalwood soap as she entered. Without its layer of dark stubble Conor's face looked even more pale and tired. He'd changed into a black t-shirt and jeans, and was studying the fireplace with a thoughtful expression. She lowered the tray, which connected sharply with the glass table. He jumped at the rattle of china and teaspoons.

"Sorry about that." Kate straightened. "The fireplace works, and we've got more wood if you feel like dragging it up the stairs. Now, I'll get out of here and let you get some rest. Leave everything outside after you're finished and I'll pick it up in the morning. I'm at the end of the hall if you need anything." She had a hand on the doorknob when Conor called her back with a question.

"What else did Phillip tell you? About me, I mean."

"Not nearly enough." She grinned, but then remembering, grew serious. "He said your mother died recently. I'm sorry."

He frowned and colored slightly. "Thank you."

"And that you'd sold your property in Ireland."

"Uh-huh. Anything else? I didn't know you had such a long chat about me."

"We didn't chat," Kate said coolly. The conversation was beginning to feel like an interrogation. "We corresponded by email. I still have the messages if you want to read them."

Seeing her irritation, he dropped his head. "No, of course not. I was only curious."

Kate relented, smiling, but before closing the door stuck her face back into the room. "While we're on the subject I should be asking what Phillip told you about *me*. I guess I can wait until morning."

The door closed with a soft click, and Conor stared at it for several seconds before turning away.

"How about—'she's deadly feckin' gorgeous'—Phillip might have told me that about you but he didn't, thanks very much."

He returned to the window seat and unzipped the insulated violin case, removing the suede-covered version inside. Then, as though unpacking a set of nesting dolls, he opened the second case to lift out the violin itself. After confirming the instrument had survived the trip uninjured he put it back, fingers brushing over the scroll in shy apology. The last time he'd played had been while standing in a field behind his farmhouse, offering up a traditional air for his mother on the last day he'd seen her alive. That was less than a year ago, and he'd been an entirely different person. What kind of sound would his hands draw from the strings now, after the things they'd done?

Setting the violin aside, Conor took a pocketknife from the duffel bag and reached again for the insulated case. He sliced along the seam near the bottom, and with two fingers dug inside to retrieve first, a pristine Irish passport, and then a U.S. permanent residence visa—a "green card." Tossing both on the window seat he bent to the travel-stained khakis he'd dropped on the floor. From the back pocket he took another Irish passport, this one stippled with airport security stickers and still damp.

He thumbed through the pages, remembering the carefully disguised fear he'd experienced each time he presented it—in Cardiff, Stuttgart and Belgrade among others, and finally on the US-Canadian border. For the past ten days, his circuitous route and modes of transport had not really been poor planning but a combination of meticulous technique and dumb luck.

At the fireplace, he marveled at this further instance of good fortune. He quickly assembled paper and kindling, and put a flame to the pile with a long-handled lighter he took from the mantelpiece. Once the fire was burning high and hot, he cast a final glance at his photo and tossed the passport into the flames. It ignited in a burst of light and the cover writhed and curled like a living thing as it melted.

"Good night, F. James Doyle," he whispered. "Rest in peace."

Maybe he was foolish to risk using his real name in this new life, but watching his globetrotting alias shrivel into cinders, his spirits rose. It felt good to be Conor McBride again.

Backing away from the fireplace he dropped wearily into an armchair and reached for the teapot, still hot under its leaf-patterned cozy. He drank off two cups and tried to ignore the craving for a smoke—a habit recently surrendered—then leaned back against the chair and promptly fell asleep.

It begins with a boy offering flowers, and he's always a stranger.

When he's awake he wonders why he doesn't recognize him, why his sleeping mind can't retain the knowledge of who he is and how the scene ends—but he never remembers. He greets the boy as though seeing him for the first time. A Hindu child. Thin, stunted, dressed raggedly, smiling up at him with a flash of white teeth, cupping a cluster of marigolds in two small hands.

Don't take the flowers, dammit.

Why not?

You know why ...

In a featureless void, the boy beams at him. He smiles in return, reaches to pick out one of the dark orange blossoms ...

Now the child disappears, and he is standing in a darkened flat. The one he rented in Dublin. The one Thomas helped him move into on a Saturday afternoon, when everything on the truck was wrapped in plastic because of the bucketing rain. His brother is gone. The flat is empty.

He stands in the living room holding a Walther semiautomatic pistol in one hand. He's sweating, shivering, and somebody is pounding on the door.

"Conor, open the door, now. There's someone wants to see you."

"Is it Frank? Tell him I won't go."

"God love you, it isn't Frank."

The door swings open and his mother stands there with the boy, her hand on his shoulder.

The small, cupped hands are lifting again and he finally recognizes him—but too late. The snow-covered pine trees in the background come into focus, the forest explodes, and the gun grows hot in his hand.

Conor bolted to his feet, heart rate still accelerating as he forced himself down to the edge of the chair, sweeping the room with a disoriented stare. He hadn't yelled this time. At least, he didn't think so. Holding his breath he listened, and exhaled. No, he probably hadn't yelled. He looked over at the clock on the bedside table and groaned. Wide-awake and wired like a watch spring at two in the morning. He rubbed a hand over his chin and squeezed his eyes shut. God, he wanted a cigarette.

3

Morning arrived with a freshly washed quality; the dew could almost be wrung from the air and sipped. Vaporous bundles of fog crouched on the pastures, and a breeze stirring the curtains of Kate's bedroom brought in the loamy smell of softening earth and everything that had crumbled into it the previous fall. She breathed in the aroma with a shiver of pleasure. Spring's grip was established and strengthening daily.

She went to the hallway of the guest bedroom and stopped short as she rounded the corner. Empty. No tea tray left outside for her. Annoyed, Kate considered giving a sharp, housekeeper's rap on Conor's door before shrugging off the irritation and heading downstairs. An aroma of coffee and warm cinnamon wafted up the staircase along with the sound of voices from the kitchen.

"Careful now, don't drip on the edges. It bakes on like concrete. Nice and—whoa! Too full."

"Are you sure you want me doing this?"

"You're managing fine, and if a little work scares you, stay in the dining room and don't be poking around back here."

"I'll try to remember that."

Kate swung through the door to find Conor standing at the stainless steel prep counter, pouring batter into muffin tins. A completed batch sat in a basket on the marble-topped island in the center of the kitchen, and with a pinch of remorse she noted the teapot and mug she'd delivered to his room were drying in the dish drainer.

"New trend, Abigail? Make the guests cook their own breakfast?"

As the clatter of the tea tray had startled Conor the previous evening, her abrupt entrance prompted a nervous, involuntary jerk in his shoulders, sending a splash of batter across the counter. Abigail spun to face Kate, smirking.

"Fine, very funny, but you should have warned him. Anyone lurking in my kitchen is fair game. I found him prowling around the cupboards when I got here this morning."

"Prowling." A muscle moved in Conor's jaw, but his face was unreadable. "I was only looking for the dish soap."

As he wiped up the spill Kate tried to judge the effect of this first, unfiltered dose of Abigail Perini. People exhibited varying reactions to her theatrical chef. Correctly anticipating when to laugh and when to apologize was a skill she'd sharpened out of vital necessity. "I hope you at least got some breakfast before she put you to work?"

"Breakfast!" Abigail bellowed cheerfully. "I should say he's had breakfast! Sausage, eggs, three rounds of toast and a big pot of tea. We'll go broke trying to keep this one fed."

"Abigail," Kate pleaded.

"I'll admit he needed some persuasion to get beyond the tea, but eventually he found his appetite."

"I don't think I'd much of a choice." Head lowered, Conor was again focused on the flow of batter into the muffin tins. Kate raised an inquisitive eyebrow at Abigail, who responded with a wink.

"I'm going down to inspect what's left of the pickles. You're in charge." The kitchen door swung on its hinges as she exited and Conor gave a low whistle.

"Here endeth the lesson."

Kate tossed up her hands. "I'm sorry, but there's nothing I can do. She came with the place when I bought it."

"Like a poltergeist?"

"Exactly." She was relieved to see a grin steal over his face. "Actually, I wish I had half as much energy as she does. We have a sous-chef who covers breakfast when the inn is open, a young Somalian man who just graduated from the culinary school, but most mornings Abigail shows up anyway. Her husband, Dominic, is our dining room manager. He'd never get a hot meal if he didn't work here. She's right, I should have warned you, and honestly Conor, you don't have to finish those."

He was lifting the muffin tins with careful concentration. "Oh, I think I do. It's as much as my life is worth getting off on the right foot with that one."

Maneuvering around the prep counter he darted a wary glance at the rack hanging above him. Like a deranged wind chime it was ornamented with whisks, ladles and other obscure tools Kate couldn't even identify. This was the central hub of Abigail's kitchen and she suffered few amateurs in her domain. Kate had to smile, watching Conor gingerly slide the tins into the oven. He clearly was off on the right foot already.

When he returned, he slid the basket of muffins in front of her and pulled forward a stool, inviting her to sit. "Cinnamon chip. She says they're your favorite."

"You could have a future in this business. You've got a flair for hospitality."

"It's genetic. Now ... coffee?"

"Oh all right, cut it out. This is my job. Here, sit down."

She went for the coffee pot and Conor sat on the stool, his reserve softened by a hint of laughter. Kate glanced at his profile as she poured. If anything, he was even better looking in the full light of day. His dark eyes were gleaming but still shadowed in fatigue. She took a seat across from him.

"I guess you didn't sleep well?" He shot her an alert questioning glance and Kate shrugged. "Seems like you'd been up for a while when Abigail discovered you 'prowling.' Jet lag?"

He plucked a muffin from the basket. "Maybe, but I'm quite an early riser, anyway. I've been a farmer most of my life."

"And a good one, I hear." Kate watched him over the rim of her mug. "I hesitate to say so, but Phillip told me as much."

Conor winced, lowering the muffin from his mouth. "Sorry. I was too knackered last night to be sensible. You've a right to expect some details about me."

"So, you're going to share a few?"

"Fire away. What do you want to know?"

"That's up to you." Kate pushed back, feeling his eyes follow her as she went to the refrigerator and returned with a ceramic jar of fresh butter. "Listen, respect for privacy is the hallmark of a good Vermonter and a good host." She took a knife from a drawer under the counter. "I try to be both, even though I'll never be recognized as a 'real' Vermonter. I'm a city transplant."

"Which city?" Conor asked.

"New York, born and raised, mostly by my grandmother. My mother died when I was six months old and my father traveled a lot. And married a lot," Kate added with a wry smile.

"Big family?"

She nodded. "Four brothers, one sister. I'm the baby and they find me hopelessly bohemian. Compared to them, I guess I am. I see what you did there, by the way. Are we back to me, now?"

Smiling, he dropped his gaze and studied his hands. "You're good at this. Okay, then. Dingle Peninsula, born and raised. Do you know it?"

Kate shook her head, taking her seat again.

"Well, some say the map of Ireland looks like a sleeping bear cub, its back toward England and its paws facing the Atlantic. The Dingle peninsula is the little claw on its right foot, on the southwest coast. Our dairy farm sits above Ventry Bay, which is shaped a bit like your lake here but a lot bigger, and with the open ocean at one end."

For several minutes Conor seemed to lose himself in the description of his home and its surroundings—its geography, the views from the upper pastures, the day-to-day operations and the layout of the farm. Captivated by the poetic lilt of his words Kate could have listened for hours, and was disappointed when he stopped with a self-conscious frown.

"More than you wanted to know, I suppose."

"Not true. It sounds beautiful."

"It was. Well, still is, sure. Anyway, that's where I grew up."

"You're going to miss it," Kate said gently.

Conor gave a humorless laugh. "I do already. Funny, since at one time I wanted nothing to do with the place. I never wanted to be a farmer. I went off to the Dublin Conservatory of Music when I was seventeen and left my brother Thomas to run the farm, but I ended up back home in the end."

"And was your family a big one?"

"No, not big at all and I'm the last. I had just the one brother. He's dead."

Conor took a long sip from his mug, giving her a weary look of appeal. Kate swallowed the reflexive follow-up question and reached for a muffin.

"I made the butter myself. What do you think?"

Since Conor had already explored the public rooms on his own—the gift shop near the front door; the living room with its fireplace, Persian rugs and baby grand piano; and the narrow, book-lined library next to the dining room—they began Kate's promised tour with a walk around the grounds. From the screened porch they went out through the perennial garden and down a staircase of widely spaced rocks in the hillside. The stairs ended in a wide grassy plateau running next to the brook, about forty feet below the house. On the opposite bank a tree-covered hill rose from the water line, and further upstream the opening between the two banks narrowed, creating a rock-strewn gorge which could be seen to spectacular effect from above.

"The last farm manager I had started this project," Kate said as they descended to the brook. "He left, so I tackled the job myself."

"Did you?" Conor surveyed the line of boulders embedded in the hill and Kate followed his gaze.

"They don't match, do they? I dragged them over here in a cart and I couldn't manage anything bigger."

The wind picked up as they walked along the bank downstream and crossed back over the meadow toward the road.

"This will need to be mowed soon." She gestured at the grass while trying to grab at the ribbons of hair whipping around her face. "I should get the tractor ready."

Fishing in her pockets she brought out a barrette that sprang open and flew from her fingers, landing next to Conor's boot. He picked it up and brushed away a piece of grass before handing it back. His face was so expressionless Kate wondered if she was tiring him out, or maybe boring him.

"You do the mowing as well? With a tractor?" Not waiting for a reply, Conor squatted down to insert a jackknife into the dirt and she bit at the inside of her lip, her concern erased by irritation. Whenever she hinted at any skill with some piece of machinery the skepticism she encountered aggravated her to the point of belligerence.

"I'm actually pretty good with the tractor." Kate heard the sharp edge in her voice, but he was rubbing a bit of soil between his fingers, oblivious. "I'm good with a tedder, too. I've even taken a few turns with a gas-powered posthole digger. I suppose you find that hard to believe? Everyone does, until they see me doing it."

"I find it hard to believe you're not dead on your feet," Conor said absently, then squinted up at her. "That was meant as a compliment. How do you stay busy when you're not making butter, hauling rocks and mowing fields? Oh, right. You manage an inn with a five-star restaurant. It's brilliant, the way you keep everything going. I can't imagine the effort."

"Oh. Well ... thanks." In confusion, Kate fiddled with the buttons of her coat. "How did you know it was a five-star restaurant?"

"I read the brochure in my room." Conor pocketed the jackknife as he rose. His face remained bland, but a tremor shivered along his cheek. "Will we have a peek at your cows, now?"

They crossed the road and climbed up to the barn. The enormous structure, built in the early 1900s, featured a stately ventilator cupola topped by an antique weathervane. A guest had once informed Kate the artifact might be worth more than the barn, the land it sat on, and the cows inside.

They picked their way through the softening mud to the barn's sliding door and Kate's spirits abruptly sank. She'd hoped this quiet stranger would be the answer to a prayer but as she heaved on the door and heard it squeal along its rusty track she realized how unappealing the entire operation probably appeared to him.

On the strength of Abigail's reputation in culinary circles the inn and restaurant had turned a profit for the last three years, but the dairy business was a perennial money pit. The farm survived on her regular personal investments and the sporadic contributions of managers who never lasted more than a season. She couldn't rely on Jared Percy much longer, and doubted a man who'd already told her he didn't want to be a farmer would find anything in the barn to entice him. She followed Conor inside, where he'd pulled up short.

"Huh. Wasn't expecting that." Arms crossed, he stared at the large corral on their left. Its design was "bedded pack," a gated rectangular space that allowed the cows to roam freely rather than being confined to stalls. "What's under the sawdust?"

"About eighteen inches of dirt on top of concrete," Kate said.

He released a low hiss. "Bloody hell. That was a job for somebody. Is this all of them?"

"The whole gang. We're milking sixteen right now, and two are getting ready to calve."

"No bulls?"

"Only the kind in a syringe." Kate's smile faltered. "And no milking parlor. They go through the gate into the tie stall section to be milked."

Conor was a step ahead of her, heading for the tie-stall area. He peered up at the ceiling and down the aisle at a small tank at the end. "A dumping station? I haven't seen one in years. You've no central milk line either, then?"

"I'm afraid not."

The rudimentary methods in place at her farm were only a few steps beyond milking by hand. Heavy portable bucket milkers were emptied into a "dumping station," a cylinder on wheels with a long hose attached to vacuum the milk into a cooling tank. Kate was no expert, but it didn't take a genius to see this was one of the reasons she had such trouble holding on to farm managers.

"It's not very efficient I guess, and a lot more work."

"A little harder on the knees and the back I suppose." Conor strolled down the aisle, giving her a reassuring wink. "But, sure it's only sixteen cows."

"How many cows did you milk?" she asked.

"About seventy-five."

Gently nudging a cow from the gate, he slipped into the pack area. Watching him, Kate felt a twinge of renewed hope. For the first time his guarded diffidence had dropped away and Conor seemed at ease, almost lighthearted. He approached one of the cows and gave her a scratch behind the ears, then crouched beside her. With a light groan, Kate saw this was the cow that had kicked her the previous summer. He probed an area around the front leg.

"Is she hurt?" She reluctantly moved closer.

"A cut just above her shank, not too bad. Have you got some disinfectant?"

She found the medical kit in the milk room but stopped outside the gate, fumbling awkwardly in trying to hand it over to him. Without comment, Conor came to take the box from her. He cleaned and bandaged the wound and then slowly circled the animal, looking for further signs of injury. Finally, he stopped with his arms resting on the cow's back and looked at Kate.

"Are you frightened of them?"

An unexpected emotion shuddered through her, dreary resignation tinged with shame. "Not really—at least, I didn't used to be. I'm not sure what happened. All of a sudden I seemed to make them nervous, and this one broke my arm with one good kick. I'm afraid they don't like me."

"That's hard to believe." Conor smiled. "But maybe they're afraid you don't like them."

"Oh, well." Kate gave a shaky laugh. "I never wanted to be a farmer either, you know. That was Michael's department."

He nodded, serious again. "Your husband."

"Yes. He died almost six years ago."

"I'm sorry."

"Yes."

With a startled horror, Kate realized she was going to cry.

4

It happened so quickly Conor had to stare to make sure he wasn't mistaken. One minute she'd been laughing and the next she was in tears. He swatted the pockets of his jeans uselessly. His old-fashioned brother would never have been caught without a handkerchief. Thomas had always insisted they served as an invaluable crutch when faced with weeping women, while Conor needled that since he wasn't in the habit of making women cry he didn't need them.

"Fuck." The oath slipped out on an exhaled sigh. "Kate, are you all right, there? Should we ... would you like to get some fresh air? Maybe?"

They emerged from the dimness of the barn into bright sunshine, and he followed her to a picnic bench placed along a tree line separating the pasture from an adjoining hay field. Kate sat down heavily. Loose in every joint, the seat skewed dangerously sideways and he braced a hand on the edge before lowering himself with more caution.

Kate had already composed herself, but the changing shade of her eyes—a sort of aquamarine in full sunlight—presented a different kind of distraction, one Conor could neutralize only by rationing his glimpses at them, like a man sipping at something he knows is too strong for him.

"That was ... weird." She sounded calm and puzzled. After considering a number of responses, he decided to risk none of them.

"I'm not usually like this." She dropped her chin to her chest. "What an idiotic thing to say. "

"It's not idiotic." Conor was grateful to offer a comment that couldn't be misconstrued.

"Have you ever been married?" she asked.

"No. I got engaged once, years ago. Didn't work out. She thought she could do better and I'm sure she was right."

"That's very gallant." She smiled and bent her head, picking at the cracked edge of the bench. "You probably think I hate those cows. I don't, but I can't say I love them, either. He seemed to, though. We found the inn on our honeymoon. How could a painter resist a name like Rembrandt, right?"

"Was he an artist?" Conor asked.

"No, I am ... was. Am." Her brow puckered. "Michael grew up on a farm in Newfoundland, but he had a falling out with his family and ended up in New York. He had a job selling software systems to restaurants and bars—high tech cash registers, basically. He still liked to call himself a 'simple Newfie farmer.' I met him at a cocktail party my father hosted at La Grenouille. He wasn't an invited guest. He'd come to train the bartender, then he crashed the party to meet me." A private smile touched her lips and quickly disappeared. "Anyway. We came back here for our first anniversary and found out the place was for sale. Eventually, we made an offer and they accepted."

Kate stopped. The sun continued climbing and a bead of perspiration trickled down Conor's back. He removed his jacket and laid it between them. After a moment she reached down to pluck one of the early dandelions dotting the pasture like pinpricks of sunlight.

"A week after his memorial service I went ahead with the closing. We'd already made the arrangements. My family called me crazy, but that's nothing new. I headed up here with a couple of suitcases. Good thing I had them because the rest of my stuff got lost. The moving van never showed up. Ever. Talk about a clean slate. But I don't regret coming here, not for a minute." She rubbed the flower against her lips and gazed at the barn. "I do wonder if keeping the farm was a mistake. I want to believe my motives were noble, but sometimes I think I'm hanging on to these cows just so ..."

She paused again, and under the influence of equally complicated thoughts Conor filled the silence without thinking. "So you can stay angry with him. For leaving you alone to deal with everything." As soon as the words left his mouth he flinched in alarm and turned to her. "Kate, I—Jesus. I've no idea why I said that. I'm sorry."

"Don't be. You're probably on to something." Kate tossed the dandelion into the grass. "It's what happened to you, right? You had to run the family farm when your brother died."

Conor didn't need to answer. The question was rhetorical, the assumption cemented, and he'd been taught to exploit such opportunities. He could shape the narrative to match what she already believed by simply remaining silent. Their eyes met ... and he couldn't do it. "Didn't happen like that, but I'm familiar with the idea of doing something you don't feel suited for, and having to learn things you never wanted to know."

"You hate farming that much?"

"Oh. God, no. I wasn't thinking about farming." Conor saw some of the sadness lift from Kate's face. "I resented it for a while, but when I stopped being sorry for myself I discovered the life has qualities I hadn't recognized, and doing the right thing brings its own satisfaction. Sort of like the Hindu idea of dharma, the obligation to fulfill your duty."

She nodded. "Making a big decision for the right reasons must feel good. I make little decisions. I build little bridges to carry me from one crisis to the next. I'm hoping the next one will be longer, to give me time to think."

The hint, obvious enough, had come earlier and in a manner far different than Conor had expected. She needed a farmer. He'd known that. It was the whole bloody point of choosing this place. He was a farmer who'd needed a place to go, to disappear. A simple concept, and he'd anticipated a straightforward, unemotional proposition, no strings attached. He had not anticipated this.

The strings were everywhere, fine strands of red gold spinning him into confusion. He recognized the danger but he was like a fly that perceives the web too late. Conor took a deep breath—the sandpaper quality of his voice evened out with a lungful of air behind it—and plunged ahead. "I'll look after your farm for a while, if you like. To give you time to decide what to do. Would that—oh, Jaysus. Please don't cry."

"I'm trying hard not to." Kate laughed a little, wiping her eyes. "I'd hoped you might help, but I was afraid once you saw all this you wouldn't stay long."

"Well, I don't know how long I *can* stay," Conor warned. "I've left a lot of things behind me, Kate, and to be honest I'm not sure they're far enough back. I'd say the last thing you should want around the place is some dodgy Irish vagabond, but you need a farmer and Phillip is right. I happen to be a good one. I won't take it as a paid position; I'll work for room and board. If you can have me on those terms, I'd be happy to have a go at your cows and see how we get on."

Kate lowered her head in furrowed concentration. As the minutes ticked by Conor grew convinced she'd send him away— certainly the prudent course of action after his outburst of candor. While waiting for her to speak, he indulged in lengthening glances at her profile.

He glimpsed a quiver in the curve of her flushed cheek, spotted two small moles below her ear when the breeze lifted the hair from her neck. In the space above her scoop-necked shirt, freckles—like a light dusting of ginger—began at the base of her throat, spreading over her collarbone and down ...

His gaze flew to the horizon as she abruptly looked up, squinting at him uncertainly.

"This is an unusual job interview."

Conor released his breath in a cough. "Yeah. Sort of unorthodox."

"Are you sure you want this?"

"Are you offering it?"

"You know I am."

"Then, I'm taking it."

She nodded, satisfied, and they sat quietly, watching a barn cat creep belly-flat against the pasture, stalking a group of sparrows. Kate tossed a stick to frighten them away and turned to Conor with a bright smile. He faced her, forcing himself to meet her blue-eyed scrutiny. He'd have to get used to it sooner or later.

"I guess now is a good time to tell you about a project I've been considering for a new breed of cow."

Oh, Christ.

He clamped his mouth shut, swallowing the expletive. He nodded for her to continue, keeping his face neutral. "What sort of breed did you have in mind?"

"Something that would work for this terrain." Kate popped up and paced a few steps along the steep incline of the pasture. "I've even got a name—Hillside Holstein."

He nodded again, patiently. "Uh-huh. Hillside."

"We'll breed them with shorter legs on one side. So they can stand up straight when they're grazing."

Conor's rigid jaw relaxed. A smile tugged at the corners of his mouth. "I see. What happens if they want to turn around and graze the other way?"

Kate regarded the pasture and looked back with a mischievous shrug. "Well, then they fall over. I haven't worked that part out yet."

He heard himself chuckle hesitantly—as though trying to remember how to do it properly—but Kate's uncontrolled mirth was a contagion beyond resistance.

"Oh my God. The look on your face. Priceless." Her cheeks coloring to a deep shade of pink, she rocked forward and literally hooted. The infectious sound caught him by surprise, prompting a helpless laughter so natural and spontaneous he almost couldn't believe it was his.

Later in the afternoon Conor settled into a sunny corner of the porch to flip through a magazine. The glossy cover of *Vermont Life* had enchanted him with a depiction of mountains saturated in color, but after only a few minutes the sun's heat had seeped into his muscles and the images on the page began swimming in a kaleidoscopic blur.

He quickly stood up and tossed the magazine aside, appalled by how close he'd come to falling asleep. One of the more harrowing aspects of his recent illness involved the regular humiliation of screaming himself awake in a London hospital bed, convinced he still lay pinned on a frozen mountain trail, gunfire shredding the trees around him. The idea of subjecting his new hosts to such a scene was mortifying to even contemplate.

He headed out into the fresh air, re-tracing the route of his earlier tour with Kate, and again ended up on the disintegrating picnic bench. The pasture seemed to grow greener as he watched, and the sound of running water was everywhere. The brook at this distance had the muted quality of white noise, but another burbling source of run-off was more immediate. Narrow rivers coursed through trenches along both sides of the road below him, echoing in the culverts and carving small tributaries that snaked into the pasture before returning to the main channel. Submerged in the running stream, flattened stalks of last year's saw grass undulated with lazy elegance.

Conor took in the view and the smell of the sun-warmed ground. The place glowed like a mythological idyll, brimming with the essence of things unseen. He closed his eyes and allowed himself to be found by the boundless thrumming presence hovering at the edge of his senses. Never far away, an elemental spirit too vast to understand waited only for a nod of permission to surge forward and wash into him. He'd spent much of his life avoiding this inherited fragment of his mother's stronger gift, but now he welcomed it—it was the one thing that brought him closer to everyone he'd lost, and those he'd left behind.

Duty. Dharma. Conor thought of another motherly figure who epitomized this concept, who'd shown by the example of her life that duty might also be a source of joy. He opened his eyes to fix on the spot where Kate had stood earlier, remembering her face, bright with laughter, and his own response—a rusty tingle of pleasure to have been the cause of it.

He didn't know when, if ever, 'joy' would be part of his vocabulary again, but if he could do something useful here, something that might offer a small measure of peace ... maybe it would be enough.

5

Conor started before dawn the next day, taking up the reins with a gusto Kate had frankly not expected, since he'd only just recovered from a serious illness. Within a few weeks he'd transformed her barn into the agricultural equivalent of a bright new penny, and had completed a project she and Abigail had often discussed but never found time for—the creation of a kitchen garden to supply the restaurant with homegrown vegetables.

He'd plowed and harrowed a parcel at the end of the meadow below the inn, fussing over the work for days before presenting the acre of dark rich topsoil for Kate's inspection. After walking its borders, marveling at the geometric precision of his work, she'd delivered her verdict with a happy smile.

"Beautifully done. Thank you. You're a little bit of a neat freak, aren't you?"

"I'd prefer to say meticulous."

"I see." She laughed at his mock solemnity. "I'm not awfully meticulous, myself."

"Really? I hadn't noticed."

"Smart ass."

While appreciative of the effort Kate had worried he might be working too hard, but all evidence indicated the pace was exactly what Conor needed. He showed an astonishing capacity for hard labor, fueled by substantial infusions of Abigail's cooking, and within weeks his gaunt frame had begun disappearing under layers of muscle.

"I covet that man's metabolism," Kate sighed one afternoon after he'd devoured two separate lunch entrees before heading out the door again. "I don't know what you're learning from this experiment, Abigail. Apparently, he's an omnivore. He'll eat anything."

Her chef had been tinkering with the spring menu and had cast Conor in the role of lab rat. With the tactful charm he used to manage her in general, he'd refused nothing, ate everything, and thus had secured his place in Abigail's wild and tender heart forever. Shuffling through a handful of dog-eared recipe cards she peered at Kate over a pair of reading glasses.

"The menu's been finished for a week."

"You're kidding. So, why do you keep giving him two meals at a time? Are you still experimenting? Because maybe Dominic would appreciate trying a few new dishes."

Originally from Italy, Abigail's husband was a dapper man with a mild and sunny temperament, who didn't seem to mind his wife spending most of her waking hours at work. They shared an odd but affectionate relationship, and as the inn's consummately professional dining room manager Dominic was an invaluable asset.

"Dom doesn't need fattening up." Abigail went back to her recipe cards. "Conor does."

"Okay." Kate nodded agreement. "But, why not pump up the volume on one entree?"

"I'm rotating through the combinations he liked most one more time."

"Why?"

With uncharacteristic calm Abigail removed her glasses and set them down. "Because it's all I can do. Don't pretend you haven't noticed, Kate—how he jumps at his own shadow and sometimes looks like he hasn't slept in days. He's getting stronger, bit by bit, but the man is clearly recovering from something besides pneumonia. You know what I'm talking about, honey. You understand this kind of thing even better than me."

Kate rested her chin on one hand and stared down at the table. "Yes. I do. He's mourning the loss of his family and home, but it feels more complicated than grief, and he doesn't seem to want to talk about it." She smiled at Abigail. "At least you thought of a practical way to help. I wish I could do as much."

Abigail gave her hand a pat and got to her feet. "I think you're helping more than you realize. Now, are you going to polish the hall floor before we open or did we give up on that plan?"

"Today. I promise." Kate slapped her palm on the table. "But I'm taking a walk to Longchamp's first. We need a new mop and I need the exercise. I'm afraid I gained weight just watching him eat."

"Uh-huh, of course I've met him." Yvette Longchamp lifted a mop from its rack and propped the handle against the floor. "He's here all the time."

"All the time?" Kate ignored the mop and returned her friend's placid gaze. With a tawny complexion and high cheekbones hinting at her French-Abenaki heritage, Yvette's face often betrayed little more than flat stoicism.

"Almost every day. Comes around ten o'clock. Gets a cruller and a cup of tea."

Kate grinned. "Crullers? Don't let Abigail know. She'll be making those for him next. He eats everything she puts in front of him."

"Doesn't seem to be hurting him." Yvette's comical leer was uncharacteristically expressive. "The man looks good in his Carhartts. They should put him in the catalogue."

"Yeah, okay. What else?"

Yvette leaned on the mop—it wasn't much shorter than she was—and considered the question. "Quiet, but friendly. You know the morning crowd here. Quiet and friendly suits them fine. Somebody's got to be the audience for these characters. He's starting to talk a little more, though. Smiles more. Fits him better. He's not really shy. Just acts like a guy trying to get comfortable with himself again."

Yvette's clipped insights were in tune with Kate's. Conor was growing more talkative with her as well, offering glimpses of a dry mischievous humor, and she was pleased he'd become a regular at Longchamp's. The local all-purpose emporium—a place where carpet tacks, dish drainers and flannel shirts could still be found under one roof—was the oldest business in Hartsboro Bend, and stood at the center of town in both the literal and figurative sense. She liked the idea of him settling into its convivial atmosphere as a member of the community.

Yvette rapped the handle against the floor, patiently amused. "Do you even need a mop?"

Startled out of her private thoughts, Kate gave a brisk nod. "Of course. That one's perfect. You still haven't said what you think of him," she added, following Yvette to the front of the store.

"Seems nice enough. Ask me again next week. We're hiking Elmore on Sunday."

"Oh? Mount Elmore?"

Another surprising piece of news. Apart from solitary walks around her thirty acres Conor had never expressed interest in any wider exploration, but then again Kate realized she'd never suggested showing him anything.

"Is Bobby going, too?"

Yvette had divorced her husband ten years earlier and Bobby Gilligan—a captain with the local fire department—was her longtime boyfriend.

"Nope, he's working." Yvette rang up the sale and handed over the mop. "Are you jealous? Because you looked a little bit jealous, just then."

"Don't get started with this."

"Not me. You started it. Sounds like you should get to know this guy better yourself."

"Enough," Kate warned. "You and Abigail double-team me with a matchmaking radar that never shuts off, and I haven't got time for it."

"No? When will you?"

"Yvette—"

"Okay, okay. I'm just saying. There's never enough time, so don't wait for that. Anyway, this Mount Elmore deal was Jigger's idea. I'll spend most of the day keeping track of him." Yvette handed Kate her change. "He's out back. Go say hello before you leave? He'll be disappointed if you don't."

Kate exited through the rear door and found Yvette's twelve-year-old son sitting at the end of the porch. His name was Andrew but he was universally known as "Jigger," a fitting nickname for the boy's special brand of excitable movement. At the moment he was unnaturally still, squinting at a guitar across his lap, but at the sight of Kate he beamed a smile of pure joy. He set the guitar aside and jumped up to throw his arms around her.

"Kate! I'm so glad to see you. I missed you!"

"Has it been that long? Well, I missed you too, honey-bun."

Kate lifted Jigger's slender figure with an affectionate squeeze. He was a sweetly handsome little boy, smaller than average for his years, with a tumble of blonde hair framing a pixie-like face.

His green eyes sparkled with a remarkably beautiful starburst pattern, and Yvette had once explained she'd known something was different about her son as soon as she'd seen them. At the age of two he'd been diagnosed with Williams Syndrome. The rare genetic disorder caused a range of disabilities, but they were often combined with unusual cognitive and verbal strengths.

Unique to this particular condition was an indiscriminately loving, empathic personality—a trait both endearing and worrisome. Jigger was as likely to offer a hug to a stranger as a friend, and this was an endless source of anxiety for his mother.

A deep affinity and aptitude for music was also common in Williams Syndrome children. With an arm around the boy's shoulders, Kate noted the string hanging loose from his guitar's tuning peg and the jumbled circle of wire lying on the porch floor.

"What's happening here, Jigs?"

"I broke a string," he said with a pensive frown. "The new string is all tangled up there. I made a complete mess of it. It was foolish of me, Kate. My hands don't work like that. I should have known."

Kate gave his cheek a friendly pinch. "Well, let's see what we can do."

They sat down together on the floor and Kate tackled the snarl of wire as Jigger described the demise of the string, including the song he'd been playing and the surprisingly loud noise as it sprang free. While listening to this intricate narrative she heard a movement behind them, and turned to see Conor coming out on the porch carrying a gallon container of murky brown liquid.

"Conor!" Again, Jigger leaped to his feet. Conor had just enough time to set the bottle down before the tow-headed bundle of love sailed into his arms.

"Oof—easy there, Jigger. Sure you'll knock the stuffing out of me one day." He rubbed a hand over the boy's tousled hair and winked at Kate. "I was told my services are required."

"I broke a string." Jigger trumpeted the news, his face buried against Conor's shirt. "Playing that song you taught me."

Kate held up the string. "Situation desperate. You're just in time. Is that teat dip? I thought we had cases of the stuff."

"Enough for two hundred cows, but sadly every bottle expired in January. I'm ashamed to say it took me nearly a month to discover. I ordered a new case."

"Good Lord. Jared didn't mention anything?"

"Not to me."

Conor dropped his gaze and Kate again wondered what on earth had happened between the two men. She'd offered to continue Jared's part-time arrangement, knowing his family could use the money, but after only a few days he'd phoned to say he wouldn't be back. In his slow, self-conscious manner he said he was needed at home but would be happy to help again "when the new fellow runs off on you like the others did." She'd been upset, worried about Conor having no one to orient him to the work, but he'd received the news with obvious relief and hadn't needed much orientation, anyway.

"Are you going to fix my guitar?" Jigger dragged him by the arm toward Kate.

"No, I'm going to show *you* how to fix it." Conor settled cross-legged on the porch, playfully pulling Jigger down with him. He accepted the string from Kate and glanced curiously at her new mop. "You walked all the way down here for that?"

"Easier when it's not pouring rain."

"*Och*, now that's a dirty dig." He laughed. "I'll run you back in the truck if you like."

"Sure. I can wait."

Kate rested against the railing and watched as he patiently helped Jigger with the guitar. When they'd finished the boy played a few chords, admiring their work. "What about your fiddle, Conor? You promised to bring it here. You said we would play together."

"Right, so. I did say that, didn't I?" Conor absently ran a thumb under his jaw. "Well, we've got the guitar for today, anyway. Have another go at the number I taught you last week."

"I've been wondering about your fiddle myself," Kate said later, when they were in the truck and headed back up the road.

"Are you going to play us a tune sometime?"

"Ah, well." Conor stared ahead at the road.

"Maybe it would help," Kate ventured, darting a look at him. She thought he wouldn't reply, but after several seconds he looked at her and smiled.

"Maybe it would."

They arrived back at the inn and pulled up next to a black Chevy Suburban in the parking area.

"I can't imagine who that is." Kate looked from the car to the front porch, where two men in dark suits had appeared, badges clipped at their belts. Abigail was right behind, looking dangerously close to detonation.

"I think I can," Conor muttered. Switching off the ignition he rolled out of the truck and they walked together to the porch.

"Afternoon ma'am, sir. Special Agents Foster and Houseman." The taller of the two indicated himself and the man next to him with a twirl of his thumb. "We're from the ICE Office of Investigations. Are you Kate Fitzpatrick?"

"Yes." Kate frowned in confusion. "Ice?"

"Immigration and Customs Enforcement," the agent clarified. He looked at Conor. "And is this Conor McBride?"

"You don't have to answer," Abigail roared. "People have rights in this country. You don't need to say anything without a lawyer."

"Steady on, Abigail. It's okay." Conor nodded. "I'm Conor McBride."

The agent was already shifting his flat gaze back to Kate. "Mrs. Fitzpatrick, we had a call to the tip line in Williston indicating you've employed an undocumented Irish laborer for your farm."

"An undocumented Irish laborer." Conor gave a low whistle. "That has a menacing 'croppies lie down' sort of ring to it."

"But, he isn't even getting—"

"Kate."

Conor put a hand on her arm and she realized the mistake she'd almost made. Announcing that he wasn't on the payroll wouldn't help the situation. Exasperated, Kate clamped her mouth shut. She'd never thought to ask about his immigration status. Why had it occurred to someone else? Agent Foster began again in a lecturing tone.

"Mrs. Fitzpatrick, I'm sure you're aware employers who hire undocumented workers face serious penalties—"

"Before you go on trying to frighten her, you might want to check that I'm actually undocumented."

The authority and cold stillness in Conor's voice captured everyone's attention. The two agents glanced at each other and Agent Houseman spoke for the first time.

"Mr. McBride, are you inferring you are in possession of a valid H-1 or H-2 class work visa? There's no such evidence from my research."

"Nor would there be, but did you try typing 'green card' into your database? Do you want to head back to Williston and do that now, or shall I go collect it for you?"

Agent Foster seemed forcibly to resist an urge to look at his partner again. "Sir, if you could produce a permanent residence visa for us we'd appreciate it."

Conor took the stairs in two steps, stopping as he reached the front door. He skewered the men with an incredulous stare. "You're going to let me wander out of sight, now? Have you ever done this before, for fuck's sake?"

"Houseman." Agent Foster jerked his head and the shorter man jumped to follow Conor.

Abigail came down from the porch and sidled over to Kate, speaking in a stage whisper from the corner of her mouth. "Seems like he's got this under control."

Kate almost laughed. "You think? My God, they'll be saluting him before it's done. Did you know he had a green card?"

Abigail shook her head. "I'd have bet money he didn't even have a birth certificate."

Agent Houseman re-appeared first. Nodding curtly, he trotted down the steps and presented the card while Conor followed more slowly, his face blank. He avoided looking at either Kate or Abigail.

"Thank you, Mr. McBride." Agent Foster handed the card back to him. "We'll run a background check just to cover the bases. I assume you don't mind?"

"Would it matter if I did?"

A flicker of interest passed over the agent's face but he left it alone, and catching the eye of his partner signaled their departure with a polite nod.

The three of them stood like mute sentinels, watching the Suburban reverse out of the parking area and coast down the driveway. Conor was first to break their motionless stupor as the car disappeared down the dirt road.

"Like a foot on the neck," he said cryptically.

Kate pivoted on her heel and headed for the house. "I'm having a drink. It's five o'clock somewhere."

6

It was a desultory scene. Kate played bartender, standing behind the mahogany bar in the corner of the dining room while her 'customers' sat on barstools in front of her. She mixed a gin and tonic for Abigail. For herself and Conor, she poured generous measures of whiskey into crystal glasses and slid one over to him. He dipped his head and accepted the drink, refusing to meet her gaze.

"I'm sorry you had to go through that." Kate put her untouched drink on the bar. "I'm the one to blame for this. I probably needed to register you or file a paper with someone."

Conor rolled the glass between his hands. "Of course you're not to blame. I am. I'm a bloody fool for not realizing this would happen. Instead of helping I put you in an impossible position."

Abnormally quiet until this point, Abigail snorted. "Listen to the two of you, thrashing yourselves. Personally, I'd like a crack at the busybody who stuck his nose where it didn't belong and called Williston. That's whose fault this is and I've a mind to go tell him so."

"Jesus, don't." Conor looked up sharply at Abigail and she gave a mollifying grimace.

"Oh, I won't do it. Just blowing off steam."

"You're saying you know who called them?" Kate saw a glance pass between them. "Both of you do?"

"Well, we can guess," Abigail said. "Can't you, for God's sake?

Jared Percy. He had the most obvious motive."

"Jared Percy?" Kate gaped at her. "What motive? I wanted to keep him on, I told him so. Conor wasn't taking anything away from him."

"I'm betting Jared thought he'd taken something."

Seeing the gimlet gleam in Abigail's eyes, Kate felt a flush spread over her face. "You can't be serious. He must be ten years younger than me."

"He's twenty-two." A wicked grin dimpled Abigail's cheeks.

"Okay, seven years." Mortified, Kate glowered at her and peeked at Conor. "Anyway, you're right. Neither of us is to blame. We didn't do anything wrong."

Conor studied his glass, looking as though he wanted to dive inside and disappear. "Unfortunately, that's not true." He drained his whiskey and set it down. "I've got to go over for the second milking but I'll be back in an hour. I need to talk with you, Kate."

"Are you going to leave?" She hated herself for asking the question, and for the plaintive note in her voice. Conor's brow contracted. He set the barstool neatly in place and stood with his hands gripping its sides.

"That will be up to you, I think. Before long those agents will finish their background check and they'll want to tell you what they found. I've got a criminal record, Kate. Not a very exciting one, for all the grief it's caused, but it's there in black and white for anyone to check."

It was closer to two hours before he got back to the house. After turning the cows into the pasture for the evening Conor walked a few miles up the dirt road, thinking there was something vaguely comedic about the situation if he could get up the energy to laugh. His new life hadn't lasted thirty days before being compromised by a jealous suitor with more imagination than he would have believed. As if he'd needed it, the fiasco was another reminder:

he was an amateur at this game and he'd elected to play it on his own.

After being discharged from the hospital and before his brief trip back to Ireland, he'd collected the green card and passports promised to him but had rebuffed any further assistance. In retrospect it might have been wiser to accept, and if he'd had greater faith in the capabilities of those offering help maybe he would have considered it more seriously.

Conor retraced his steps back to the inn, dreading the approaching encounter with Kate. In the kitchen, Abigail had left a covered plate on the counter along with a note giving instructions for re-heating the meal. A line scrawled at the bottom read: *Don't do something stupid. You belong here.*

He put the plate in the refrigerator and went upstairs to Kate's apartment, where he found her sitting in the living room facing the window. The bottle of whiskey and two fresh glasses had migrated from the bar to her coffee table. She saw his reflection and looked back over her shoulder.

"I was beginning to think you'd already left."

"I'm sorry. I went for a walk." Conor eyed the immaculate wheat-colored carpet and wiped his forehead, realizing how dirty and sweaty he was. "I'll just clean up a bit. I won't be long."

When he returned, his anxiety was tempered by inquisitive interest. Although he passed the living room every day he'd never ventured inside. The handsome space was lit by artfully arranged lighting, and its pale yellow walls glowed in the deepening twilight. Although the carpeting provided a muffled ambiance, the overall design seemed more formal than he would have expected. Everything was tasteful and complementary, but too pristine and strangely inexpressive of what he knew of Kate's personality.

"This is a gorgeous room." He paused in front of the large window framing the lake in the distance.

"Thanks. Anna designed it—my latest stepmother." Kate glanced around the room. "Actually, her interior decorator did. She wanted to help. I had to let her do something but I didn't anticipate the consequences. I feel like I'm visiting someone else's house when I sit in here."

"I know what you mean. Maybe this will take the edge off." Conor splashed some whiskey into one of the glasses, and with the bottle poised over the second looked at Kate. She nodded. "A Jameson's drinker." He poured and handed her the glass with a smile. "I don't think I would have guessed that."

"Well, there's always more to learn about someone."

"Touché."

He sat in one of the two leather club chairs anchoring either side of the couch, considering how to begin. As he'd completed the walk back to the inn Conor had begun piecing together a story—something to spin the facts into a benign tidy package and seal off further avenues of inquiry. The strategy involved a fair amount of dissembling. Looking at Kate's solemn face as she sipped her drink, he couldn't do it. His appetite for pretense had never been strong, and grew weaker the longer he remained anywhere near her. Without any backup plan he started talking, praying he'd know when to stop.

"The trick is knowing when to stop," he blurted aloud, and after a stab of panic realized he'd begun a more authentic story than the tale practiced earlier. "With the drink, I mean. That's where my brother got into trouble, after I'd left for Dublin. Our father had been dead for years, and our mother ... "

An image of Brigid McBride rose in Conor's mind and pain bloomed in his chest like the kinetic flare of a match. "She was a rare one, a sort of half-pagan, half-Catholic mystic. A lot of the time she seemed to be living on the threshold of some other place. She was easy to love but not always easy to live with, and I never realized how lonely it was for Thomas until I got a taste myself. Not hard to end up spending your evenings with a bottle when you've nothing better to do. I was lucky I had the fiddle." Conor took a sip from the glass and shot Kate an apologetic glance. "Sorry. Getting off to a slow start, here. I'll come to the point, eventually."

She nodded, drawing her feet up to the couch and tucking them beneath her. He waited until she'd settled again before resuming.

"Thomas hired two farming assistants. From Northern Ireland. He started getting drunk with them on a regular basis, and they went to work on him. They connected him with someone they said had a scheme for building Irish pubs in places that didn't have them—Asia, Africa. They said this fellow wanted partners who could come up with capital. Thomas got seduced by it all, the idea of having a different kind of life in some exotic country. He was an easy mark. One night they got him completely fucking scuttered and he signed off on papers for a business loan."

Conor still remembered his own incredulous anger at first hearing this tale—a textbook scam, and one that had a nasty twist buried inside.

"At least, they told him it was a loan," he continued bitterly. "Turns out he'd submitted an application to the European Union for an agricultural grant with barely a word of truth in the bloody thing. The EU made the award, but pretty soon they twigged the farm didn't have nine hundred head of cattle and didn't have sheep at all. They filed a warrant with Interpol, and the Garda— that's the Irish police force— went to arrest him, but when they got to the farm Thomas had disappeared. So, they came looking for me."

"I don't understand." Kate frowned.

"I was co-owner, and I'd signed the application forms as well." Conor put his unfinished glass down, sliding it across the coffee table. "I didn't even read them. They came in the post with a typed note telling me to sign and send them on to an address in Tralee. I saw it was to do with the farm, so therefore I didn't give a shit, and I always did what my big brother wanted. A few months later the Garda took me out of my flat in handcuffs and I got convicted for conspiring to defraud the EU. That ended my days in Dublin, and my career with the National Symphony Orchestra."

"You went to prison?" Kate had shifted to the end of the sofa near Conor. Uncomfortably near.

"I went back to the farm, which seemed like prison right enough, at first." Conor sat farther back in his own chair, seeking respite from her clear-eyed attention. "My solicitor made a deal for repaying the money in installments, and the farm was the only way I could earn enough. The debt's been paid—I had help in the end—but the record stands for anyone who wants to look for it."

"Did you ever see Thomas again?"

Kate's question was a natural one, but Conor wished she hadn't asked. It took the story in a direction he couldn't allow. Before he could form an answer she made it more complicated.

"You were with him when he died."

He kept his face still, suppressing a tremor of surprise. He'd learned something about her impulsive nature and inclination to draw conclusions from fragments of data. He hadn't realized how good she was at it.

"Yes. I was with him."

"Tell me what happened."

From someone else this might have struck Conor as vulgar curiosity, but the compassion in Kate's eyes suggested a different motive. She had figured him out—seen more than he intended to show, heard more than he meant to say. Instead of being sensibly alarmed she was offering to listen to him, to be a channel for safely releasing the pressure he cradled inside himself like a combustible gas.

"I can't do that."

She nodded, unsurprised. "But, did you make peace with him before he died?"

"Jesus, Kate." A strangled hiccup—more sob than laughter—lodged in Conor's windpipe. The choking fit gave him time to harness the emotion she'd innocently ignited. "You're quite a skilled interrogator, you know." He dropped the fist from his mouth with a sigh. "Bloody ruthless."

"I'm sorry."

"No, you're all right. Sure it's the one good thing to come out of the whole business. It was okay between us. He was a decent man – simple, strong and loyal. Yeah, we were okay in the end." He stood up and moved back to the window, trying to put more space between himself and the temptation to go on testifying. "I'm sorry for all this. I ought to get out of here before causing you more trouble."

"What kind of trouble?" Kate asked.

Conor gave an evasive shrug, but the truth was he didn't know himself. That was the hell of it. "I can leave in the morning. If you want me to?" He studied her in the window's reflection. Her face was calm and utterly fearless. She smiled.

"If I said 'yes', where would you go?"

He turned to her with a soft laugh, shaking his head. "Good question."

7

After a day of fieldwork under the hot August sun Conor entered the kitchen through the back door, weary, sore and ready for supper. He almost always came from work too ravenous to wash and change for dinner, but with his clothes redolent of the barnyard the inn's dining room was off-limits. An alcove off the kitchen was the only acceptable place for him, and his arrival had been anticipated. A bowl of gazpacho sat waiting and Dominic was coming forward with a basket of bread.

"*Prego*," he called out in his rolling Italian accent, gesturing for Conor to take a seat. A slender man in his fifties with a neatly trimmed mustache, Abigail's husband had negotiating skills that might have earned him a good living as a diplomat, yet he seemed content using them to manage the fragile alliance between the dining room and kitchen staff—and between all of them and his wife.

"She started asking where you were an hour ago. 'He works too hard,' she says. 'He doesn't sleep enough,' she says." Dominic clapped a hand on his shoulder, giving Conor a sympathetic smile. "She's got worries, *amico*. She's got *questions*."

"Oh, bloody hell. Thanks for the heads-up, Dom."

Conor had grown fond of Abigail over the past several months and was touched by the maternal interest she took in him, but her fussing sometimes strained his patience. This was the price to be paid, he supposed. With Kate's encouragement he'd remained in place, and only time would tell whether the decision was sensible or delusional. In the meantime, he'd become rooted in a community of people who cared—and worried—about him. He could hazard a guess at the source of Abigail's latest concern. A few minutes later she arrived with his dinner, and confirmed that he'd nailed it in one.

"Darla said she ran into you at Copley Hospital earlier today." She put the plate down in front of him—diver scallops on a bed of risotto with a side of hanger steak—and waited.

Darla Barstow was the inn's housekeeper, a petite high-strung woman of twenty-three who reminded Conor of some form of feathered wildlife, always twitching and chattering.

"I figured she wasn't likely to keep that to herself." He reached for the salt.

"That doesn't need salt." Abigail plucked the shaker from his hand. "So? Are you sick?"

"Of course not. Do I look sick?" Conor bent over the plate to hide his irritation.

"You look tired."

"Sure you're always telling me that."

"Because it's always true. You were at Copley once already at the beginning of May. I gave you directions."

"And didn't quiz me, as I recall. Keeping a diary now, are you?" Instantly, Conor regretted his ill-humored sarcasm. Abigail flinched as if she'd been slapped. She turned away and he caught her by the hand.

"Abigail, I'm sorry. Listen, they're just check-ups. I need to go once a month for a while to make sure my lungs heal properly. They take an X-ray, I spit in a cup and it's done. I'm fine, and I'm not as tired as you seem to think."

"I'll take your word for it." She allowed herself a grudging smile. "Baked potato?"

"Have I ever refused one?"

She brought two, and left him to finish his dinner, but returned later carrying a covered plate on a tray. "Since you're so fit and rested I'm sending you up to deal with Kate."

Conor hadn't seen Kate at all during the day, which wasn't uncommon given their divergent schedules, but in the evening she often took a minute to bring him a pint of something from the bar. Concerned, he frowned at the tray. "What's the matter? Is *she* sick?"

"In a manner of speaking. She's in her studio. I think she was there all night and the only thing she ate today was a chocolate bar—for breakfast." Abigail set the tray on the table. "Take this to her and make sure she eats. I'm holding you responsible."

Conor rubbed a hand over his mouth. "Listen, if she's in her studio I imagine she'd rather not be bothered. Artists can get pretty absorbed—"

"No, you listen, Conor. You've been here four months and you've been a godsend, but it's time to make yourself useful in a different way. Kate needs to talk about what she's going through to somebody who understands. She needs something I can't give her. You can."

"Jesus ..." Conor squirmed under her gaze.

"I understand you're afraid," she added softly, "But this is what you need too, sweetie. Stop fighting. A second chance only counts if you recognize it when you see it."

He stopped fidgeting and grew still. "I can't start down this road, Abigail."

"Of course you can. It's the only road worth starting down. Now, go. Get out of my kitchen."

As always with Abigail, he had little choice but to obey. Filled with conflicting emotions he lifted the tray and left, threading his way through the busy dining room. On an intuitive level, he understood Kate's struggle. A few weeks earlier he'd ended his own self-imposed penance and had begun playing his violin again, practicing in a shed next to the barn. The initial effort had been excruciating. Consumed with self-doubt, he'd struggled with pacing and mechanics as well as memory. Entire sections of concerti he once could play in his sleep escaped him, or came out in the wrong order. The first session was painful and more than a bit frightening, but when finished he'd flexed hands that had not been stretched in such a way for nearly a year and felt their responding ache with a wave of contentment. It was like having a limb rejoined with his body—the point of attachment was tender and raw, but the parts knew they belonged together.

Unlike other aspects of his life the experience was one he could discuss without mystery or evasion, but he hesitated to open this line of conversation. Kate had shared few details about her own creative paralysis, and none about its cause. Given his own reticence he had no right to probe, and as a rule he avoided topics which might become too personal. As Abigail had clearly discerned, his friendly affection for Kate was threatening to spill beyond the boundaries he'd set, and the effort to contain it was taxing enough without further complications.

He reached the third floor and moved past her bedroom to the studio door at the end of the hall. With the tray balanced on one arm he took a few deep breaths and knocked. A muffled movement sounded within. He waited, then rapped again more loudly.

"Kate? I've got a bit of supper Abigail asked me to bring for you."

"Thanks. I'm not hungry."

Her voice, just on the other side of the door, sounded tired. Uncurling his hand Conor rested his palm against the door and tried again, this time with some light banter. "Well that's fine, Kate, but listen to me. If you send me away my only choice is to bring this tray back to the kitchen and get abused for a feeble effort. So, in the interest of saving my backside will you ever just open up? I'll pass the works through like a hero and you can do what you want with it."

The door swung open. Kate stood aside and motioned for him to enter. He walked in and placed the tray on the only available surface he could find, a table littered with drawing paper. The room was larger than he'd expected and engulfed in clutter, but it held no interest for him as he turned to her. Dressed in jeans and an oversized white shirt with the sleeves rolled up, Kate looked as deflated and miserable as he'd ever seen her. She frowned at the floor, her eyes hidden by a curtain of dark red hair.

"Are you all right?" Conor asked softly.

"Yes. I'm just not hungry."

He picked up a napkin and wiped a smudge of chocolate from the corner of her lip, resisting the alarming impulse to sift through the curls falling around her face. "Must have been some chocolate bar. Breakfast of champions, was it?"

A shadowy smile touched her lips, but faded under heavy weariness. She lifted the cloche from the tray and they both examined the plate underneath. Abigail had prepared a Caesar salad topped with grilled shrimp. A generous slice of raspberry pie sat on a separate plate.

"I can't eat all this," Kate complained.

"Hmm. I could maybe give you a hand with the pie."

"Oh, really?" Her smile lingered a bit longer this time. She passed over the plate and nodded for him to sit, then she sat down next to him and he handed her a fork. They began eating in silence.

The pie disappeared in four bites. Wiping his mouth, Conor swung around in his chair with awakening curiosity. The room was unlike any other in the house, infused with Kate's spirit in a way her tastefully correct living room was not. It had the evocative character of the classic "atelier"—long, narrow and high ceilinged, with three windows along its length facing the road. All were open to the evening breeze and between two of them an old sofa sat on a worn Persian carpet. The floor was wide planked oak and dotted with paint-stained drop cloths.

In the center of the room a large blank canvas balanced on two easels, partly obscured by a black cloth draped over its corners. Conor took it all in, along with the faint odor of turpentine mixed with the fragrance of old wood. The room was spectacular.

"I can imagine what you're thinking." Without looking at him Kate speared a shrimp and pointed her fork at the jars and paint tubes in front of the canvas. "You're thinking it's no wonder I get nothing accomplished in a mess like this."

The unfamiliar edge in her voice startled him. "Your imagination is pretty far off track."

"Well, you can't be thinking this looks like the studio of a serious artist," she insisted with heavy sarcasm. "More like a children's nursery. All it needs is a box of blocks thrown on the floor."

He shifted to address Kate's averted face. "You're making a lot assumptions about what I'm thinking and you haven't got one right yet."

"The place isn't usually this messy."

"So what if it was?"

"Excellent point." She huffed a bitter laugh and plunged the fork into another shrimp. "So what if it's messy, or clean? Doesn't make a difference, right?"

"Kate—"

"Watch the artist in her milieu, consistent output under all conditions."

"Kate, stop for God's sake. Bullying yourself isn't going to help. I've tried and it doesn't work, believe me."

She put the fork down and finally looked at him. "Are you sure? Because nothing else I've tried is working, either." Her blue eyes appeared darker than usual and the derisive glint had disappeared, leaving them full of sadness and exhaustion.

"Do you want to talk about it?"

Kate gave him a dubious glance, then slumped against the chair. "I got an email yesterday from an art collector who bought one of my pieces at a juried show eight years ago. A painting called *The Three Graces*."

She pushed aside a pile of papers and picked up a large print from the table, handing it to him. Conor accepted it with a solemn nod, no stranger to the anxiety involved in the deceptively simple gesture. In the practice of any art there was such a fine balance between the desire to be heard or seen or understood, and the terror of exposure. He assumed an impassive expression and angled the print against the window for a better view.

The work was magnificent. The scene depicted three women, lithe and elegant, wrapped in long formal dresses, all so similar as to suggest the same figure arranged in different poses. They stood slightly apart, turned away from each other. Only one faced forward, wistfully staring out at him with an upturned head and a wise reserved smile. Set in a moonlit landscape the women appeared to float within the scene, and beneath the composition's visible brushwork the hue and texture of the canvas remained as an underlying glow. A sense of contemplative movement inhabited the work, as though each woman had been captured in the midst of her own slow, solitary dance.

"This is gorgeous," Conor began, before lapsing back into stunned silence. He didn't know what he'd expected, but somehow knew he had not guessed at this level of talent. He realized his thoughts were transparent when Kate's face relaxed into its first sustained smile.

"Such astonishment. You're surprised I was actually good at this?"

"Well, no, it isn't that, exactly."

"Oh, come on. You can admit it. I haven't been much of an advocate for myself, so why wouldn't you be surprised? You didn't expect it."

"I ... no. I did not," Conor said reluctantly. "And it's a mortal embarrassment. I should know by now not to underestimate you."

Kate dismissed his confession graciously. "I almost wish I hadn't shown it to you. I'd prefer being underestimated. It's painful when people think you're wasting your talent—not quite so much if they think you don't have any. The art collector isn't operating under either impression. He wants to commission a companion piece."

"And you don't think you can do it." From her responding glare Conor saw he'd touched a nerve.

"I don't *think* I can do it? I *know* I can't do it. I believe I've mentioned this before, Conor. I can't paint." She flung an arm at the blank canvas across the room. "I can't even bring myself to put a mark on it. It sits there and I come in every few weeks to dust it, for God's sake. I've tried therapy, meditation—I even tried hypnosis, if you can believe that. Nothing works."

"What about focusing on art, instead of yourself?" Conor asked. "Have you tried that?"

"Have I tried focusing on *art* instead of *myself?*" Kate looked stunned, and then extremely angry. "I suppose to you this all seems like some self-induced, navel-gazing melodrama?"

"Ehm, no, that's not—"

"You insensitive bastard!"

She came out of her chair, gathering wits and breath for a withering explosion. Conor knew it would concuss any second and silently cursed Abigail for setting off this crisis. His question had been intentional, but not skillfully phrased. He didn't have a lot of time to get it right.

"Okay wait, wait. That's not exactly what I meant to say." He rose from his seat as well, hands waving in self-defense, and took a step backward. "Will you ever let me explain before you eat the head off me?"

With exaggerated patience Kate stood in front of him, eyebrows raised in wordless, hostile inquiry. He took another step back, collided with the arm of the sofa, and abruptly sat down.

"Holy Mother, what am I like?" He caught himself before he pitched over backwards. "Listen. I didn't mean to be insensitive. I actually do understand how it feels, when the one thing you thought you were born for seems completely out of reach."

The chilliness in her eyes warmed a degree, encouraging him to continue.

"You get the idea that everything has slipped away from you. You can't remember where it came from in the first place, or how to get it back, and then you start wondering if it's gone for good ... " He trailed off, looking at the blank canvas. Enveloped in its shroud-like covering it presented an uncomfortably obvious metaphor. Struggling for composure, Kate finished for him.

"That's the most terrifying thought of all, isn't it?"

"Yes," he whispered.

Silently, Conor prayed for the moment to pass, not knowing what he might do this time if she cried, but she found a distraction, picking up wadded balls of drawing paper from the floor. With a soft groan he swung his legs over the sofa and sank into the cushions, knowing he was snared and that he'd half-consciously set the trap himself. He should have avoided coming close to her like this, but he couldn't; he should refuse now to be drawn in deeper but when she came and sat next to him, he knew he wouldn't.

"I don't know what to do."

Hearing the weariness in her voice Conor automatically circled an arm around her shoulders. "I'd say the first thing is to get away from this bloody canvas for a while. Gives me the fear, the way it's looking at us. Do you fancy a bit of music? I've something in mind that works best at sunset."

8

S quinting up at the setting sun Conor chose a spot for them, pointing his violin case at the top of the pasture across the road. They reached the picnic bench and sat with the case lying open on the grass in front of them, revealing a much older instrument than Kate had expected. Gleaming with a brandy-colored finish and nestled in a cocoon of green velvet, the violin rested inside like a rare antique, too brittle to be touched.

"How beautiful." She spoke as though cooing into the cradle of a fragile newborn.

Conor lifted the violin and began tuning, hands brisk and self-assured. As he ran a bow over the strings the instrument came alive with drones and animated squeaks, dispelling some of Kate's intimidated awe.

"What would you like me to play?" He frowned down the length of the fingerboard, giving the tuning pegs a few final tweaks.

"Oh. I don't know. Your violin seems too grand for a hoedown tune."

"Not at all. She's perfectly happy with whatever I play—reels, Mozart, pub songs—but I've no idea what a 'hoedown tune' is." Conor's face cleared in a smile. "Local expression?"

"I guess so." Kate laughed. "Something like a reel, or a jig?"

"Is it a jig you'd like? Or a reel?"

She didn't want to admit she couldn't tell the difference

between the two. "Play whatever you want. You said you had something in mind."

"I do. Let's sit on the grass. We need to wait a couple more minutes."

They settled on the ground and Conor finished tuning with a flourish of scales as the sun descended. When its bottom edge brushed the mountaintop in the distance he tucked the instrument back under his chin, lifted the bow, and stopped. The corners of his eyes creased as he stared at the mountains. "My father taught me this. He called it the tune to put the sun to sleep. Now, close your eyes 'til I'll tell you to open them."

Kate lifted her face to the warmth of the sun and let its glow pulse against her eyelids as the violin begin to speak—slow notes in a minor key, like a soft, keening moan. They circled back and the phrases repeated, filling the air with mournful lament, and after a moment Conor's voice whispered close to her ear.

"Open your eyes, Kate."

She opened them with drowsy reluctance as the music changed pitch with a set of clear piercing notes, desolate and urgent. Tethered to the rising sound, Kate felt her heart straining to float up to it. Before her an expanse of cloud in technicolor blue and pink spread like a bruise toward the horizon, hovering in a sky of radiant gold while the sun slipped lower, in sleepy obedience to the tune. Gradually, it melted into the mountains until only a sliver lingered above the peak, and then winked out.

The music had ended, and Kate turned to see the violin already tucked back in its case, as if the entire episode had been an acoustical fantasy. With his knees hugged to his chest Conor sat watching the color intensify in the afterglow.

"Not too bad, then? The sound was okay?"

"Seriously?" Kate stared at him. "My God."

"You liked it?"

"Of course. The sound was amazing."

"Thank you."

Kate considered the strange paradox of the man as they enjoyed a stillness neither seemed anxious to break. In some ways he was easy to know and in others, impossible. He'd revealed only a piece of his past—and that only out of necessity—but although Conor had drawn a veil around any further details of his troubled history he seemed a reluctant enigma, and with his music he'd shared something deeply personal that seemed to invite a closer glimpse.

"When did your father die?" she asked gently.

He stirred and shifted to face her. "Almost twenty years ago. He died of pulmonary disease when I was twelve."

"And he taught you that tune? You've been able to play like that since you were twelve years old?"

He smiled at her astonishment. "Not exactly, but I've played some arrangement of that air since I was six. He gave me a fiddle when I turned five and once he realized I had the knack he got fairly serious with the lessons. Before he got too weak he dragged me to every fiddling contest in the west of Ireland, but sure we only went for the *craic*—a bit of fun. He'd usually be getting me out of school, serving up some desperate rubbish for the teacher."

"Did you win them?"

"A fair number. I stopped going when he died. I couldn't play at all for a long time. I had the fiddle with me everywhere, by then. I couldn't leave it alone and I couldn't bear to play. Sound familiar?" He smiled at her. "My mother figured out what to do. Classical music—same instrument, different art altogether. I had to start at the beginning and learn everything all over again. She found a Czech master who gave lessons in Tralee. This violin belonged to him—an 1830 Pressenda he left to me when he died."

Kate took the instrument from its case and held it up to the fading light. She turned it over and ran a finger over its back. The gorgeous striated pattern resembled the skin of an exotic animal.

"Demonstrate." She handed the violin to him. "Play something Classical."

Conor's expression faltered. "I'm not exactly at the top of my game. Until a few weeks ago I hadn't played the thing for almost a year."

"I promise not to wince."

He rose to re-tune, pacing in front of her, and without warning launched the bow over the strings in a staccato burst of notes. In contrast to the slow air this tune was hectic, played at a frenzied pace. Assuming a more formal posture, Conor had transferred his entire attention to the violin, and after he'd plucked the final two notes with his fingers his eyes slowly re-focused on her.

"And?" He cocked an eyebrow.

"Was it supposed to sound like mosquitoes on speed?"

He laughed, settling back on the ground next to her. "Wrong bug. It's called the 'Flight of the Bumblebee,' although your description is better."

Kate imagined any idiot would recognize Conor's skill, but from her own creative perspective she saw the intangible element transforming his talent into something sublime—virtuosity pushed beyond technical brilliance, becoming art. The source was a mystery impossible to teach or easily explain, and as she knew from painful experience it could leave without warning.

"What made you stop for nearly a year?" Envy lent an impatient bite to her abrupt question.

"Guilt, I suppose—imagining I'd lost the right to the pleasure it gave me."

Without thinking, Kate let her emotions override any sense of discretion. "What a load of self-indulgent bullshit. You have a miraculous gift; you can't bottle that up and pretend it doesn't exist. It deserves more respect. To be nurtured and shared. How could you think you'd lost the right to play? You don't have the right not to."

Conor had again circled his arms around his knees with the violin in one hand, and for a long moment he stared at the ground. The light was nearly gone, but when he turned his mischievous grin cut through the darkness.

"You mean focus on art, instead of myself?"

"I mean— " Kate's brain caught up with her spleen and her argument trailed off into confusion. "Oh."

"Do you see what I did there?" he teased softly.

Flustered, she was quiet for a moment, but then her eyes narrowed. "Are all Irishmen as devious as you?"

"Of course, darlin'. You've always to be watching us. We can't help ourselves."

For just an instant the light in Conor's eyes held something at odds with his lilting humor, a flare of heat that disappeared so quickly Kate could sense only its effect on her—a sudden tickle in the center of her abdomen. Startled by the unexpected ripple of energy between them she waited for him to say something, but Conor swiveled his head to the horizon, and after a moment of awkward silence Kate stretched and rose from the grass.

"Time to go face Abigail. I've deserted my post for long enough. Thank you for the concert—and for schooling me. Both helped."

"Right. Grand." He glanced up at her and dropped his eyes away again. "Be sure to tell her you ate all your dinner. I'll be expecting a gold star."

After watching her descend the pasture Conor reclined on his back against the hillside and stared at the sky. "You're an awful feckin' eejit, McBride. You can't go there, and you know it."

He rested a hand on the violin lying on his chest, grateful to have at least one avenue of fulfillment available to him. His fingers fidgeted on the fingerboard, reveling in the restored connection, itching for something more. He stood up again and lifted the instrument to his shoulder. The bow hovered shyly over the strings then gently moved down over them in a loving stroke. After the first few notes he recognized what he was playing: the Brahms concerto, Adagio.

The performance was far from polished, but he played through to the end. As he bent to pick up a square of chamois from the case a white card fluttered out and fell to the grass. He retrieved it and ran a thumb across the embossed lettering: *Frank Emmons Murdoch*. One of many cards the cagey, silver-haired cipher had always been handing out, usually with something scribbled on it. He angled the back of this one into the starlight for a better view.

Lanesborough Hotel bar - Wednesday, 6 o'clock

Naturally. The one that started it all. Drinks in a London hotel, a memorable dinner the following evening, and then the improbable journey that had led to his brother. He'd found Thomas only to lose him again, and in the process had lost part of himself.

Conor tilted his head back, nodding a salute to whatever power inhabited the star-streaked sky. This was how retribution worked. It waited not only in nightmares where it was expected but also in quiet moments, slicing into temporary zones of peace, reminding him that every step in the direction of grace would carry a price. He picked up the case and started back down the hill toward the house.

The mills of God grind exceeding small.

They did, indeed. It was right that they should.

*S*omething is coming. He can feel it on the road moving toward him. It doesn't seem far away.

He turns to look and something in between clouds his vision, but he can see a small figure, hands held up, shoulder-high. Carrying something.

The thing between them is heat, bending in the air as he watches, making everything he looks at ripple in a spastic dance. It's too much heat, too hot for Ireland.

He turns again and faces a long pasture leading up to a stone farmhouse. Home. He can see it there, but the road billows with a kind of dust that looks like it belongs somewhere else, and the sun hammering into his head is the burn of a different climate.

"What's in your pocket?"

A whisper he doesn't recognize in the air around him.

"What's in your pocket?"

Now, he does. His own voice.

He reaches into his pocket and draws out a small marigold blossom, dark orange, wrinkle-petaled. Again he looks behind him, and the child is moving forward with the same smile. The same handful of flowers. Not far away at all.

Now, he is on his back, eyes closed, perspiration tickling over his scalp like a warning. He turns his head to one side, opens his eyes ... and the boy stands next to his bed, mouth stretched in a soundless howl, a hideous parody of his brilliant smile. Arms held forward, he presents his offering of marigolds but their bright color is ruined. They are soaked in blood.

Conor was up and at the opposite wall before coming fully awake and realizing the thing he'd blindly reached out to clutch was the mantelpiece in his bedroom.

The nightmare was the first he'd had in a while. They'd ripped him awake almost every night for weeks after he'd arrived, but gradually a daily routine of manual labor had ensured he went to bed too tired to dream about anything. Having fewer post-traumatic stress episodes in his life had seemed like a relief. Now, he questioned whether trading frequency for virulence was an improvement, and wondered what had triggered this one. Perhaps it was nothing more than the memories evoked by the sight of Frank's card earlier in the evening, but deeper in his mind he registered a sense of climbing tension, of an arrow being drawn to its point of release.

His hands slid over the marble of the mantelpiece. It seemed greasy under his jumping fingertips and Conor felt a pool of hot saliva collect in his mouth. He lurched back and doubled over, breathing in shallow gasps to force down the nausea. After several minutes the wild pounding of his heart subsided and he slowly straightened. He looked around the room, half-expecting a small figure to dart from a shadowed corner, and pressed a hand to the back of his neck. The skin was slick with sweat and still tingling.

"I told him to go home. God help me. Why didn't he go home?"

9

He'd lost it again. Conor swept his fingers under a swaying tower of paper, not surprised the pencil kept disappearing on him. More unnerving was the thought that this was Kate's idea of a tidy work area.

"I cleaned off the desk for you," she'd announced before leaving for a season-ending sale at a greenhouse in Cabot. With four sets of guests scheduled to arrive, Conor had agreed to staff the front office until Darla came on duty at noon.

He had a project to keep him occupied—graphing a year's worth of animal nutrition data—but progress proved a challenge since he had only sixteen inches of surface area for the task.

Conor wheeled back, searching for the pencil under his feet without success. "Well, for fuck—ah, oops." He bit down on his lip. He was doing his best to cut down on the swearing—especially around the guests—but the Irish had spent centuries perfecting the art of cursing as poetic expression, and he found the habit more difficult to kick than cigarettes.

When he pulled his gaze from the floor the young couple who'd arrived Saturday stood at the front desk. He sprang from the chair wearing a guilty smile and came out to greet them. "Now. Are you all right, there?"

They needed tourist maps, and he obliged by pulling an assortment from the shelves beneath the desk. "We've every kind of map going. Cycling maps, hiking maps, maps for finding cheese, here's one for wineries."

By the time he'd armed them for an outing under any possible theme, two of the expected arrivals had come through the door. Both men, and the elder of them was one of the largest human beings he'd ever seen. He stood at least five inches taller than Conor and every vertical inch balanced against an impressive spread of muscle. He looked to be in his mid-fifties, with a strong angular face and hair like teased-out steel wool. Like a genial, fairy-tale giant he stepped forward, hand extended in greeting.

"We have arrived much earlier than expected, I think. I hope this is not inconvenient?" His voice rumbled, a deep *basso profundo* ornamented with a German accent.

Stunned, Conor recovered in time to take the enormous hand while discreetly eyeing the list on the desk. "Not at all. Welcome. I'm guessing you must be Dr.... ehm, von Hahnemann?"

"Excellent," the man rumbled. "This is it, exactly correct pronunciation. I am Dr. C. Eckhard von Hahnemann and here is my associate Leonard Belkis. Delighted to meet you."

"Yes, you as well, Dr... sir."

"C."

"Sorry?" Conor angled his head politely as he extended a hand to Leonard. Like a sapling in the shadow of a redwood, the young man seemed small and colorless by comparison.

"Professor C is the sobriquet people find most convenient for addressing me. I have grown accustomed to this and I invite you to make use of it."

"Thanks, that is a bit easier."

"I assume you must be Conor McBride, the Irish musician I was told I would find here."

Conor's smile froze. "Who told you that?" he asked quietly.

The man took his time responding, appearing to enjoy the tension he'd created. "Why, Mrs. Fitzpatrick." His grin widened. "Who other than she? I am a conductor with the Salzburg

Philharmonic. Leonard is an accomplished keyboard artist from Manhattan."

"Primarily harpsichord," Leonard clarified with remote, condescending patience.

"We are guests of the symphony orchestra in Sherbrooke, Quebec. With leisure time available I was eager to visit Vermont. The scenery is often compared with my homeland."

"Well, you've a great day for touring. So, two rooms. If you could sign these and—right, thanks."

Conor focused on the check-in procedures, trying to convince himself the heat spreading along his nerves was not a prickle of warning.

"Looks like we've got you in rooms three and five. They're on the right at the top of the stairs. The dining room is closed tonight but breakfast starts at half-six—sorry, six-thirty—tomorrow morning. Just the one night, then?"

Professor C nodded with a humorous pout. "Sadly, yes. All too brief a trip, although I hope to have the pleasure of hearing you play before leaving. I understand you are quite a remarkable virtuoso."

"According to Mrs. Fitzpatrick, I assume?" Maintaining eye contact and a bland smile, Conor slid the keys over to Professor C.

"Of course, Conor. Who other than she?"

The two men headed for the stairs, declining his offer of assistance with their bags, and Conor returned to Kate's office. Dropping into the chair he found himself staring straight at the long lost pencil. He picked it up and then threw it down again, wheeling backwards and kicking a booted foot against the desk.

"Fuck." The curse emerged with unrepentant energy.

Dr. C. Eckhard Von Hahnemann might be who he said he was, but there wasn't a doubt in Conor's mind he'd come for some reason other than sightseeing. He had no idea what it was, but thought he knew exactly who had sent him.

Kate swiveled from the computer screen, looking for any excuse to stop tinkering with the Rembrandt Inn's website. Since returning from Cabot she'd spent the last hour trying to book a room at her own property, but the online software kept spinning her into oblivion. She swung back to her desk, admiring the alterations produced by its most recent occupant. While discreetly maintaining whatever doubtful system might be in place, Conor had transformed her piles of chaos into neat stacks that seemed to double the size of the desk.

"Is the site working yet?" Darla called out breathlessly from the registration desk—for the third time in an hour. The young woman was kindhearted, but she fixated on the smallest crisis with ghoulish urgency. She also had an insatiable appetite for gossip and tiresome questions. The mere hint of her approach could make Conor disappear like a skittish house cat.

"Not yet." Kate emerged from her office. "Don't stress, though. I'm not. Do you know where Conor is?"

Darla sucked her breath over her teeth and bit her lip. "He seemed really distracted when I got here and then he ran off so I never had a chance to talk to him." She cocked her head—a quick, bird-like movement—and frowned in concern. "Is everything okay? Nothing's wrong, I hope?"

"Not that I'm aware of, Darla," Kate said patiently. "He must be around somewhere. I'll find him."

After searching for him in his room, the barn and his practice studio, Kate found Conor crouched in the garden tying up tomato plants. With a jackknife clamped in place between his teeth he hiked his chin in silent greeting at her approach, and continued working.

His t-shirt and jeans were covered in dirt, but with a Phoenix

Feeds cap shading his eyes and perspiration accentuating the muscles of his tanned arms he appeared even more eye-catching than usual. Kate took in the view with an appreciation she'd lately discovered was no longer quite as disinterested. Only when she drew closer did she notice the pinched distraction Darla had mentioned.

"Is everything okay?" she asked, unconsciously mimicking her young housekeeper.

He took the knife from his mouth and glanced up at her. "Fine. Why? Hand me the string, will you?"

"You look sort of hot and bothered." She handed the spool to him. "I think you're working too hard. You should take a rest."

"Don't you be starting on me as well." He shot her an abashed grin, softening the retort. "One house physician is all I can handle. How was the flower sale?"

"I got some great deals. Thanks for holding down the fort. Darla is staying late so we're clear for our picnic. She and I met C. Eckhard von Hahnemann earlier, and his friend Leonard. 'Professor C'. What a character. I've never seen anyone like him."

"Yeah." Conor scowled, cutting a length of twine and shuffling to the next plant. "Quite the force of nature."

"You don't like him?" Kate studied him, trying to understand why he was so abnormally grumpy. "I thought you would enjoy talking with them—him being a conductor and Leonard a pianist."

"Primarily harpsichord," Conor corrected, a pitch-perfect imitation of the young man's pedantic tone. He shrugged. "Conductors make me nervous. I generally steer clear of them outside a concert hall."

"Uh-oh. I didn't know that." Kate braced herself, anticipating she was about to make his cranky mood even worse. "I invited them to join us tonight with Yvette and Jigger."

Conor pivoted on his heel, giving her a hard stare. "You're joking me."

"He said he wanted to hear you play." Kate plucked at the twine around one of the plants in front of her. "I told him we were hiking up to the pond and you'd be playing later, and they were welcome to come listen. I'm sorry. I should have asked you first, but I just thought—well, I guess that's the trouble. I wasn't thinking."

"Never mind about it." Conor lifted her fingers from the plant and gave them a squeeze. "I don't think they'll come."

"Why not?"

"Because I think Professor C has something else in mind." Conor released a long breath of weariness. "I apologize for raising this tedious issue again Kate, but did the two of you talk about me when he rang to book the room?"

"Of course not." Kate's eyes widened. "He didn't call. He booked through the website, back when it was working, that is. He knew you were here? Do you know who told him?"

"I've a pretty strong hunch."

The obvious next question hung in the air between them. Avoiding it, Conor lifted the bottom of his t-shirt and wiped his face, peering down at the result. "I look about three-quarters dirt, don't I? Have I time for a shower before we go?"

Yvette and Jigger arrived while Conor was showering. Once he was ready he shouldered the backpack containing their picnic—allowing Kate to carry his violin—and they started out for the pond. Kate and Yvette walked slowly, chatting about perennials, but Jigger stepped out at a quick march across the long field behind the inn. Conor stayed close behind him, happy to be diverted from an unproductive train of thought.

He'd know soon enough if the enigmatic Professor C wanted something other than a recital from him, so he pushed the mystery aside to concentrate on the immediate prospect of dinner and music, and kept an eye on the retreating figure in front of him.

Jigger had already reached the edge of the field where a tractor road began. The route wound steeply up through the woods, ending in a wide hilltop meadow with a spring-fed pond at its center. As the boy disappeared into the trees Conor jogged forward.

"Don't get too far ahead, Jigs," he called. "The water's not running away from you."

He signaled to Kate and Yvette then started up the path, catching glimpses of the bobbing, fair head through the trees. After a few minutes of climbing he came around a loop in the trail and found Jigger squatting in the dirt twenty feet ahead. His compact figure was lit by the fractured sunlight bending around the surrounding branches and leaves. Before he could speak the boy stood up, turned to him, and extended his cupped hands with a delighted, radiant smile.

Like a switch being thrown, Conor was hit with a salivating panic he was helpless to control. He felt himself collapsing—stomach hollowed out, heart hammering. With blood roaring in his ears he stumbled to the nearest tree and swung an arm around it as his legs gave out. He slid down the slender trunk as though slipping down a fire pole and landed hard, hitting the ground with a gasp.

In almost every circumstantial way, the boy in front of him was not at all like the child haunting his dreams. The two shared nothing in terms of culture, condition or physical resemblance, but in the space of an instant they had fused into one. One pair of hands extended in offering, one innocent smile of welcome and pleasure, one small bundle of fragile humanity. The same bass-line theme repeated with a slight variation. Like a chaconne.

For most of his life Conor had been immersed in the canon of his mother's mystical philosophy, one that saw porous borders between worlds and understood many things passed over them, in both directions. He couldn't dismiss the waking replication of a dream as mere coincidence. He recognized a portent when he saw it.

Groggy and still disoriented, Conor became aware of Jigger, frantic on the ground next to him, fluttering hands patting him everywhere.

"Please tell me what it is, Conor. Does it hurt somewhere? It looks terrible. Oh, it looks like it hurts. Can you breathe? Are you going to throw up?"

"Yes, I can breathe, and no, I'm not going to throw up." He came sufficiently to his senses to pull the boy into an embrace and prevent him from bursting into empathetic tears. "I'm all right. Sorry for scaring you, boss. It's the heat, maybe. I went bleary-eyed for a second and I think I tripped on a rock. See it, sticking up over there? How did you manage to miss it?"

He was still resting by the tree with Jigger at his side when Kate and Yvette appeared. They registered the scene slowly and then hurried forward.

"What's going on?" Kate looked down at them. "Are you okay?"

"Yeah, yeah, fine. Got a bit doze-y for a minute." Conor held up a half-emptied bottle of water. "I probably haven't drunk enough today. I'm re-hydrating."

She exchanged a glance with Yvette, who extended a hand to Jigger and pulled him to his feet. "Come on, hon. Let's blaze the trail and these two can catch up."

Before they were out of sight Kate hunkered down in front of him, lightly resting her hands on his knees. "Okay I'm worried, so cut the shit. You're white as a sheet and you've been acting weird today. What is it?"

Conor took a pull from the bottle and began a reprise of his excuse, but then stopped. He put his head against the tree and closed his eyes. "I'm not sure. Never happened before. A sort of flashback, I guess. I can't ... I'm sorry, but I can't tell you more than that."

Another half-truth, another apology. He wondered how long it would be before he'd exhausted her patience for this, but apparently she could endure a little more. He felt her grip on his knees tighten—the only sign of her frustration—before she dropped her hands.

"All right, how can I help? Do you want to go home?"

He opened his eyes. "Jaysus, no. I'm starving and I've lost half my weight in sweat. I want a swim and I want my dinner. What color do I look now?"

"A little pinker." Kate shook her head, laughing a little.

"See? You've helped already." Conor pulled himself up and adjusted the backpack. "Let's go. Don't forget the fiddle."

When they reached the place on the trail where Jigger had been standing, Conor bent to pick up—not a marigold blossom but the small skull of a squirrel. He pocketed the brittle totem, and they continued up the hill.

10

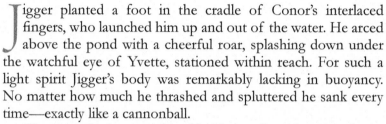

Jigger planted a foot in the cradle of Conor's interlaced fingers, who launched him up and out of the water. He arced above the pond with a cheerful roar, splashing down under the watchful eye of Yvette, stationed within reach. For such a light spirit Jigger's body was remarkably lacking in buoyancy. No matter how much he thrashed and spluttered he sank every time—exactly like a cannonball.

The scene had repeated itself a dozen times, but the players performed with such gusto it continued to be entertaining. Kate watched from her perch at the end of the dock, envying the boy's exuberance, not to mention his disregard for the pull of gravity. Her gaze wandered past Jigger to the wooden raft floating farther out in the middle of the pond. Rocking with the turbulence created by all the activity it seemed to be nodding an invitation, taunting her immobility. She looked quickly away and ran a hand over the front of her bathing suit—a flattering black one-piece, as dry as the paintbrushes in her studio. The irony did not escape her. Two neuroses, same symbolic characteristic.

Since the day her husband had drowned—six years ago this week—she hadn't ventured into any body of water deeper than a bathtub, but in more recent years with every visit to the pond she tried to conquer the phobia. She never got far before fear caught up to her, slithering along her nerves like venom, freezing her limbs in place until her whispered surrender relaxed them enough to allow a retreat.

She had a long history of such failures, but had reason to hope for a different result tonight. The anniversary of Michael's death had come and gone two days earlier. For the first time, half the day had passed before Kate remembered its significance, and when she did, she waited for the crippling sense of loss and panic that always followed. To her surprised relief, it didn't come. She'd felt a startled catch in her throat, but nothing more. If the grief cycling through her like a chronic illness was at last loosening its grip, she hoped its related symptoms might recede as well.

She'd set out that evening determined to force the issue, but her demons were too clever for any direct assault. They were practiced in the art of avoidance, and the incident on the trail with Conor provided a convenient diversion. Instead of forcing herself down into the water she continued sitting on its edge, thinking about him, wondering where his demons came from and if he'd ever tell her.

When she looked up again Yvette and Jigger had scrambled ashore to head for their picnic site while Conor lingered behind. She'd been alarmed by how shaky and ill he'd appeared earlier, but the horseplay with Jigger had revived him. Sleek as a seal, with his wet black hair sculpted against his head, he swam toward her and stood up as he neared the dock. Kate made an effort not to stare. She assumed the hefting of forty-pound milk buckets held the secret to abdominal muscles most men only achieved with a gym fee.

Oblivious to the new sort of distraction he was causing, Conor waded forward and stopped in front of her. "We're coming to the end of August. Might be the last time we get up here this summer." He angled his head, leaving the question implied but unspoken.

She nodded, acknowledging the hint. She'd confessed her fear of water to him during their first visit to the pond earlier in the summer, but had not revealed the source of her phobia. He'd accepted her silence with tactful understanding, never mentioning the topic—even indirectly—until now.

Lifting her foot, Kate kicked a few drops of water at him. "Between the two of us we'd keep a therapist busy for years."

"No argument there."

"Listen, I'm not trying to pry and this is only a suggestion, but I know one if you're interested."

"So, we're back to me, now?"

Kate laughed, dropping her eyes again. "I did go to him myself for a while."

"Did it help?" Conor asked.

"Not much," she admitted. "That might have been my fault. He's supposed to be very good, and of course trustworthy. Maybe you could tell him things you can't tell me."

"Kate." He came closer and put a hand on the dock. "I hope you aren't thinking I don't trust you. You couldn't be more wrong."

"No, no, I understand. I only meant ... well, it would be sort of like the confessional. Oh, I know a priest too, that might be better? He wasn't much help, either, though."

"Ah, that's grand, isn't it? You want to saddle me with all your cast-offs."

Smirking, he pushed away and swam back to the middle of the pond, but soon returned. He came up out of the water below her and Kate's breath stuttered at the unexpected pressure of his palms against the soles of her feet.

"I shouldn't have been flippant," he said softly. "I do appreciate the offer. How about we skip the priest and the therapist. Maybe we can help each other. We could start now, if you like?"

Kate let him move her feet in slow circles, but when he reached a hand to her she reluctantly slid her foot free and poked a toe at his stomach. "We shouldn't keep the others waiting, and since you were starving half an hour ago you must be ready to faint by now."

Without answering, Conor watched her face for another

moment, then nodded and lifted himself up to the dock. Disappointed with herself, Kate handed him her towel and they walked back across the field.

When they'd finished eating, Conor and his young protégé settled on a broad flat rock with their audience on the picnic blanket in front of them. He'd taught Jigger guitar accompaniments for several traditional tunes and had been stunned by how quickly he'd learned the basics, assimilating and adapting the technique to new material as soon as Conor presented it. They played them all, producing a nearly seamless set that had Kate and Yvette on their feet doing an unorthodox jig in front of them. As the music died away the two collapsed, breathless and giggling at Conor's feet.

"What was the last one called?" Kate asked.

"The last one? 'The Old Hag at the Kiln.'" Conor smiled at her incredulous snort. "Yeah, we're not always poetic."

With sunset approaching, Kate went to collect a t-shirt left by the pond. Jigger curled up on the blanket, head propped against his guitar case, while Conor and Yvette worked around him to pack the remains of the food.

"Feckin' loaves and fishes." Conor grappled with the backpack's zipper and straightened, wiping a line of sweat from his lip. "How did she get all this in here?"

Yvette ignored the complaint, her attention elsewhere. "She's going to try again."

He turned and saw Kate standing in ankle-deep water, her back straight and her chin lifted, pointing at a boundary only she could see. "Do you want to go to her, Yvette? It might help."

"Me?" Yvette's flat affect betrayed a hint of sarcasm, but then she nodded in understanding. "She hasn't told you."

"No, and it didn't seem right to ask."

"Since you have so many secrets yourself?"

Conor winced at her mild tone of challenge, but Yvette merely shrugged. "Her story isn't a secret but it's hers to tell. You just have to let her know you want to hear it." She gazed at Kate, her brow creasing. "She usually wants to do this alone, though. This could take a while, and it's getting late."

"Go." Conor gave her shoulder a squeeze. "I'll wait for her. Can you manage all right with Jigger? He's falling asleep."

"I'm not asleep." Jigger smiled at them drowsily, fighting to stretch heavy-lidded eyes, and climbed to his feet.

His mother kissed the top of his head and laughed. "He'll be okay once we start walking."

The sound of their footsteps scything through the tall grass faded as they crossed the meadow. Conor hunkered down against a rock facing the pond. The crickets trilled and the fish had begun their twilight feeding. The liquid sound of their mouths breaking the surface carried to him as he watched, and waited. He was in no hurry to leave the place with its magical light and natural music, but when Kate moved back to the end of the dock to sit on its edge his restraint gave way.

After his sunset recital for her, he'd spent the past two weeks in a state of perpetual resistance, afraid of being pulled into an orbit he'd never escape. He couldn't do it any more. He couldn't let her struggle alone and he was tired of plotting every move in his life like a game of three-dimensional chess. He decided to let God move the pieces around for a change.

Conor entered the water quietly and went to stand in front of her. Kate raised her head, her smile dying before it reached her eyes. "Will you tell me?" he asked.

She tensed, regarding him uncertainly, and leaned a shoulder against the dock's corner post. "You've probably never heard of the Thimble Islands? They're in Long Island Sound, off the coast of Connecticut. My father has a house on one of them but

Anna—my stepmother—prefers the Hamptons, so they hardly ever go. Michael and I went there six years ago this week."

Her brow wrinkled. "Things hadn't been great between us. We'd fallen out of sync, somehow. We needed this vacation to get back on track, but then Phillip showed up at our apartment one night and Michael invited him to come with us. Classic avoidance tactic. They spent every afternoon sailing together. I was livid, and Phillip tiptoed around me like I was a bomb about to blow. The poor guy knew he was caught in the middle of something, but he was so kind to me later. Which reminds me ..." Kate gave Conor a pointed glance. "You never answered my side of this question: what did Phillip Ryan tell you about *me*?"

"Not nearly enough."

"He didn't tell you about any of this?"

"Only that there was an accident. I didn't realize he was with you."

Kate nodded, lips pursed. "We were all on the boat together that day, and we stayed out pretty late. It was dark and the water was getting choppy. Phillip was at the helm, but Michael got up to take the wheel back—he was nervous about a sloop sailing too close to us—and he sent me down below to make sure everything was secure. The boat heeled over hard while I was down there and I went flying. I don't even know what I hit, but by the time I had my breath back and got up on deck Phillip was at the wheel again, screaming, and Michael was gone. I don't remember much after that. Phillip said he'd thrown out one of the boat fenders on the side where Michael had gone overboard, but we couldn't see him and the boat was still moving. He said I just went berserk and jumped into the water."

Kate touched her fingers to her lips and closed her eyes. "I do remember the water. So cold. Nothing around me. Nothing I could touch. And then suddenly, Phillip was there. He wasn't much of a sailor, but he'd finally managed to bring the boat into the wind and stop fairly close. He tried to throw me a lifeline, but I was hypothermic and nearly unconscious by that point. He jumped in after me and somehow got me back into the boat."

"What about Michael?" Conor asked.

She shook her head, her eyes still closed. "Gone. He wasn't wearing a life jacket. Someone called in the Coast Guard, and they gave me first aid and told Phillip to get me to the hospital while they searched. Hours later when I woke up in the emergency room, Phillip had to tell me they hadn't found Michael, and there wasn't much hope left that they would. I screamed at Phillip, I blamed him. He let me rage at him—hit him even—and then he held me while I cried. He never left my side that day, but he hardly ever said a word. He left as soon as I was released the next morning." Kate opened her eyes, and they were clear and calm. "What's he doing, now that he's not working for you?"

"He's got a place on a ferry run, taking tourists to the islands off the Dingle Peninsula."

"On a ferry. Good for him. He wasn't afraid to go back on the water." She gave an approving nod. "I lost so much that day but I want some things back, and I think I've waited long enough."

"I think so, too." Conor took a step forward and put his hands on the dock. "Will you let me help you?"

Kate frowned and indicated the shallow water near the shore. "I usually start back there."

"I've seen that. Let's try something different." He brought his hands to her waist, bracing to lift her, but seeing the panic in her eyes, paused. "No? Should I stop?"

"No."

Conor lifted her, easing her down into the water, and immediately the color drained from Kate's face. He felt her muscles shudder and lock in terror. Alarmed, he moved to lift her back on the dock, but she took his hands from her waist and held them in a crushing grip.

"Don't," she whispered. "Let's go. Farther out."

He moved slowly backward, praying he wouldn't trip over something. Kate stayed rooted in place, but when her arms were almost fully extended between them, she took a step. And then another. As the water reached her collarbone they stopped, and Conor held her lightly by the elbows. She trembled, her breath coming in uneven gasps, but gradually grew quiet. After a few minutes she stepped away from him and turned in slow circles, a tranquil, dervish-like movement that reminded him of the figures in her painting.

"Maybe it's enough for now?" he suggested, when she stopped. She was calm, almost serene, but still pale and shivering. Again, she shook her head.

"No. Not enough. I want to float. Some day I want to swim out to that raft and jump up and down on it, but for now I just want to lie on my back, look at the sky ... and float."

She tried on her own, but couldn't bring herself to lift both feet. Conor finally took her up into his arms and she pressed her face into his neck, fingers tight on his shoulders. He held her for a long moment, and as she gradually relaxed he lowered her to the water. Eyes shut, she floated there, her hair washing around her face like an exotic sea grass.

Slowly, Conor removed his arms and withdrew, stepping several yards to the side. As he drifted backward, Kate opened her eyes and looked at the sky with a smile that took his breath away. A tear swelled and grew bright before spilling onto her face. He watched, and felt changed. As though he had become the single drop of water sliding down her cheek, carrying its taste of salt to the sweet water of the pond, dissolving without struggle.

11

Darkness hid their faces as they moved, descending through the woods and across the field. Kate carried the flashlight. She focused on the juddering beam teasing them along the path, absently alerting Conor to obstacles as they appeared.

"Rock. Roots. Hole." The terse warnings were the only conversation she could manage as her mind lingered over a long-awaited epiphany, probing the outline of something taking shape inside her.

Conor had lifted her up and rested her on the water, and with his hands anchoring her the terror of being weightless and unmoored had finally disappeared. He'd held her for as long as she'd needed, but had known enough to release her, and when she'd realized his hands were gone the sensation of freedom had been staggering.

With outstretched limbs holding her in balance, her body was like a tightened fist that had unclenched and stretched for the first time in years. She was grateful for his intuitive understanding—allowing the moment to be hers alone—but in its aftermath she found herself torn between an instinct to nurture a hard-won liberation and the desire to feel his hands beneath her again.

They came through the door into the kitchen, and in the fluorescent glare of its light she looked at him and saw her own uncertainty reflected back at her. He emptied the contents of the backpack onto the prep counter and Kate put the leftovers into the refrigerator, and then they stood staring at the flattened bag until she finally broke the silence.

"You're always helping me—so much, and so often. Won't you let me return the favor?"

Conor offered a fleeting smile. "I wish it could be that easy."

"Are you saying my 'phobic disorders' don't compare with yours?" Kate feigned outrage, teasing him, but Conor's face remained pensive.

"No, Kate. I'm saying you're braver than I am."

She stepped forward, yielding to impulse, and stretched up to kiss him on the cheek. He stiffened, hesitating, then his arms circled her waist and he drew her against him.

"I think we each have what the other needs." She rested her head on his shoulder. "But it will only work if we can accept what the other offers."

"I know. I'm sorry."

"You apologize too much." Kate drew back, smiling. "It isn't only you. I need some time as well—to understand how much I'm able to trust, and what I'm willing to risk. Does that make sense?"

"How can it not? It's the story of my life." He gave her waist a final squeeze before stepping back. "Do you need any help here?"

"You've helped enough for one day. Are you heading upstairs?"

"Not yet. I'm going down to the brook to play a little longer."

The moment of intimacy was slipping away, and she felt reluctant to let it go so abruptly. He picked up his violin and Kate caught his arm as he moved past her. "Conor, I don't want to lose whatever this is."

He reached out to sweep the still-damp hair from her face and gently kissed her forehead.

"Nor do I."

Following several false starts Conor took the violin from his shoulder in frustration. His objective was the diffusion of passion, not its escalation. He should have known the murmuring undercurrents and shadows below the inn would confuse that effort. The air itself was enough to unsettle him. With an aroma of newly cut grass on its breath, a breeze whispered against his face while the moon lit up the brook like a showcase of crystal.

He was in love with her. One minute he was telling himself to relax a little for fuck's sake, and the next minute he was in love with her. Just like that. His shoulders slumped and he dropped his head. No, not really 'just like that'. The truth was, he'd been tumbling a little farther every day from the moment he'd met her.

The undeniable reality of being in love was all the more unnerving for being alien. His mind wandered back to his years in Dublin and his short-lived engagement to a fellow musician named Maggie Fallon. Such memories were so remote they seemed like the history of someone else's life.

Despite assurances to the contrary—sincere at the time— he'd never been in love with Maggie. Until now he hadn't acknowledged how short of the mark he'd been. He'd assumed his arrest and conviction had prompted her to leave him, but maybe her letter would have come anyway. Maybe Maggie had realized what he was holding back, and now he did as well. He also knew what he was holding back from Kate, and what he stood to lose by it. For the first time he began fearing the consequences of secrecy almost as much as disclosure. Christ, he needed to stop thinking about it.

He shook himself into a more formal posture, and raising his bow like a whip set to crack, he glared at the moonlit brook and launched into Paganini.

He played caprices, the musical equivalent of a long run in the rain. Moving through them without pattern, his mind emptied of everything that was not concerned with the placement of his fingers and the movement of the bow. He stopped when his arm was limp and burning, and when he could no longer ignore the additional distraction lurking in the darkness behind him. Conor massaged the back of his shoulder and spoke without turning.

"Care to offer a critique? I'd say the pace was a bit ragged myself, but I wasn't planning on an audience."

"Ragged perhaps, spirited nevertheless." The soft voice with its deep mellow notes easily carried above the sounds of the brook. "I'd hoped not to disturb you. I'm sorry you perceived my presence."

"Just as well I did. I tend to react badly when I'm startled." He turned from the water and walked toward Professor C, who was sitting on the garden bench next to his violin case.

"I took such care to be silent, but you are more accomplished than I in these matters, yes?" Professor C winked at him.

"If it makes you feel any better I didn't hear a thing. I smelled the smoke." Conor sat down, nodding at the cigarette perched between the conductor's muscular fingers. "Give me one of those, will you? I've an idea I'm going to need it."

The conductor produced a silver case and lighter. Conor hesitated after picking out a cigarette, already regretting the lapse of willpower, but he put it to his lips and accepted the offered flame in surrender. The first smoky exhalation ended in a groan and Professor C smiled.

"Better than sex?"

Conor breathed a laugh. "Hard to tell. I've gone without that for a while, too." He read the label stamped below the filter tip and studied his companion's face. "Same brand. How is he, then, our mutual friend?"

"He is well, and pleased at hearing you also are well."

"How did he find me?"

"Are such things important?"

"Might be, yeah," Conor replied evenly.

"In truth, I do not know." A brief flash of annoyance gave credence to the assertion. "I am merely the courier. My role is quite limited."

"Uh-huh. What about your sidekick?"

Professor C pursed his lips in distaste. "Leonard is a boring young harpsichordist, nothing more. I would have happily left him in Sherbrooke but he quite conveniently had a car, while I—inconveniently—do not drive."

"Do you do this kind of thing a lot?"

"I prefer not to, but as you are aware our friend's charm and power to persuade can be devastating."

"I think you find it more charming than I ever did," Conor said. "So, what's he want?"

"To deliver a message to you."

"I gathered as much. What is it?"

"He wants to see you."

Conor shifted impatiently. "Oh, for Christ's sake. We're going to be at this all night. What does the man want and why isn't he here to tell me himself?"

"I don't know. Yes, yes." Professor C raised a hand, anticipating Conor's irritation. "For both of us this is frustrating, but I can give only the information presented to me. He wishes the meeting to be discreet; he wishes it to take place elsewhere." He drew a small, narrow envelope from his shirt pocket and handed it to Conor. "Tomorrow evening. Arrive at six o'clock. You will look for a pair of low folding chairs, in red-and-white striped canvas. You will sit in one and wait."

"Will I?" With a thumb and forefinger, Conor parted the envelope and squinted at the ticket inside. "Suppose I choose not to show. What then?" Receiving no response, he looked up and saw Professor C's smile of weary patience.

"Forgive me, but truly this is not a serious question, Conor.

I have delivered such messages before. You are no different than the rest. All of you fear something and cannot afford the indulgence of choice. All of you come when you are called."

Conor absorbed this assessment—brutally honest and accurate—without visible emotion. He dropped the cigarette to the ground, grinding it beneath his heel. They sat in silence until Professor C heaved an expressive sigh and stood up, offering him the silver case.

"A parting gift. Accept it with my apology. I have presented you with an unwelcome task."

With a small grin Conor declined the offer. "Another indulgence I can't afford. I accept the apology, though."

"Excellent. I hope we may meet again—perhaps on the concert stage, a milieu I believe we each find more suitable to our talents."

Conor hoped so as well. He watched the enormous figure gradually merge with the darkness, climbing the stone steps in the hillside like one of Jacob's angels. A mystery only partly revealed.

12

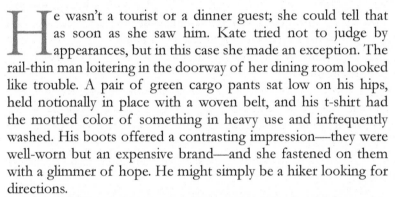

He wasn't a tourist or a dinner guest; she could tell that as soon as she saw him. Kate tried not to judge by appearances, but in this case she made an exception. The rail-thin man loitering in the doorway of her dining room looked like trouble. A pair of green cargo pants sat low on his hips, held notionally in place with a woven belt, and his t-shirt had the mottled color of something in heavy use and infrequently washed. His boots offered a contrasting impression—they were well-worn but an expensive brand—and she fastened on them with a glimmer of hope. He might simply be a hiker looking for directions.

She motioned for him to wait and finished seating a table of four before returning to the restaurant's check-in desk. He watched her approach, squinting in weariness, and although the evening was warm he shivered a little.

"I need to speak with Kate Fitzpatrick. You, I'm guessing?"

Okay. Not a hiker. She met his eyes—they were an unsettling shade of nickel gray—and gave a composed smile. "Yes. How can I help you?"

The man's rigid stance relaxed and he swayed to the left. He caught himself, frowned and stiffened again. "I'd appreciate a glass of water before anything else."

"Of course." Kate eyed him with cautious concern. "Maybe you should sit down in the living room and I'll bring you one. Are you feeling ill?"

"Starting to." He pushed away a portion of straight blond hair falling across his eye. "I've got about an hour before it gets worse. The living room won't work, though. I need to talk to you about Conor McBride." Digging into the pocket on his right thigh, he pulled out a slim wallet and flipped it open for her. "Curtis Sedgwick. Special Agent with the US Drug Enforcement Agency."

"I see."

At least they keep sending the 'special' ones, Kate thought. Her wan amusement lurched into queasiness as she examined the ID. The number of federal agencies tangled up in Conor's life had just doubled, and she wondered how many more might be waiting in the wings.

"If you're looking for Conor he isn't here." She masked her unease behind a cold formality. "And I honestly don't know where he went. He left word with my chef not to expect him back until late."

"No worries, I know where he is." He pocketed the wallet again.

"If that's the case, you should go find him there. I don't know how I can help you, Agent Sedgwick."

"I don't need to find him. He'll be back soon enough, and in a bad mood I imagine." The lines of fatigue in the agent's face deepened in amusement. "Just plain 'Sedgwick' is fine. Nobody calls me Agent-anything unless they're dressing me down."

"I don't know how I can help you—Sedgwick," Kate repeated.

The sardonic smile widened, but faded as he angled his head in appeal. "How about that glass of water? And two or three of whatever you've got for a headache. If we start there I'll be in better shape to tell you."

Reluctantly, Kate steered him into her office, to a chair across from the desk. She asked Dominic to take over for her and returned with a pitcher of water and some ibuprofen. She found

Sedgwick standing at the antique breakfront behind her desk, eyeing the contents of its shelves.

"Handsome piece of furniture," he observed without turning, casually opening one of the side drawers. "Matches the desk. Victorian?"

"Biedermeier," Kate said curtly. She gave him the ibuprofen. "If you're going to search my office, don't you need to show me a warrant?"

"I'm not actually searching. Just snooping." Sedgwick shook three pills from the bottle and accepted the water she offered. He drained the glass while sauntering around the room, his eyes like a recording device, sweeping over the braided oval rug on the floor, the green-and-cream striped sofa in front of the window—another Biedermeier—and the framed Audubon reproductions on the walls. After this tour he returned and silently presented his glass. She poured again, then pointedly took a seat behind her desk and waited, trying to appear calm.

For many reasons Kate had accepted Conor's secrets on faith, assuming his grounds for keeping them were sound and honorable. Her belief structure was not yet under active assault, but she felt the chill of a threat.

The agent emptied the glass a second time. Placing it on the desk, he brushed a few fingers against chapped-looking lips and releasing a slow breath sank back into the chair.

"Thanks. Helped more than I expected." He crossed his arms and regarded her speculatively, a scrutiny she wasn't prepared to tolerate.

"Well? If you want a question answered you need to ask one."

"What do you know about Thomas McBride?" he asked.

"Very little. If this concerns Thomas you need to wait for Conor to come back. I'm not comfortable answering questions about his brother."

"I didn't come here to interrogate you." Sedgwick was still

watching her with a trace of laughter. "I'll be doing most of the talking. I'm just trying to get a baseline so we don't waste time. What did he tell you?"

"That his brother was tricked into stealing money from the European Union and Conor was convicted as a conspirator, that Thomas disappeared, and that he's dead." Sedgwick flinched, a muscle rippling along his jaw. "Oh. You didn't know?"

"Yes. I did. Did Conor mention Thomas disappeared into India, and that he went there looking for him?"

"Thomas died in India?" she asked.

"Jammu-Kashmir. From a gunshot wound."

"Did you shoot him?"

"Of course I didn't shoot him, for God's sake."

"Well, I'm sorry," Kate shot back with equal intensity. "How was I supposed to know? I don't know anything except what I just told you."

"That's okay, Kate." Sedgwick's glare softened to a sly grin. "I'm here to fill in the blanks."

"Maybe I'd prefer to leave them empty," she countered weakly.

"Sorry, not an option. I need your cooperation but first I have to brief you on what's going on, so you've got to hear it."

She briefly considered trying to stop him anyway, instinctively knowing their conversation would carry consequences beyond anything she could predict. Despite her outburst, she felt unequal to the task of matching wits with the lean, weathered professional in front of her. He was a different specimen than the freshly laundered agents from Williston. Like a tempered blade that had seen its share of battles, he looked sharper and more dangerous.

The setting was beyond spectacular. Its backdrop was a series of gently rounded mountains nestled in uneven rows receding into the distance. In the foreground a performance tent floated above the field like a dollop of meringue, its roof plucked into stiff white peaks. Colors and convivial sound spilled out in front of the stage as concertgoers continued to arrive, spreading blankets and chairs, opening baskets, uncorking wine.

Conor was in everyone's way. He'd paid little attention to his surroundings while parking the truck, concentrating instead on the yellow-vested volunteers waving him along, but once he'd arrived on the threshold of the Trapp Meadow he'd been struck motionless, utterly gobsmacked by its beauty.

This was one of the things he was coming to love about Vermont, because it reminded him so much of home. Every craggy corner was stuffed with unanticipated wonders, and whether natural or manmade they radiated an indescribable spirit, mirroring the soul of its people.

And those people were, to a large degree, tolerant and unhurried—additional characteristics he admired. They'd arrived for this concert in a caravan of cars, winding their way up from the village of Stowe, past the alpine grandeur of the Trapp Family Lodge, to arrive at a rapidly filling meadow. Now, his immovable body stood at the gate between them and their destination, but with only a few curious glances they patiently streamed past him like water around a boulder.

Collecting his wits Conor stepped forward to present his ticket. Once inside he moved away from the foot traffic to scan the crowd, half-hoping not to find what he'd been told to look for, but the two empty chairs jumped out at him immediately. A rush of adrenalin propelled him down the field, but after sitting alone for fifteen minutes his heart rate had slowed and his attention wandered to a wicker basket the size of a steamer trunk placed between the chairs. He was inspecting the contents packed inside when he heard a familiar voice above him.

"You've not drunk up all the wine, I hope. It's rather a special vintage and I've been looking forward to a glass all day."

"I might have done, if you'd been much longer." Conor paused as he peered up over the basket's lid, grinning at the novel sight of the elegant Frank Emmons Murdoch in a red polo shirt, khaki shorts and sandals. His silvered hair gleamed in the afternoon sun but he seemed younger than Conor remembered, perhaps because the summer attire revealed him to be surprisingly toned and fit.

"How are you, Frank? You're looking well. The all-American style suits you."

"As it does you, my boy. You positively glisten. Quite an improvement from the haggard shell I dropped on the curb at Heathrow five months ago." He dipped into the basket and came out with a chilled bottle and corkscrew, both of which he handed to Conor. "Do the honors for us now, and we'll toast our reunion."

"Hmm. An Austrian Riesling." Conor shot Frank a deadpan stare. "Who recommended that, I wonder?"

"Yes, this was all Eckhard's idea. Marvelous, isn't it? I keep expecting a pink-cheeked child to spring from the woods singing *Edelweiss*." Still emptying the picnic hamper, Frank hesitated. "What did you think of our illustrious conductor?"

"I was prepared to dislike him, but it didn't take." Conor pulled the cork from the bottle and sat back. "The two of you have a lot in common."

Frank nodded, amused. "He's extremely cross with me at the minute and I don't wonder. His family are friends of the von Trapps, and with the symphony playing tonight—well, I do regret his disappointment. I really ought to have let him come, I suppose."

"Why didn't you?"

"Because it's not all fine wine and music, I'm afraid. You and I have private business to conduct."

"How's that?" Conor asked. "As I recall, last time we talked you said MI6 had released me."

"Did I? How odd." Frank gave a perfunctory smile. "We never let anyone go, Conor. Now, let's enjoy some refreshment before we start. It likely won't taste as good to you later."

The ceiling fan above their heads was rotating at its lowest setting, barely stirring the humid air, but Sedgwick appeared chilled and uncomfortable and his shivering had become more pronounced. He pointed at the fan, wincing as he pulled himself upright.

"Do you mind if I turn that off?"

"Let me." Kate got up and tugged the chain to cut the motor. As the rotation slowed, she caught one of the blades and gave him a worried glance. "You must have a fever. Should I get you a jacket from the gift shop?"

"I doubt it would help much." His eyes squeezed shut against another tremor and he nodded sheepishly. "Might help a little."

Once zippered into the fleece jacket she brought him, Sedgwick irritably refused her suggestion of hot tea. "Sit down. We don't have a lot of time."

"You're *welcome*." Kate added some acerbic weight to the remark, wondering if she should throw him out after all, or if she even could. She had no idea what kind of jurisdiction these federal agencies had. Ignoring her attitude, Sedgwick drew in his shoulders and again crossed his arms.

"The story starts with the guy who conned Thomas, the mastermind of the scheme to rip off the EU. He calls himself Robert Durgan—probably an alias. We still don't have a firm identity for him, but rumors say he broke from an IRA fringe group to start a money-laundering business for developing world mafias, running the operation through a chain of Irish pubs. He was looking to get started in Mumbai, and decided grant fraud was an easy source of capital. So, he got a few old friends from Northern Ireland to find him a patsy, and they found Thomas."

Kate's mouth had dropped open at hearing the words "IRA," "money-laundering" and "mafia" in one sentence. Sedgwick narrowed his eyes.

"Is any of this familiar?"

"No. It's just ... not what I expected."

He peered at her, thrumming his fingers against his arm, and finally continued. "Thomas wanted to turn himself in, but Durgan's men convinced him it would be 'healthier' for him and his family if he did what he was told. They got him out of the country just ahead of the Irish authorities and a month later they had him placed in Mumbai, using the grant money to open a pub and run the business as a laundromat for Pawan Kotwal, the city's biggest Hindu mafia boss. Okay, what now?"

Kate thought she must look like a grazing goldfish. Her mouth kept opening and closing in stupefaction. "Hindu mafia? I wasn't aware there was such a thing."

"Why would you be?" He scowled. "Google it on your own time. Let's stick to the main story."

"I'm not the one who keeps interrupting it," Kate snapped, her dazed compliance shattering. "And you haven't explained why you need to tell it to me, but I don't have a lot of time either. I've got a business to run."

As if on cue, a tentative tap sounded and the door opened. Dominic's apologetic face appeared around its edge. The question was regarding a group booking for an anniversary dinner the next evening. After a whispered conversation he withdrew with a discreet, curious glance at her guest.

Sedgwick had twisted in his chair to observe the exchange. Seeing his cool amusement as she turned to face him, Kate's hostility began to work up a head of steam. She resented his presence and his hard-edged arrogance, and she resented Conor for whatever he'd done to bring these furtive characters out of the woodwork like questing termites. Most of all, it was humiliating to hear this story from the curled lip of a stranger when she should have demanded it directly from the source a long time ago.

"What?" she challenged, glaring furiously.

"Seems as though I've miscalculated. You're not easily intimidated by authority are you?"

"I was earlier but it's wearing off, and frankly it's hard to find you menacing when you're quivering like a tuning fork. You said you need my cooperation, and from the shape you're in you're going to need a bed and more of my ibuprofen, so maybe you should give up on intimidation and try a little charm instead."

"Maybe you're right."

"What's wrong with you, anyway? This is an odd time of year for the flu."

Unexpectedly, her vehemence drew a genuine, spontaneous smile from the agent, which startled her. Because it did make him look quite a bit more charming. Almost boyish.

"You're just like him," he said. "No wonder he's hung around here so long. Can we leave that question alone, for now? We'll get off track and I don't have a lot of gas left."

Kate spread her hands in sarcastic consent. She sat down, relenting as she watched him burrow into the jacket, searching for warmth. "Can I get you anything?"

"No." He glanced up and smiled again. "No, *thank you*. Where was I?"

"Thomas. Laundering money through an Irish pub in Mumbai. For Pawan Kotwal, the Hindu mafia boss."

"Right, which is how I met Thomas. The Special Ops division of the DEA was in Mumbai, setting up a sting operation to bring in a Russian named Vasily Dragonov— a big-time drug and arms dealer. We needed someone with the right profile to pose as a buyer, so we were building a relationship with Kotwal."

"You were working *with* the mafia boss," Kate clarified.

"Yeah, exactly. Covert ops are a daily slog through ambiguous shit like that."

"Again, I don't understand why you're telling me about a covert operation."

"Does it make me seem more menacing, or charming?"

"It makes you seem crazy."

Sedgwick gave a weak laugh. "You're not the first to think so. Anyway, Kotwal agreed to play ball but he wanted to keep everything at arm's length, and his firewall was his money launderer. He told us to run the whole thing through Durgan. The DEA agent in charge of our operation was Greg Walker, and he met with Durgan in Geneva, saying Kotwal had recommended him as the right man for a piece of new business. Didn't go well. Durgan was an asshole and Walker decided we couldn't work with him, but we discovered he had a guy in Mumbai managing the flow of Kotwal's money through the pub. So I started schmoozing Thomas. After a while he trusted me enough to tell the story of how he'd been fucked by Durgan, and I got him on board by promising to take the guy down if he'd help us with Dragonov. It was a multi-year operation, went like clockwork, but just as we were ready for the sting MI6 staggered in and got everything fucked up good."

"MI6?" Kate asked.

"British Secret Intelligence." Sedgwick rubbed his fingers against his eyes. "They'd picked up the line about an IRA dropout who was washing money for international mafias. They didn't know who the hell he was but they followed the trail leading to Thomas, and sent a man to Mumbai to find him and persuade him to inform on his boss. As luck would have it, they asked me to babysit their operative while he was in Mumbai. I was one of MI6's non-official cover agents in India." Seeing Kate's exasperated confusion, Sedgwick paused. "I guess I just lost you."

"You told me you're with the DEA," she said.

"Which I am." He gave his pocket a slap. "Want me to show the badge again? At one time though, I was a contractor, kind of a freelance operative-for hire. MI6 didn't realize I had a job with the DEA. We couldn't risk telling them about the Dragonov operation, or let them have Thomas, so Walker asked me to run their agent in circles, which turned out to be fairly easy. London sent a fat douche bag they had to recall after he drank his way through Mumbai and blew his cover. We're not sure when or how Durgan got wind of the whole fiasco but we think he must have a mole inside MI6, because a few months later he passed a piece of information directly to Thomas. The British were training a new agent to send to Mumbai, and this time their operative was an amateur—his own little brother. Conor McBride, the fiddle-playing farmer."

Stunned, Kate sat back in her chair, fumbling for the armrest. For reasons that had never been simple, it had suited her to minimize the importance of Conor's opaque past, but this was far different than anything she'd imagined. The dark-eyed man with the lilting voice who managed her farm, played lullabies, flirted with her chef—and who had stirred something in her she was only beginning to understand—was someone she really didn't know at all.

Struggling to find a germ of comfort in the revelation, she focused on the innocence implied in the word "amateur operative," but as though reading her thoughts Sedgwick exploded this effort immediately.

"I figured an amateur would be even easier to get rid of, but I was never more wrong in my life. They gave him ten weeks of training before throwing him out to me like cannon fodder, and he turned out to be one of the purest talents I've ever worked with—unflappable, good at almost everything. For a while I distracted him with a side job I managed, collecting intelligence on Kotwal's rival drug gang. I had him doing some pretty nasty shit but he just kept coming back. I couldn't shake him. In the end, we had to come clean and bring him into the DEA's operation." He lifted his eyes to look past Kate, fixing on a point near the ceiling behind her head. "Might have been a mistake. We made a lot of them."

His face grew slack and Sedgwick stopped, appearing to lose the thread of the story, and Kate tried to decide if she should discourage him from continuing. Whatever ailment he was suffering from, its severity was beginning to alarm her. The fever had surfaced patches of crimson on his face and his ears glowed like red-hot coils. She wondered if a 911 call was going be added to the interesting events of the evening.

At the very least she'd have to put him to bed in a guest room. She doubted whether he could make the trip on his own, which meant she'd be hauling a ragged, incapacitated man through the lobby and up the stairs at the peak of the dinner hour. Perfect.

"Maybe you should stop now," she suggested.

"The operation was compromised." Sedgwick abruptly pulled his gaze from the wall and continued as though she hadn't spoken. "We'd finally landed a face-to-face with Vasily Dragonov at a mountain resort called Gulmarg, in Kashmir, promising a twenty million dollar transaction. Unfortunately, one of our own DEA team members, an analyst named Tony Costino, figured he could profit by switching sides. He tipped off Dragonov, so we ended up running straight into a trap instead of springing the one we'd planned. There was a firefight and Thomas took a bullet in the side. We carried him down through the woods to the car so Conor could take him to a hospital in Srinagar. I arrived later, but they hadn't shown up. I never saw either one of them again."

His face twitched convulsively—reacting to something other than fever, Kate suspected. He reached for the glass, needing both hands to hold it steady, and she rose to pour more water.

"Is this why you're here? To find out what happened to Thomas?"

"No, I know what happened to him." He choked out a hollow laugh. "But I'm sort of curious about what happened to the twenty million dollars he and Conor transferred out of the DEA's bank account that day in Gulmarg. Hopefully, our talented Irish lad has the answer, because I'm not the only one wondering, and I'm not the only one who knows he's here."

13

Forewarned is forearmed.

He didn't remember who coined the aphorism, but it was bloody good advice that always failed him in the presence of his MI6 recruitment officer. Perhaps because Frank Murdoch seemed so clever at *dis*arming him—primarily through the use of alcohol.

Conor drank a small amount of the crisp white wine—enough for the obligatory toast—before moving on to a local stout fished from the bottom of the cooler, confident the bottle had been stocked with his tastes in mind. The brew tasted all the better for not being too cold. Americans had a puzzling aversion to unchilled beverages.

After beguiling him with food and beer, Frank continued the campaign with newsy updates from the professional world of "Classical Violin", a world Conor felt quite disconnected from now. He had to admire Frank's attention to detail—Gil Shaham's establishment of his own record label, the release of a re-mastered compilation of Kreisler—all this esoteric information spilled from his lips with impressive ease.

Conor reclined in his lawn chair, and as they talked he flipped through the program book and watched their surrounding neighbors. To their left an older couple sat on a beach towel, pulling a simple meal of pita and hummus from their backpack, while in front of them a party of "patrons of the arts" handed wine glasses around a low, cloth-covered table complete with candles and a wildflower centerpiece. None encroached on their established boundary. The enormous blanket spread beneath his and Frank's chairs provided a discreet but effective no-man's land on all sides, ensuring privacy for whatever business was forthcoming.

The conversation followed a meandering course and Conor played along. Frank never came at anything directly—he preferred to promenade around its edges until his quarry was too tranquilized to struggle. He was also in no hurry because he'd already been warned the fun wouldn't last, and he found himself enjoying the reunion. Frank's motives didn't necessarily match his own, but Conor never succeeded in sustaining any level of antipathy toward the man. He had to admit he enjoyed his company. Frank held him in high regard as well—his fondness was palpably sincere—but Conor would not make the mistake of expecting affection to trump the agent's cold-blooded professionalism.

"Wait, what's that about Fort Monckton?" He snapped alert at the mention of the MI6 training facility in Gosport, England. This signaled the first hint of a shadow on the sun, and a good indication of a change in course. He gave a wistful glance at the program book, doubting he'd still be around for the concert scheduled to begin in less than an hour.

"I said I went down a few days ago." Frank offered a patient smile. "Your reputation among your trainers lives on, you know. You made a strong impression on them. A feat not often achieved."

"Uh-huh, I'm sure." Conor braced himself, a white-knuckled flyer preparing for descent as the old pro banked a turn for his final approach. "Why were you in Gosport?"

"To see our friend, Curtis Sedgwick."

And, ka-boom. Conor imagined Frank could gauge the

precise instant when the bottom fell out of his stomach.

"So, he's alive."

Frank clucked and peeled a scholar's eye at him. "Well, I hadn't said so. I might have been viewing his mortal remains, after all. Your sloppy inference is correct, however. Is the news surprising, pleasing, disappointing?"

"It's a relief," Conor replied. "I left him in a tight spot. How is he?"

"Much the same as I remember." Frank sniffed. "Unkempt, surly, and profane."

"He wasn't unkempt the last time I saw him." Conor pulled at his lip, struggling to articulate a question he didn't want to ask. "Did he seem ... I mean, were you able to tell—"

"I've no idea. I did not inquire and I don't care. He seemed lucid and reasonably healthy, for whatever that's worth, though I still find it astounding the DEA would take him on board."

Conor nodded, wishing he felt reassured. He understood what the disastrous operation in Gulmarg had done to *him*, both physically and emotionally. The memories lived with him every day and he was finding a way to deal with them, but Sedgwick had a more complicated personal history, one riddled with coping mechanisms that had often brought him to brink of annihilation.

"Why did you meet with him?" Another question he didn't want to ask.

"His request, to compare notes," Frank explained. "Since you two last met, Sedgwick has been tracking the DEA's black-hearted traitor Tony Costino, who in turn is keen to track a certain twenty million dollars he thought had been transferred to Vasily Dragonov but instead went curiously missing. The snafu has put a strain on his relationship with Dragonov. Believing you and Thomas hold the key to a puzzle he needs to solve, he'd like to locate you. Toward this end, he's accomplished something MI6 can't seem to manage. Costino found Robert Durgan, and while the fate of your brother is apparently still a mystery Durgan hasn't penetrated, we've discovered he almost certainly knows what became of you."

"Jesus Christ." Conor gaped at him.

"Yes. Quite," Frank agreed drily. "Through a spectacular piece of misfortune, it appears the unidentified mole within MI6 who leaked your recruitment to Durgan last year is keeping him updated on your present location."

"How? How could that happen? I didn't even tell *you* where I went."

"Ah, well." Frank's easy manner faltered. He blushed and frowned, twirling the stem of his wineglass between his fingers.

"Frank." Conor spoke in quiet warning. "How the fuck did your unidentified mole find out where I am?"

Frank offered a mild shrug. "It was meant for your protection, really. At least in part. The conditions our American friends set for your green card stipulated your public records would remain unpurged and accessible to US authorities. The most I could do was have them electronically flagged to receive notice if anyone accessed them. When US Immigration and Customs Enforcement pulled your arrest record at the beginning of May, I obtained an electronic copy of the report filed by the agents detailing their visit to the Rembrandt Inn, and within hours flew to Vermont to meet with one of them. I returned home satisfied the matter was entirely innocent."

"But it wasn't?"

"Yes, of course it was. That wasn't the issue." Frank waved his hand. "The problem occurred at the London end. I'd no idea ICE would also express a classified hard copy of the report to me. Since I was sitting in the Burlington airport when the file arrived in my UK office, it passed to the next officer with the proper security clearances for triaging. I received a copy through internal channels weeks later. I interrogated the chap responsible, but he'd no recollection of when or how it had been cleared off his desk."

"Someone else had their hands on my file, and you didn't think the information worth sharing. You obviously knew where to find me." Conor's toneless composure perturbed the agent at last.

"You're offering a bravura display of your considerable skills, my boy."

"It's that 'talent for repose' my trainers mentioned. No doubt it made a strong impression."

"No doubt," Frank snapped, "but this façade of restraint isn't necessary with me."

"Good, because it's nearly exhausted. Why didn't you tell me?"

"Perhaps I should have done; yes, all right, certainly I should have done," Frank sighed. "I knew what would happen, though. The risk seemed small and for once I allowed emotion to cloud my judgment."

"You didn't want me disappearing again," Conor accused. "You wanted me to stay pinpointed on your radar screen."

"I wanted you to be happy," Frank countered wearily. "I looked at the website for the inn. The setting is glorious, and the entire state is like a Lake District paradise, or a slice of Irish countryside. I couldn't imagine a more perfect sanctuary for someone so in need of recuperation. I didn't want to take it from you."

Conor held himself still, and for a while couldn't think of another thing to say. After unsteadily hitching in his breath, he got to his feet. "Right. Well, it's gone now. I'm off."

"Not just yet, I hope." Frank smiled up at him, recovering some of his aplomb.

Conor pulled his keys from his pocket. "For God's sake, Frank. I need to go back to the inn, collect my things and get the hell out tonight."

The agent reached out and gave the low empty chair next to him a gentle shake. "Sit down. You act quite certain about what you need to do but your confidence is misguided, I assure you. You're not thinking clearly just now. Disappearing is not the wisest or safest plan of action, and it deviates from our strategy."

"Deviates how? Whose strategy? What is it?" Conor telegraphed his mistrust, glaring at Frank.

"One devised by Sedgwick and myself, of course." Entirely restored now, Frank looked maddeningly pleased with himself. "We've enhanced our inter-agency cooperation quite a bit since last year. Embarrassing fiascoes tend to produce this sort of salubrious effect. I'll be happy to share our plans with you, just as Sedgwick—presumably at this moment—is sharing them with the lovely Kate Fitzpatrick at the Rembrandt Inn. We'll want her cooperation of course, so we needed to bring her up to speed."

Conor plummeted down to eye-level, landing on his haunches. He grabbed Frank's chair, and with his face inches from the man's carapace of impeccable silvered hair, hissed into the agent's ear.

"What the fuck have you done, you manipulative son of a bitch?"

14

The drive along the curving scenic byways between Hartsboro Bend and Stowe had taken a good hour and a half when Conor—preoccupied but unhurried—made the outbound trip earlier in the day. The return took exactly fifty-eight minutes.

He still had plenty of time to cycle through the grim scenarios he might face at journey's end, and by the time he arrived and Dominic had directed him to Kate's office his brain was thicketed with an entire network of conditional responses. All of them grew obsolete the minute Conor strode across the lobby and threw open the door. He stumbled into a scene far different from what he'd expected, and froze on the threshold.

In front of the office couch, dripping with perspiration, Kate knelt with her arms wrapped around the limp torso of a man on the floor. Her eyes stared in alarm at the sound of Conor's entrance. She went limp with relief when she recognized him, but as he continued to stand mute and immobile, her expression hardened.

"Come in or stay out, but for God's sake close the door." She dropped her arms and sat on her heels, passing a hand over her forehead. "If anyone catches sight of him they might think he ate here."

Conor closed the door and walked into the room until he stood directly over the man who had served as his MI6 control in Mumbai—the man who'd begun their relationship with a lie, spinning him into the web of chaos that had taken his brother's life. He wanted to despise Curtis Sedgwick, but their shared history was too complicated for such purity of emotion. Circumstance had forged a tenuous bond, strengthened by the deeper truth connecting them: they both had loved Thomas, and he had loved them.

As though sensing the weight of his gaze Sedgwick shivered and lifted his head, displaying a weak smirk before letting his chin drop to his chest. "Welcome home, McBride. Enjoy the concert?"

Conor had never seen him in this condition, but thought Thomas had been all-too familiar with it. His brother's antidote of tenderness and violence in equal parts had secured for the agent what he couldn't achieve alone—a lasting respite from self-destruction.

Promise me you'll take care of yourself.

Those were the last words Thomas delivered to Sedgwick as they settled him in the car for the drive to Srinagar, a trip they all knew would take too long. Conor turned from the agent, emotion thickening in his throat, and shifted his attention to Kate, who avoided his gaze with a tight frown.

"He couldn't manage the stairs. I tried to get him back to the couch and we both ended up on the floor."

"How long has he been here?"

"I'm not sure. An hour, I guess. Long enough. He seemed sick when he got here and it's been getting worse. Whatever it is. He wouldn't tell me." She darted a reproachful glance at him. "He was more interested in talking about you than himself."

He nodded, offering to help her up, but she twisted from his outstretched hand. "Move out of the way now," Conor said quietly.

"He's heavier than he looks. Just get on the other side and help me."

"I said move out of the way."

"Yes, I heard what you said." Kate rounded on him, pinning him with an anger that darkened her eyes to violet. "Sorry to be in the way. How far would you like me to go?"

Conor clenched his jaw. "Please, Kate."

She held her ground for several seconds, then got to her feet with a shrug of dismissal and moved to lean against the desk. Conor put one hand under Sedgwick's arm, getting a grip on his belt with the other, and with an abrupt jerk he wrenched the agent from the floor and slammed him onto the couch. Sedgwick crumpled sideways, chortling feebly as his head came to rest against the padded arm.

"Still quick with your hands, dude. What are we at now, three rounds to one? Not a fair fight this time, though."

He tipped off-balance as he struggled to lift his legs. Conor gathered up a handful of his stained t-shirt and shoved him back into place. "What have you done to yourself, you selfish bastard? He only wanted one thing from you. He sat there with the life bleeding out of him and asked for one fucking promise. That was too much, was it?"

Sedgwick stared up at him, all trace of amusement gone. In its place Conor saw a haunted grief he recognized well; he faced it in the mirror on many a morning.

"What about you?" Sedgwick whispered. "What did he want from you?"

Something he almost couldn't bear either, Conor thought. His anger faded at the memory of a flashlight hanging from a hook in the darkness, and of his brother's hand gripped between both of his own as the Kashmir night deepened around them.

"To hold onto him until he was safe. I kept my promise."

"I kept mine, too."

"Horseshit." Conor scowled at the agent. "Look at you, shaking yourself to bits. You're coming off of something. What happened? Ran out of needles or money, or both?"

"Try 'neither' you self-righteous asshole," Sedgwick snapped. "I've got malaria. The only thing I've been on is chloroquine, which apparently didn't work."

"Malaria?" Conor squinted, unconvinced. Behind him, Kate snapped to attention.

"Malaria! Holy shit, malaria?"

"Relapsing malaria is more precise." Sedgwick glanced at her. "Not contagious, don't worry." He fumbled a small bottle out of his pocket and threw it at Conor in exasperation. "I bought them off a kiosk in Bangalore. The label says choloroquine but the fucking pills are either counterfeit or past the expiration date. All I can tell is, they're not working. So, unless your corner store here in East Overshoe carries anti-malarials I guess I'm in for a rocky night."

Following a terse exchange, Kate returned to her post in the dining room and Conor retrieved a box of primaquine from his medicine cabinet. The anti-malarial drug was one among a sackful given to him upon discharge from Kings College Hospital. Most were for the regimen he'd followed every day for months, but other prophylactics had been thrown in as a precaution. His doctors had pegged him as a tropics-wandering daredevil who needed ongoing protection. After returning to Kate's office and administering the first dose, he managed to haul Sedgwick up the stairs and into a guest room without attracting notice.

He got him into bed, and sat guard to keep the agent from falling out as he lurched in a delirium punctuated by self-recrimination—seemingly a catalogue of every weakness and every wrong he'd ever committed.

"Will you ever leave off, already," Conor sighed. He lifted Sedgwick's head and pressed yet another glass of water to his lips. "Stupid git. Even I don't think you're as bad as that."

When the fever broke, coherence returned. Flattened against the mattress as though ironed into it, and with lines in his face deep enough to put a finger into, the agent resembled a sculpted effigy. Conor offered no quarter for his glazed exhaustion. As soon as he saw evidence of lucidity he started the interrogation.

"What did you tell her?"

"Everything, pretty much. The basic facts, I mean." Sedgwick studied him, eyelids at half-mast. "Relax. I left out the gory details. I think she could have handled them, though. She's quite the piece of work. Quite the piece of something else too, isn't she? Is she a natural red—"

"Shut the fuck up."

"Hmm, yeah. Thought so."

Conor ignored the remark. "What happened after Thomas and I left Gulmarg? On the path?"

They exchanged a long look of understanding. Sedgwick was the first to grimace and glance away. "Leave it alone. I said I would take care of it, and I did."

"But, how—"

"Leave it alone."

"Fine." Conor held his breath for several seconds—shamed by the thought of it escaping as a sigh of relief. "What happened back up at the resort?"

"Frank was supposed to tell you." Sedgwick settled his head deeper into the pillow and closed his eyes.

"He never got the chance. I left in a hurry. Wake up and give over. What happened?"

"Bloodbath." Lips pursed, Sedgwick frowned at the ceiling. "By the time I got back up the hill the only ones still alive were two Srinagar police officers."

"What about Greg Walker?" Conor had last seen the senior DEA agent sprinting in the direction of the gunfire as they carried Thomas away.

"Dead. AK-47 spray. Most of his face was gone."

"Costino?"

"Disappeared. I tore most of the town apart looking for the double-crossing piece of shit. Eventually, I discovered he'd hiked down to Drung village and paid someone to drive him to the nearest rail station. Then he went to ground, which seemed weird at the time. He would have assumed Walker and I were both dead, because the news stories about the Gulmarg shootout reported no survivors. He probably figured you and Thomas had left the country, and anyway he had no reason to think anyone had guessed what he'd done. He'd just helped an arms dealer score twenty million and presumably earned a nice commission. Why hide? Unless he'd somehow lifted the twenty million for himself and was hiding from Dragonov. The trail went cold for months but he finally made a mistake, which is when I discovered I was only partly right. He was hiding from Dragonov, not because he'd stolen the money but because it was missing. So, where was the twenty million? Only one explanation made any sense and it knocked me back a little."

Conor deflected the agent's inquisitive gaze with a glare. "Is this what it's all about for you, trying to get the DEA's money back?"

Sedgwick worked at the sheet covering his chest, gathering it into his hands and releasing a slow breath. "For God's sake, Conor. Is that what you think?"

"I don't, no." He regretted the remark, recognizing it as a bit of opportunistic redirection. "We didn't take the feckin' money," he said flatly.

Sedgwick raised his head, looking more alert. "Care to elaborate?"

"Not at the moment."

Conor got up and moved to the room's open window, which offered a view of the parking lot. A group of dinner guests stood chatting in the moonlight near their cars, reluctant to call time on a pleasant summer evening. He leaned an arm against the sill, listening to their relaxed laughter mingle with the piercing call of nighthawks, feeling like a man staring from a prison.

"You said he made a mistake. What was it?" Getting no reply he turned and saw Sedgwick dozing off again. He returned to the bedside, giving the agent's leg a light slap, and repeated the question. Sedgwick's eyes opened more slowly this time.

"We set up an email account at the beginning of the DEA operation to communicate with Dragonov's people. Costino and I both had access; we wrote the messages and signed them as Thomas. Obviously, Costino used a different channel once he decided to rat on us, but I still checked our original account every day. Earlier this month it paid off, but he didn't write to Dragonov's people. He sent a message to Robert Durgan, and I traced Tony's IP address to an internet cafe in Bangalore."

"Tony knows where Durgan is?" Conor asked sharply. Sedgwick looked dubious.

"Not sure we can assume that much, but he knew how to reach him. Costino was the one who contacted Durgan to set up the meeting with Walker in Geneva. He got the email address from Pawan Kotwal."

"Yeah, since we're on this topic—it wasn't Durgan who showed up in Geneva."

Sedgwick squinted at him. "What do you mean? I told you about the meeting. Durgan was an asshole. Walker said he'd never be able to trust him."

"Wasn't him," Conor insisted. "Thomas said Durgan suspected a trap so he sent a stand-in named Desmond Moore, one of the farm assistants who conned my brother into the grant fraud. When he figured out later that Desi had bollixed the meeting he tortured and killed him, and sent Thomas the photos as a warning."

Sedgwick was too weak to muster more than a fretful

complaint. "Why didn't Frank fill me in on any of this?"

"How the hell should I know? Anyway, come on, now." Conor mopped the agent's face with a wet cloth to keep him awake. "Costino contacted Durgan. What did he say?"

"Okay, okay." Sedgwick swatted the cloth away. "This time he tried a threat. Told Durgan his man in India had screwed up, said you and Thomas had stolen federal government money and if Durgan didn't cough up your location a team would be mobilized to bring him in and string him up. Risky move, but Tony knows he can't hide from Dragonov forever. He's betting Durgan knows where you are, and thinks if he can find you he'll find out what happened to the twenty million dollars. To be honest, I can't argue with his logic."

"What happened?" Conor asked, ignoring this pointed remark.

After an appraising stare Sedgwick settled his head back on the pillow, all remaining energy sapped. "Durgan actually replied. Said he had no information about Thomas but might have an address for you. The threat didn't scare him, though. He said Costino would have to make his cooperation worth something, and told him he'd be in touch again later. His message was the first confirmation I had you were even alive ... and that Thomas probably wasn't. By this time I was on the way to Bangalore. I watched the internet cafe around the clock for a few days, but Costino never showed and didn't access the email account again. Then I got malaria. Thought I had food poisoning at first, since I puked most of the day. When I finally got off my knees it seemed more important to find you than to waste any more time crawling around Bangalore, so I got in touch with Frank."

"When was this?" Conor asked.

"Two weeks ago. Should have contacted him a long time ago, I suppose. Never trusted the old son of a bitch, but in the end I had no one else to call."

"What about the DEA? Aren't they interested in finding Costino as well? You must have reported back to them?"

"Yeah, funny thing. I tried but they didn't want to hear it."

Sedgwick's lips were barely moving now, and before this tantalizing bit of information could be explored he crashed into sleep. Conor let him go this time and slumped against the chair, equally exhausted by a narrative that had raised as many questions as it answered. Within minutes sleep had pulled him under as well, but at the touch of a hand on his shoulder, he snapped awake with a gasp.

"Shit. What's the time?"

"Calm down. It's only eleven o'clock." Kate stood in the circle of light cast by the bedside lamp, holding a covered plate in one hand. "How is he?"

"Should be okay, assuming my drugs work better than his." Conor gestured at the plate. "He's probably not going to eat anything for a while."

"I brought it for you," Kate said.

"Oh. You did?"

"It's just a sandwich."

"No, that's ... thanks." He reached forward but Kate swung away, plate firmly in hand.

"Let him sleep, now. You can eat upstairs. While we talk."

"Right. Okay."

Conor watched her disappear into the hallway, his hands gripped on the arms of the chair. He pressed hard against the back of it and the dovetailed joints strained against the wood, releasing a high-pitched creak. E Minor, he thought mechanically. After a minute, he stiffly rose and followed her.

In Kate's apartment they faced each other across a tiny café table in the kitchenette—an alcove more than a room, barely big enough for both of them. To buy a little time Conor forced down some of the sandwich, but the bread churned in his throat like wet concrete, nearly gagging him. He gave up after a few bites, which fortunately left his airway clear when Kate addressed him with icy precision.

"You used me, and you used my home as a hide-out."

God knows he'd had enough time to prepare, but the accusation and its undeniable truth left Conor searching for breath. In one simple sentence she'd captured everything. He'd used Kate to his own advantage—used her need, her compassion and her tolerance—and betrayed her trust. He'd violated her home by cowering in its safety, hiding from her and everyone else, including himself.

"I suppose this is my fault as much as yours," Kate went on bitterly. "I asked but I never demanded, and I projected on to you what I wanted to be true. I thought we shared something in common, because I assumed we were talking about trauma and grief, not spies and secret operations."

"Those things aren't mutually exclusive." Conor dipped his head at her responding stare. "No. I understand that's not the point."

"How long did you think you could do this, especially after last night ... at the pond?" Kate's voice caught. "Didn't you realize silence wasn't going to work forever? That you'd have to give me something? Even if it was a lie?"

"That's what they trained me for, sure." Conor picked at the sandwich, unconsciously crumbling the bread into a pile of rubble on the plate. "To lie, and become good at being somebody I'm not. I wanted to believe I'd be lousy at it. Turns out the whole business slips over me like a comfortable old coat. A perfect fit. I got used to lying, and yes, I figured I'd be giving you more of the same—but I didn't. I never did lie to you, Kate. I've wriggled like a snake, trying to keep you in the dark, but I didn't lie. From the minute I ever laid my two eyes on you I knew I wouldn't be able to."

He risked a peek at her face, and the anguish he saw did him greater damage than her anger.

"Maybe you didn't lie, but you weren't honest. Not really."

"No," he acknowledged. "Not really. Honesty wasn't an option. The only thing I could do was leave, which I should have done a long time ago, but—"

"I wanted you to stay. I asked you to."

"And I convinced myself it would be okay. I was tired of losing things, tired of leaving everyone I care about behind me and just ... feck it. Tired."

Conor sensed control escaping him by degrees, like air whistling through a knife-pricked hole. Pushing up from the table as though yanked by an unseen hand, he picked up the plate and stared at the wreckage.

"Jesus. I've made a mess of this. Sorry."

Recognizing the irony, he looked at Kate and gave a miserable shrug. Her responding smile—brief and sad—hinted at the possibility of forgiveness, a gift so generous it shuffled him that much closer to the edge. She rose and took the plate from him, pressing him back down into the chair. After tossing the mangled bread into the garbage and leaving the plate in the sink, she returned to her seat.

"There are some things you need to tell me, now."

Conor nodded, and winced at the pain throbbing in his head.

"Did you take the money—the twenty million dollars these people are trying to find?"

"Not exactly." The equivocation lit a dangerous spark in Kate's eyes that he rushed to subdue. "The meeting with the Russian arms dealer—Dragonov—was supposed to include an electronic transfer of the money from the DEA to an account they shared with him. Costino was the operation's legal analyst and he'd convinced Greg Walker—the senior agent in charge—a transfer had to happen to make the case stick in court. Now we know why. It was a convenient way for him to make sure Dragonov got his money. Even at the time the idea sounded mad altogether and Thomas didn't like it, so he opened an account at a bank in South America to receive the transfer instead. He asked me to set the password but I don't even know what country he picked, much less the bank. I never imagined I'd need to. It was all so we'd be able to transfer the money back, not get blamed for losing twenty million dollars if something went wrong. Of course, it did— everything went wrong."

Conor stopped. He couldn't control what happened in his dreams, but many months had passed since he'd allowed his waking mind to exhume the chaos of that day in Gulmarg. The passage of time had not softened the panic cascading along his nerves, a sizzling fuse racing toward ignition. He rocked forward, catching his head in his hands, and surrendered to the weight of memories.

Somewhere beyond the ringing in his ears Conor heard Kate murmuring his name. He felt the pressure of her hand massaging the back of his neck, but couldn't respond. The tableau was repeating again and he was powerless to stop it—as he always was. The figure in white comes into focus, turns to him in astonishment, and the forest explodes.

15

Kate made it until ten o'clock the next morning before giving in to curiosity and aggravation. The previous evening she'd felt embarrassed and ill used, and had been spoiling for a fight with Conor—an objective frustrated by his immediate capitulation. In the end they'd both been too worn out to take the argument further, so she'd settled for Conor's account of the meeting with his MI6 superior, Frank Murdoch. At midnight, she'd left him still mumbling apologies outside his room while she made a brief trip downstairs to check on Sedgwick, who was also mumbling—in his sleep.

Her own sleep had been fitful and uneasy, and as the morning wore on Kate grew increasingly on edge. She'd been cheated of the opportunity to vent a cleansing fury, and now had been excluded from whatever discussions she presumed were going on without her. Neither of the two "agents" sheltering under her roof had made an appearance as yet. For once, Abigail had taken the morning off, but Ghedi, the Somalian sous-chef assigned to the breakfast shift, reported Conor had not shown his face at all, nor could Kate find him in any of the usual places. She assumed he and Sedgwick were holed up in the agent's room, exchanging information they may or may not choose to share with her.

After seeing off her final overnight guests her patience and her nerves had stretched to a filament. She double-timed it up to the second floor and down the hall to Sedgwick's room, storming the barricade with two firm raps. The door abruptly swung open and the force of it nearly sucked her inside.

"Oh. It's you." Sedgwick planted an arm against the doorframe and grinned at her. "Afraid I was dead? Or hoping I was?"

He'd showered and dressed—a clean pair of khakis and a blue polo shirt—and apart from a lingering pallor he seemed largely recovered. Caught off guard, Kate fumbled for an opening line before hitting on the most obvious one.

"How are you?" She looked beyond him, confirming he was alone.

"Not too bad. Joints are kind of achy. Not sure if that's from the fever or from McBride throwing me around the room. Did you want to come in?" He swung the door wider. Deflated, Kate walked in, thwarted again in her effort to be incensed.

"I thought I'd find Conor here with you." She flopped into the chair near the bedside table. "Plotting or scheming, or doing whatever spies do when they get together."

"Plotting and scheming pretty much covers it." Sedgwick sat down at the foot of the bed. "I only woke up an hour ago. Haven't seen him."

Kate cast about for a topic of conversation, wondering what she hoped to accomplish before impulsively posing a question she hadn't expected to ask.

"What went wrong that day?"

"He still hasn't told you." The softness of Sedgwick's tone surprised her.

"He tried, I think he wanted to, but he couldn't." She dropped her gaze to her hands resting in her lap. "He has nightmares. I've heard them a few times, but he doesn't know."

After a long silence she looked up at Sedgwick, who absently rubbed a hand over the globe-shaped finial of the bedpost, as if it were a crystal ball that might provide answers for both of them.

"Everything went wrong," he said, echoing Conor's words. "He had to run away from all of it. There was no other option, but that's hard to remember when you're sweating it out in the middle of the night. He'll tell you when he's ready."

Kate nodded, looking restlessly around her. Odd, to sit like a tourist in one of her own guest rooms, evaluating the amenities from an outsider's perspective. Were the curtains as clean as they should be? Her attention settled on an edgeless lucite picture frame sitting on his bedside table. The photograph inside showed a beautiful, smiling Indian girl with a lustrous braid pulled forward over her shoulder. She wore a red school jacket and white skirt, and held the handlebars of a dusty bicycle.

"Is she your daughter?"

Sedgwick gave a self-deprecating snort. "No, luckily for her. I'm an honorary *bhaiyya*—elder brother—and a stand-in if I'm honest. McBride still reigns as Number One *bhaiyya*."

"Who is she?" Kate picked up the frame and studied the photo more closely.

"Her name is Radha. Her father sold her to a dance-bar pimp in Mumbai when she was twelve years old. McBride bought her back so to speak, and nearly got himself killed in the process. One of his little adventures. She's at a convent school in Agra, now. I visited her three months ago and she wanted me to send the photo to him. At the time I didn't know if he was dead or alive, but I wasn't about to tell her."

Sedgwick laughed, a grudging sniff of appreciation. "He can be as cold-blooded as he needs to be, has some amazing talents, but self-protection isn't one of them. He won't put on the armor. Leaves him vulnerable to everyone and everything that wants to stick to him—needy children, old ladies, tuberculosis—"

"Tuberculosis?" Kate glanced up sharply.

"Oops. Shit. Forget I said that." Sedgwick made a wry face and changed the subject. "Where the hell is he, anyway? I figured he'd be hoisting me out of bed at daybreak."

"Off somewhere, I guess. I can't find anybody who knows. Tell me what you meant by—"

"Wait. You're saying nobody's seen him?"

"Maybe he walked into town. He can't be far. The truck and my car are still here."

Sedgwick was up and at the window before she'd finished. He looked down at the parking lot and then turned to study her, the cool speculation she'd seen the previous evening dropping over his face like a mask.

"Well, *my* car is gone. Fortunately, there's a tracking device under the hood."

She couldn't believe Conor would run away, but the evidence and Sedgwick's conviction were hard to challenge. He tore into his duffel bag and came out with a laptop and a slightly larger square device, then ran from the room with Kate close behind, chasing him down to the ground floor.

"Get me your keys," he said over his shoulder.

"I'll drive. I'm coming with you."

"No, you're not."

"Then I won't give you the keys."

Sedgwick pulled up at the foot of the stairs and glared at her. "You think I can't start a car without keys?"

She was composing a scathing retort when the front door opened and Conor stepped into the lobby, balancing a large white box on one arm. Before the moment could elude her again Kate gave voice to her pent-up wrath.

"Where the hell have you been?"

Conor froze with his hand on the doorknob. The box wobbled at a dangerous angle and he steadied it, staring at the two of them.

"At the bakery in Montpelier. Abigail asked me to collect the cake for the anniversary group booked in tonight. She didn't tell you?"

"It's morning. She's not scheduled to be here."

"Since when does that matter?"

"Why did you take his car, for God's sake?" Kate hiked a thumb at Sedgwick.

"It's a Mustang." Conor shrugged, as though further explanation would be superfluous.

"It's government property you dickhead, and it's got a trunk full of surveillance equipment among other things." Sedgwick did a slow-motion collapse on the stairs, looking weary. "If you'd been stopped for speeding we'd be dealing with a shit-storm right about now."

"Jaysus, really?" Conor smiled faintly. He pulled the keys from his jacket and tossed them over. "Good thing I wasn't, then. Don't leave those lying around in your pockets from now on." His dark eyes lost their glitter when they shifted back to Kate. "So, I guess you thought I'd scarpered for the border, or the airport or someplace. That's what you expected from me?"

"Not as much as he did." Kate was still fuming. "Don't try throwing me on the defensive, Conor. You've got no right to the high ground. You told me you had pneumonia last winter, but this one is telling me it was TB. Who's lying?"

Conor glared at Sedgwick. "Thanks very much."

"Sort of slipped out."

"You can't pretend you didn't have time to tell me all this yourself." Kate paused, seeing Conor's annoyance abruptly darken into something more threatening. Without further warning, he exploded.

"And what exactly was I supposed to say, Kate? Lovely of you to have me here, and by the way I'm an undercover MI6 agent, just off a badly fucked up black ops project with the DEA?" He slammed the box on top of the registration desk. "Yes. I got TB in Mumbai. Last winter."

"How?" Kate asked.

"I suppose I caught it off someone else," Conor snapped. "As one does. People get tuberculosis in India, along with malaria and cholera and a bunch of other biblical diseases we don't much worry about in Hartsboro Bend. Then, while I was hiking around in the fucking snow in Kashmir, I caught pneumonia as well. So, nobody was lying and now you know; and can I just say that if you'll be going off your nut like this every time a new fact emerges, you should probably start drinking a lot more than you do now."

Kate had never seen him so angry. Instead of fueling her own rage it gave her an irrational urge to smile. Avoiding his eyes she approached the desk and peeked into the box, relieved to find the cake still intact. She turned to his scowling face, and a belated sting of anxiety erased the inclination to laugh.

"Tuberculosis is curable, right?"

"Not always, but in this case, yes. Thanks for asking." He took a deep breath, and continued more calmly. "I did a six-month therapy with shed-loads of pills and was cleared a few weeks ago at Copley Hospital. Darla saw me there, ask her. She haunts the place."

"Good." Kate closed the cake box and smoothed her fingers over the top, calming the atmosphere. "Are you hungry?"

Conor squinted at her, as though suspecting a trap. "Ehm, yes?"

"What about you? Breakfast?" Sedgwick gave a nervous start as she spun around to face him. He was still perched at the bottom of the stairs, in neutral territory.

"Yeah, sure. Whatever. Coffee, anyway."

"Well, come on, then." She picked up the cake box and started down the hall, and like obedient school boys the two of them fell into step, following her into the dining room.

"Sorry to screw up your love life, dude." Sedgwick shot Conor a skeptical glance. "She's sort of out of your league though, isn't she?"

"Feck off." Conor plucked a strip of bacon from the agent's plate. "You'd best be nice to me if you want any more of my primaquine."

"I was wondering where those pills had gone."

"Nicked them. When I went for your keys."

"Nice to know you haven't lost your edge."

Kate appeared, coffee carafe in hand, and frowned at Sedgwick's plate of half-eaten pancakes. "You're not doing a very good job of keeping up."

Sedgwick rolled his eyes. "Look who you're comparing me with—he eats like he's going to the chair."

She twitched a glance at Conor's empty plate before sitting down and pouring herself a cup of coffee. "What have you been discussing? You weren't supposed to start without me."

"Just trading insults," Conor said. "You haven't missed anything."

He was trying to keep up, also—to find a balance in the shifting terrain of Kate's mood. Since last night he'd seen her move through anger, bitterness, anguish and tenderness, and then back to anger again. He'd made the rounds through most of those as well. With anger put aside—at least for the moment—he detected a renewed smidgen of warmth between them, but also the sense of a retreat, as though they'd each pulled back to opposite corners, measuring out a safe distance from which to avoid being hurt. He decided not to dwell on what that felt like, or what it meant. He turned his attention to Sedgwick.

"Last night you said the DEA wasn't interested in hearing your report. Why?"

"Wish I knew." Sedgwick pushed the remains of his breakfast around his plate. "They flew over an officer to deal with the transport of Walker's body and settle down the Srinagar police, who naturally wanted an explanation for why they'd just lost six officers. I expected the guy to debrief me on the spot but he told me he didn't have clearance to hear anything, and he told the police their answers would be coming through diplomatic channels. He seemed genuinely in the dark. Privately, he said DEA headquarters was freaking out, and he'd seen a few characters in the hallways who smelled a lot like CIA. His official purpose was to put me on administrative leave until further notice."

Next to him Conor heard Kate abruptly shift in her chair with a small sigh of distress. She appeared tired and shaken, but managed a smile in waving off his concern. "Of course. The CIA. Why not?"

"Sounds fishy," Conor remarked.

"You think?" Sedgwick shot him a sarcastic glance. "What else would send me running into the arms of Frank Murdoch? For better or worse I'm buddied up with him on this gig, flying under the radar to hide the fact from my own agency." He poured himself a third cup of coffee before continuing with clipped efficiency. "So, this is where things stand. First we've got Tony Costino, desperate to deliver the twenty million dollars he promised Dragonov, which he thinks you have. Then we have Robert Durgan, who most likely got your location from a mole inside MI6, and he's essentially been told you and Thomas cheated him out of a huge piece of business. He's only waiting for a guaranteed return on investment to justify the risk of coming after you. Dragonov's assassins might find Tony before he can close a deal with Durgan, although we can't depend on it. We need a strategy for both defense and offense, but first let's go back to the question you dodged last night, McBride." Sedgwick put his mug down and rested his elbows on the table. "Where the hell is the DEA's money?"

"Haven't a clue," Conor admitted. "We did the transfer to a bank account Thomas set up in some South American country."

"Uh-huh." Unlike the previous evening the agent's gaze was focused and alert. "A country like Brazil, for instance?"

"Sounds as good a guess as any, I suppose. Why Brazil, in particular?"

"He used to launder some of Kotwal's money through a bank manager in Porto Allegre. Why did he do it?"

Conor explained his brother's foresight in questioning the idea of putting twenty million dollars into an account Dragonov could access, and Sedgwick's face brightened.

"It must be the bank in Porto Allegre." He thumped a fist on the table. "Excellent. You've got the password for the account?"

Conor met his eyes without flinching. "Nope. He didn't tell me."

The decision to lie and its actual delivery was an instinct that formed in the space of an instant, before he even understood why he was doing it. In keeping with his training in this particular art, the words fell from his lips without hurry or hesitation, but Conor was less anxious about Sedgwick's reaction than Kate's, since the statement was a direct contradiction of what he'd told her earlier.

Sedgwick spat an obscenity, dropping his head in frustration while Conor extended a booted foot under the table to carefully rest on top of Kate's. So much depended on how she would respond, and he had no idea what to expect. She had already turned her head to him, her mouth opening to speak, but stiffened as she felt the pressure of his foot. He could only risk a glance, serving as an implicit plea. It was enough. Kate pressed her lips together and began gathering the breakfast dishes.

Eyes down, he slid his plate over, grateful she could still offer this degree of trust. It was a privilege he had not earned.

"We've got to tell Abigail."

It was after midnight and Kate was stretched flat on her living room sofa. Sedgwick had checked in as an official guest by this time—insisting on the government rate—and their relationship had crystallized into an ongoing contest of wills. Earlier in the day he'd emptied his car trunk of its stash of technological wonders, but Kate had flatly refused to have them installed. She was in the hospitality business, she argued. She couldn't operate as a guarded fortress, spying on her guests. Conor supported her on this point, although she suspected he too would have preferred to have every inch of the inn bristling with revolving cameras and hidden microphones.

He and Sedgwick were sprawled in the club chairs flanking her, the rejected surveillance equipment piled on the coffee table in the middle. All three of them were weary after several hours of argument. She'd yielded on the demand for remote access to the inn's reservations system, but intended to extract a concession in exchange.

"It's too awkward." Kate turned to Sedgwick. "She didn't believe you're a soil scientist from the USDA and I can tell she's upset."

Conor sat forward and groaned. "Bloody hell, Kate. Can't we tackle this fight later? It's nearly one o'clock in the morning. I've got to get up in three and a half hours."

"I'm not fighting that one anyway," Sedgwick said tiredly. "Go ahead and tell her."

Astonished, Kate sat up, wishing she'd demanded something else now. "You don't care if she knows?"

The agent gave her a vicious grin, clearly pleased at having outsmarted her, but then grew serious. "We've got no idea what a Durgan-Costino alliance might cook up—if one ever takes shape. I'm heading back to India to try and pick up the trail on Tony, so I'll be out of the picture for a while, and since you won't accept the security detail Frank wanted to arrange, McBride will be adding guard duty to his list of chores. Given all that, it's smart to have another person in the house who can be trusted to take direction and act as needed. If you trust her, then let it be Abigail."

There was no one Kate trusted more. Whether Abigail would take direction was another matter, and whether she'd share the story with Dominic—which Sedgwick had strictly forbidden—was yet another. The first question was how to approach her with the news. After fretting through the night she determined the best plan was to let Conor handle the matter alone. When the restaurant closed the next evening she left the two of them sitting in the kitchen, working their way through a banana cream pie while he told his story.

Sedgwick departed the following day, looking much healthier than he had upon arrival. After upending their lives in one short visit his final assault on their nerves came as they stood in the driveway, listening to him deliver final instructions like a worried parent.

"Trust your instincts—if anything seems suspicious get in touch with Frank. He'll be able to mobilize something pretty quickly. MI6 has a few general staff officers placed at the British embassy in New York, and he's got a personal connection with some higher-up in the FBI. That's how I ended up with this car. He's got a few connections of a shadier variety too, which is how I ended up with this other little item." Sedgwick reached under the seat of his Mustang and came out with a zipped leather bag. Kate saw Conor immediately stiffen and take a step back as the agent held it out to him.

"No. I can't. I won't."

"Conor, don't be an idiot." Sedgwick spoke with surprising gentleness. "You know you have to. Take the damn gun."

The tension of shared secrets passed between the two men, mysteries that had not been revealed in Kate's initiation. The pain in Conor's face tugged at her heart, but the past was not her concern now. She moved to his side and put a hand on his arm.

"Take it."

16

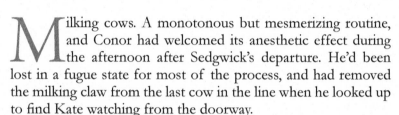

Milking cows. A monotonous but mesmerizing routine, and Conor had welcomed its anesthetic effect during the afternoon after Sedgwick's departure. He'd been lost in a fugue state for most of the process, and had removed the milking claw from the last cow in the line when he looked up to find Kate watching from the doorway.

"Hey," he greeted her, surprised. "How long have you been standing there?"

"Just a few minutes."

"Sorry. I didn't notice."

A trace of amusement skittered over her face. "No kidding. If I'd set myself on fire you wouldn't have noticed. Go ahead and finish. I'll wait for you on the bench."

He joined her, and for a moment neither of them spoke. He imagined them both remembering earlier, happier trips to the same spot.

"You're wrong," she said finally. "I didn't believe you'd run away, but I've been giving it some thought and I think maybe you should, Conor. Just go, and don't tell anyone. Not Sedgwick or Frank Murdoch, or even me. If someone turns up looking for you I can say you're gone and I don't know where. Which would be the truth."

Is that what you want? Conor kept his face composed and resisted asking the question aloud, afraid of the answer. "Suppose they wouldn't believe you? What's worse, suppose they thought you knew about the money and how to get it? Don't send me away now Kate, even if you'd rather see the back of me. I can't leave your safety to a roll of the dice."

Kate swung around to straddle the bench, facing him directly. "I figured you'd say something like that, so I have another idea. Get Frank to spread some disinformation around his office, say you're somewhere else, and if a mole is keeping Durgan informed he'll pass the news and they'll be off on a wild goose chase."

"You *have* been giving this some thought." Conor smiled at her and shook his head. "Frank wouldn't do it."

"Why not?"

"Because he wants Durgan to know where I am. Frank didn't want me to leave Ireland. He hoped I'd sit at my farm like bait in a trap with a few security agents guarding the perimeter, but I ran off instead. This time he's made sure you're well tangled up in the trap too, counting on the idea that I won't run again and leave you sitting alone in it. Frank wants Durgan. There's something personal about his obsession I can't figure out, but he wants him badly—and to be honest so do I. Durgan and Costino, both. My brother's blood is on their hands, and while I spent the last four months hiding, Sedgwick has been tracking them down."

"Why did you lie about the password to the bank account? Don't you trust him?"

"I trust him well enough," Conor said, "but the password is my only leverage in this game. I won't give it up until I can get something in return."

He passed a hand over his eyes. He felt tired and fearful, but oddly relieved as well. He'd done things he couldn't forgive himself for, but hoped some form of atonement might still be possible.

Like bait in a trap. Fine, but when the prey wandered close enough he would become the hunter.

In the following days, Kate initially regretted her naive refusal of surveillance and security. She began each morning at a baseline level of anxiety that ratcheted up by the hour. By evening it seemed to float above her like ectoplasm—as if dread had become a sort of mystical, out-of-body experience. She found it hard to function, fixed in an orbit of taut vigilance, but as the weeks passed with no further word from either Sedgwick or Frank her nerves gradually settled—just in time for the annual touristic juggernaut known as the Fall Foliage Season.

Unfortunately, it proved to be the coldest, wettest autumn Kate had ever experienced in Vermont. The driving rain stopped only long enough for an oppressive fog to coat everything with a layer of condensation, making Hartsboro Bend seem like the stereotypical setting for a horror film, where locals share nervous glances as something unholy prepares to descend on them. By the time a windstorm ripped the trees bare in a single night, Kate felt she'd be happy to take a smaller bottom line just to have the season finished.

The current set of bedraggled guests included a couple with two children they made no attempt to control, and a sullen collection of senior citizens that even Conor's Hibernian charm was powerless to crack. After setting up card tables for them in the library on the second showery morning of their stay, he met Kate putting on a sweater in the hallway and rolled his eyes.

"Horrible old wagons. The looks they're giving off, you'd think I'd personally pulled the leaves off every feckin' tree in the state."

Unlike her, the past several weeks had taken a heavy toll on him. He'd operated as a one-man physical security system, until his hollow-eyed exhaustion made Kate reverse herself and insist he install the remote-alarm tripwire devices Sedgwick had left behind. The intervention helped, but the strain on him was compounded by the demands of the season—he'd often been pressed into bartending and butler duties—and his current week was ending with an excess of farming drama. The storm had knocked out the barn's archaic electrical system, resulting in two days of dumped milk, and a heifer was due to calve at any moment. After spending the past two nights on obstetric duty Conor was tired and grouchy, and fighting a cold that only made him more so.

"A sweater won't do the job in this weather." He scowled at her. "Where are you off to?"

"The store. I told Yvette I'd run the cash register for her today and pick up Jigger from school."

Yvette was another casualty of the month's foul weather. She'd slipped on the wet leaves covering her porch a week earlier and had broken her shoulder. Kate added a raincoat on top of the sweater and surveyed Conor. "What about you? You sound awful."

"I'm all right. I'm going to meet whoever Green Mountain Power sends over to prop up the bloody grid. If I have to throw one more bucket of milk down the drain I may weep." He cocked an eyebrow. "And how's your week going?"

"Okay I guess, but I plan to drown the children in the brook later today."

The tiredness in his eyes shifted to a mischievous twinkle that had become too rare of late. "About bloody time. Will I give you a hand?"

"I'm not sure I need help." Kate pursed her lips. "I can just kick them over the edge."

They exchanged a facetious glance before her involuntary snort tipped them into hilarity. A healing laughter, it dispersed the simmering tension of the past several weeks and continued until Conor's painful-sounding cough made them both wince. Abigail equated its percussive depth with the noise of a two-by-four in a wood chipper, and knowing his medical history she and Kate were openly nervous about it—which added to his irritability.

"Don't look at me like that."

"Like what? Like I'm afraid you're headed for the sanatorium?"

"Do they still have those here?"

Kate smiled at his startled consternation. "Of course not, but I hear doctors are still in fashion." Opening the door to a furious downpour, she plucked two umbrellas from the corner and held one out to Conor. He dismissed the offer, tugging a Penzoil cap from his pocket instead.

"Another one? Where do you come up with those?"

"The store. Sale table." He grinned, pulling up his collar and using the cap to wave her through the door ahead of him.

She returned in the late afternoon. The inn was wrapped in a pleasant hush typical for that time of day, disturbed only by the muffled clinks and rattles of the kitchen staff preparing for the evening shift. Kate went straight up to change before the restaurant opened. Leaving her bedroom to return downstairs she met Abigail coming down the hall, carrying a tray of food and looking troubled.

"Whatever he's got, it's not letting go. When the man won't eat, you know something's wrong."

"I thought the same thing earlier," Kate said. "Has he been in bed all day?"

"Should have been. He fussed over that damned cow for hours. Breach delivery. Turned out fine for her but he looked like death on a cracker when he got back—wheezing, feverish, shirt covered in blood and afterbirth." Abigail brightened a little. "He scared hell out of one of the old ladies."

"Go on ahead. I'll peek in on him before I come down."

"I just did that," Abigail pointed out. "He's asleep."

"Well, still ..."

"Sure, honey." Abigail headed for the stairs, hiding a smile. "Go peek in on him."

Kate put her head around his door and confirmed Conor was indeed still asleep. He lay in a damp tangle on top of the bed, covers askew, pillows scattered. His room was otherwise as tidy as the day he'd arrived. His violin case and a folded music stand stood near the fireplace, a pile of musical scores sat neatly stacked on his bureau, and a number of Vermont-themed books had been added to the mantelpiece. She tiptoed across the room and stopped to browse the collection—Robert Frost, Howard Frank Mosher, field guides and farming manuals, and a history of Vermont. Kate glanced at Conor's sleeping face, thinking about his own startling history, wondering why she'd thought it made him such a stranger to her and realizing she didn't seem to believe it anymore.

She settled on the window seat and indulged in a long, uninterrupted study of him. He still wore his jeans but the offending t-shirt had been dropped on the floor next to his boots, and he'd pushed away all except a corner of the patchwork quilt covering him. His hands rested on his stomach, moving with the rise and fall of his chest, and they seemed to symbolize the contradictions she'd been struggling to reconcile. His fingers had the graceful elegance of a virtuoso, but years of manual work had weathered them, and the prominent tendons running up into his wrists hinted at a hard, concealed strength. Like everything else about him, Conor's hands contained layers of meaning not easily discovered. They lay deceptively relaxed against the coiled muscles of his abdomen, and looking at them Kate acknowledged what was useless to deny—mystery, risk, danger—however hazardous it might prove to her peace of mind and wellbeing, all of it only increased her attraction to him.

She rose to peer outside before leaving. The rain had

tapered off at last and hints of watery sunlight burned through the thinning clouds. Behind her Conor's measured breathing changed, and when she turned from the window her own breath caught. He was awake, dark eyes fixed on her.

"You look nice." His sleepy voice contained more air than sound.

Kate glanced down at her selection for the evening—a simple, long-sleeved black dress—feeling the color rise on her face. "Thank you." After an awkward pause she offered him the glass of orange juice Abigail had left next to his bed but Conor groaned, shaking his head.

"I've had enough juice, thanks very much. She's been throwing it into me all day. My tonsils are floating." He squinted at the clock next to him. "Damn. Is that four o'clock already?"

Kate set the glass on the table. "Never mind the cows, I'll call Jared. Don't be stubborn, or bite my head off about it. You know this could be dangerous if you're not careful." She hesitated, worried and conflicted. "I'm supposed to leave for New Hampshire tomorrow morning. Maybe I should tell them I can't go."

"Oh, no." Conor lifted himself to sit against the headboard. "Don't use me as an excuse to avoid your family. Especially after they've been calling all week."

Kate had to admit canceling was out of the question. Each year, the charitable foundation her grandmother had founded showed its appreciation with an extravagant dinner at her favorite resort—the Mt. Washington in Bretton Woods. All of Kate's siblings had called during the week to confirm her attendance, and she understood why. The dinner this year had been planned to coincide with her thirtieth birthday, which was coming up on Sunday but she hadn't mentioned that to Conor. Her family had a horror of anything that smacked of vulgarity, so she was sure the event would be marked with no more than a discreet cake at the end of the evening. The milestone itself was one she'd been secretly dreading, and she was anxious to discuss it with her grandmother. Also, she'd promised to take Jigger along with her to give Yvette a chance to rest.

"All right." Kate tucked the quilt up around Conor's shoulders. "I'd better not come home and find you in the hospital. Or the barn."

"Well it's late, so if you're going to call Jared you should go do it, otherwise that's where I'm headed." Peevishly, he pushed the quilt down again, and seeing her exasperation offered a sheepish grin. "Sorry. I'm the most churlish invalid you'll ever meet."

"Yes, I'm beginning to realize this." She gave him a light cuff on the head and headed for the door. "Go back to sleep. I'll send up some soup later."

"Send up a pint," Conor muttered. "I'm more likely to drink that."

"Soup," she said, bringing the door shut behind her.

"Guinness is good for you," came the insistent, muffled reply.

17

Christ, that can't be right.

Conor swiveled his head to the window and met a blast of morning sunlight before swinging back to the clock—it was a little after eight in the morning. He couldn't remember the last time he'd slept past five o'clock, let alone three hours beyond.

With some effort he rolled upright, and sat listening to the wheeze carrying on inside him like an independent life form. He'd downplayed the symptoms with everyone else but wasn't so foolish as to ignore them. He'd phoned his pulmonologist the previous afternoon, hoping for reassurance, and after a fashion the physician had tried to provide some when she returned his call later in the evening.

"Probably just pneumonia again," she said, and told him to report for an examination the following day.

Brilliant. Just pneumonia. Again. He wondered if all his past misadventures would keep repeating themselves like this—a series of open cadences without resolution.

Conor drew in breath for a long sigh of self-pity. Bad mistake. Once he'd stopped hacking he had another depressing thought for the start to his day—he sounded like his father, a pretty fucking uncomfortable idea to be sure. He'd been grateful to have inherited the musical talent of Thomas McBride, Sr., but he could do without the crap pulmonary genes.

A long steaming shower revived him a bit, and down on the ground floor he was relieved to find the place deserted. In the kitchen he drank a few mugs of tea, then after inspecting the barn and resisting the urge to clean what Jared had not—beggars can't be choosers—he drove off to Copley Hospital for another round of x-rays and antibiotics.

He was back a few hours later and ready for a nap, only to find Darla on the scene. He tolerated her effusive concern with what patience he could summon before excusing himself, shaking his bag of pills in apology. That worked only for the moment. As he lowered himself onto the couch in Kate's living room, Darla's face loomed over him.

"I come bearing gifts," she said brightly. "Abigail is on her way, but she called and asked me to heat up this nice bowl of chicken soup for you. Doesn't it smell wonderful? Don't you think you could eat a little?"

"Thanks very much, Darla. Sure I'll do my best. Maybe you could leave the bowl on the counter down the hall. I'll tackle it after I've had a rest."

"I think you'd better eat while it's hot—no, don't get up. I can manage."

The tray was heavy looking and she was a tiny thing, but Darla maneuvered with little effort in setting it down on the table in front of him. She irritated the hell out of him but Conor had to admire her spunk, and her manic, wiry strength. He obliged her by slurping up a few spoonfuls of the soup while she moved to the picture window, still chattering.

"What a beautiful day after so much miserable weather! Perfect for a drive to Mt. Washington. I think Kate's family will be so happy to see her. She didn't go last year you know, but they weren't going to let her get away with it this time. Seemed like every time I picked up the phone this week another one was checking in to make sure she was coming. I told Kate she might want to get a second phone for the front desk. Not that I mind answering a few personal calls—no, no, I don't at all. But it would be easier not to run into her office all the time, and then when a guest needs to use the phone—they can never get their cell phones to work here—I have to send them in and hope they don't run up the long-distance bill. Some of them take their sweet time, too ..."

Conor abandoned the soup and sat watching her blather on, trying to identify which avian species she most resembled. Nut hatch? Shrike? He sank back into the cushions and closed his eyes, not caring anymore how long she might stand there, talking.

Someone is listening.

It was like the air speaking into his face, riffling his hair, covering his hot skin with a puff of coolness.

Wake up, love. Someone is there. Someone is listening.

Not a puff now but a gust—a short, sharp hurricane piped directly into his ear, raising a line of gooseflesh up his back.

Wake up, Conor.

"I'm awake, Ma."

And he was. Completely awake. Wide awake. Conor remained still, his ear tuned to an interior conversation for about ten seconds before he leaped up, nearly falling over the coffee table where the bowl of soup sat, cold and gelatinous. He raced from the room, taking the stairs two at a time down to the lobby. When he exploded from the staircase next to the front desk, his face shining with sweat, Darla received him with a jittery scream.

"Who's been using the phone?" She stared at him, speechless for once in her life, and he slammed his palm against the countertop with a crack like a gunshot. "The bloody phone, Darla. You were talking about the phone in Kate's office. Which guests have been using—oh fuck it."

He came around the desk and flew past her into the office, pulling the phone line from the wall and grabbing the cordless handset from its base. Darla found her voice again, shrieking as Conor ransacked the drawers. He pulled out a letter opener and went to work on the phone, and heard Abigail's voice at the front desk.

"What the hell is going on out here?"

"I have no idea!" Darla wailed. "He's delirious! He looked ready to murder me!"

The letter opener merely bent in his hands. He threw it to the floor and picked up the granite paperweight near Kate's computer, bringing it down on the phone with a crash. He pulled the half-shattered remains apart and the electronic bug fell out into his hand.

"Jesus help me." Staring at it, Conor dropped heavily into the chair. "And we thought nothing was going on."

With his elbows on the desk he rested his hands over his eyes, and when he removed them his face was flat and composed. He got up and walked to the doorway where the two women stood staring in at him.

"Darla, I apologize for frightening you," he said evenly. "Abigail, I need a favor. I'll meet you in the parking lot."

Head twitching, Darla appeared ready to pose a shower of questions and Abigail seemed as though she wanted to speak as well, but Conor closed the door on both of them. He went to the breakfront behind the desk and unlocked the combination safe inside. The small leather bag seemed to wriggle in his hands as he removed it, the innards shifting and sliding against each other. He swept the wreckage of the phone into a drawer and opened the bag, spilling the contents onto the desk. A Sig-Sauer this time, he observed grimly. He pulled up his shirt to mop his face then briskly assembled the pistol, sliding the magazine into place with a click both familiar and repellant.

He found Abigail outside leaning against the truck, arms folded, wearing a battlefield expression that prompted him to come to the point without mincing words. "The phone's been tapped. For all I know the whole house is bugged and the cars as well."

Abigail popped away from the truck as though it had burned her. "Son of a bitch. How did you know?"

"A sudden intuition," Conor said.

"Who did it? And when?" she demanded.

"I don't know, and I don't have time to speculate." He swiped again at the perspiration beading on his forehead. "The point is, Durgan's people have been here already, and since they chose not to carry me off with them they're playing a trickier game than I figured. Do you have a mobile phone?"

Abigail shook her head. "They usually don't work up here, anyway."

"I need you to get to a phone somewhere off the property and try calling Kate to tell her I'm on the way."

"You think Kate's in danger?"

He nodded, rigid with the effort of standing still while every muscle in his body screamed for movement. Conor wished his mother's ethereal voice had blown something more helpfully specific into his ear but it hadn't, so he was operating on little more than inherited prescience, which was telegraphing a simple, repeating signal that Kate was in terrible danger.

"Tell her to stay where she is and to stay in a group, or at least in public. She shouldn't go anywhere alone, even to her room." He took out his wallet and removed Frank's ivory-colored calling card. "After that I need you to call the number on the back of this card. They'll ask for a password—it's Kreisler."

"Chrysler," Abigail repeated. "Like the car?"

"No, like the violinist, Fritz Kreisler." Conor rocked on his heels restlessly. "Listen, doesn't matter. Recite the bloody thing for whoever answers. They'll connect you to the agent I told you about—Frank Murdoch. No details. Tell him you're calling for me and I want to know what time his friend will arrive. That's the signal to get someone up here. He'll send an MI6 general staff officer from the embassy in New York, but this is a London number so you have to—"

"I know how to dial a London number. I'll call from home." Abigail snapped the card out of his hand. "Now, do *you* know how to get to the hotel?"

"Bretton Woods. I've a map in the truck, I'll figure it out."

"You look ready to pass out."

"I'm okay."

"You'd better be. I love you honey, but if anything happens to Kate I'll kick you until you're dead."

Her threat, delivered while throwing her arms around him, had little credibility. Conor returned the embrace before stepping away.

"Abigail, if anything happens to Kate I'll be begging you to."

Bretton Woods wasn't as far away as he'd feared and Conor made good time, especially after hitting the interstate in St. Johnsbury, a scenic but not heavily traveled section of highway. For long stretches his was the only vehicle in sight and he pushed the battered farm truck to its limit, cursing it for not being a Mustang. In a little over an hour he'd exited onto Route 302 and was sweeping through the White Mountains, only dimly aware that the landscape around him was magnificent.

He passed the sign welcoming him to Bretton Woods and began scanning the road on either side, anxious not to miss any clues as to the direction of the hotel. He needn't have worried. As he came around a tree-lined curve the resort abruptly materialized in the distance on his left, looking like a massive cruise ship on dry land—white-faced, red-roofed, flags flying.

Conor slammed on the brakes to make the turn onto the entrance road, and after leaving the truck in the parking lot he paused on the sloping driveway to take stock of his appearance. Not great. To hide the gun riding in a holster against his back, he'd layered a black-and-gold checked flannel shirt over a blue t-shirt. Both articles carried their share of mysterious stains, and his jeans were a long way from clean. He returned to the truck for the black duck jacket he'd left on the seat. It made him too warm but looked better than anything else he was wearing.

Walking onto the massive veranda and through the door of the Mt. Washington Hotel was like stepping onto the creaking floorboards of an earlier era. The cavernous lobby was typical for the grand hotels of the Gilded Age. It was an unusual combination of elegance and mountain rusticity—from the central chandelier and rows of stately columns to the rugged stone fireplace with its moose-head trophy. The space was generously furnished with deep sofas and wingback chairs, and in one of them near the fireplace Kate was sitting with her face to the entrance.

Overcome with relief, Conor's knees buckled slightly as she rushed across the lobby and into his arms. She circled his waist, and when her hands brushed against the gun through the fabric of his jacket she hitched in her breath, letting her face rest against his chest.

"I was so worried. Abigail said you seemed ready to collapse when you left and I've been sitting here freaking out since she called. This doesn't make any sense, Conor. Why would anyone be coming after me?"

"I don't know." Conor held her close and brushed his lips against her hair, breathing in its fresh scent.

He had to admit her skepticism was justified. He could think of nothing Durgan would gain by targeting Kate and complicating his main objective, and allowed himself to consider the possibility of being wrong. The phone surveillance was real but the bug on Kate's phone might have been incidental, another means of gathering intelligence about him. Maybe he was delirious—he felt hot enough to be—and maybe this rescue operation was a neurotic over-reaction. What was he supposed to tell her? That his mother had whispered to him in a dream and it sounded like truth? That he believed its murky warning even now, despite the lack of any rational explanation? Kate stirred in his arms.

"You're trembling," she said.

"I think we both are." He rested his chin on top of her head.

"But you're the one with a fever. You're not trembling with emotional derangement."

"Don't be so sure."

She pulled back and examined him. "Do you think we're in danger right now?"

Still holding her by the elbows Conor let his eyes travel around the lobby, realizing its majestic size and an accumulation of furniture had created a false impression of emptiness. He counted eight guests sprinkled amongst the sofas like artfully arranged bric-a-brac. Studying each of them—golfers, senior citizens, a few mothers with young children—he found nothing menacing for even the most paranoid mind to fix on as a threat. Frustrated by his own uncertainty and aware that the circumstances made him appear unhinged, he dropped his hands and took an unsteady step away from Kate.

"I guess not right now. Nothing looks dangerous, anyway."

"Did you eat anything today?"

"Darla heated up some soup."

"A clever non-answer which I'll take as a 'no'." She circled her arm around his and drew him forward. "Come on, they're serving lunch on the back veranda. If you don't sit down and eat something you won't be able to protect either of us from anything."

Having satisfied his concern for Kate's immediate safety, Conor could spare a bit more attention for their surroundings. He spent a moment leaning on the back veranda's spindled railing, looking out at a panoramic view of the Presidential Range. The epic bulk of Mt. Washington dominated the scene, trails drizzling down its sides like lines of rainwater. Below him the hotel's back lawn rolled down to a brook about a quarter-mile away. It was spanned by an arched footbridge that connected the resort to its golf course, which sat in a bowl-shaped valley in the middle distance. Before returning to the table where Kate was already seated he swept a gaze over the veranda. Along its length guests were sitting in similar groupings, in wicker chairs arranged around low tables. Some were eating, others chatting or simply admiring the view. All of them clearly innocuous.

"You didn't bring Jigger along after all?" he asked, sitting down across from her.

"Oh, he's here." Kate accepted a menu from the waitress who came to take their order. "We were just heading out to the Cog Railway when Abigail called. My sister took him instead, along with her kids."

Conor declined to take a menu and smiled at the young woman. "Just a cup of tea would be grand, thanks."

"No, not grand." Kate plucked the menu from the server's hand and presented it to him. "Eat something."

He ordered a BLT, and when the sandwich arrived he ate a little before sitting back, tired from the effort. Watching him Kate nibbled at her thumbnail, looking as if she was trying to decide what to do with him.

"What now? Do you want me to go home with you?"

"Oh ... ehm, I hadn't thought that far ahead." Conor realized he'd given no thought to anything beyond the priority of having her in his line of sight again.

"Should I ask them to add another place for dinner?"

"Jesus. No." The thought appalled him. "Look, just go ahead and have your party and I'll sort of hang about, keep an eye on things and on ... well, you."

"How? By hovering behind my chair like a bodyguard?"

"Something like that, I suppose. I'm not exactly dressed for a fancy dinner with your family."

"And how long are we going to need to do this?"

"How the f—, how should I know? I'm making this up as I go along." His exasperation brought on an alarming cough, which threatened to get away from him until he smothered the spasm against his jacket.

"Okay. I'm sorry." Kate lowered her voice and put a hand over his. "I'm not trying to upset you, but I need to be honest. You're the one who's got enemies, not me. You've had to stay alert for weeks, trying to guess what they'll do and and when, trying to keep everyone from getting dragged any further into your nightmare. You're under a huge amount of stress, you're exhausted, and you're sick. Isn't it possible your mind is playing tricks on you? That it's created an illusion of danger around me that doesn't exist?"

"Yes. It's possible, of course." Conor dropped another slice of lemon into his tea and took a swallow. "You want evidence and I don't blame you, but all I've got are ghosts and dreams, and a bit of my mother's sense for the uncanny. I was never comfortable with it, but I've learned to respect it."

Kate sat back, staring at him. "God almighty. You're like a Napoleon pastry; layers without end. Are you telling me you're clairvoyant? On top of everything else?"

Conor squirmed in his chair, wondering whether the spark in her eyes indicated skepticism or amusement. "It's not really like that. Listen, I'm not asking you to believe in any of this. I'm just asking you to humor me."

"I understand." Kate signed for the lunch and got to her feet, extending a hand to him. "And as a matter of fact, I do believe in it. Come on up to my room and rest. We'll figure something out later."

No longer dozing in its mid-day hush, the lobby and its protesting floorboards had come alive with new arrivals. After they'd dodged a rumbling luggage trolley and navigated around the front desk's gathering crowd, Conor sensed a presence looming close behind them and quickly turned.

"Katie! Have you seen Jeanette and the kids?" A stocky man of medium height came to an abrupt stop to avoid running into them. Impatience masquerading as concern flashed across his face. He rubbed a palm over thick black hair that stood up from his head like a piece of manicured topiary while Kate gave him a teasing smile.

"Cog railway, Richard. I was there when she told you."

"Ah, jeez. Okay." Richard relaxed. "I just wasn't sure what suit to bring in from the car. She brought two for me. Are your Dad and Anna here yet?"

"No." Kate pulled an ironic face. "They'll swoop in at the last minute. I'm surprised they're staying this year. Daddy doesn't see the point of grand old hotels. He only likes things that are new."

"Right, right." Richard looked between the two of them with an ingratiating tilt of his head. Before Conor could decide what to do, Kate was talking again.

"Oh Richard, you remember my friend Conor? The Classical violinist from the Dublin Conservatory?"

Conor immediately stuck out his hand. "Good to see you again."

"Well of course, of course. How are you, Conor?" Richard crushed his hand and gave his shoulder a manly thump. "What brings you up to the mountains?"

"A surprise." The words burst from Kate's lips and she paused, giving Conor a nervous glance that he returned in kind, wondering what in the name of God was going to come out of her next. She took a breath.

"For Oma. She loves music. He's going to play during the cocktail reception. He came as a favor to me."

"Sounds wonderful." Richard was already looking beyond them at a group of golfers coming through the door. "I'm sure the princess will enjoy that. Will you both excuse me? There's a fellow I want to catch before he leaves."

"Either a donor or someone he hopes will become one," Kate said as they watched him cross the lobby. She giggled. "I do that to him all the time. Introduce him to people he's never met like they're old friends. He's a Massachusetts state senator. He can't afford to admit he doesn't know everyone."

"Yeah, that's hilarious *Katie*," Conor said drily. "Can we talk about this plan you've hatched without telling me? Fair play, the idea's not a bad one, but where am I supposed to get a violin? Or even a suit?"

"Milton can help us." She pulled him toward the elevator behind the stairs. "He's the head concierge and he's been here forever. A suit and a violin? Piece of cake. He won't even break a sweat. We just need to get you rested and ready."

"'Oma.' That's your grandmother, yeah?" Conor allowed himself to be dragged forward without protest. He was beginning to feel quite sleepy. "Why did he call her a princess? Is she a bitch?"

"No, not at all. Far from it. Her name is Sophia Marie." Kate punched the elevator button and said nothing more. Conor raised an eyebrow and she dropped her head with a sigh. "My grandmother is part of Luxembourg's royal house of Nassau-Weilburg. Her father was the last crown prince of Bavaria."

During the stunned silence that followed the elevator arrived. It was a real antique, manually operated and claustrophobically small. It looked like the first elevator ever invented. Avoiding his eyes Kate stepped in and Conor followed, taking up a position against the opposite wall. He watched a telltale flush of pink spread up her neck and over her cheeks, and gave her a broad grin.

"What's so funny?" she asked in a small voice.

"No, nothing. This is just an interesting sort of treat for me, discovering you've got secrets of your own."

"I would have told you, eventually." Kate shrugged. "As you can imagine, these are not the circumstances under which I thought I'd be introducing you to my family."

Conor put his back against the wall of the elevator, still smiling, pleased by the idea she'd thought about introducing him to them at all.

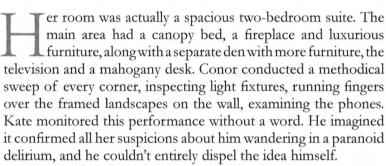

18

Her room was actually a spacious two-bedroom suite. The main area had a canopy bed, a fireplace and luxurious furniture, along with a separate den with more furniture, the television and a mahogany desk. Conor conducted a methodical sweep of every corner, inspecting light fixtures, running fingers over the framed landscapes on the wall, examining the phones. Kate monitored this performance without a word. He imagined it confirmed all her suspicions about him wandering in a paranoid delirium, and he couldn't entirely dispel the idea himself.

Once satisfied the room was "clean" he collapsed on the sofa in front of the fireplace while Kate went to phone Milton, the concierge. Conor's operational discipline relaxed into dull exhaustion as he gazed around the suite, trying to make sense of the fact that an ordinary farmer from Dingle—not entirely unrefined or lacking in unconventional skills, but still, of humble origin—could be in love with a product of European royalty.

He put his head back and closed his eyes. *Bloody hell. What would the neighbors say?*

He lapsed into a doze until Kate returned and dragged him up from the sofa, insisting he move to the bed. Conor felt ridiculous lying beneath the fussy-looking drapery, but the pillowcases had a pleasant alpine scent and the bed was irresistibly comfortable. He sank into the mattress as he would a hot bath, and made no fuss as Kate settled the comforter under his chin.

"You must feel lousy. You're not being difficult."

"I wouldn't dream of hassling a princess."

"Don't." She ducked away, hiding an uneasy frown. "Please. Not even as a joke."

"Why so sensitive? Where I come from you can't throw a rock without hitting some plonker who swears he came from kings."

"This is different," Kate insisted. "My grandmother has been in this country since the 30s. She married a scientist from Boston, and then my mother married a hedge fund manager and I married a cash register salesman. There's nothing 'royal' about any of us, but the bloodline is real, and the heritage, and of course the European relatives. It's a challenge to navigate. I try not to get too involved."

"Right, so." On the edge of sleep, Conor nodded. "I promise not to call you a princess. I'll just think of you as one."

He woke some time later and slid a hand under the pillow, confirming the gun had not wandered out of reach, then cradled the second pillow against his ribs as his rumbling cough sent pain like the sharp end of a knitting needle through his chest. While recovering, Conor became aware of a more insistent but less agonizing sensation—a pinch on his right big toe, and then the same on his left. Conor lifted himself up on one elbow and saw Jigger at the foot of the bed.

"It worked." The boy laughed. "Hi Conor."

"Hi yourself. What's the idea, abusing my toes while I sleep?"

"Kate said to wake you up at five o'clock, but she told me to be careful when I did."

"Where is she?" Conor sat up, instantly alert.

"Taking a bath."

"Oh."

His sigh aggravated the feathery, tickling thing in his chest and Conor dropped amongst the pillows, using them to muffle the racket. Empathic instincts awakened, Jigger hurried forward to rub his back, woeful and fascinated.

"Kate thinks you have pneumonia. I think she's right."

"Which makes three of us, then. Unanimous vote."

"And she said you're going to play some music for her grandmother, but you left your fiddle at home."

"Also correct."

"You seem to have a lot of troubles, don't you?"

Conor choked out a laugh and pulled himself upright. "You've noticed that as well, have you?"

"Yes. I've noticed." Jigger pointed to a violin case tucked into a corner on the sofa. "Kate's friend Milton found a fiddle for you. Do you want to look at it?"

He carried the case to the bed like a tray of fine china and placed it in Conor's hands before bouncing up to sit next to him. Conor flipped opened the lid and they both peered inside.

"Pretty shiny," Jigger remarked. "And not old, like yours."

"No, but we won't hold that against it." He tuned the instrument and ran off a few scales before peeking through the f-hole at the label inside. The violin had come from the Naples workshop of Vincenzo Anastasio, a contemporary master luthier. Impressive.

He was in the sitting area, amusing Jigger with an interpretation of *I Am The Walrus* when Kate emerged from her bath. She wore a silk dressing gown of sky blue, her head turbaned in a towel, and as far as Conor was concerned she might as well have been ready to go. He couldn't imagine what she could put on to look any more beautiful. Kate met his gaze with an equal measure of concentration, and appeared less satisfied with what she saw. She sat on the sofa next to them and tugged on Jigger's ear.

"Your turn, kiddo. I've got the tub all ready for you. Bubbles piled high." When the bathroom door had closed she moved closer to Conor. "I'm having second thoughts about this plan. I think we should get you home. I'll make up some excuse."

"And be disappointin' yer poor aul' gran?" Conor asked in an exaggerated drawl. He took her hand and rested it on his knee. "I'll be fine. I'm sort of looking forward to this, to be honest. A shower and a shave and I'm a new man. Just wait and see."

Kate seemed unconvinced, and anxious. While doing his best to hide it he was worried as well.

Something is coming.

The whispering chant of his dreams clicked against his brain like the relentless tap of a metronome.

Something is coming.

He believed it. He could feel its approach. It wasn't far away.

This time the shower didn't produce the restorative effect Conor had hoped for, but the suit did. Milton the concierge was clearly a "fixer" of the first order. He'd come through with a full dress, tuxedo tail package complete with white vest and matching bow tie, studs and cufflinks.

It had been years since he'd worn white tie and tails. By the time he'd finished snapping and buttoning himself into the entire kit a burst of energy pulsed through him. After fitting the gun with its clip-on holster into a comfortable spot under the tailcoat, he combed his hair, took a generous pull from his bottle of prescription cough syrup and stepped from the bathroom.

"Oh my." Kate rose from the sofa, one high-heeled shoe dangling from her hand. "Who are you, and what have you done with my farm manager?"

"I pass inspection, then?"

"Pass? My God, you've aced it. You look perfect. It looks like it was made for you. You look—" Kate stopped abruptly. Unable to resist teasing her Conor waited, head tilted.

"You look very handsome," she finished quietly.

"And you look like a ..." He grinned at her squint of warning. "Like a movie star."

In truth, neither "princess" nor "movie star" captured it. She was stunning in a strapless, floor-length gown of pale gold overlaid with a pastiche of autumn colors. It was like a gorgeously rendered canvas, accenting her hair, which she'd tamed into a shining coil. He thought she more nearly resembled a high queen of Celtic legend but held his tongue, aware that it would sound rapturous and might test her patience even further.

Jigger bounced in from the adjoining bedroom, shoeless but otherwise dapper in a white jacket and red bow tie. "You both look like something from a fairy tale," he exclaimed, having no qualms about sounding rapturous. "I think we're all beautiful, don't you? Kate, remember you have to help me with my shoes. I can get them on but I can't tie them. I'm excited to meet your grandmother and hear the music. Are we ready to go?"

Shoes tied, he bolted for the door and then the elevator while they followed him down the hallway.

"Is your family prepared for the social dynamo about to descend on them?" Conor asked.

Kate nodded. "I laid the groundwork but I'm not worried. Cocktail party chat is right up their alley, and right up his. He'll be a big hit."

With effort, Conor had mastered an urge to caress the glowing skin of her bare shoulders, but when the elevator reached the ground floor he instinctively placed his palm on the small of her back as the door rattled open. Kate leaned against the pressure of his hand before she stepped out, smiling at him.

The pre-dinner reception took place in the Conservatory between the main lobby and back veranda. The room was an airy, circular colonnade, topped by a rotunda with a celestial blue ceiling featuring a tiny, soaring gull at its center. Around twenty people had gathered so far, all dressed in sparkling evening attire, drinks in hand. Jigger had trotted ahead and was already talking to a group settled in front of the fireplace.

In quick succession Kate introduced Conor to her brothers, their wives, her sister Jeanette, a small girl named Emily who wasn't identified as belonging to any of them, and an aunt Winifred.

"Have you got all that?" she teased, steering him toward the next wave of relatives.

"You'd be surprised," Conor said. "I'm good at memorizing things."

"Natural talent, or training?"

"A little of both."

Having met the siblings and spouses—all of whom smelled of money—and having surreptitiously examined the exits, the waitstaff and the random guests on the porch, Conor stationed himself beside the grand piano. He watched Kate chatting with her relatives as he tuned, and inspired by the hues in her shimmering dress launched into a solo version of the Grappelli and Menuhin arrangement of *Autumn Leaves*. Jazz standards seemed a good fit for the setting, and since he'd long ago mastered the Grappelli and Menuhin catalogue he carried on with *Skylark*.

The room filled, and its atmosphere had warmed to a festive buzz when the guest of honor arrived, flanked by a couple Conor assumed were Kate's father and step-mother. Her grandmother was easy to recognize as she stood in the doorway. Tall and slender, Sophia Marie had a smooth complexion and long silver hair pulled into a bun secured by a diamond brooch. Wearing a beaded gown of forest green she moved with aristocratic grace, but the air of nobility was softened by lively blue eyes and a warm smile that so reminded him of Kate that Conor momentarily lost his place in the tune he was playing. With a poise that managed to be both regal and self-effacing, the Bavarian-born princess swept in to general applause.

He continued serenading the room while observing the family dynamic. He'd noted Kate's stiff formality in introducing him to her three oldest brothers, and her more relaxed attitude now, chatting with her sister and Peter, the youngest of the brothers. Around her the guests revolved in a slow-moving orbit, the scent of their mingled colognes circulating with them as they moved.

Conor was no stranger to events of this sort. The well-groomed individuals here provided a familiar backdrop that could anchor similar scenes around the world. In his former life he'd spent many an evening performing recitals and concertos for the bejeweled, tuxedoed upper crust in Dublin, London, Paris and Rome. He'd chatted up the conspicuously wealthy at obligatory post-performance gatherings, drinking their Champagne and eating their exquisite hors d'oeuvres, and unlike many of his countrymen he harbored no automatic antipathy toward them. Like any other people, some he found interesting, others dead boring, and a few had made his blood boil. The only constant was that he'd always been happy to excuse himself after a polite interlude to search for a more filling meal and easier conversation in the nearest pub. Trailing in the wake of the "splendid set" wasn't his idea of a fun evening, and—he had to admit it—discovering Kate was a card-carrying member unnerved him a little.

She introduced him to Princess Sophia Marie, who welcomed him with grace and charm, and to Douglas and Anna Chatham, Kate's father and step-mother. From a cursory study Conor surmised that her gaunt, worried-looking step-mother was an anorexic with a compulsive tanning habit, and her short, balding father was a cocky little gobshite who liked hearing himself talk.

"Irish, eh? Markets still raging over there—Celtic Tiger, right? Won't last, you know. You people are way over-exposed. Investors are fools to put anything in Ireland, now."

Kate pulled at her father's arm, shooting Conor an apologetic glance. "Daddy, I don't think we need to—"

"Remember it was me who told you," Douglas commanded, his face a picture of smug satisfaction. "Hard times ahead."

"Sure that'll be nothing awfully new for us, sir," Conor said smoothly. Sophia Marie circled an arm around Kate's waist, and as the group prepared to move on she touched his shoulder.

"I'll be back with a request. I'd love to hear some Schumann."

When she approached a half-hour later, Conor segued from what he'd been playing to the swaying lullaby theme of Schumann's *Traumerei*. She put a hand to her lips, surprised and pleased, and took a seat on the window ledge behind him. He finished the piece, and turned to acknowledge her applause with a droll bow.

"How did you know?" she asked.

"A hopeful guess. Truth is, the rest of my Schumann is pretty dodgy."

A member of the waitstaff entered the room playing a set of chimes, calling everyone to dinner, but Sophia Marie inclined her head, indicating the space at her side.

"You're looking very flushed. Come and sit down."

Conor left the violin on top of the piano and obediently sat next to her.

"You've become quite an indispensable fixture at the Rembrandt Inn, I understand. Kate has been telling me all about you." His flinch of alarm was mostly for comical effect, and she smiled. "That makes you nervous?"

"Depends what she's been saying," Conor replied, with perfect candor.

"Only the best things, trust me, and even the things she doesn't say I can see on her face. She's hoping for my good opinion, I think."

Oh, God help me. Conor's stomach tightened as though preparing to resist a blow. A matchmaking interview with

Kate's royal granny was exactly what he didn't need. The shot of adrenalin propping him up had peaked a while earlier and perspiration was streaming down his back like a small river. He slipped a hand into the pocket of his trousers and surprised himself by coming out with a handkerchief.

"Did you know her husband? Michael?"

Startled, he shook his head while wiping the back of his neck, offering hosannas for the incomparably gifted Milton. "I didn't. When I got ready to emigrate a good friend of mine in Ireland provided an introduction for me with Kate. He was a cousin of Michael's."

Conor stopped, hoping his silence would be enough to nudge the conversation elsewhere. It wasn't.

"I didn't care for him."

"Ah." He gathered the handkerchief into a soggy ball, flexing it inside his clenched fist. Sophia Marie nodded sadly.

"Kate and I have always been very close. She often stayed with me for months at a time as she grew up. So, when I disapproved it became hard for both of us. And then, he died ..." She lifted her arm and let it fall helplessly to her side. "I felt so guilty. I wished I could have liked him better. I don't know why I didn't."

There was absolutely nothing to be said in reply to such a remark. Conor was mercifully spared from attempting one by the timid advance of Kate's step-mother. She stopped several yards in front of them and stood on tiptoe, nervously tucking a lock of honey-blonde hair behind one ear.

"Sophia?" Anna spoke the word with brittle uncertainty, as though expecting to be contradicted. "We're going in to the Sun Dining Room, now."

"Yes, dear. We're coming." The older woman turned back to him. "You'll join us for dinner, of course?"

"Oh, I've eaten already," Conor lied, distracted as he searched for Kate in the exiting throng. "I was hoping to go in and play some dinner music for you though, if that's all right."

He spotted Kate following her father and two of the brothers out of the room and relaxed a little. She had a hand on Jigger's shoulder and was bending her head to him with a smile. No doubt the boy was recounting the life histories of everyone he'd met so far. Conor turned back to Sophia Marie, who was standing now, regarding him with that same, nearly identical smile.

"There. You see I never saw *him* look at her like that. Yes. Please come. I'd be delighted to hear more of your dodgy Schumann."

Close to eighty guests were still filing across the floor of the main restaurant into the private dining room. Conor took advantage of the bottleneck to duck into the men's room and throw some water on his face. It helped, which was good because the antibiotics clearly hadn't. His fever was spiking again, and beginning to make him dizzy. He hovered over the basin, taking cautious snatches of breath, then emerged to join the last group as they passed through to dinner.

The Sun Dining Room shimmered, lit solely by candelabras placed between magnificent floral arrangements along each of four long tables. The guests, still in reception mode, milled around the tables instead of sitting at them, their conversation amplified to a garbled roar in the high-ceilinged room. The candlelight dazzled Conor. It bounced off the windows, reaching up to illuminate panes of stained glass near the ceiling, and stretched to raise dramatic shadows in the corners. The effect was spellbinding, but he soon discovered something fundamentally wrong with the scene. Kate was not in it.

19

"Where is Kate?"

Hearing his own question made audible Conor at first failed to note its external source. When it came a second time, cutting through the conversational din around him, he turned to face her brother Peter. He was a handsome, dark-haired man—probably close to his age—and from his glazed, horizon-searching stare Conor deduced him well on the way to being squiffed.

"I'm wondering myself." He forced a smile. "I thought she was here."

"She *was* here. I thought she went to get you." Peter rattled the ice in his glass, gesturing vaguely to his left. "That waiter came and said you needed her on the porch."

Holy Christ. Conor made an effort not to fasten onto the man and shake him. "Which waiter? Where is he?"

"Well, that one ... oh, no. Not the guy. Don't see him." With exaggerated slowness Peter rotated in place from right to left, but Conor had heard enough.

"No bother. I'll fetch her back. Just hold this for me, right?"

He thrust the violin into Peter's hands and ran through the main restaurant, nearly colliding with a tray of drinks, then re-traced his steps to the Conservatory and staggered out its rear door. The broad veranda was deserted, and the outline of its dramatic vista was barely visible under a cloudy, moonless night.

Conor dropped his hands to his knees, wondering whether he should—or even could—run a circuit of the porch. It comprised nearly a thousand feet of floorboards wrapped around the hotel like an apron. While considering the option and trying to catch his breath, a flicker of brightness beyond the veranda caught his eye. He crept forward, staying low, and squatted to peer between the railing's spindles. About thirty feet below him the fabric of Kate's dress was like an organic form of light, a tapered prism glowing against the darkness. She was halfway down the sloping back lawn, stumbling along the walkway and across the grass. Her eyes, mouth and hands were bound with strips of cloth, and she was straining to escape the grip of the muscular figure in a white waiter's jacket who was dragging her forward.

Conor reached beneath his tailcoat for the Sig-Sauer as he ran for the staircase, channeling a surge of panic into action. At ground level he moved to the right, away from the lower portico, remaining first in the shadows of the hotel's L-shaped footprint then using the lawn's sculpted shrubbery as cover. He did his best not to focus on Kate's increasingly frantic struggles and concentrated on gathering what information he could from the size, shape and movements of her captor. He was big but clumsy, stopping frequently to adjust his hold on Kate, and from the way he held his right arm Conor guessed a gun was holstered on that side, which meant he was left-handed. The cadence of his voice drifted up the lawn, revealing something else: he was Irish. Armagh accent. From the direction he was taking, it became clear he intended to cross the footbridge spanning the brook to the golf course on the opposite side. As Conor prepared to leave his crouched position of cover, he heard a tread of rapid footsteps descending the hill. He swiveled on his heel and peered up toward the sound.

"Oh, fuck."

Dropping the pistol, he lurched forward to sweep his arm

around the pelting form as it came alongside him on the walkway. In a single scooping movement, he snatched Jigger from the path and clapped a hand over his mouth. They fell back behind the hedge and Conor lay panting for several seconds, hand still in place, before rolling him gently onto the ground and putting his mouth against his ear.

"I need you to be very quiet and run along back inside, now. Don't make a sound. Understand?"

Eyes saucer-wide, the boy nodded, but as Conor removed his hand Jigger grabbed his head and pulled him closer.

"What is Kate doing with that man?" he whispered. "Is it a game? I'm supposed to tell her to come back to the party."

"I can't explain right now buddy, but we'll come as soon as we can. It won't be long."

Conor stripped off the tailcoat and dropped it on the ground, hiding the gun as he slid the weapon back into the holster. When Jigger had disappeared into the shadows of the portico he stepped out on the walkway and started down the hill, reaching the edge of the footbridge before Kate's abductor noticed him. They had reached the opposite side and he was hissing a ferocious stream of obscenities while pulling her toward a golf cart parked behind a stand of trees. He was older than Conor had first assumed, looking like a prizefighter several years past his prime—square face and small eyes, head covered in a fuzzed stubble the color of concrete. Seeing Conor he grunted in surprise and fumbled to reach the holster with his left hand, trying to control Kate with his right.

"Now, you bloody bitch," he crooned. "Here's your boyfriend come to rescue you, and if you don't stop your fuckin' squirming I'll put a bullet between his eyes right now."

Abruptly, Kate grew still and seemed to wilt a little. Conor raised his hands and fought to remain steady as he watched her face tilt upward, searching for him through the blindfold.

"Let her go. I'm the one you're after, anyway. I've got what Durgan is looking for, so let her go and I'll give it to you. You'll be the hero of the day."

"Jesus, listen to you." The older man waved his gun in a show of nonchalance. "As if you had anything to bargain with, mate. Did you think he wasn't coming after you next? But, true enough. Two treasures in one night—he wasn't expecting that. Fuckin' right I'll be a hero. Get your ass over here."

"Let her go," Conor repeated, "and I'll start walking. You don't need her if you've got me."

The man dropped his shooting arm, looking at Conor in disbelief, and then gave a shout of laughter. With his right arm wrapped around Kate's shoulders he shook her and growled suggestively into her ear.

"What about it, Red? Sounds like you haven't told the laddo what you're getting for your birthday?" Kate went positively rigid in the man's grasp as he turned away from her, still chuckling. "What did you get for *your* thirtieth, McBride? I'm fairly certain I got a bottle of Powers, and that eventually got me a fist in the face just like every other year. This little cherry-top though, she's coming into something a lot better tomorrow, aren't you, love?"

"Look, I don't know—"

"Oh that's pretty clear, McBride. You don't have a feckin' clue. You've been arsing around with a forty-million-dollar heiress and you didn't even know it, and Jaysus, here's your little friend come to the party as well. What's he got to add, I wonder?"

With a sick sensation, Conor turned to see Jigger emerge from the darkness. Oblivious to any danger, he was striding toward them in anxious determination.

"You said this wasn't going to take very long, Conor. They'll be pretty mad inside if we don't hurry up."

"Christ almighty, Jigger." In fear and desperation Conor knelt and took the boy roughly by the shoulders. He whirled him around and pointed him back up the hill. "What did I tell you? Get inside, now."

"Whoa, there. You just stay right where you are, little man."

Conor stared at the flat, expressionless face across the bridge. "You can't be serious."

"I can be, and I am."

"He's a twelve-year-old boy."

"I don't care if he's a crawling infant. He stays right where I can—"

"He doesn't even know what's going on, for fuck's sake."

"Shut the fuck up and bring him over here!"

"I will in me arse. Go ahead and shoot me, if you think Durgan's going to thank you for that."

When improvising strategy in the midst of peril, recognizing the line between constructive chaos and a complete shambles is of vital importance. The first helps an agent gain the initiative; the second gets him killed.

Conor could almost hear the drawl of the MI6 trainer who had schooled him in that particular piece of wisdom. He hadn't appreciated its importance until now. In this case he didn't know which side of the line he stood on, but for a brief moment he thought he'd found the sweet spot.

The man in the murky darkness across from him had lost his temper, in effect had lost control, and Kate was the first to realize it. With a violent twist, she tore herself from his grasp while at the same time shoving blindly at his chest with her bound hands. He staggered sideways, arms waving, and she ran from him, clawing at the strips of cloth around her face.

Conor quickly drew out the Sig. Kate had run only a few yards before tripping and falling headlong to the ground, but there was plenty of daylight between them now and he intended to make the most of it. The burly Irishman had seen the threat; he was regaining his footing and raising his firing arm. Conor brought his gun into position and locked onto him, but then a sudden blur of white crowded the edge of his vision. A nauseating sense of deja vu poured through him. Before he could move Jigger was advancing on the footbridge at a dead run, directly in the line of fire.

"Kate! Kate! Are you all right? Are you hurt?"

"No." Conor's throat convulsed on the word as he sprinted for the bridge. "No! Jesus Christ, don't shoot!"

He made a desperate dive at Jigger, connecting with him as an explosion signaled the release of the first bullet. They landed together on the cement below the apex of the bridge's arch. It provided at least a sliver of cover. The metal railings surrounding them popped and sang with the ricochet of gunfire as Conor flattened the boy beneath him, scrambling for an angle to launch a volley of his own. He got off two shots, burying both of them in his adversary's right thigh, and that proved to be enough. The man went down in a heap, but sprang up immediately. He began dragging himself to the golf cart and Conor continued firing at the retreating vehicle until his magazine was empty.

For a time after that he lost the sense of his surroundings, not unconscious but somehow suspended on the edge of becoming so. When he struggled to his knees the gun had dropped from his hand, and his surging fever sent spangling dots of light across his eyes. An eerie, high-pitched whine muffled the sound of everything around him—shouts in the distance, doors slamming, and somewhere closer in front of him he sensed Kate, but he couldn't concentrate on her because of this other frightening noise. At first he didn't recognize it, and then he did. It was his own voice, straining in hopeless, unending lament.

"Oh please God. Not again. Please not again."

On the ground a huddled form lay wrapped in white, and covered in blood.

20

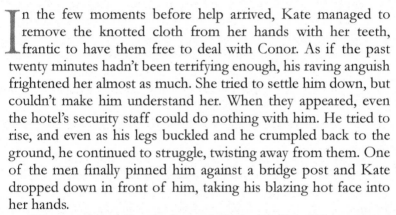

In the few moments before help arrived, Kate managed to remove the knotted cloth from her hands with her teeth, frantic to have them free to deal with Conor. As if the past twenty minutes hadn't been terrifying enough, his raving anguish frightened her almost as much. She tried to settle him down, but couldn't make him understand her. When they appeared, even the hotel's security staff could do nothing with him. He tried to rise, and even as his legs buckled and he crumpled back to the ground, he continued to struggle, twisting away from them. One of the men finally pinned him against a bridge post and Kate dropped down in front of him, taking his blazing hot face into her hands.

"Conor, please. For the love of God, sit still and listen to me. Can you hear me? Do you understand?"

He grew quieter, but Conor's delirium and grief continued spilling from him with every irregular gasp.

"Why won't it stop? He shouldn't have been there. I told him to go and he keeps coming back. And I don't see him in time. I can't ever stop it in time."

"Conor, you did see him. You did stop it. He's okay."

She'd reached him at last. His eyes fixed on her. "Kate. Where's Jigger?"

"They've taken him inside to calm him down and clean him up."

He grew agitated again, struggling to his knees while Kate applied all her strength to holding him in place. "Inside where?

Where did they take him? He's bleeding."

"No, Conor, he isn't. You are. Quite a lot, it seems."

"I'm bleeding?" He blinked at her, perplexed, and then looked down to inspect himself, which was more than Kate could bring herself to do at this point. She'd already seen the blood saturating the front of his tuxedo, and had watched while most of his shirt was cut away to expose a great deal more. It pooled and flowed down his left side, making it impossible to judge what kind of wound lay beneath. Kate kept her attention fixed on his lowered face, and on his grateful relief when he raised his eyes to her.

"It's only me, then? Thank God."

He rolled forward into her arms and Kate caught him, ignoring the lacquer-red stain that began spreading over her dress, burying its dappled autumn hues under a smear of rude color.

The resort had a team of certified first responders on staff who took one look at Conor and radioed for an air transport. They packed the wound with sterile gauze while he remained stretched on the surface of the bridge with his head in Kate's lap, slipping in and out of a feverish doze.

The back lawn became crowded with the curious and anxious and the hotel security team formed a protective zone in front of the bridge to keep all except a few family members at bay. Kate recognized the voices of her father and sister somewhere close by, but she kept her head bowed over Conor, focusing on every shallow sip of breath, willing him to take the next.

When the Dartmouth Advance Response Team arrived they worked with undisguised urgency to stabilize Conor and transfer him to the helicopter. Seeing Kate's determination, they allowed her to climb aboard without argument.

She was buckled into the seat opposite the flight nurse, a

slender man with a military bearing who appeared fit for a tour of duty anywhere in the world. He secured the gurney and started oxygen before putting a stethoscope to Conor's chest.

"No evidence of a lung puncture." He glanced at her. "Has he been sick? Sounds like pneumonia."

"He's had it before. He also got TB last winter, in India." The nurse's eyes widened and Kate hurried to explain. "He got treatment, and the doctor said he was cured. TB can't come back, can it?"

"Unlikely, if the drugs were effective and he followed the therapy correctly." The nurse gave her a reassuring smile.

Police cars began arriving as they prepared for take-off and the sirens, screaming from all directions, added to the general chaos. The interior of the helicopter was an oasis of calm, the deafening sound of rotors reduced to a muted, rhythmic thump. Just before they lifted off, her sister Jeanette appeared and the pilot opened the door to allow her to pass through a canvas bag.

"Your purse and a change of clothes, and Conor's jacket," she shouted over the roar. "I'll take care of Jigger. Call as soon as you can."

Once they were airborne the frightening cyanotic tint around Conor's lips and nose receded as the oxygen took effect. A few minutes into the flight he came awake with a shudder. Fumbling with the oxygen mask he saw the nurse and flinched, immediately alert and agitated.

"Try to relax. You're okay." The flight nurse tried to put the mask back in place but Conor knocked his hand away.

"Who the fuck are you? Where's Kate?"

"She's here on board, buddy. Sitting right behind you. We're in a—" he broke off as Conor bucked against the gurney's restraints, his struggles threatening to pull the IV from his arm. The flight nurse gave Kate a quick nod. "Switch seats. He needs to see you."

Conor relaxed as soon as Kate was beside him. He remained silent for a moment then beckoned her closer, whispering into her ear between panting breaths. "We left a crime scene behind us, and we're the only ones who know what happened. The police will want to question us, and if they do my cover is blown. You have to tell Frank. As soon as you can. He'll get his FBI friend to fix this. Abigail has the number. Can you do that?"

"Of course. Just rest now."

His burst of energy spent, Conor nodded, but his eyes filled as she kissed his cheek. "I was nearly too late. A minute longer and I'd have lost you." He traced a finger down her jaw and frowned. "You've got blood on your neck. Did he hurt you?"

Kate stroked his face, trying to contain her own hysteria. "That's just more of yours. You ruined my party dress, too." She attempted a smile but couldn't manage one and dipped her head away from him. "Conor, I'm such an idiot and I'm so sorry. It seems obvious now, but I still don't understand. Very few people have been told about the money, most of my family doesn't even know. My grandmother set up a trust fund for me after my grandfather died twenty years ago and when I turn thirty tomorrow, control of the entire portfolio shifts to me. The money came mostly from my great-grandfather. He invented something to do with refrigeration."

"And made forty million dollars? He must have invented ice." Conor brushed a tear from her face, a wistful smile tugging at his lips. "Tomorrow's your birthday. I wish I'd known."

His eyes closed and his hand dropped weakly to his side. Kate rubbed away another tear, but more followed and she couldn't hold them all back. When Conor drifted off again she stopped trying. Across from her, the flight nurse looked undecided as to whether he should offer comfort or pretend not to notice. Kate turned to the window, giving them both some relief, and stared out at the black night surrounding them.

"How could they have known?"

She addressed the question in a whisper to her own pale reflection. The face looked so much like a stranger she half-expected it to speak, but it only stared back at her—a tear-stained apparition with no answers.

She was separated from Conor as soon as they landed. The medical crew rolled him up a ramp and out of sight, leaving Kate on her own to find a restroom and deal with the blood-stained ruin of her dress. It took enormous amounts of soap and hot water, but once she was in the clean clothes Jeanette had provided in the canvas bag Kate felt a little less like Lady Macbeth and more like herself.

She checked in with the ER staff and learned they would have no updates on Conor for a while. As required for violence-related injuries they had already reported his arrival to law enforcement, so she decided to put some distance between herself and any officers who might be on their way to investigate. She wandered out to the medical center's central mall—a soaring promenade of skylights and open balconies—and stopped in a quiet alcove outside the chapel to carry out Conor's instructions to contact Frank. As if anticipating her purpose, she suddenly heard her cell phone vibrating with an incoming call.

The phone was at the bottom of her purse, and the purse had fallen to the bottom of the canvas bag, and all of this information became clear to Kate only after the phone had stopped ringing. She groaned after snagging it up from between her wallet and checkbook. The screen indicated she'd missed four other calls along with the most recent one—all of them from the inn's main number. She should have called hours ago to let Abigail know Conor had arrived safely at the hotel. Kate stabbed at the "call back" option, and when the phone was answered on the first

186 | THE SECRET CHORD

ring she nearly wept at the comforting predictability of Abigail's worried rage.

"Are you all right? Is Conor with you? What the hell is going on and why didn't you call earlier?"

Kate took a deep breath, preparing to launch into the narrative, but then remembering, stopped. "Abigail, is it safe for us to talk on this line?"

"It damn well better be," Abigail thundered. "Reginald Effingham from the British Embassy has torn apart every phone and light fixture and half of them still aren't working. He found some kind of satellite transmitter behind an electric socket in your office. Other than that he says the place is clean, and he's been climbing up my backside every ten minutes asking if I've received your 'coordinates'. So give them to me, right now."

"We're at Dartmouth-Hitchcock Medical Center."

Abigail's indignation evaporated in a gasp. "Oh dear God, honey. What's happened?"

Kate forced the words past the pressure in her throat. "Someone shot Conor."

"Someone shot him! Who? Where? How badly is he ... hey!"

The demand for details was abruptly cut off, followed by a muffled, heated argument for control of the phone. Abigail lost the battle, and the next voice on the line was young and British.

"Mrs. Fitzpatrick? Reg Effingham here. Can you confirm whether or not Mr. McBride is alive at this moment?"

"Confirm? I'm not ... Yes. He's alive." Kate felt she'd somehow know if this wasn't true.

"Excellent. Thank you for that. Bear with me."

Kate heard him furiously typing on a computer keyboard. When he resumed, his reedy tone strained for an obligatory note of sympathy. "I do apologize for being brusque, but it is imperative we keep our conversation brief and to the point. Describe the circumstances if you would, please."

Kate provided a recap of the evening's events thus far, with Agent Effingham humming encouragements at each pause. When she'd finished he pounced with a number of follow-up questions.

"Threat assessment, please. Are you safe in your present location?"

"I guess so, yes." Uneasily, Kate scanned the empty alcove and hallway beyond. With her focus entirely on Conor she hadn't even considered the possibility of an additional threat.

"Excellent. Anyone with you? Family members? Friends?"

"No. They're all at the resort." Kate lowered her voice as two young women who appeared to be sisters emerged from the chapel. Their eyes, patient and sad, met hers and she gave them a nod of sympathy.

"And has Mr. McBride—have either of you—been questioned by the police as yet?"

"Not yet. Conor told me I should get in touch with Frank about that. He said—"

"Yes, quite right. Excellent." Reg Effingham repeated this favored word in a preoccupied drawl and Kate could almost picture him, fresh-faced and self-assured, dutifully ticking through a checklist to pass on to his MI6 elders.

"I'm not sure what's so 'excellent,' Mr. Effingham," she said coldly.

"Of course not. Awfully sorry. Mrs. Fitzpatrick, please remain where you are and monitor your phone. I'll ring you back shortly." Without further ceremony the line went dead.

Feeling like she'd been swung round the room and thrown against the wall, Kate at first obeyed the young man's directive literally, staring at her phone with fixed attention. As the minutes ticked by and the screen remained dark, her vise-like grip loosened. Not knowing where else to go she slipped inside the chapel and slumped down with the canvas bag at her feet—a frightened, bewildered refugee.

The room was dim and empty, and well supplied with tissues. She sat staring at the stained glass window on the opposite wall, lightless against the black night sky, then lifted Conor's jacket from the bag and laid it across her knees.

The first item she pulled from its pockets was a bone-handled jackknife. It was old, the decorative carving on its brass bolsters worn with age, as was the monogram "TDM" etched in an elegant script. She lifted the blade, which came up easily. The hinge was well oiled, the edge razor-sharp. She knew it instinctively, without an instant of doubt: his father's knife.

Kate ran a finger over the handle, her breath catching in her throat, then placed the knife on the seat next to her. She continued to slowly empty the pockets, pausing over the ordinary bits and pieces that emerged, each with some unique characteristic clinging to it. A few plastic-wrapped maple candies from the bowl on the inn's front desk, reminding her of his astonished delight the first time he'd popped one into his mouth. A slip of paper with notes in his nearly illegible handwriting—slender looping swirls he described as "Catholic school penmanship gone heretical." A receipt from the Copley Hospital pharmacy for the antibiotics he'd picked up that morning, which seemed like a hundred years ago.

His slim nylon wallet came out last. She added it to the pile on the seat and looked at it all, this small tower of treasure. The mundane odds and ends evoked something she hadn't quite permitted herself to recognize, something that escaped now as a stammering epiphany, evenly balanced between confession and prayer.

"I'm in love with this man. Don't take him from me."

She put the jacket on and pulled it tight against her shoulders, trying to draw out and absorb whatever part of him still lingered in the fabric.

21

An hour later Kate's phone lit up, and its buzzing vibrations quickly sent it skittering off the chair onto the floor. In the struggle to retrieve it from between the chair and the wall she nearly missed the call again, but Reginald Effingham was still there when she answered. After confirming she had no updates for him, he moved quickly to a solemn pronouncement worthy of Marley's Ghost.

"Three visitors will be seeking you out at your location, Mrs. Fitzpatrick. Expect the first two within the next few hours, and the third by morning."

"Who are they?" Kate asked.

"Friends," he replied, simply. "Friends concerned with ensuring the safety of Mr. McBride and yourself. Please meet them in the Emergency Room area."

"What about the police? What should I tell them?"

Agent Effingham prefaced his reply with a complacent hum. "That matter has been handled by Mr. Murdoch. I will relay your best wishes and the relevant information to your friends here, and I trust you will liaise with our associates who will arrive on scene shortly regarding further updates. All the best, then. Bye."

Following his incongruously cheerful sign-off, a roar of protest sounded in the background before the line went dead, and Kate tried to imagine the unrest foaming at the other end of its severed connection. Unless Reginald Effingham possessed a more imposing physical presence than his voice suggested, he'd be lucky to survive this assignment.

The ER waiting room had grown crowded in Kate's absence, and continued filling as the evening progressed. She did her best to follow the counsel of the hard-pressed staff—namely, to sit quietly and wait for the updates that began dribbling out from random sources.

The injury had been evaluated by a specialist. A surgeon had sutured the wound. A pulmonologist had been called in for a consult. Conor was in transport to X-ray. Conor was in transport back from X-ray. The X-rays were being evaluated by a specialist.

Although grateful for every kernel of news, and for the kindness of those who came forward to deliver these updates, Kate had no idea who any of them were, what they weren't telling her, or what roles they played in the backstage area they appeared from and returned to like characters in a play.

After two hours of staggered bulletins she'd begun pacing the hallway, seconds away from punching the ward's wall-mounted door opener and charging through, when a voice spoke behind her.

"Are you Kate Fitzpatrick?"

"Yes?"

She spun around to face a man with a head full of curly brown hair in a blue oxford shirt and chinos—surely too young to be a doctor, but the lab coat with a photo ID clipped on indicated otherwise. He offered a smile and held out a hand.

"Greg Burton. I'm one of the physicians on-call tonight. Sorry to keep you waiting so long. Do you want to sit down?"

"Do I need to sit down?" Kate felt reduced to little more than a heartbeat. Its hammering rhythm throbbed everywhere. The doctor registered confusion.

"No, you can stand. I mean, we don't have to sit down if you don't want to."

"Let's sit down." Her legs collapsed like a folding ruler, and by a lucky chance Kate landed in a chair. "How is he?"

"Better than when he got here. It appears to be a ricochet wound; the bullet carved a ten-inch furrow along his rib cage. Lucky angle. He did lose a fair amount of blood so we gave him a couple of pints after suturing the wound. He's in no danger from it, although he's experiencing pain as the local anesthetic wears off."

The news should have come as a relief, but as Doctor Burton continued the report Kate took little comfort from his guarded tone.

"I've consulted with his doctor in Vermont. We're running tests to be sure, but neither of us think we're dealing with a recurrence of TB. He does have a serious bacterial pneumonia in both lungs, complicated by residual scarring from past infections. The current organism resisted the initial antibiotic so we're trying a second line. We're going to monitor him in the ER overnight to make sure nothing develops to require transfer to the ICU. Do you have any questions?"

None Kate dared to ask, and Dr. Burton correctly interpreted her silence.

"I know this sounds scary, but we've got a good plan. I'm hoping for results in the next few hours. Conor is awake and breathing more comfortably. I can take you back if you're ready to see him? He's certainly anxious to see you."

Kate had only been permitted brief glimpses at the inner sanctum of the emergency ward, but the automated doors swung wide for her now with a wizardly flourish. Stepping through them was like lifting the cover from a beekeeper's hive, revealing the industrious colony beneath. The atmosphere was heavy with purpose and the pervasive odor of disinfectant, but sporadically lifted by laughter and the conversation of colleagues. The sights and smells collected around her, slowing her steps as she followed Dr. Burton further into the ward. Kate was surprised it had taken so long to register. She had lain in a place just like this six years ago, and by morning had known how much she'd lost. More than the memory, the dread of enduring another loss sent a convulsive shiver down her back. The doctor's voice continued as a fuzzed background noise.

"I ordered pain medication but so far he's refused any. After you've had a chance to talk maybe you can persuade him. He needs to get some sleep." He pulled up at a doorway on his left and looked back, surprised to find her several yards behind him. "Are you okay?"

"I'm fine." She hurried forward, thanking Dr. Burton before scooting past him. Behind the exam room curtain Conor lay in a bed propped to an upright angle, an intravenous tube in his right arm, the clear plastic oxygen cannula still in place under his nose. A sheet covered him up to the waist, and from the available evidence he wore nothing beneath. A pale green hospital gown, wadded together with a blanket, lay at the bottom of the bed. He looked haggard and feverish, but he was alive. Seeing her, his face brightened.

"Finally. I was ready to crawl out of here and go find you myself."

"Not without coverage, I hope." Kate picked up the twisted hospital gown. "Aren't you supposed to be wearing this?"

"Too hot."

She let it drop back onto the bed and came closer, shyly examining the wide gauze bandage taped against his side. "Does it hurt?"

"Not too bad. Comes and goes."

"You told me you'd never lie to me."

"I don't think that's exactly what I said." Conor gave her a faint smile. "So, where do we stand? Did you speak to Abigail?"

"Sort of, but she didn't get to say much."

Kate shared the details of her brisk discussions with Reginald Effingham. Conor, relieved that Frank's FBI connections appeared to be as good as Sedgwick thought, speculated the promised visitors would likely be a protective detail. To Kate's question of who they might be he could only respond with a weary, apologetic shrug.

"Never mind. You should rest. The doctor prescribed something for the pain. I'll go find someone."

"No, not yet." Conor caught her arm and pulled her back. "Come here. Sit down."

He shifted on the bed, grimacing and losing a little more color in the process, and patted the empty space next to him. Kate gingerly climbed up and settled next to his hip, taking care not to interfere with any tubing. He remained quiet for a moment, tensed in pain, then his face relaxed and he took her hand.

"*We dance round in a ring and suppose, but the secret sits in the middle and knows.*" He ran a thumb over her fingers. "Robert Frost. That's the whole poem. Says all he needed it to."

Kate nodded, wondering what he expected from her. "You know all my secrets now," she offered uncertainly. He surprised her with a tender grin.

"Somehow, I doubt that. It wasn't yours I was thinking of, though." His smile faded. "He was such a little boy, probably no more than ten years old. Hindu," he said softly. "I don't know his name. We were in a hurry and I didn't take the time to ask. For a while I thought that's what made everything worse, but I was kidding myself. What made it worse was feeling I knew him entirely, in that one instant. As if his soul flew up out of him and showed me everything he was, everything about him. Except his name."

"Don't do this," Kate whispered. "Not now. It's too much."

"It's not too much. More like not enough. You run as far as you can from the thing you're trying to escape. In the end you realize you've only been circling it." Conor looked up, sad and resigned. "I've nowhere else to go, except back to the middle. I have to get there while I can, and no matter what you might think of me later, I need to tell you."

Kate laced her fingers between his and felt the tremor running through him like a current of electricity, reaching for her, presenting no choice but to flinch and pull away or be frozen by its embrace. She raised Conor's hand to rest against her cheek, and held tight.

He could remember the congestion in his chest as they climbed that morning, worsening with every step, but he didn't think it had ever reached the crackling pitch he was trying to ignore now. Conor gripped Kate's hand, his centering stake in the ground, and let his mind drift backward.

At the time, the state of his lungs was just one more thing to worry about as he followed Thomas, slogging up through the Kashmir woods to a doomed meeting with the lieutenants of Vasily Dragonov. Preoccupied and jittery, he'd fallen behind as they approached a small, dilapidated Hindu shrine. When the boy suddenly appeared, cupping a handful of marigolds, it startled him, as though a pint-sized spirit had risen from the snowy path. He couldn't resist the child's bright, engaging smile.

"Even now, I wonder about those marigolds—how he could have gotten them, with the ground still frozen."

Conor leaned back, allowing himself a short respite. Outside the room the business of emergency medicine continued along its course, moving to a tune of electronic tones and low-tech rattles, and the occasional unexpected crescendo. He listened, drawing strength from the compassion in Kate's eyes before continuing.

He'd obliged the boy by taking a few of the flowers, giving a handful of rupees in exchange, and after depositing his offering at the dancing feet of Shiva in the shrine's niche, he'd removed the long white scarf from his neck to wrap around the boy, and told him to run along home.

"It was freezing out, and he looked so cold." Conor worked his lips into a faltering smile. "I suppose something in saffron would have been better. He was an acolyte, after all, no matter how tiny. But white seemed to suit him as well."

What followed after was a dimly lit recollection—of moving forward and waiting and moving forward again, of rehearsed conversations in an antiseptic hotel room, of improvisation and, ultimately, of mayhem. When the mission exploded and his brother was shot, he and Sedgwick carried Thomas down the path, but after they'd laid him in the car two of Dragonov's men had arrived on the road, armed to the teeth. They managed to get between them and the car, and before Conor knew what was happening Sedgwick was dragging him back into the woods.

"Evasive maneuvers. We tried to lure them up the path, get them into a position so they weren't between us and the car. It almost worked."

Almost, but not quite. They were sprinting back down to the road when Dragonov's men pinned them down behind a boulder, opening fire from a point farther up the path, somewhere near the shrine.

Here, his memory was something more than just vivid. It was an endless present moment, always with him, never faded. He heard the relentless burst of automatic weapons, of bullets cracking against stone. He saw the trees around him, trunks torn apart, exposing the soft, shredded wood. He smelled the pine pitch.

And he could feel his jumpy, tingling nerves wrap themselves around the gun in his hand, felt his panic and desperation to move, to do something, to make it stop. Then, in the midst of chaos, a break— a breathless lacuna drawing Conor forward, away from his cover and onto the path, gun already raised, already firing.

And in this eternal sliver of time he saw it—the flash of white skating across the path, the wide, astonished brown eyes, and so much more. He saw everything, understood it, and knew what he'd done.

Why was he there, a small innocent running through the center of havoc? Why had he not gone home as he was told? Who could answer such questions? Who but the god Shiva, whose dancing idol had slipped from a small pair of hands, landing upright on the path where it had toppled, one bell-clad foot poised in the air, ready to ring down onto the icy earth. To destroy it all, and create it new.

The secret sits in the middle. Now, so did he. Conor sat there with it and let everything else spin around him. He felt so far away, and so very tired. But still, there was a hand in his, cool and soft, that hadn't let go. And that was something.

In fact, that was everything.

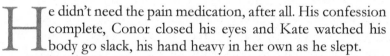

22

He didn't need the pain medication, after all. His confession complete, Conor closed his eyes and Kate watched his body go slack, his hand heavy in her own as he slept.

Without taking her attention from his face she eased herself away from him, down into the chair at his bedside, and folded her arms on the mattress. At some point her head dropped on top of them, and there it remained until the pressure of a hand on her shoulder pulled her from sleep.

She sat up, muscles protesting as she unwound, and turned to face a muscular gray-suited stranger. He had a dark, precisely trimmed goatee, but not a follicle of hair on his perfectly formed head. It gleamed like rich polished mahogany, a warm contrast to the antiseptic light of the exam room.

"The spirit that was foretold?" Kate asked. The quizzical cast of his eyebrow indicated it wasn't the greeting he'd expected. He pulled a photo ID from his jacket.

"Agent Reynolds, Mrs. Fitzpatrick, and my partner Agent Levine." He inclined his head at a second, far less imposing man who stood by the door. "We're with the Diplomatic Security Service, providing assistance at the request of the British Embassy. We arrived about three hours ago, and I apologize for waking you but I've been told we need to leave."

"Leave? Why? What's happening?" Kate turned back to Conor who lay with eyes closed, pale and motionless. His breath came and went in rapid puffs, a sluggish piston straining to keep up with its work.

"No further details, except that we should return to the waiting room," Agent Reynolds said.

"I'm not returning anywhere until I know what's going on."

"I'm afraid I don't have that information for you, ma'am."

"Well then, let's find someone who does."

"Yes, ma'am."

The two appeared to accept her remark as a mission-critical directive, but before they could act an unseen hand drew the privacy curtain back and three clinicians entered the room. Frightened and disoriented, Kate longed for a familiar face.

"Where's Dr. Burton?" she demanded. An attractive woman with purple-rimmed glasses stepped forward.

"His shift ended earlier and he didn't want to wake you. I'm Lucille Kim. I'm afraid we're not getting enough traction with the current line of meds and Conor's condition is becoming critical. We're going to transport him to the ICU and try a different therapy." The doctor gave her a sympathetic smile. "You've been here all night. Why not take a break and get something to eat? There's no immediate danger and we've got your cell number. Give us an hour or so to get him settled and then you can see him again."

The idea of eating generated only nausea, but for lack of a better plan Kate wandered over to the cafeteria, her impressive bodyguard trailing behind her while his partner remained with Conor. She bought a cup of coffee and offered to buy one for Agent Reynolds.

"No thank you, Mrs. Fitzpatrick. I'm good."

"Please call me Kate."

"Yes, ma'am."

"Yes, *Kate*," she said, exasperated.

"Yes, Kate." The agent allowed himself a fractional smile and touched a hand to his chest. "Gideon."

They made their way to a table by a bank of windows filled with the first wool-gray light of morning. Kate glanced at her watch—five o'clock. She wondered if Jeanette had brought Jigger back home by now, and whether Reg Effingham had been offered a guest room for the night or been shown the door. It was too early to call anyone. She swirled a spoon in her untouched coffee and watched the people filtering through the cafeteria. From the variety of uniforms—scrubs, hair nets, lab coats—she presumed most were hospital employees, but occasionally her attention locked on a few individuals who didn't laugh or talk with their companions but sat quietly pushing food around on their plates. They were like ghosts at the banquet, and she drew a guilty consolation from their tired faces. She was one of their number— another anonymous servant to the fear surrounding illness and loss.

*B*reathe.

Not too deep. Just a little one.

Go again.

Life was simple for him on this level, where only a few rules mattered. The rest had all been incinerated into ash along with every hope or desire that fell subordinate to the one goal and its supporting objectives: To draw a breath. To keep the intake shallow and even—that minimized the pain. To coax his bloodstream into absorbing the wisp of air and its tiny cargo of oxygen. To draw another breath.

This was his universe, and it demanded singularity of purpose, but a pressure on his forehead kept disrupting his tempo, a stroke in counterpoint to the established rhythm. Conor's eyes fluttered open to squint at the distraction. He squeezed them shut and tried again. Still there. The vision might be a side effect of delirium, but it wasn't going away.

"Good morning, Conor. I seem to recall we've played this scene already."

Although its breeziness seemed forced Frank's mellifluous baritone rolled over him like a soothing melody. Conor's reply disappeared as it left his lips. Frank leaned in closer, and he tried to add a larger measure of sound on the next exhalation.

"Sorry to bore you."

"Ah, you are never a bore, my friend. Many things, but never that." Frank's face quickly sobered. "Do you know who did this?"

Conor's brow creased with the effort of patching together an oral brief. "Fella ... from Armagh. Heard the accent. Big fucker. Crew cut. Shot ... shot him twice. Right leg ..."

"Yes, all right. Well done." Frank ran a hand over his forehead again, the cool touch an instant of luxury, too quickly consumed by the furnace burning through his skin. "We're coming very close now, Conor. Our elusive wizard has bungled his position. He's lost the initiative, and we'll not let that advantage slip away."

Conor managed a small nod and closed his eyes. He had no more strength to spare, but as he slipped back to focus on his goal of sustained respiration he realized he'd neglected something—the most critical piece of information in his whole report. The thought provided a short-lived jolt of adrenalin. His eyes shot open and fixed on the agent.

"He wasn't after me. He wanted Kate. She just inherited a fortune. Durgan found out, somehow. Don't let anything—swear to me, Frank. Swear you won't let anything happen to her."

He struggled to hold onto consciousness for a few more seconds, but he'd exhausted all his reserves. Conor fell into darkness, still waiting for Frank's promise.

From the corner of her eye Kate noticed Gideon removing a

phone from his pocket. As he spoke to the caller, his eyes met hers and glanced away. Something was wrong. Her shoulders trembled as she tried to read some message in the agent's flat expression. He clapped the phone shut and turned to her.

"What's happened? Is something wrong?"

"No ma'am." He spoke in the same emotionless tone, either oblivious or impervious to her state of mind. "The gentleman you've been expecting just arrived."

"Who? What gentleman?"

"Unknown."

Kate scowled. "Gideon, can we please talk like normal human beings for a minute? What does 'unknown' mean?"

This time the agent offered her a wide, apologetic smile. "It means I don't know the guy's name, Kate, but he's on his way down so we'll both find out soon."

When he did appear she had an immediate hunch as to his identity, but doubted her instinct. The handsome, silver-haired figure didn't look like someone who'd just flown through the night across the Atlantic. He carried a leather briefcase shined to a glossy finish, and the suit draping his lean frame fit with tailored perfection. A regimentally folded handkerchief peeked from its breast pocket and his shirt—snowy-white shot through with pin-striped burgundy—was equally precise. Not a single crease appeared where it should not. He stopped to confer with Agent Reynolds and Kate came forward to greet him.

"Frank Murdoch?" she asked doubtfully.

Offering a slight bow, the older man smiled and took her hand. He regarded her in silence for a few seconds, his hazel eyes meeting hers with a mixture of irony and warmth. "Ginger-haired, indeed. Eckhard mentioned as much, but I'd no notion it would be so beautiful. Your blouse sets the color off to marvelous effect."

"I ... thank you." Kate ran her hands over the shirt, attempting to smooth its wrinkles. "Can I offer you something?" She indicated the various stations of the cafeteria.

"Please allow me to offer *you* something." Frank took her elbow and led her back to the table. "I believe you could do with a bit of breakfast."

"No, I'm not hungry, and I have this coffee I haven't even touched."

"Nonsense." He gave the cup a frown of distaste and turned on his heel. "Agent Reynolds, would you be so kind? Bring whatever appears least gruesome. Buttered toast perhaps, and a quantity of hot tea, preferably in a pot of some sort." Having handily dispatched the federal agent Frank turned his attention back to Kate. "Now, shall we have a chat? I've just come from Conor, who offered brief comments before inconveniently falling asleep."

"You saw him? How is he?"

Frank paused before offering a reassuring smile. "Well he's looked worse, my dear. Tell me what the doctors are saying."

She attempted a dispassionate narration, but exhaustion and fear finally caught up with her. The words tumbled from Kate in a monologue fractured by sobs, and once begun they seemed unstoppable. Frank offered the pristine handkerchief from his pocket and put an arm around her, murmuring encouragements that gradually succeeded in calming her. When she was quiet he guided her into a chair and poured out cups of tea. With dull surprise, Kate realized Gideon had managed to find a stainless steel teapot.

She sipped the tea and nibbled at the toast Frank insisted she eat, and at his gentle prodding began describing the events of the past twelve hours. By the time she'd finished, the cafeteria had filled. Outside over the mountains a pale autumn sun burned through the mist, and although it was still quite early the breakfast aromas of eggs and toasting bread began subsiding under a pervasive smell of stewing tomatoes.

Frank removed an envelope from his briefcase and placed it on the table between them. "Kate, I realize this is all extremely frightening, but the window of opportunity for action is shrinking and I must ask for your assistance." He slid the envelope across the table, his hand still pressed on top. "These photographs represent classified documents, but I need you to tell me if the man who tried to kidnap you last night is in any of them. You mustn't ask about the subject or content of the photographs, and you must tell no one you've seen them. Do you understand all this?"

Kate nodded, and Frank removed his hand. He sat back in his chair and crossed a leg over his knee. She unfastened the clasp and slipped a dozen photographs out on the table. All featured men in groups of two or three, taken in a variety of settings, at different times of day. A few were interior shots in what looked like a bar.

The first six photos contained faces she'd never seen before, but when she flipped to the seventh Kate immediately shuddered. A group of three men stood under the Guinness sign of an Irish pub, and she recognized her kidnapper as the one in the middle. The man on his left was a stranger, but as she focused on the third figure in the photograph a deeper chill shook through her. Even turned slightly in profile the face was unmistakable.

"My God," she whispered. "It's Phillip Ryan."

"What? Phillip Ryan?" Frank sat forward, startled.

"Yes." Kate turned the photo to give the agent a better view. "This man in the middle is the one who tried to kidnap me last night, but this man on his right is Phillip Ryan. He's Irish. He was my late husband's cousin and he lived over here for a while, but later he became the manager of Conor's farm in Dingle. He's the one who first wrote to me about Conor."

"This man?" Frank pointed, watching her closely. "You're

certain it was this man? When did you see him last?"

"Six years ago." Kate felt lightheaded. "We exchange Christmas cards, and he sent an email last April saying Conor needed a place to stay. I don't understand. What is Phillip doing with the man who—"

"Just a minute," Frank said sharply. He pulled the photo closer, staring in silence, then abruptly pushed it back at her. He removed a slim notebook from his briefcase and uncapped a fountain pen. "Phillip Ryan." He wrote the name at the top of a blank page. "Tell me everything you know about him. Everything. Quickly."

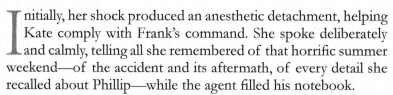

23

Initially, her shock produced an anesthetic detachment, helping Kate comply with Frank's command. She spoke deliberately and calmly, telling all she remembered of that horrific summer weekend—of the accident and its aftermath, of every detail she recalled about Phillip—while the agent filled his notebook.

The constrictive daze gradually lifted, and as the significance of what she'd learned sank in Kate lost focus. Her eyes shifted, irresistibly drawn to the photograph. He'd saved her life and had been so kind to her, but Phillip Ryan was not who he'd appeared to be. What had he really come for that week? Had he known about her money, even then? And how?

The questions cascaded, leading to the one her mind barely touched before scuttling back in horror. Was her husband's death an accident? Or had he learned something about his cousin that week? Something that made him an unacceptable threat.

"It's him, isn't it?" She pushed back from the table, fighting an urge to run, to get away from the photograph and all it represented. "Phillip Ryan is Robert Durgan. A murderer. Conor said he had someone tortured and killed. A man named Desmond."

"Desmond Moore." Frank rested a finger next to the one face in the photograph Kate had not recognized. "The other man—your would-be kidnapper—is Ciaran Wilson. Both from Northern Ireland. Armagh."

Kate looked up at the note of strain in his voice but he gazed past her, bemused and sad.

"How did I miss this? I ransacked every department in the service, looking for a mole that never existed. It was the bloody farm manager all along." He glanced at the photograph with a puzzled frown. "And who the hell is he, I wonder?"

"Conor's best friend. Are you going to tell him? He's already so weak and this will break his heart."

"Certainly not." Frank swept the photographs together and back into the envelope. "Far better for this to remain between us two at present. I need to make a number of phone calls. You've confirmed Wilson as your abductor, and I'm eager to provide information to the local authorities to ensure his capture."

He rose from the table and nodded at Gideon, who had seated himself at a discreet distance. The agent immediately stood and came forward.

"I'm sure you're anxious to return to the patient's bedside." Frank smiled at her. "When I'm finished, perhaps I'll join in the vigil, if you'll allow me? I'm rather fond of the fellow myself, you know."

"Please do. I'd appreciate the company."

Kate accepted the hand he extended to lift her from the chair, her heart unexpectedly warming to the man. His manner was cloaked in a theatrical persona he'd clearly taken pains to perfect, but a twinkle at the corner of his eye suggested humorous self-awareness, and occasionally a flash of something more pensive.

She arrived at the ICU to be introduced to another new set of faces who provided an update even more somber than she'd feared. With Conor's soaring temperature a source of increasing worry, they'd started a fresh combination of drugs, but he'd grown progressively weaker. Before leaving her alone with him a large, muscle-bound nurse with tattooed arms and a diamond earring tried to provide a few words of comfort.

"He's tired, but still battling." He set a chair down for her. "Just keep encouraging him. He may not respond, but he'll know you're here and I'm sure that's going to help."

Kate thanked him with a smile. She stood next to Conor and took his hand, its heat quickly absorbing the chill from her own. He didn't move or open his eyes, but she sensed a faint answering pressure when she kissed his forehead and began speaking softly.

Flowers again. Always marigolds.

So many this time. Feathery bunches pillowed beneath his hands, yielding to his fingers. Spread all around, under his arms, over his chest.

Like a bright blanket of light.

Like the offerings of Taj pilgrims on the tomb of the Mughal empress.

He's with her now, a pilgrim with only himself to offer. He feels the stone-cool air moving in the darkness of the lower crypt. The relief of coolness. Darkness. He can press his hot face, his blistered lips, against the smooth, polished marble. Touch row upon row of scripted calligraphy. Trace out the ninety-nine names of God.

He can rest.

He hears her, the beloved ornament, in her seclusion. In her everlasting loneliness. Calling him.

Stay with me. I love you. I've waited so long. I've waited for you.

Like a gentle wave, caressing and retreating, pulling him with her.

Repeating over and over for as long as she needs to.

Until he finds the way.

The conversation floated above Conor like a ghostly radio signal—fuzzy, but growing stronger as he emerged from a world of fog and curious dreams.

"I'm telling you, I've never seen a fever break like that."

"Unbelievable."

"Seemed like he just punched his way out."

"Looks like he punched through Hoover Dam. He's drenched."

"No shit. Been going on for twenty minutes. He was headed

down, all his levels dropping, then all of a sudden his back arches right up off the bed. Next thing, the sweat just starts pouring out of him. He fought hard for twelve hours but I didn't think he had anything left."

"Fighting Irish, huh?"

"Seriously."

"Where's the girlfriend?"

"Went to call home with the good news. I'm not sure she's the girlfriend, though. He muttered some crazy shit for a while, and she and I both tried to figure it out. Sounded like some other girl's name. Awkward, right? And crazy, 'cause if he doesn't want her ... you know what I'm saying?"

"Yeah, yeah. Calm down."

"Anyway, whatever. I thought this one was gone. Figured we'd be calling it in another hour."

"Okay, Danny. Shut up. Look, he's awake. He can hear us."

Conor blinked, trying to clear his eyes, but water kept streaming into them, stinging and blurring his vision. Where was he? Where was Kate? Where was all this fucking water coming from?

A towel descended, scrubbing at his face and neck. When it was removed he stared up at a bull-necked, red-haired man in scrubs, with a diamond stud in one ear. Conor drilled him with a hard stare.

"Where is she?"

The question came out as an abraded rasp, but had some energy behind it. A snort of laughter erupted from the foot of the bed.

"Tough luck, Danny. Sounds like he wants her."

When Conor opened his eyes again several hours later everything seemed a little sharper, a little less inclined to spin and pixilate into shapeless color. In the chair next to him Kate slept with a blanket pulled to her chin. He stared at her arm resting next to his on the bed, wanting to touch her, torn between wishing she would wake up and wanting the drowsy, peaceable moment to go on forever.

"*They say that her beauty was music in mouth.*" The line of poetry came out in a whisper, and moving his hand closer—he couldn't help himself—he allowed a finger to settle against her wrist.

"*And O she was the Sunday in every week.*" The voice, soft and resonant, set off a disorienting prickle of confusion until he turned his head to discover Frank sitting in a chair on the opposite side of the bed. Conor gave him a weak grin.

"Thought you were a ghost."

The agent smiled. "You wouldn't believe how often I've heard that."

"You've finally convinced me, Frank. Anyone who can give out a line of Austin Clark must have some Irish in him."

"A rare victory for me at last."

"What's the time? How long have you been here?"

"It's just gone six o'clock. I've been in and out through the day, offering succor to my lovely fellow guardian. Allow me to speak for her in saying how delighted we are you've decided to remain with us."

"Good to be here." Conor slipped back into a whisper. His aching throat had grown as dry as an acre of sun-baked sod; every word scraped like the tines of a rake. Stretching his neck, he shifted his weight then gasped and coughed as a scalding pain spiked up his side. Frank stood to pour some water.

"How do you feel?"

"Leathered. Top to bottom." He accepted the cup, took several long gulps, and sighed in relief. "Thanks. And thanks for being here, Frank. For staying with her."

"Hardly an onerous burden I assure you, but I'm glad you're

awake as I'm just preparing to leave. I've a rendezvous with the FBI in Nashua."

"Your man came through, then?" Conor asked. "The FBI agreed to help?"

Frank nodded. "Rather a strain on our relationship, I'm afraid. He wasn't at all pleased to hear an MI6 agent was wandering loose in America, but the director of the New Hampshire state police is a friend—something to do with ties formed at the FBI National Academy—so the jurisdiction was transferred with a single phone call."

"So, what's going on in Nashua? Did they find the guy?"

"They did, yes. The manhunt proved anti-climactic in the end. Ciaran Wilson, or the 'big fucker' from Armagh as you aptly called him, was apprehended there about an hour ago. An FBI agent found him in his car, bleeding and unconscious, in the parking lot of a shopping mall. The local hospital is pumping pints of blood into him and he'll be ready for questioning in the next few hours. I'm eager to get his thoughts on a particular line of inquiry. After that I'll fly back to London, but I'll be in touch again once things have been ... clarified."

"Will he cooperate?"

Frank's hazel eyes flashed with a cold metallic glint. "Oh I think so, Conor. Yes, I feel certain he will."

Although he tried not to, Conor drifted off again before Kate woke up, and remained asleep through the night and into the next morning. Once fully awake his passage from peaceable contentment to restless boredom was swift. For one thing he was alone now, apart from the circling presence of the Diplomatic Security Service. Agent Levine reported his partner Gideon Reynolds had driven Kate home the previous evening for some much needed rest. They would return later in the day. Conor found little in his surroundings to interest him, but diversion arrived in the early afternoon—a therapist, leading him in an unpleasant session of lung-clearing exercises. A frighteningly youthful nursing aide followed shortly after, wanting to help him shower.

The combination of activities left him literally dizzy and breathless—especially the bathing ordeal, which involved fierce negotiations around what he'd be allowed to do by himself. He was back in bed, washed and bandaged, trying to fend off more unwelcome attentions when Kate appeared in the doorway. The nursing aide sang out to her.

"Come on in, we're almost finished." She squeezed a dollop of lotion on her palm. "Just sit forward a little Mr. McBride, so I can get this on your back."

"You know, I don't think I need any—ouch. Right. Okay." Conor cradled his ribs and pitched forward. *Get me out of here,* he mouthed at Kate, his desperation only half-facetious.

"Between this and the lung-clearing therapy I'm afraid we've tired you out." The young woman settled him back and winked at Kate as she departed. "Don't be surprised if he falls asleep on you."

"I hope not. I've waited three days to catch him with his eyes open. Lung-clearing therapy?" Kate asked, lifting herself to sit on the bed next to him.

"Best not described."

Happy for the first time all day, Conor studied her—the practical, unpretentious innkeeper, gifted artist, and forty million dollar heiress of royal lineage. At the moment she was a very weary looking heiress. "You look so tired, Kate. You shouldn't have come all the way down again, today. They're telling me I'll be out by Wednesday."

"They told me Wednesday at the *earliest.*"

"A distinction without a difference, as far as I'm concerned.

How's everything up north?"

Much calmer since the departure of Reg Effingham, Kate assured him. They talked for a while about Frank and the events of the past few days. Conor was amused at how thoroughly the agent had worked his way into her affections, but Kate was distracted, not noticing his playful teasing. She was also reluctant to muse on where Frank's interrogation of Wilson might lead, or how Durgan had discovered so much about her circumstances.

Conor thought he understood the source of her uneasiness. He knew she cared for him—a miracle in itself, considering all he'd told her—but warm feelings aside, his presence in her life was a rolling disaster. He'd appeared at her door dragging his troubles behind him, and on top of the sins he'd arrived with he could add another to the pile—introducing a murderous criminal to a prize even larger than the one he'd originally sought. A peculiar way to conduct a romance.

"I need to talk to you about something," Kate admitted at last, "but I don't want to upset you."

"Sure. Whatever you like. I won't be upset." He hoped that was true.

She regarded him for an indecisive moment, then asked, "Did you have a serious relationship with a woman you haven't talked about, yet?"

Jesus. What?

He started to answer, heard himself stutter, and closed his mouth. Possibly a calamitous reaction but he couldn't help it. The question was so monumentally unexpected. Conor swallowed and began again.

"I'm not sure. That is ... we've never talked much about any of my relationships with women. Which," he hurried to add, "I wouldn't say have been unnaturally numerous."

"I guess that's fair." The edge in Kate's tone suggested otherwise. "I'm not asking you to break down your record for me, and I realize you were engaged once—"

"Which ended years ago."

"Yes, I understand. What I'm asking is whether there was something more recent, and serious."

"More recent, yes, but serious? No." Confident in his honesty, he was hurt by her lingering doubt. "What is this about, Kate?"

"You were calling a woman's name, Conor," she said softly. "You were delirious and most of the time just mumbling gibberish, but you kept calling for her and it's hard to believe that doesn't mean something."

Before he could say anything a nurse came in to check his IV line and deliver another injection. Appearing sensible to the fact she was interrupting, she worked without extraneous conversation, completed her task and retreated quickly. She left some juice in front of Conor and he stared at the plastic cup, sliding it back and forth between his hands on the tray table.

"Are you going to tell me the name?"

"I was hoping you would say it," Kate said.

"Right. I see. So, in fact you *are* asking me to break down the record."

"You're getting upset."

"Well it's hard not to."

"Astor." Kate threw out the word like an incantation, as though expecting something or someone to materialize in front of them. "Even the big nurse with the diamond earring heard you. Astor. He asked if it was my name, which was a little awkward, as I'm sure you can imagine."

"I suppose I can," Conor shot back, "but does it matter at all I don't know who you're talking about? My ex-fiance's name is Maggie, and if it's a list you want I'll give you one, but there's nobody called 'Astor' on it."

His insistence, so vehement and genuine, seemed to hit its mark. Kate looked startled. Whatever else she might be thinking he could see she believed him.

"Actually, something you said did sound a little like 'Maggie', but more like 'McGee'. Her last name, I thought."

"Oh for Jesus' sake, you're killing me with this." Conor pushed the tray table aside and rubbed his hands over his face. "I never had any dreams about Maggie Fallon. Ever. It's hard to believe I'd start now, or that I'd have them over somebody named Astor McGee who I've never—"

He stopped and abruptly dropped his hands, gazing at the opposite wall as the light bulb pinged in his brain. "Astor McGee. Oh my God." Conor looked at Kate and laughed out loud.

"So, you do know her." She recoiled and jumped down from the bed. "And you're laughing. Why is this funny?"

"Wait. Come back here, and I'll tell you." The quick movement made Conor wince as he circled an arm around her waist, drawing her to his side. No longer laughing, he tucked a lock of hair behind her ear. "Gibberish, you say. My own native tongue. Here's me, in the article of death, crooning out fine poetry in Irish, and you thought it was gibberish. I suppose I'll forgive you. Sounds strange when you're not used to it."

He watched Kate's brow wrinkle in adorable astonishment. "Irish? You think so?"

"Only one way to be sure." He put his lips to her ear. "*A stór mo chroí*. Was that it? Is that how it sounded?"

Her body relaxing against him was the only response he needed. "You weren't far off, Kate. It is a sort of name. *A stór mo chroí*. It means 'heart's treasure'." He cupped her face in his hands, stroking its warm flushed skin, and gave her head a gentle shake. "It means you. I was calling for you."

She blinked away a few tears, and Conor thought he'd be happy to spend the rest of his life trying to put a name to every color he saw in her eyes.

"I was calling for you, too," she whispered.

"I know, love. I heard you."

He started with her forehead, then moved to her ear, her cheek, her chin and her lips, taking his time, savoring each new discovery— the warm, spicy taste of her mouth, the quiver of a heartbeat at the base of her throat. With every kiss he added a few new words to her vocabulary, wreathing her in the poetry of an ancient language—the first he'd ever learned, the one that best captured what he most wanted to say.

A mhuirnín. Oh, darling.

A chuisle. Oh, pulse.

A stór mo chroí. Oh, heart's treasure.

Bí liom. Be mine.

Gach orlach de do chroí. Bí liom.

Every inch of your heart. Be mine.

24

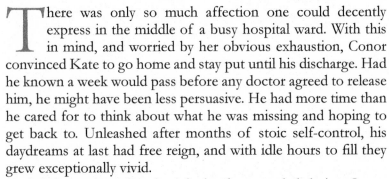

There was only so much affection one could decently express in the middle of a busy hospital ward. With this in mind, and worried by her obvious exhaustion, Conor convinced Kate to go home and stay put until his discharge. Had he known a week would pass before any doctor agreed to release him, he might have been less persuasive. He had more time than he cared for to think about what he was missing and hoping to get back to. Unleashed after months of stoic self-control, his daydreams at last had free reign, and with idle hours to fill they grew exceptionally vivid.

When not brooding in a funk of suspended desire, Conor spared some time to reflect on the previous week's many dramas, and to wonder at Frank's lengthening silence. After providing security at both the inn and the hospital for several days, the Diplomatic Security Service had recalled its agents. Agent Levine explained they'd received word from London that "evolving circumstances" made any further threat against Conor and Kate unlikely.

This vague communication provided little reassurance, leaving Conor uncertain about how much trust to place in the secretive maneuvers of his MI6 superior, and wondering how long he should wait in passive ignorance. He found himself giving in to operational instincts—those natural-born talents he'd been taught to use in a different way, boosted by acquired skills he could never unlearn.

Discharge day came at last and Kate arrived, rested and glowing, her hair loosely pulled into a curling ponytail, looking more beautiful than anything he'd conjured in her absence. She wore a pair of snug black corduroys and a bright blue sweater—a scoop-necked, close-fitting article highlighting every exquisite curve.

They greeted each other with a chaste kiss, both gripped by a shy, blushing awkwardness. Conor noted the flush in her cheeks and thought perhaps he hadn't been alone in his unbridled daydreaming. With no immediate prospect for testing the theory, as she pulled the Subauru onto the interstate he shifted to a more practical topic, one they'd avoided until now.

"Have you spoken with your family since last Saturday?"

Kate hesitated before responding, and when she did all evidence of shyness was gone. "I talked to Jeanette and my father. And to Oma."

"What did you tell them?"

She shrugged. "Well, I couldn't exactly tell them the truth. I said you'd needed fresh air after playing during the reception, so we walked down to the brook ... and you were accidentally shot by an illegal hunter."

"Ah, go on. You're joking." Conor darted a suspicious squint at her, but Kate's eyes held the road without faltering.

"Not joking. Nope."

"They believed it? That some fella was wandering 'round the golf course of a posh resort—in the dark—jacking deer?"

"These are people who never leave the city. If it's north of New Haven they call it wilderness. The idea of rampant, plaid-wearing men shooting off guns isn't a stretch for them."

"If you say so." Conor studied her profile before adding, "What about Jigger? You said your sister brought him home. Have you seen him?"

Kate adjusted her hands on the steering wheel, locking them down at ten and two o'clock. "I went to Yvette's on Sunday night, but Jigger had already gone to bed and I haven't had a chance to go back yet." Kate turned to him, a touch of defiance in her face. "I told her everything, Conor. Oddly enough I didn't mind lying to my family, but I thought Yvette deserved the truth. I'm sorry for not telling you sooner, but I'd do the same again."

He took in this confession thoughtfully. Although the idea of having more people familiar with his past—and now, present—troubled him, she had a valid point, and Yvette's reticent nature was a safer bet than that of the combustible Abigail. As Conor's silence continued, Kate's defiance wavered.

"Are you angry?"

"No. Of course not." Tentatively moving his hand to her thigh he added, "Are you?"

Kate looked surprised. "What? Angry? No. Did I seem angry?"

"I wasn't sure." He smiled. "Makes me a bit nervous but I understand why you told her. Her son got shot at; she didn't deserve to have that explained with a lie." After a slight pause, he changed the subject. "I don't know why, but Frank apparently thinks we're out of danger, at least for now. I hate to admit it, but I'd still feel safer if I had my gun. Do you have any idea what happened to it? Did someone from the hotel security staff take it?"

Kate shook her head. "They didn't know you had one. I never told them."

"Didn't they see it, though?"

"You blacked out for a minute, and before anybody came I threw it off the bridge into the brook."

"You threw my gun into the ... " Conor trailed off, staring at her. Having just escaped kidnapping or worse, and in the midst of a chaotic situation, she'd had the instinct and presence of mind to do exactly what he would have done. "The police must have searched around the bridge. They probably found it."

"Maybe, but I heaved the thing pretty far upstream, into the weeds." Kate glanced at him, enjoying his reaction. "We can get to the resort in an hour and a half. Do you want to find out?"

"I do," he admitted. "How did you know?"

"I guess I'm a mindreader."

"I guess so." Conor watched the slow spread of her incomparable smile and moved his fingers over the velvet nap of her corduroys, letting them slide to the inside of her leg. "What am I thinking now?"

Maybe they'd come back too soon to expect any cathartic release from a return to the scene, but Conor was surprised by his aversion when Kate turned the car onto the hotel's access road. Surrounded by the rust and lavender hues in the landscape, the building loomed like an unsettling mirage beneath an overcast sky. After she'd parked they both sat, seat belts still fastened, riveted by the intermittent ticks of the cooling engine.

"I feel like throwing up," Kate said. "I'm not actually going to," she added in response to Conor's wide-eyed glance.

"No, I get it, believe me. Do you want to wait here?"

An obligatory suggestion, predictably refused. Much like ripping off a Band-Aid Kate pulled the key from the ignition. "Let's go. We'll need to come back some day with smudge sticks or something. I spent most of my summers here growing up—it means too much to me."

They skirted the main entrance, following a service road past the tennis courts that looped around the southern end of the resort and straightened as it ran along the brook. The golf course was deserted, as was the lawn of the hotel, and although a few guests moved on the back veranda, none were lingering long in the chilly air.

They had a spirited discussion over which of them would

venture into the icy ankle-deep water, an argument that lasted longer than the search itself. Kate prevailed, and after kicking off her shoes she rolled up her pants and darted into the stream some distance from the bridge. After a few minutes of searching in the weeds on the opposite bank she returned with the dripping Sig-Sauer hidden under her sweater. While she was putting on her shoes, Conor wandered onto the bridge. He stopped just below the apex of the arch, guessing at the approximate spot where he'd pinned Jigger beneath him. Everything looked so different in daylight.

His side was healing quickly, but had been extremely painful for several days. At one point he'd removed the bandage himself to inspect the source of his discomfort. He'd been startled by the extent of the injury—a long, neatly stitched furrow running through a collage of lurid bruises— and amazed to have been so oblivious when the shot hit him.

Conor rubbed the toe of his boot over the surface of the bridge. The cement showed no trace of blood now, but he remembered his madness in seeing the dark splash pooling beneath him, and remembering experienced some echo of it again.

Were the heavens satisfied? A bizarre, mind-warping reenactment and a claw-like rip along his chest—would it serve as a worthy penance? Would anything? He thought about the legend of a secret chord, a tone so perfect and true it could melt the heart of God. He'd offer it up and play for all he was worth, if he only knew how to unlock its mystery.

Behind him, Conor heard Kate step onto the bridge. She hesitated, but walked forward when he looked over his shoulder with a rueful smile.

"I won't ever understand how it feels." She came closer and slipped a hand into his. "Nothing I can say or do will make it better, but I hope I can help make it bearable."

Conor bent to her face, giving her lips a lingering kiss. "That's not true, actually. You do make it better, and that makes everything else bearable."

He wrapped his arms around her. If a secret chord existed, the mystery lay beyond the limits of his art, but she was the living expression of what it represented—the tonic note that gave the discordant cadence of his life a place to resolve and rest. He held her tight, afraid she might somehow slide from his grip, and while kissing her slipped a hand under her sweater and removed the gun. A sad self-awareness sank in as the weight settled in his palm like an old familiar ache. Nothing could be unlearned, or undone. This was who he was now, and until the heavens decided otherwise, this was who he would be.

Sound asleep for most of the ride back, Conor reacted in typical fashion when a hand prodded him awake. He launched himself at the windshield in a half-conscious burst of adrenalin. Functioning as designed, the seat belt locked and snapped him into place, which in turn set off his lingering cough. Kate looked both amused and concerned.

"I was afraid that might happen. I almost left you here to wake up on your own." When his thunderous fit had subsided she added, "Should I be worried about this?"

"Lung-clearing therapy. You'll get used to it." Conor laughed at her stare of alarm. "Relax. I'm only messin'." He unwrapped one of the maple candies from his pocket, tossing it into his mouth, and seeing her suddenly tender expression he gave Kate a questioning smile.

"Nothing." She shook her head. "Just glad to be home. Let's go in through the kitchen so Abigail can fuss over you. I know your low tolerance for pampering but try to be patient. She's been bottling it all week in anticipation."

"Does she know—ehm, have you told her ... ?"

"That I have a new boyfriend?" Kate grinned, blushing up to her eyebrows. "Not yet. I haven't figured out how to tell anyone without sounding like a teenager."

As predicted, Conor had not quite breached the doorway before Abigail was steaming toward him. He managed to take the brunt of the impact on his right side, swallowing a yelp of pain while she held him in a crushing embrace and erupted in tears.

"A bit melodramatic, isn't it?" he teased, but then realizing she was crying in earnest he kissed the top of her head and rocked her gently. "Sure it's all right, don't cry, darlin'. I'm after returning from the brink, will you destroy me now with tears?"

Once she'd calmed down, Conor meekly submitted to her closer examination and fretful remarks about his coloring (hospital gray), and weight loss (admittedly significant). The scrutiny complete, Abigail pressed him into a seat next to Kate and served tea—sweet and strong, just the way he liked it—along with a bowl of hot apple crisp, swimming in cream. It was good to be home.

They lounged in the bucolic homecoming atmosphere for only a few minutes before Abigail's apologetic grimace brought them to earth. "I suppose I'd better tell you. The British are here again. Frank Murdoch checked in about two hours ago."

This time Kate fell into a choking spell, while Conor lowered his spoon and carefully placed it next to his empty bowl. He nodded for Abigail to continue.

"I told him you were expected back any time, gave him tea in the library, and then he went up to his room. He looks like he hasn't slept in a week, but he wanted you to come get him as soon as you got here."

Hasn't slept in a week, Conor repeated to himself. Not like Frank to appear tired and disheveled, and that did not bode well.

25

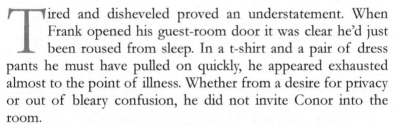

Tired and disheveled proved an understatement. When Frank opened his guest-room door it was clear he'd just been roused from sleep. In a t-shirt and a pair of dress pants he must have pulled on quickly, he appeared exhausted almost to the point of illness. Whether from a desire for privacy or out of bleary confusion, he did not invite Conor into the room.

"I'm not sure I care for your looks," Conor said by way of greeting, reprising an old joke between them. Despite his exhaustion, Frank received the jibe in good spirit, smiling.

"You, by contrast, are a sight for sore eyes."

"Glad you approve." Conor affected a slight bow but then dropped the banter. "Sorry to wake you, only Abigail said you wanted to know when we got back. Are you all right, Frank?"

"Pretty well, for what's left of me." In weariness the agent's voice slipped, betraying his heritage more effectively than any ease with Irish poetry might. Conor had occasionally discerned vestigial hints of this accent, but never had it sounded this distinct.

"Jaysus, you've a brogue on you like a Ballybay shopkeeper. That alone says you must be knackered. Do you want to wait and talk in the morning?"

His face growing pink, Frank cleared his throat and straightened. "No, quite impossible," he said, British inflection firmly in place. "I'll need to leave early. Just give me half an hour to shower and change. Where shall I join you?"

"One floor up. Will I have a bracer ready? Seems as though you could use one."

"By all means. Laphroaig, if you have any. I'd suggest one for yourself and Kate as well."

Conor didn't move from the doorway. "It's bad, isn't it?"

"I'm afraid so, Conor. In a way I never anticipated."

When Frank arrived in Kate's living room, he'd changed into a green cashmere sweater and camel-colored trousers. He appeared somewhat restored and acted more like himself, which made dealing with him in this setting all the more disorienting. He greeted Kate with affection and a continental kiss on both cheeks, then they gathered around the coffee table where the Laphroaig waited. Conor didn't much like scotch, but that seemed beside the point. He poured out a generous slug for each of them and sat on the couch next to Kate, while Frank took the chair to their left.

Kate reached for Conor's hand. She seemed sad, and a little nervous. "I have to confess, I think I know what's coming. Frank had me go through some photos at the hospital—"

"Kate," Frank interrupted gently. "Best to wait, I think."

He had two manila folders in his lap, and after swallowing half the contents of his glass he slid the first of them over to Conor. "This is the photo Kate pulled from the others I showed her." He flipped open the folder. "She identified Ciaran Wilson, the figure in the middle, as her attempted kidnapper. The man to his right she identified as her husband's cousin, Phillip Ryan."

Conor stared down at the photograph. "I don't understand. That's impossible. It doesn't make any sense."

Kate put a comforting hand on his knee. "I thought so, too. He seemed like such a—"

He jerked from her touch, a wild panic shuddering through

him. "How could he seem anything to you? You didn't even know him."

"No, not the way you did. I realize it's hard to think of Phillip as——"

"For Christ's sake, Kate! This isn't Phillip. This is my *brother*."

Kate glanced at Frank, looking suddenly worried. "Conor, Thomas is dead."

"Of course he's dead!" Conor surged to his feet. "He's under a pile of rocks by a Kashmir roadside. I buried him myself. So how could you have met him? What the fuck is going on?"

He took a fumbling step away from the couch and Frank rose to grip his arms with unexpected strength.

"Conor, stop it at once. Your reaction is understandable, the stakes for you are enormous; but you are an MI6-trained operative and however personally excruciating it might be, this is an operational briefing. Now, get your emotions under control, because there's more to come."

The order had its intended effect. Sitting down, Conor drew a long breath. With a hand still clasped on his shoulder, Frank placed the second folder in front of him and briefly tightened his grip.

"The wizard."

Conor sat motionless, his eyes following Frank as he returned to his seat. He'd watched countless moods pass across that aristocratic face, but had never seen it contain such an aspect of ... grief? Dread mounting, he reached for the folder.

He heard Kate's soft gasp when he opened it, and then for a while, nothing else. As his brain raced toward comprehension his only thought was that he wanted it to stop, but more quickly than he could bear he'd absorbed enough of the truth to feel his heart breaking at the exposure of a betrayal so grotesque.

Kate was beautiful in the picture, but on the whole Conor thought her more beautiful now. A winsome gaiety played about the face looking out at him across the space of years. The bright smile and laughing eyes held an innocent joy with an expectation of more to come, but something essential was missing: the aura of maturity, of hard-won wisdom from battles fought, of suffering encountered and transcended.

He preferred Kate as she was now, but still, he could look at the photograph and wish he could have been there that day. That it could have been him she leaned into with casual affection, resting a hand on his arm. He wished he'd been there to save her from the pain she would endure later, and Jesus, he so deeply wanted to protect her from it now. His vision blurred. The photograph swam out of focus.

"Conor," Frank called gently.

"I know." Conor wiped his eyes. "I know. Just give me a minute."

Kate had been watching silently, and he wondered how much of the truth she'd already guessed. He placed the two photos side by side on the table, pointing to the first one. "This man introduced himself to you as Phillip Ryan, but that was a lie. This is my brother, Thomas." Conor picked up the second photograph—Kate's wedding picture—and handed it to her. "This man—your husband—used that alias as well. This the man I knew as Philip Ryan. He was my best friend. He lied to both of us. His name wasn't really Michael Fitzpatrick or Phillip Ryan. This is Robert Durgan, and he's ... at least I assume—"

"He's alive." Kate's voice was flat, expressionless. "You're telling me my husband is alive."

Conor looked at Frank, who nodded a confirmation.

"I see." The shock was transparent in Kate's face, but her voice remained steady. "I have a framed print of this picture on the nightstand in my bedroom. Where did you get this one, Frank?"

"From a moving line's shipping container, hidden amongst

others in a warehouse on the outskirts of Dingle. I brought several boxes of personal items along with me. They're in my car. I can arrange for the container's remaining contents to be shipped back to you."

"So, that was him. He robbed me." Kate's face began to crumple, but she bit down on her lip and steadied her composure. "He booked the company in advance. For moving up here. I spent two months trying to track that moving truck. Finally, I just took the insurance money. I lost everything. Family antiques, some original oil paintings from the Hudson River School, photographs. I got the wedding album back, though. My sister called the photographer and had it reproduced for me. I also lost almost all of my own canvases. It was as though everything I'd ever done was a mirage." She rose from the couch. "Is your car unlocked?"

Frank pulled the key from his pocket and Conor got to his feet. "Do you want me to help?"

She turned to him, her gaze opaque, as though looking at a stranger. "No. I want you to—" She caught herself, and walked from the room without another word.

After watching her leave, Conor picked up his scotch, drained it, and then—like an elderly invalid—slowly lowered himself onto the couch. His face was still in his hands when he heard Frank open the bottle and refill his own glass.

"Shall we get drunk, my friend?"

Conor dropped his hands, and without looking up, pushed his glass forward.

Fueled by booze, the operational debriefing continued until midnight. Despite Frank's many sleepless nights in pursuit, Robert Durgan had not been found, but a file which had remained thin was thickening rapidly. The name he'd been born with turned out to be a hybrid of his working aliases. Robert Ryan Fitzpatrick grew up at Twinbrook, a republican-leaning housing estate in West Belfast. Fitzpatrick was a known commodity, a wanted man who'd been missing for years. He'd been a key figure in a paramilitary group called the Irish People's Liberation Organization, infamous for violence and criminal activity of all varieties. Many of its recruits came from the ranks of those fallen from favor in the IRA. On October 31, 1992, the Provisional IRA wiped out the IPLO, killing its leader and several members in a series of raids around Belfast. Fitzpatrick was not among the killed or injured.

"He simply dropped off the face of the earth," Frank said. "The strong suspicion within IPLO circles is that he informed on his colleagues to the IRA—who might be found at what time, in what pub—in exchange for an altered identity and safe passage to the United States. No UK authority or intelligence service chased it up. Christ, British intelligence might have helped the business along. At any rate, why should we care? A distasteful element had been sorted, and everyone was making nice in support of the flowering peace process."

The agent flipped open one of the manila folders and referred to a sheet of paper. "Had we been looking, we might have easily found the record of an arrival from Shannon at the New York port of entry on October 28, 1992. IPLO member Robert Ryan Fitzpatrick had become American citizen Michael Fitzpatrick, complete with a valid US passport and a bright new legend—birthplace Newfoundland in 1968, matriculated at New York University in 1989, US citizenship in the same year. Digging a little deeper, we'd have turned up a 1996 marriage license for himself and one Katherine Chatham, and perhaps even the Coast Guard's report from August 22, 1998, detailing the boating accident and presumed death of Michael Fitzpatrick in Long Island Sound."

He paused to let the information sink in and then asked, "Do you remember when Phillip Ryan turned up in Dingle?"

"About two months later. Middle of October is when I met him, anyway. In a pub." Conor poured another measure of scotch into his glass.

"The wedding photograph in Kate's bedroom. You never—" Meeting Conor's stony gaze, Frank cleared his throat. "Obviously, she never showed it to you."

"No."

Frank nodded, tapping a finger against the manila folder. "I didn't make the connection immediately, but I realized the farm manager was the key as soon as Kate identified your brother in this photograph as a man named Phillip Ryan. For some reason Thomas had pretended to be her husband's cousin, which meant her husband had lied to her. At some point whilst keeping watch at your bedside the significance of her married surname dawned upon me, and the penny finally dropped. Her husband and your farm manager were the same man—the infamous, long-lost Robert Ryan Fitzpatrick. I puzzled over this a bit during my drive to Nashua to sit in on Ciaran Wilson's interrogation. Wilson and his associate Desmond Moore had been loyal members of the Armagh branch of the IPLO, and Fitzpatrick had betrayed them. Why would they be working for him?"

"So, why were they?" Conor asked.

"Wilson and Moore never met the man in person. He recruited them by phone two years after the elimination of the IPLO, and they knew him only as a Canadian-born American named Robert Durgan. A stroke of genius, the Newfoundland cover. He apparently affected a convincing American accent, but would attribute any slips to his 'Newfie' origins." The agent gave a thin smile. "Imagine Wilson's consternation at discovering who he'd been working for all these years. He was quite eager to cooperate, once he knew. He said he'd never been keen on the kidnapping assignment. Their main project with Durgan had been grant fraud and money laundering. Wilson and Moore recruited accomplices willing to sign their name to EU grant applications in return for a cut of the money. The cash would get flushed through a select group of New York restaurants and bars—clients whose money Durgan already laundered under the alias of Michael Fitzpatrick, purveyor of restaurant cash management systems."

"Thomas wasn't a willing accomplice," Conor objected.

"No," Frank agreed. "Wilson conceded Thomas was an anomaly. They simply deceived him. The strategy from the start was for Thomas to get caught, and for them to 'rescue' him. Durgan had indicated he wanted someone in New York for a special job."

"Why did Wilson and Moore target Thomas in particular?"

"I don't think they did, Conor," Frank said sadly. "An accident of fate. They were passing through Dingle, simply looking for the nearest farmer. Had he stayed away from town that night or left the pub a bit earlier, they would have picked someone else, and Thomas might never have run into two strangers who stood him six shots of Jamesons before convincing him to give them a job."

"Sure, he was an easy mark for Durgan, or Fitzpatrick. Ryan. Whoever. Ah, Christ." Conor got up to pace the room with his hands on his head, trying to loosen the stiffened muscles in his side. "A poor culchie from the heart of the Gaeltacht who wouldn't recognize an IPLO traitor if one bit him in the arse."

"Precisely." Frank took a sip from his glass, squinting and frowning at the wall as he swallowed. "I'd prefer to stick with 'Durgan' if you don't mind. I've been using the bloody name for years and haven't the time or staffing resources to re-label everything."

Conor expelled a bitter laugh. Dropping his hands, he stopped pacing and eased himself back onto the couch. He noted without much interest that the alcohol was having an accelerating effect. He'd had a lot to drink and little to eat, and was dosed with medications carrying instructions to do exactly the opposite. He gazed through the large living room window in front of him as a car glided up the road toward the inn. As he stared at them, the twin beams from its headlights bobbed and merged into a single fuzzy glow. Reservations at eight. Table for two. Candlelight and music. All going on just two floors below him. Two floors and a universe away. He heard the soft clink of glass on glass as Frank placed his drink on the coffee table.

"I mentioned Durgan laundered money for a number of New York clients." He steepled his fingers and sat back in his chair. "The list included a chain of upscale Indian restaurants called Bombay Masala. Care to guess the owner's name?"

Conor pulled his eyes away from the window and rolled them toward the ceiling. "Pawan Kotwal."

"Our favorite Indian mafia boss. Extraordinary how the puzzle comes together so nicely when you understand where the pieces are. I surmise Durgan perceived some opportunity in Kotwal's broader interests in Mumbai and wanted his own reliable 'smurf' placed onsite to handle the cash deposits—Thomas. I haven't worked out where Durgan went after the manufactured boating accident. We know Thomas was in Mumbai a few days later. Perhaps Durgan traveled ahead to help build the pub and get the business running. At any rate, as you already confirmed, two months after the incident he appropriated the Phillip Ryan alias for his own use and presented himself to you for employment. Brilliant in a way, because if Thomas attempted to escape his situation, surely his family would hear from him. Seems an odd cover—self-imposed isolation with an identity as a lowly farming assistant, maintained over a period of years; but he was biding his time, of course. He had a particular goal with a hard deadline: Kate's thirtieth birthday."

"And after all this you still don't know where he is." Conor didn't intend the comment as an accusation and the agent didn't take it as such, but he sensed Frank's helpless frustration.

"I'm afraid not. I'd hoped to use Wilson to trap him, but unfortunately they spoke by phone after he left Bretton Woods, and when Durgan learned the extent of his failure he severed all contact. Until then, he'd remained in his rented house on the outskirts of Dingle, continuing under the 'Phillip Ryan' alias, but by the time we'd mobilized the local authorities he'd gone. The closest neighbors in the vicinity hadn't seen his motorbike in the driveway for several days. Some documents he left behind led us to the shipping container with Kate's possessions, but I imagine everything of value got fenced long ago."

Conor ran a finger over the rim of Kate's glass of scotch. "I understand the Mumbai money-laundering piece, but why did he need Thomas to come to New York and pose as his cousin? Why fake his death at all, when he might have just disappeared? She nearly died, Frank. He left her broken and traumatized. What was the point of such cruelty?"

"A question only he can answer," Frank said. "I'm sure the plan somehow advanced his plans for getting her money, once she reached the age of inheritance. He was her husband, and of course she must have confided her circumstances to him before their marriage."

"Her husband." Conor reached for her glass. "Her husband, my friend, and as surely as the man who put the bullet in—my brother's murderer. And I am a trained MI6 operative who will just as surely see him dead."

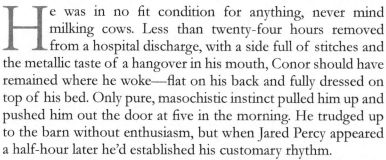

26

He was in no fit condition for anything, never mind milking cows. Less than twenty-four hours removed from a hospital discharge, with a side full of stitches and the metallic taste of a hangover in his mouth, Conor should have remained where he woke—flat on his back and fully dressed on top of his bed. Only pure, masochistic instinct pulled him up and pushed him out the door at five in the morning. He trudged up to the barn without enthusiasm, but when Jared Percy appeared a half-hour later he'd established his customary rhythm.

Determined to finally bury the hatchet with the young man, Conor expressed admiration for his clever bits of work in the barn and offered profuse thanks for all his efforts. He insisted he could take the first shift on his own, but asked Jared to come back in the afternoon. Even if Kate hadn't sent him packing by then, he'd never manage the second milking. With his shy smile Jared offered a handshake before departing, and Conor tried not to worry he'd just made his last friend in Hartsboro Bend. After a short rest he got back to work, letting familiar routine produce the usual, zen-like trance.

He finished an hour later, and had become a sweating, trembling collection of parts he could barely control when Frank stepped into the barn, wearing a jacket and tie. He cradled a large thermos and two mugs in one hand, and carried his briefcase in the other. Conor hiked an eyebrow at the green thermos, obviously an old and well-used artifact.

"I take my mugs as I find them," Frank explained, "but one should never leave home without a proper thermos. The Stanley model is one of America's greatest contributions to civilization. Shall I pour? I'd hoped for a visit amongst your livestock, but perhaps you ought to sit down. I don't suppose you have a break room or some such?"

"No." Conor smiled. In the most grueling of circumstances, his boss never lost the power to amuse. "Let's get you out of here. My head is hammering as it is. Touring you around my cow barn will make it explode altogether."

They sat on the picnic bench, side-by side in friendly silence, sipping their tea and watching the morning fog roll up off the pasture.

"What's your stake in this, Frank?" Conor kept his eyes fixed ahead, setting his mug down between them. "I'm remembering our first dinner at your club in London. You talked about getting intelligence on a global money-laundering operation that props up terrorist groups. That was a load of shite and you knew as much, even then. It wasn't any global operation, no network of smurfs running around throwing cash into off-shore accounts. No international wizard. This is small beer, really. One criminal fucker and his two pathetic sidekicks snookered a man into breaking the law and joining them. A job for Interpol and local police. Why would MI6 care? If there's intelligence to collect and analyze it's like shooting a gnat with a feckin' howitzer. So why is British intelligence even involved in this? Or are they?"

Conor faced Frank, steeling himself for the answer to that last question. The agent's initial reaction was unsettling. He closed his eyes and dropped his head with a smile, looking relieved at finally being caught.

"Ah, Conor. As if you haven't suffered enough you have the torment of wondering whether all along you've been under the finger of a rogue agent, operating off the ledger. Not the case, I assure you. The mission has always been officially recognized by MI6. I will admit however, I used my position and seniority in the service to make it so."

He reached down and picked up his briefcase. Conor thought he would leave without further explanation. He'd experienced that sort of anti-climax before. Instead, Frank pulled out the folder from the previous evening and passed the photograph to him.

"The third man in the picture. Desmond Moore. You know his name, but not all of his story. He was a hard-living, hard-drinking criminal who drifted into the Irish National Liberation Army, and then to the Armagh branch of the IPLO. Unbeknownst to him, he was also an informant, passing information to British intelligence on the groups' ties to the international drug and arms trade. Desmond Moore was my younger brother."

"Holy mother of God." The blood drained from Conor's face before quickly flowing back in a rush of irritation. "You didn't think this was something I deserved to be told?"

Frank shrugged. "The story was tangential to your mission, and to be perfectly honest I was ashamed to tell you. I supported Desi, just like a big brother should. Money for him, and money for his causes. In return—although he never realized it—he supported me. My career became cemented on the back of my access to those two paramilitary organizations. When the IRA disbanded the IPLO, Desi mucked about with illegal bookmaking and small-time drug dealing and we fell out of touch. As you correctly observed, those sorts of activities are of small interest to MI6. Several years later he came to me, wanting drinking money for a trip to Geneva. He'd been recruited into a project so secret he wouldn't even tell me, but he was childishly excited. The matter didn't seem worth much attention. When he returned I dutifully tried to ply him with money and whiskey, and then more money, but to no avail. Later he disappeared, and I was relieved. He represented an unpleasant weight on my conscience. Then, a few years before you and I first met, someone discovered the remains of a mutilated body on the edge of an Armagh construction site."

Frank took the photograph back and slipped it into his briefcase. "Desi was no Thomas McBride. He was not a good man. Along with being a criminal he was a cruel and uncouth bigot, but he was my own brother. My blood. I assiduously betrayed him over a number of years then tossed him aside when his value no longer compensated for my discomfort. After the discovery of his body I set about unraveling what he'd been getting up to, going back to the first period when I lost touch with him, which eventually led me to a pub in Dingle, and a story about a couple of lads from Armagh who had corrupted Thomas McBride and ruined his little brother's life."

He finished his tea, and brushed a few invisible specks of nothing from his trouser leg. "So you see, there is something personal for both of us in this journey, although mine is largely one of atonement."

"You're not alone in that either, Frank," Conor said.

They shared a long silence, each of them wandering in memories, until Frank sighed and rose from the bench. "My flight leaves Burlington in less than three hours." Watching Conor brace his hands against the bench and struggle to his feet he added, "You'd do well to crawl back into bed. We can talk when you've had a few days to recuperate from all this."

"No. Don't pull this on me again." Conor straightened. "Don't just disappear like the last time and leave me wondering. You have to deal me in on however this is going to end. I've earned that much."

"Of course you have, Conor. That, and a great deal more." Frank regarded him fondly. "Very well. I'll tell you the latest. Sedgwick has had some luck in picking up information on the

DEA's traitor, Tony Costino. We believe the next move in this chess game centers around him. Costino hoped Durgan would help in finding you, but that was over two months ago, and Durgan's most recent aggression was not actually against you. This suggests he's been withholding assistance. Now things have changed. His master plan is off the rails and he must assume Ciaran Wilson, his last trusted associate, is in custody cooperating with the FBI. Since the Garda raided his house in Dingle he realizes his real identity has been exposed. We've located and frozen all his bank accounts, both legal and illicit, so he's living on whatever cash he had on hand when he disappeared. The Garda haven't the manpower for ongoing surveillance, but they've been doing regular evening rounds on his house as well as your old farmhouse in Dingle, but he's not turned up at either of them. He's on the run, trapped in Ireland, which is too small a place to hide for long. He needs help, and the only bit of leverage left to him is the information about you that Costino is looking for. I expect they will connect again soon, if they haven't already. If Sedgwick can find him, I'm quite confident he'll be able to 'persuade' Costino to lead us to Durgan. I'll be conferring with him in a few days and I promise to keep you involved. In the meantime, take good care of the lovely Kate, and for God's sake take care of yourself. She will need your support in the weeks ahead."

Conor looked down at the bench, a different sort of pain slicing through his chest. "I doubt she wants anything from me."

"Nonsense. Who do you suppose sent me over with the tea? I mentioned you were not in your room and she instantly knew where you'd gone. She was quite alarmed." Frank smiled. "A little time and space my boy, and patience. You are a challenging package of oddities to be sure, but Kate is a woman of spirit, and you are far too good—and far too handsome—for her to give up on you."

In the week following Frank's departure, Kate slept little, usually waking with a dull headache and a jaw so clenched she had to coax her brain into letting it loose. She spent the better part of each day in her office with the door closed, emerging only to escape into the twilight for a restless hike through woods and meadows.

Her predominant emotion during this time was anger. Not a blistering rage—that might have blazed hot and fast and burned out more quickly. Her anger seemed like a low fever she tended daily, a symptom to indulge when the underlying disease is too frightening to tackle. It took root with the first glimpse of her wedding portrait lying exposed on the coffee table as a bloodless piece of evidence, and it became the only firewall she had to prevent the revelation from destroying her.

Irrational and unfocused, nothing wandering within its radius was exempt from her resentment, including Conor. She made no pretense about her intention to avoid him, but on the rare occasions when their paths did cross she didn't ignore him—she did something worse. She managed their exchanges by playing the role of the quintessential innkeeper asking after her guests. How did he feel? Was there anything he needed? Her superficial tone clearly hurt him, but she couldn't seem to stop. Conor didn't complain, and since she treated him like a guest he behaved as one. He kept mostly to his room as he convalesced, playing his violin softly in the mornings, and she often heard his lilting voice in the lobby outside her office, charming the real guests into senseless enchantment.

Abigail served as their reluctant envoy, passing messages and providing updates in sad confusion until Kate at last confided in her. The situation once more proved the solid worth of her friend. Kate had always known Abigail's blustering theatrics were a salt meant to flavor the environment as needed. She understood when to grind the mill, and when to put it away. With tensions running high Abigail provided quiet leadership, comforting the inn's skittish staff and offering a listening ear for its two most miserable occupants.

The crisis reached its tipping point after eight days, on an evening of cold rain. Kate had stopped in the relative shelter of some pine trees, near the composting remains of the garden. She saw Conor coming across the meadow with a closed umbrella, his capped head bent against the icy downpour. Reaching her, he offered the umbrella with a tentative smile, but she crossed her arms and gazed beyond his shoulder.

"You're being foolish." She sniffed. "You shouldn't be out here in this."

"I might venture to say the same. Here. Take this if you're going to stay outside."

She took the umbrella roughly from his hand. "Why don't you ever use one yourself for God's sake?"

He stuck his hands into his pockets and shrugged. "Because men are feckin' eejits. We'd sooner be caught naked than under an umbrella."

"That's ridiculous."

"Yeah."

At least she'd managed to stop talking to him like a robotic hostess, but Kate couldn't bring herself to go further. She stood under the umbrella, signaling him with stony silence.

"Kate, I understand you don't want to talk to me. I suppose I just wanted to tell you how sorry—"

"Conor, stop." She held up a hand, frowning impatiently. "Look, a lot of this isn't even about you, so don't try to take it all on and be a martyr to some misplaced sense of guilt. You do that, you know."

"Right, but—"

"No." She motioned again for him to stop. "Shut up and

listen. You didn't lie through two years of marriage or let me nearly drown in the ocean, or do anything to try to hurt me. You don't own that guilt, so leave it alone. But you did bring this down on me. Of course you didn't intend to, but because you showed up at my door I'm dealing with something I might never have needed to know, and you know what? That would have been fine. He lied to me, he nearly got me killed, he robbed me and was ready to try again, but however unintentional, the one kindness Michael did for me was to let me think he was dead. What good does it do me to know the truth? What the fuck am I supposed to do with it? I've got all this unwanted reality and for that, yes, you're right to apologize. For that, you need my forgiveness."

"Will I ever get it, do you think?"

"I don't know."

Conor's head had been bowed throughout this tirade, his face obscured by his cap. Now, he pulled the bill more firmly over his eyes, and without looking up turned and walked back to the house.

As soon as he'd left her, Kate realized the anger that had fortified her was exhausted, expelled into the night with one furious outburst. In its place, confusion and sorrow finally came forward, like a distant relative at a funeral, waiting in the corner until recognized.

She'd committed to a life with the man she knew as Michael Fitzpatrick because she thought it offered more meaning than the lifestyle her family embodied. She'd treasured the memory of every happy time they'd shared, but now she reflected on the moments of unease she'd banished from her mind, of his aloof moods and unusual limitations. Of disappointments she'd accepted. She'd too easily assumed responsibility for everything. Her own privileged upbringing had created a sense of self-conscious guilt, something that seemed like the opposite of entitlement. He'd seen her vulnerability, and had used it against her.

What could she infer from any fonder memories, now? Those times when they'd been happy together. Had any of his attentions been sincere, or merely tactics employed to advance an end? Was anything they'd shared genuine? Had he loved her at all?

The sobs came at last, and she was relieved to finally give in to them. Kate turned and put her face to the rough, cracked bark of the pine tree, surrendering to the pain her soul must accept if it was ever to heal.

She returned long past the dinner hour, slipping in through the front door. Being Monday, the dining room was closed, the ground floor quiet. The darkness was softened by pools of light from the few scattered lamps that remained on through the night. Kate heard the muffled movements of guests overhead, and she smelled bacon, which meant Conor must have eaten breakfast for supper again. A "fry up" as he called it, was about the sum total of his cooking prowess.

She retreated upstairs, took a long hot shower, and put on a pair of silver silk pajamas. Then, she crept back down to the kitchen to fix herself a sandwich and a cup of tea. She left the lights off and sat eating in darkness, listening to the wind and the occasional creaks of the settling house, at peace for the first time in weeks.

She paused on the way back to her room, seeing the light still spilling from a crack under Conor's door. She thought of his face as she'd railed at him—bleak and compliant, as if her negation was no more than he deserved.

He hadn't deserved it, of course. She'd perversely withheld forgiveness for something that wasn't his fault. After a few seconds of indecision Kate walked to his door. She knocked, and entered at his quick invitation.

Conor reclined on the bed with a book propped open on his

chest, in the same V-necked sweater and gray khakis he'd been wearing on the day she met him. He looked well; his color was good and his eyes had recovered their dark glitter. He seemed surprised and hesitantly pleased to see her, but now that she was inside the room Kate wasn't sure how to begin.

"I noticed your light. I just wanted to make sure you were okay. You were insane to go out in the pouring rain, Conor. The doctors warned—"

"Right." He cut her off quietly, a flash of disappointment in his eyes. "The summary of what the doctors have warned me about is already well represented, and repeated often. Thanks for checking, though. I'm fine."

"I'm sorry. I didn't mean to start out like that."

She considered leaving, but then came in and closed the door behind her, leaning against it. Conor swung his legs from the bed and sat up to face her. He looked wary, and she didn't blame him. Almost too afraid to go on, she stalled for time.

"What are you reading?"

Without taking his eyes from hers he shut the book and showed her the cover. Robert Frost. "The man to go to. Sort of like Vermont's version of Yeats."

"The secret sits in the middle." She gave a shaky laugh. "I'd never heard it before, and now that poem seems like the theme to our life."

Our life. The inclusive pronoun was not lost on him, and seeing his hopeful smile Kate's eyes filled. She'd been damaged, and had paid dearly for her misplaced trust—but so had he. They each had what the other needed.

"Will you help me?" she whispered. "I can't sit there alone with it."

He was on his feet before she'd finished. Kate lifted her arms to circle his neck and sank her fingers into his hair, feeling his chest expand in a grateful sigh as she kissed him. It was long and deep and she was the first to come up for air. Undeterred, Conor moved down her neck, his breath stuttering as her hands slipped beneath his sweater, pressing against the warm, hard muscle of his stomach before sliding down under his belt.

Shaking, she fumbled with buckle, button and zipper while his fingers moved up her sides until the slippery silver top was lifted off over her head. He explored every inch of her with slow intensity, his mouth lingering on each susceptible area and landing at last on a place that turned her legs to water. With a hand on the small of her back, he pulled her against him with a jerk, and she felt as much as heard his gravel-edged hum of satisfaction.

"Come here to me, *chuisle*. You've more sweet spots than a honeycomb. Let's see how many more we can find." They stepped from the tangle of clothing on the floor and he drew her down onto the bed. As her hips settled against him, he took in a sharp breath.

"Did I hurt you?" Kate gently ran her fingers over his side, and Conor exhaled a quiet laugh.

"Not there. And not the way you think."

He rolled her beneath him, his mouth covering hers while his calloused fingertips began a slow passage over the curve of her breast and down her stomach. The indescribable sensation pulled a husky, unfamiliar sound from her throat, and as her back arched, Kate felt something dig into the back of her shoulder. Without pausing, Conor reached behind her and pushed the book to the floor. It landed with a ponderous thud as his musical voice sounded close her ear.

"Good night Robert, aul' fella. Promises to keep, don't you know."

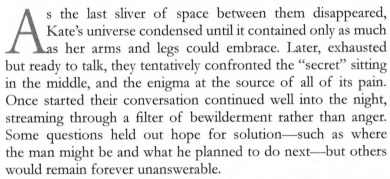

27

As the last sliver of space between them disappeared, Kate's universe condensed until it contained only as much as her arms and legs could embrace. Later, exhausted but ready to talk, they tentatively confronted the "secret" sitting in the middle, and the enigma at the source of all of its pain. Once started their conversation continued well into the night, streaming through a filter of bewilderment rather than anger. Some questions held out hope for solution—such as where the man might be and what he planned to do next—but others would remain forever unanswerable.

"He sent me a Christmas card every year," Kate said. "A money-laundering, paramilitary fugitive, my fake dead husband, sent his fake widow a Christmas card every year. What kind of bastard does that?"

"A sick bastard." Conor lay spooned against her with his hand resting on her stomach. Kate felt his chest moving in a deep, regular rhythm against her back.

"Are you falling asleep?"

"Absolutely not."

His hand started traveling south. Kate smiled and captured his fingers, and since their electrifying texture was a matter of some fascination for her, she lifted them up for closer inspection.

"I wonder if he thought this would happen. Between you and me." She brushed her lips along the top of each of Conor's fingers. "He set the whole thing up for you to come here. Why? Wasn't it a risk?"

"Risk be damned. I think he can't resist fucking with people's lives. I was actually the one who suggested coming here. He'd mentioned this place a few times over the years—what a laugh it was, his cousin's widow trying to run a farm. I'm sure he had another laugh when I gave him an easy way to keep tabs on both of us. And here was me, sick with guilt and so grateful for his help. Good old Pip Ryan."

"I don't even know what name to call him anymore." Kate said.

"I can think of a few."

"You know what I mean."

"Right." Conor sighed. "Let's follow Frank's lead and stick to Robert Durgan. The name for a man none of us knows."

"What about me? He was declared dead. Am I still married? Or was that even legal?" Without warning, Kate felt close to crying again. "What do I call myself?"

He swept aside her hair to deliver a warm kiss behind her ear. "I can think of a name there as well."

Kate twisted in his arms to face him, smiling sadly. "Is this a proposal?"

"Only if you're ready for one, but I'm guessing you're not."

"When I am, will you ask again?"

"I'll go on asking for the rest of my life. If that's what it takes." Conor's face was the very image of transparent sincerity. No mystery. No equivocation.

"Don't be ridiculous." She snuggled in closer, tucking her head under his chin. "It's not going to take that long."

With eyes still closed Kate shifted, rolling into the kiss lightly brushing her cheek while a hand on her waist stopped her momentum. She felt his lips curve into a smile.

"Careful, love. You'll end up on the floor."

Kate forced open one sleepy eyelid to focus on Conor, already dressed, kneeling by the edge of the bed in the pre-dawn darkness.

"Sorry for waking you. Go back to sleep."

"What time is it?"

"Only half-four."

"Oh my God." Kate burrowed drowsily under the covers. "How can you stand doing this every day?"

He laughed, and kissed her again before getting to his feet. "I've got to admit, it just got a bit harder."

After he left she drifted off, but woke less than an hour later with her arm stretched across the mattress, as though straining for something just out of reach. With the passage of years she'd grown accustomed to the emptiness next to her, but now after being warm and full for one night, the space seemed colder and twice as wide as she remembered. She pulled her arm back to the warmth of her side and decided there was no point in lying in bed any longer.

She showered and dressed, but instead of heading downstairs Kate brewed coffee in the french press she kept in the apartment's kitchenette. She wasn't ready to put on her public face just yet, or confront any new challenges, or do anything that might resurrect the pain she and Conor had managed to subdue. Lingering in the moment, and hoping it could stretch around the clock to give them at least one normal day, she carried the steaming mug into her studio, drawn irresistibly to the window framing the barn on the opposite hillside. Through the darkness a light from the milk room beamed a watery fluorescent glow.

After first ignoring them and suffering the consequences, Conor had obeyed the hospital's discharge orders and remained idle for a week before returning to work a few days earlier. Kate gazed at the square of light, visualizing him in the barn. The radio would be on—WDEV for the morning, VPR in the afternoon—its soundtrack occupying only half his mind while he moved in rhythmic, prayer-like stillness.

A movement on the road caught her attention, and as Abigail's car turned up the driveway Kate realized she'd been staring and daydreaming for longer than she'd thought. She left her mug in the sink and headed downstairs for a second cup of coffee with her chef before beginning her own routine.

Productivity eluded her that morning. Kate couldn't manage to concentrate on anything, but she finally switched on her computer and while it chugged to life she made a half-hearted attempt to organize the piles surrounding her, which gave her another excuse to think about Conor. She badly needed his flair for bringing order to chaos, and decided to find some ploy to put him on desk duty one day soon.

She reviewed the registration system for the day's arrivals and checked the dinner reservation list, and then opened her email. The first item in her inbox had been sent at two o'clock that morning. Kate clicked on it with a sense of foreboding, and needed only an instant to read its terse message.

"Crap." She sat back and sighed, her tender fantasies colliding with reality. It was seven o'clock in the morning, and the "normal" part of her day was already over.

"Ghedi, did you remember to pick up soy milk?" Abigail asked the question without turning from the stove. "We're due any minute for the special order I told you about yesterday. Oatmeal with raisins. Soy milk only."

"Soy milk, ma'am? Oh yes, yes. Yes. Oh dear."

Waiting for his breakfast at the kitchen island, Conor looked up from his newspaper. The Somalian chef's dark, liquid eyes had fastened on him in stark panic. He gave the young man a reassuring wink.

"It was on the list, mate," he murmured. "Door of the fridge, red carton."

"Something I need to know?" Abigail pivoted to confront them. Ghedi's face, which had been subsiding into relief, froze again.

"Only that his baby girl was running a fever yesterday, so I collected the shopping while he went to the doctor's." Conor tossed the sports section aside—American papers never covered sports he actually cared about—and smiled to see Abigail's face predictably crumpling in sympathy.

"Poor little Ayanna. Is she all right, Ghedi?"

"Yes ma'am, thank you. It is an ear infection, but she is much better."

"Well, why on earth didn't you say something when I—"

"Abigail," Conor said mildly. "Are those my pancakes you're waving about? Could I ever have them before they're cooled entirely?"

As Abigail was putting the plate in front of him, Kate swung through the door with a tray of dirty dishes. "Oatmeal-with-soy-milk is here. Please, tell me we can do that."

Ghedi offered a bright smile. "Of course, ma'am. Straightaway."

Conor swung around on his stool to face Kate, bursting with the knowledge of a secret shared and curious to see what she'd do with it. She saw him and stopped short, flicking a nervous glance at Abigail.

"I didn't know you were back," she said in a neutral tone.

"Just got here," he replied, equally bland.

She set the tray on the counter next to him, and as Conor prepared another banal remark she suddenly stopped him with a long, demonstrative kiss. His muffled laugh escaped around her lips, and over her shoulder he watched Abigail's rounded amazement crinkle into delight.

"Thank God that's finally settled," she muttered, heading back to the stove. "Took them long enough."

Kate reached into her pocket and reluctantly presented him with a folded piece of paper. "Arrived early this morning. And I was hoping for a quiet, normal day."

Conor accepted the paper without looking at it. A quick glance confirmed Ghedi was busy with his soy-spiked oatmeal, well out of hearing range.

"Is this going to put me off my breakfast?"

"I don't think so. It's pretty short."

Dubious, he peeled back the corners of the paper as though defusing a bomb, and read the email message.

Have him call me this morning ASAP. On his cell. My number is the same.

"Is he still in India?" Kate asked.

"Last I knew. Frank was supposedly coordinating strategy with him."

"I didn't think you had a cell phone."

Conor looked up from the note, grinning. "I don't, actually. The MI6 lads took it off me when they debriefed me in the hospital last March. They were glad to have something back. I'd lost or broken everything else they gave me. I suppose I can get one cheap at the WalMart?"

"Wow. WalMart. Where the discerning spy shops?" Kate gave him an arch look. "You're a regular James Bond, aren't you?"

"Seems like you thought so last night."

His impertinence earned him a vicious poke in the shoulder, but the laughter in her wide blue eyes was worth the punishment.

The smoke-gray sky was unloading a style of precipitation

he'd never seen before. It wasn't snow, nor was it exactly hail or freezing rain. Sitting inside the truck, Conor was transfixed by the perfectly round dots bouncing off the hood, obsessed with the challenge of putting a name to them. He noted the sudden squall had not cast the same spell over his fellow shoppers. They continued across the parking lot, their stolid gait signaling this was not a weather event of any interest to them. Maybe because Vermonters knew what to call it. Maybe—like the Inuit—they had a rich vocabulary for types of snow. Conor tried to think of how many words the Irish had for rain, but decided their talent lay more in describing what the rain was actually doing—lashing, teaming, pissing, bucketing ...

He was stalling. On the plastic bag next to him, WalMart's iconic smiley face beamed its idiocy at him, looking jaundiced against the filmy blue background. The phone was inside the bag, activated, charged and ready to go, but having a premonition of what was coming, Conor was not.

He delayed the inevitable for a few more minutes before finally plucking the phone from the bag. After connecting to the international bridge Conor dialed from memory and slumped back, waiting for something to happen. He'd only called the number once before, and briefly thought he might be as unsuccessful as he'd been the first time, but on the fifth ring he heard a click, an obscenity and a muffled cough, and then Sedgwick's flat mid-Western twang.

"You do know what time it is over here, right?"

"Night-time. You did say ASAP."

"I said ASAP hours ago. Christ, this could have been a disaster; I fell asleep waiting for you. What took you so long?"

"Had to run an errand," Conor said.

"Oh, right. God forbid we alter the flow of happy village life." The sizzling snap of a lighter cracked over the line. "I've got eyes on Costino."

"Right now, like? Does that mean he's in bed with you?"

He heard Sedgwick take a long drag from his cigarette and release his breath slowly. "Okay, Conor. 'Uncle'. I yield. I haven't slept in three days, so can you cut me a break?"

"Yeah, of course. Sorry." Conor wrapped his fingers over the steering wheel, watching whatever the heavens were still unloading onto the asphalt. "Been a busy month here as well."

"So I'm told, buddy," Sedgwick said, without sarcasm. "The whole thing is pretty fucking unbelievable. Anyway, I'm in a hotel in Bangalore. Costino's in another one up the road and I need you over here. How are you doing, by the way? Are you healthy?"

"Sure. Fighting fit. What's the plan?"

"I'll tell you when you get here. You leave this afternoon. Frank's got you booked from Burlington to Newark under your own name, but the guy in the seat next to you will have alias info for the flight to Mumbai—passport, credit cards, cash, and whatever crap they throw in to pad the legend. The Brits love pocket litter. He'll leave an envelope in the seat-back pocket, so just pull it out when he goes to the john. From Mumbai you fly to Bangalore, and I'll meet you outside the arrivals hall. Don't stand me up like the last time."

Conor detected the smile in his voice and grinned as well, remembering his first chaotic arrival in India almost a year ago. "Promise. When is the flight from Burlington?"

"1:30 on United, so you don't have much time. You'd better pack and get on the road now."

"Bloody hell, I can't make that," Conor sputtered. "I'm not even at home. I'm at a mall in Berlin. It's forty miles at least, and on secondary roads. I can't get back in time to pack and get to Burlington."

"What the fuck are you doing at a mall in ... shit. Wait, Berlin, Vermont. That's right off I-89. Sedgwick hurried on without waiting for confirmation. "Look. You need to make this, so get your ass on the interstate and head for the airport right now. From where you are, you're less than an hour away."

"No, hang on a minute, I can't—"

"You have to," Sedgwick said flatly. "Your documents are all on that flight, McBride. You can't miss it. Do you hear me?"

"Yeah. I hear you." Conor slumped back, defeated. "I won't miss it."

28

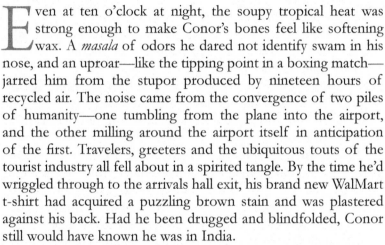

E ven at ten o'clock at night, the soupy tropical heat was strong enough to make Conor's bones feel like softening wax. A *masala* of odors he dared not identify swam in his nose, and an uproar—like the tipping point in a boxing match—jarred him from the stupor produced by nineteen hours of recycled air. The noise came from the convergence of two piles of humanity—one tumbling from the plane into the airport, and the other milling around the airport itself in anticipation of the first. Travelers, greeters and the ubiquitous touts of the tourist industry all fell about in a spirited tangle. By the time he'd wriggled through to the arrivals hall exit, his brand new WalMart t-shirt had acquired a puzzling brown stain and was plastered against his back. Had he been drugged and blindfolded, Conor still would have known he was in India.

A cluster of service providers waved him through the door as though escorting an arriving dignitary, but their ranks soon dwindled and the few remaining grew plaintive in their appeals for his business. He ignored them, positioning himself near the doorway and scanning the area, determined not to miss the rendezvous.

"City of Bangalore is welcoming you, sir. You are wanting taxi? Excellent hotel? First-class womens?"

He turned in the direction of this more familiar voice and saw Sedgwick maneuvering toward him, twisting around the crowd in a series of athletic bounces. The agent had gained a few badly needed pounds since their last meeting and seemed to have caught up on his sleep.

This was more than Conor could say for himself, but he managed a smile as they shook hands. "They say memory always exaggerates—not really possible with this place, is it?"

"Not that I've noticed." Sedgwick pushed away one of the touts arguing his case with too much persistence and proximity. "*Arrey*, back off dude. This one's mine." He grinned at Conor. "You look all right for someone who's almost died twice in one year. Flights okay? Make any new friends this time?"

"A family of touring Australians. Becky, Sam and baby Jake, visiting their mates in Pune. The baby honked his dinner all over me, but otherwise no drama."

"Lunatics. Only Australians would bring a baby on vacation to India." Sedgwick started down the sidewalk. "Come on. Our ride's down here and we've got about a three-hour drive. You can sleep in the back."

Sweaty, tired and petulant, Conor swore under his breath and picked up his duffel bag—another artifact from his lightning round at WalMart. "A three-hour drive to where, please, and more importantly will we find any food at all when we get there?"

Without stopping, Sedgwick merely twirled a finger in the air, signaling Conor to follow, but when they reached a battered toy-sized cargo van he slid open the side door and indicated a backpack on the floor inside.

"Food for the road. Knowing you and your hollow leg, I brought plenty. I put in a futon too, and it's mostly highway driving. Should be pretty smooth. Climb aboard."

Conor didn't move. "A Maruti van? What happened to the SUV?"

"Wasn't right for the job," Sedgwick said cryptically.

"Hmm." Conor frowned at the dented exterior. They were big dents, and there were a lot of them.

"How are the brakes?"

"Good horn, good brakes, good luck. That's all you need in this country. Get in the fucking van, McBride. I want to check out how it rides with you in the back."

Once inside, Conor settled against the steel-cage partition separating the driver's cab from the cargo area and opened the backpack. Along with two-litre bottles of water, he found a package of *sheekh kebabs*, a larger one of *chapatis* to wrap around them, and an enormous tin of chicken *biryani*.

"Careful with the *biryani*." Sedgwick lit a cigarette and started the van. "They throw in more chilis down here." After merging with the traffic exiting the airport, he glanced in the rearview mirror. "Did you tell Kate where you were going?"

"I did, of course." Conor took several long swallows of water.

"How did that go?"

"Pretty feckin' rocky. Let's leave it at that."

Neither of them spoke again for a while. Sedgwick smoked and concentrated on the road, threading the van through openings only he could see, while Conor polished off a large share of the provisions. He tried not to think about Kate's face or voice, or the taste of her skin, or anything else that would only remind him how far he was from her.

He'd called her during his high-speed drive to Burlington, and the conversation had been as difficult as he'd dreaded—full of confusion, anger and awkward silences. By the end he'd heard her tired acceptance, and a catch in her voice suggesting she thought herself foolish not to have expected something like this, which troubled him most of all. Conor knew he didn't have a lot of wiggle room with Kate, nor did he expect much. The last man in her life had left her in dramatic fashion, inflicting a psychological violence she'd already been brave enough to survive once. While picking her way through the minefield a second time, she'd reasonably hoped for some small zone of stability and he'd failed to provide it. His only comfort came when she rang him back right before he boarded the flight to Mumbai. The call had been short.

"That Irish thing you say when people are leaving."

"*Slán abhaile.* Safe home." Hunched over in a hard plastic chair, Conor had pressed the heel of one hand to his forehead, aching for her.

"Yes." After a short silence, she'd added, in a whisper, "*Slán abhaile,* Conor."

The back of the van—dark, claustrophobic, smelling of *biryani* and diesel—had no side windows. Conor could only assess their surroundings by peering beyond the cage barrier and through the front windshield. Not that he would have recognized anything. He'd covered a lot of ground in India, but he'd never been this far south. Directly ahead of them he faced the terrifying spectacle of a young woman sitting sidesaddle on the back of a motorcycle, holding on to nothing except the infant in her arms. He averted his eyes, but had nowhere else to turn them other than on a sea of cars and auto rickshaws and the occasional ox cart. Conor stretched out on the futon with his head on the backpack.

"Are you going to tell me where we're off to, or is it a secret?"

"No secret," Sedgwick said. "Just waiting for you to stop sulking. We're going to Mysore. I've discovered Costino is splitting his time between two hotels—one in Bangalore and the other in Mysore. He's managing them."

"Managing hotels? What's that about?"

Sedgwick grunted a laugh. "Seems Tony has a few more brain cells than we gave him credit for—he's got your brother's old job, working for our friend Pawan Kotwal."

Conor shot upright, connecting the dots instantly. "He's laundering Pawan-bhai's money through the hotels?"

"Big time. After he found out Dragonov's twenty million

was missing, he thought you and Thomas had teamed up with Kotwal and pulled a rope-a-dope with the money. Where do you suppose he'd go first for information?"

"The pub in Mumbai."

Sedgwick nodded. "But by the time he got there, Frank had debriefed you in London and knew about it, and he'd already rained a world of shit down on that pub. He had MI6 and the Mumbai police crawling all over, looking for something to lead them to Durgan. For his next brilliant move, Costino went directly to Kotwal, which didn't go as planned. Hang on, here's the expressway."

Conor narrowly avoided being thrown against the opposite wall as the van executed a series of sharp left turns. A less congested road rolled out in front of them, and Sedgwick relaxed.

"Of course, Pawan-bhai had nothing to do with the missing money, and he was bullshit about the pub. He had the Mumbai authorities breathing down his neck, his local money launderer— Thomas—had deserted him, and Robert Durgan, the mastermind of the whole pub operation, wouldn't return messages. Plus, his DEA buddies who'd been so eager for his help on the Dragonov sting had disappeared. So, when Costino showed up he found himself in the cross hairs of one highly pissed off mafia boss. To save his own skin, he struck a deal with Kotwal. He agreed to fill in for Thomas and relocate the money-laundering to this area, and in return Kotwal agreed to provide protection from Dragonov and keep an eye out for you and Thomas. All right, I've got a free hand now—any food left?"

Conor wrapped up a few *kebabs* and slid them through one of the narrow squares in the partition. "And you figured this out, how? I'm guessing it didn't come to you in a dream."

"Almost that good. Pawan-bhai dropped a dime on him."

"No shit." Conor whistled. "Why would he grass on his own man?"

Sedgwick laughed. "Sick of him. Just like us. I questioned Kotwal back in the spring. By then he'd already made his deal with Costino and wanted nothing to do with me, but when I tried him again a few weeks ago he spilled the whole story. He'd warned Costino I was alive and looking for him, then in August he had to warn him Dragonov's people had come sniffing around. That's when Tony contacted Durgan, desperate for some angle to track you down and get the target off his back. He also started demanding more protection from Kotwal—fancy surveillance equipment, extra bodyguards. Pawan-bhai had an inkling he'd put himself on the wrong side of a Russian arms dealer and Costino was a problem he couldn't afford. Now, he wants us to handle the little weasel before he has to."

"This is going to somehow lead us to Robert Durgan?" Conor asked.

"Not quite. It will lead Durgan to us. Make yourself comfortable and I'll tell you how."

Apart from a few clarifying questions, Conor allowed Sedgwick to divulge the plan without interruption, and let the details settle in over a distance of several miles before voicing an opinion. "Sounds overly complicated."

Sedgwick gave a derisive snort. "Life is complicated."

"Exactly. Life is extremely bloody complicated, which is why plans should be simple. That was the take-away wisdom from our last fiasco together."

"It wasn't our fault we got set up. That plan was good and so is this one, and it's not up for discussion."

"I figured as much. I just want to go on the record. 'Overly complicated'." Massaging a cramp in his calf, Conor put a finger through the partition and rattled the wire cage. "Look, I've had enough of the 'prisoner in transport' game. Will you ever pull over and let me come sit in the good boy's seat, now?"

They reached the royal city of Mysore a little after one in the morning. Even in the darkness, Conor could sense a charming old-world appeal in the quiet tree-lined boulevards, but as with most urban centers in India the sporadic street lights revealed more than a few figures sleeping on the sidewalks and in doorways. Motionless in the shadows, they bore an uncomfortable resemblance to shrouded corpses.

From his many months in Mumbai, Conor had grown adept with Hindi, but here most of the storefront signs displayed the rounded decorative script of the Kannada language. It served as another reminder that he'd come to unchartered territory—a southern region where Hindi, and its more recognizable linear script, was not dominant.

They turned at a traffic circle where the statue of a maharajah stood under a golden-domed pavilion, draped with a necklace of fresh marigolds. Beyond the roundabout, a carved stone gate with large, scalloped archways led to a palace that was nothing short of a Moghul emperor's fantasy come to life. The elaborate structure glowed under the moonlight, studded everywhere with domes of rose-colored marble, looking like evenly spaced pomegranates.

"Does somebody live there?" Conor craned his neck to look back as they sped away.

"No clue," Sedgwick said, "but I've got a guidebook in the hotel room and you'll have all day to read it."

A few minutes later they'd left the city center and were in a more thinly settled area. Sedgwick pulled the van off the road and parked next to a waist-high concrete wall marking out a wide, rectangular boundary. Inside, a wider expanse of concrete and a few fragile trees formed a courtyard, serving as a second perimeter. A building shaped like a cinder block sat in the center, four stories tall.

"Hotel Tamarind," Conor read aloud. The neon sign, running down one side of the building in electric pink, was all that relieved the scene's barren ugliness. "He's inside right now?"

"I would have heard something if he wasn't. Come on, let's check in with my partner." Flashing an enigmatic grin, Sedgwick pulled himself up and over the wall, and when Conor had followed he added, "That's him in the auto rickshaw."

Except for a distant echo of barking dogs, there wasn't a sound anywhere around them. A small cluster of cars was parked at one end of the courtyard and the hotel was completely dark, no light or stir of activity even in the lobby. About twenty yards ahead, the rickshaw sat in the shadow of a tree, snugged up to its trunk and facing the front entrance. The figure inside was clearly a large man, although he couldn't be seen in full. He'd stretched one leg out of the vehicle to brace a booted foot on the ground, and his hand had reached up to languidly grasp the rickshaw's yellow canvas roof. The body language was of someone relaxed but ready to spring, and something about the posture looked eerily familiar. When the man shifted, the light from the hotel sign glinted off a thick iron bangle circling his wrist—one of the articles of faith worn by men of the Sikh religion. Conor sucked in a soundless, astonished whoop and pivoted to Sedgwick.

"What the hell is wrong with you?" he hissed. "Why is he here?"

"He wanted to help, and I needed some. We drove down from Mumbai in the van together."

"How is that even possible? He never trusted you."

"Still doesn't. Not much, anyway."

"Nor do I at the moment," Conor snapped. "You shouldn't have dragged him into this. He has a family, for fuck's sake. He has teenaged daughters."

"He also has a drawer full of commendations and medals from the Indian Army. He's more than meets the eye, as I only recently discovered myself."

Conor swallowed an automatic retort and took a breath. "Bishan Singh is in the army?"

"Was," Sedgwick corrected. "Sikh Light Infantry, an elite regiment. He retired with full honors eight years ago after some counter-terrorism action in Assam. Feats of heroism and three bullets to the gut. Wouldn't say much about it. Blushed like a little girl when his wife brought out the medals."

This Conor could easily picture, and he smiled in spite of himself. Bishan Singh, the Mumbai tour guide he'd met on his first day in India, was a brave, humble man of deep emotions, and a good friend who'd helped him out more than once.

"What were you doing at his house?"

Sedgwick dropped his head back to stare at the sky and spoke with exaggerated patience. "Again, I was looking for you. No stone unturned, right? I went to him six months ago and left the poor guy sobbing, thinking you were dead. First chance I had to go again was when I got back from Vermont last month. I gave him the good news, and one thing led to another ..."

"And you told him everything." Conor dismissed the rest of the story with a wave of resignation, already walking toward the auto rickshaw, moving quietly until he was close enough to whisper inside. "*Arrey.* Are you sleeping in there, *yaar*? What sort of watchman are you?"

The auto rickshaw pitched violently as Bishan Singh emerged with great energy but little noise.

"Here he is, mind-blowing MI6, 007 man." His voice was a hushed, melodious rumble. "Something shocking I tell you, absolutely. It's good to see you are still living, my friend."

He wore a turban of jet black, and a matching shirt stretched over his powerful chest. As always, his beard was immaculate, and his smile flashed bright in the darkness. He seized Conor's forearms at the elbows and held them in a tight grip. A restrained display of affection, but so heartfelt it carried more impact than a bear hug.

Although still appalled to think his friend had been drafted into the operation, Conor had to admit he was glad to have him on board. His friend matched gentle affability and compassion with an imposing physical presence, giving Conor more confidence for the whole enterprise. Military service was a celebrated part of Sikh heritage; he shouldn't have been surprised to discover his erstwhile tour guide was a decorated veteran.

"It's good to see you as well, Bishan Singh. Sorry I didn't call or write."

They reminisced quietly for a minute, until Sedgwick abruptly shut them down. "Yeah, this is really touching, but Bishan is still on duty." He dropped his cigarette to the ground and stepped on it. "Since I'm relieving him at six in the morning, I'd like to get some sleep. Let's go, McBride. Bishan booked the room but they lock up at midnight. We'll break in through the back and sneak up the stairwell."

With a long-suffering sigh, Conor turned to follow, then looked again at the deserted courtyard and the dark, silent hotel.

"Hang on." He grabbed Sedgwick's arm, pulling him to a stop. "Let's do this now. Why wait?"

"Why wait?" Sedgwick snorted. "How about because I don't want you falling asleep in the middle of everything. You've been traveling for almost twenty-four hours. The plan is for you to get a good night's sleep—"

"I slept on the plane," Conor lied.

"And we'll make sure you eat a nice big breakfast—" Sedgwick continued as if he'd not spoken.

"And then we'll sit and watch a cricket match on the telly? Waiting for two in the morning to come around again?" Conor shook his head. "Come here now, listen for a minute and look around you. It's dark and dead quiet. We're all here and we know our man is inside. The conditions are brilliant. They'll never get better, so why risk them getting worse? Let's do this now."

Scowling, Sedgwick took a few steps away and surveyed the courtyard. After a tense moment he looked at Bishan, grinning sheepishly.

"Son of a bitch. He's right. The fiddle-playing farmer is right." He reached into his pocket and pulled out the keys. "Go get the van, Bishan. I'll open the gate."

The muscular Sikh caught the keys in one hand. Conor heard him chuckling as he walked toward the van, shaking his head.

"Mind-blowing MI6 man."

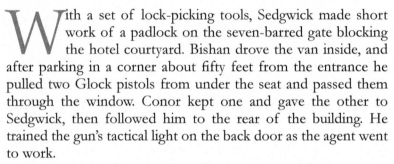

29

With a set of lock-picking tools, Sedgwick made short work of a padlock on the seven-barred gate blocking the hotel courtyard. Bishan drove the van inside, and after parking in a corner about fifty feet from the entrance he pulled two Glock pistols from under the seat and passed them through the window. Conor kept one and gave the other to Sedgwick, then followed him to the rear of the building. He trained the gun's tactical light on the back door as the agent went to work.

"I sent Bishan in yesterday to book a room and do the recon," Sedgwick said. "The manager's suite is on the ground floor, down a hallway next to the front desk." He swiveled the tension wrench, and the bolt slid soundlessly back into its assembly. "He says the place is a block of hollowed out marble, everything echoes. So, be light on your feet and don't even whisper."

They crept into the hotel, which was like entering a mausoleum—everything faced in polished white marble, lobby walls glistening as though under a curtain of water. By contrast, the front desk and wall behind it were of stainless steel, combined with tiles in the same electric pink that appeared on the building's exterior. The air, clean and cool compared to the humidity outdoors, carried a slight aroma of incense.

Sedgwick moved behind the desk to the end of the wall and held up a fist, signaling Conor to stop. He slid an eye around its edge, uncurled his hand to show two fingers, and sketched a quick outline in the air. Two bodyguards, posted at the door. He turned to Conor, and with a contemptuous smirk crossed his arms over his chest. Sleeping.

Tucking his Glock behind his back, Sedgwick held out a hand and Conor handed over his own gun. The agent grabbed the muzzle, cleared his throat loudly, and stepped away from the wall, hands raised. Getting no reaction from the sleeping pair he impatiently knocked the butt of the Glock against the wall's stainless steel edge, raising a sound like a gong being rung, and got immediate results. Conor heard sluggish exclamations and a scrape of chairs.

"Hi, boys. Speak English? Hindi? Marathi?" Sedgwick offered the options with a few words in the corresponding languages before adding in English, "I hope at least one of those works because I can't speak a friggin' word of Kannada."

"Who are you?" A throaty voice challenged him in English. "Throw the gun away! Throw it away!"

"How about if I lay it down?" Hands still raised, Sedgwick slowly crouched and placed the weapon on the floor. "Okay? We're good? Maybe you can stop pointing that one at me?"

He wiggled one finger for emphasis and Conor nodded. Only one gun.

"I've got a friend with me," Sedgwick continued. "We want to talk to you for a minute. Don't shoot him. He's not armed."

Conor took a breath, and raising his hands stepped away from the wall. The men at the end of the hallway shifted nervously as he came into view. Their faces were indistinct but he could make out their general shape—not as big as he'd feared, not as small as he'd hoped.

"It's all right. Pawan-bhai sent us." Sedgwick added quiet words of reassurance as he started down the hall. Conor matched his pace, hands still raised, chest-high. Gradually, the features of the bodyguard in front of him grew clear—large, but more fleshy than muscular, pockmarked face, one droopy eye pointing at the wall while the other one stared at Conor. He was also the one with the gun. When they came within four feet, Sedgwick stopped, and offering both men a casual smile murmured, "Okay, now."

Conor went for the hand holding the gun, cracking the back of it on the doorjamb, and used the side of his other hand to deliver a hard chopping blow to the Adam's apple. The man made no sound, at first. His droopy eye popped wide open as he staggered back, and by the time he'd gathered enough breath to begin gagging he was pressed face-first against the wall with his own weapon jammed under his ribs. Conor looked down to his left and saw Sedgwick squatting on the floor with one knee on the second bodyguard's back. Unlike his older colleague the man was young and fit, but with a gun pointed at his head he appeared eager to obey the command to remain still.

"*Shabash*," Sedgwick said—the Hindi expression for "well done"—and grinned up at Conor. "I'm guessing yours is the guy in charge. Turn him around." Conor obliged, keeping the gun in place, and Sedgwick addressed the older man in a conversational tone. "Look, sorry to ruin your snooze, but we're taking the manager on a trip, with Pawan-bhai's blessing. I don't expect you to take my word for it, and since car chases aren't really my thing, let's give the big boss a call, make sure we're all on the same page. Sound good? Here, you can use my phone. Save your minutes."

The man accepted the mobile, fumbling as he continued to choke and groan pitifully. He placed the call, and from the conversation it appeared he was moving through Pawan Kotwal's command structure. At last, he stood a bit straighter, listening.

"Yes, *bhai*. Thank you, *bhai*." He forced some energy into his strangled voice. "Good night, sir." He closed the phone and nodded to the young man on the floor, then dug a hotel room key from his pocket and offered it to Sedgwick. "Late night food bazaar is there, near railway station. We will be taking chai for some little while."

"Fantastic idea." Sedgwick beamed at him. "Just the thing for a sore throat."

"Pawan-bhai is saying your friend is lucky you reached first. Others will be coming."

"Thanks. Good to know. Sounds like he's about to be in hot demand."

With muttered resentments, the two bodyguards retreated up the hall and out the back. Conor retrieved his own gun from the floor near the front desk and Sedgwick eased Costino's door open. It moved a few inches before catching on the chain lock.

"Aha." The agent gave the chain a playful poke. "I guess we're done with the quiet part."

Conor's ears were still ringing from the marble-amplified explosion of Sedgwick's foot on the door when he heard the agent—already at the far end of the suite—send a boot crashing against another one. Hurrying to catch up, Conor raced over the polished floor of the living room, dodging an obstacle course of rattan chairs and glass-topped tables. He followed Sedgwick into the bedroom and found him already pulling Tony Costino— naked and terrified—from a cocoon of yellow silk sheets. The agent dragged him across the king-sized bed, dumping him on the floor and delivering a kick to his abdomen. Costino cried out and rolled into a fetal position, his face hidden. Sedgwick bent to grab a handful of hair and lifted him up to look in his eyes.

"Surprise, Tony," he said, low and sinister. He slammed Costino's face down and straightened. "Love the Sasquatch thing you've got going on. Put on some fucking clothes. We're taking a ride."

Conor could see the man was in fact a wilder, hairier version of the DEA agent he'd met in Mumbai, ten months earlier. At their first disconcerting meeting, Tony Costino had appeared as a neatly pressed bureaucrat with a 1950s haircut, complete with a razor-sharp part down the side. Slender, apple-cheeked, eager to please—the type of dark-suited young man who turns up on doorsteps, offering pamphlets. Now, he appeared older, and had gained at least ten pounds of paunch. His light-brown hair had grown into a waving mane that almost reached his shoulders, and a thick beard obscured his face and neck. Small, half moons of pink skin peeked out below his eyes, which appeared unchanged. Round and pale blue, they'd often defaulted to a deceptively credulous expression—the gentle simpleton amazed by everything he sees—but they seemed genuinely stunned when they came to rest on Conor's face.

"I was told you'd left India." He gasped a little as he climbed to his feet. "Where's Thomas? Did he come back with you?"

Conor slowly shook his head, and slammed a right hook against Costino's jaw. It toppled him backward, and his skull connected hard with the marble floor.

"No," he said, breaking the silence he'd maintained since entering the hotel. "Thomas isn't coming back."

"Might have been better if you hadn't knocked him senseless."

Sedgwick was at the wheel of the van once more, Bishan in the seat next to him, and Conor was again sitting cross-legged in the rear with little visibility, but he recognized their route as the one they'd come in on when the Gothic structure of St. Philomena's church loomed ahead of them.

"I seem to remember you getting in a few shots as well. Anyway, I'm fairly sure he's faking now." He braced a foot against Costino's back to keep him from rolling off the futon. The captive remained unresponsive, lying with his face to the wall of the van, wearing the handcuffs Sedgwick had slapped on after they'd managed to get him dressed. When they were into the more remote village areas with Mysore a half-hour behind them, Bishan offered a suggestion.

"Perhaps you could be sharing some water with him, *yaar.* Good refreshment for head-clearing, *na?*"

Taking a bottle from the backpack, Conor pulled at the thatch of beard and splashed a little water into the open mouth that appeared. Costino wrenched away and bolted up, coughing with melodramatic force.

"You're waterboarding me."

"If you call that waterboarding, I don't think you know how it works." Conor offered him the bottle. "Drink some, asshole. Might help the headache. And get busy talking. We want the status of your relationship with Robert Durgan."

Costino gave him a blank look. "That guy Walker met in Geneva? The one Thomas was working for? Don't know him."

In a swerving move that threw them all off balance, Sedgwick pulled the van to the side of the road and stopped. He put an arm on the back of his seat and turned to stare at Costino through the steel mesh barrier. "Listen. I doubt waterboarding was part of McBride's operational training. Even if I'm wrong he's got too many scruples to try it on you. But me? You know me better, don't you, Tony? What you also need to understand is that there's a stagnant pond two miles up this road. It's probably got a thousand kinds of bacteria that will eat you from the inside out, and in five minutes I'll be throwing the shit down your throat in buckets if you don't stop dicking around. Think you can help us out, here?"

Costino slouched in submission and nodded. "Sure. Why not? I'm so damned tired of all of this."

"Excellent." Facing forward, Sedgwick put the van in gear. "Your witness, Agent McBride."

"Let's not waste time on what we already know," Conor said.

"You sold out the DEA's operation to capture Dragonov—" The shaggy head begin wagging in protest and he grabbed a handful of Costino's tangled hair, pulling his neck back sharply. "Spare us the Little Boy Blue act, you minging wanker. You sold out your team; two of them are dead because of you—your boss and my brother, and a lot of other people besides. Dragonov promised you a cut of that twenty million I'm sure, but you found out pretty quickly he never got the money, that the whole thing was a massive fuck-up and that you were in trouble."

"Because you and Thomas stole the money instead."

"We didn't steal anything."

"Where the hell is it, then?" Costino shouted.

"You're the one in handcuffs, Tony." Conor released Costino's hair and sat back. "You don't get to ask the questions. So, you wanted to find us, and at the end of August you sent Durgan an email saying you'd make life difficult for him if he didn't help you. He said he'd get back to you. What happened next?"

"This isn't even the right place to start, but fine. Whatever." Sighing, Costino rubbed a hand against his head and winced. "After I got his first response I set up a more secure communication channel, and after that he gave me the run-around. Told me you'd gone to Ireland at the end of March before leaving for the States. He knew exactly where to find you, but you were too close to something he had in the works and he wouldn't risk having me come in at the wrong time. He said I'd have to wait for a couple of months."

"Until after her birthday," Conor said under his breath.

"Whose birthday?"

"Never mind. What happened next?"

"I tried some arm-twisting but I think he could tell I had no leverage. He stopped communicating, and I figured I was screwed. Then, he got back online with me a week ago. Said he'd trade information for a passport and some cash, and a plane ticket. I guess he couldn't travel under the name that—" Costino faltered, appearing undecided about how to continue, before finishing with a shrug. "So that was the deal. He needed someone to hook him up."

"And he thought a DEA agent desperate for his help could do that for him."

"Sort of, but not exactly." Costino gave an odd, ironic smile. "Like I said, this isn't the right place—"

"Yeah, sure, not the right place to start. I got that the first time," Conor replied acidly. "And so why don't you stop smirking and feck-acting and tell us where the right place is."

Instead of a reply, the next thing Conor heard was a remarkably explicit obscenity from Bishan Singh. He felt a transient weightlessness as Sedgwick—also swearing—hit the brakes. Conor sailed forward, stopping only when his shoulder bounced off one of the steel posts on the wire-caged partition. Costino tumbled up next to him and caught a knee against his recently sutured left side, landing in the exact spot that was still the most tender. Conor doubled over, gasping, and chimed in with his own piece of profanity.

"What the hell is this?" Sedgwick said, when the van had fishtailed to a stop.

In front of them a car sat sideways across the road surrounded by at least a dozen people, all of them talking and gesturing in animated bursts. The car was a white Ambassador, nearly as common on the roads of India as the yellow-topped auto rickshaw, its vintage bulbous shape a copy of the UK's beloved Morris Minor. Although the vehicle appeared undamaged the driver's side door was open, and a man—presumably the driver— was propped on the ground against the rear tire. If injured, he was getting little assistance. The onlookers were paying the man scant attention, but as Sedgwick snapped on the high beams to illuminate the scene they all suddenly took a keen interest in the

Maruti van. Bishan sucked in his cheeks and released them with a smack. He growled another oath in Hindi and put a restraining hand on Sedgwick's arm.

"*Arrey*, don't be leaving the car, man. This is some rubbish going on, here."

Sedgwick nodded. "I get it, don't worry. It's like a Bollywood set piece. Problem is, I don't think we can go around them."

"What's happening?" Conor rubbed a hand over his ribs and gave Costino an irritable shove.

"Traffic accident scam," Bishan said. "A racket for some of these villagers. This chap lying down is playing hurt or dead. They will be saying we have done this, and will demand money for injuries or funeral. If we refuse, they will threaten with police and lawsuit, and maybe more if we are getting outside this car. So remain inside, Conor, and lock the door."

"Stay in and stay down, but lock and load," Sedgwick added. "Both guns are in jail back there with you, in the backpack. Operational failure. My bad."

"Jesus and Mary." Conor pulled the bag forward, the zipper squealing a pointed note of protest as it scraped over the metal floor. "Overly complicated. As I think I said. Overly. Bloody. Complicated. Oh, and by the way, the lock on this sliding door is broken."

"Undo these and let me have one of the guns." Costino rattled his handcuffs. "I can help."

"Steady on there, Jesse James." Conor pointed with the Glock to the rear of the van. "Shift yourself that way and keep your head down."

While Costino scuttled to the back Conor peeked through the partition, warily eyeing the villagers as they milled in and out of the headlight beams like circling moths. How many were active participants and which merely spectators was impossible to judge, as was the question of whether any of them had weapons.

Most of the figures were wrapped in colorless homespun shawls that might be concealing anything.

For a few minutes, it appeared the thing would be resolved without any more drama than was already in play. Sedgwick rolled down his window to the apparent ringleader—a youth who seemed to fancy himself an action hero. He wore tight-fitting jeans, and a red-and-blue madras shirt unbuttoned to his navel. The effect was undermined by his narrow, skeletal chest.

The discussion proceeded in Kannada with Bishan translating for the young man, who described a predictably implausible scenario. His uncle had been blinded from afar by the van's bright headlights. He'd struck a boulder, had lost control and was thrown from the car. He was gravely injured, and it would need some twenty thousand rupees to make him well.

At this, Sedgwick laughed out loud. "Tell him to knock off a zero and we'll have a deal."

Bishan translated the counter-offer, which got an immediate and extremely negative reception. The crowd surged forward and Sedgwick hastily rolled up the window as they started rocking the van back and forth, beating at its sides. The handle next to Conor began to turn and he shot out a hand to hold the sliding door in place.

"Maybe you should up the offer," he suggested.

"I was going to need to take a collection for the first one. I've only got about fifteen hundred in my pocket." Sedgwick looked at Bishan, who offered a placid head wag.

"At most, three hundred, but this is expected. They will be wanting to drive one of us to nearest cash machine."

"Hmm, I wonder if that's why the black sedan has been tailing us." Sedgwick peered into his side rearview mirror. "I picked it up ten miles back, and it just pulled over about twenty yards behind us. Time to get your Rambo on, McBride. Are you up for it?"

At that, the side window next to Sedgwick exploded under the blow of a steel-tipped stick and several pairs of hands fastened on the agent's head and shoulders, trying to drag him through the shattered opening. Bishan grabbed him around the waist to hold him inside, spewing threats and invective, while Conor, releasing his grip on the handle, had barely enough time to spin onto his back and raise his feet as the door slid open with a violent crash. He planted both boots squarely in the solar plexus of the figure who appeared in the doorway, and launched himself out. The man cried out, hurtling backward and taking down those directly behind him. Belatedly, Conor remembered the second Glock. He put his left hand back, scrabbling along the floor, and snatched up the gun before Costino reached it. He slammed the door shut and turned to brandish both weapons at the crowd, firing two rounds into the ground and giving what he hoped sounded like a convincing vengeful roar.

However it sounded, he was offering hotter action than the villagers had in mind. They began scattering off the sides of the road, melting into the darkness, except for the ringleader. Conor quickly circled around the front of the van to the driver's side, and found Sedgwick half out of the window with his head against its frame, the point of a kitchen knife pressed to his neck. Agitated, the young man was babbling at Bishan in Kannada.

"He's afraid you will shoot him," Bishan explained. "He says if you don't surrender the guns he will cut Sedgwick's throat."

"Right. Tell him he's got it arseways. If he doesn't drop the knife, I *will* shoot him."

Bishan translated this proposition, appearing to add several thoughts of his own in a stern, commanding tone. Conor kept a close eye on the knife, but suddenly saw two bulky figures ahead in the darkness moving into crouched positions. Not villagers. He was pretty sure they were not even Indian.

"Get down!" Conor hit the ground himself, urgently waving

at the youth. "Bishan, tell him to—"

The first shots sounded before he'd finished. Luckily, they went wide of the mark, since the young hoodlum in front of him was frozen in place. Returning fire, Conor crab-walked forward, yanked him down and rolled him under the van. One of the figures had slumped to the ground, but the other had disappeared, darting behind the back of the van.

Conor pitched one of the Glocks up through the shattered window. "A little help here, Bishan. One is down, and the second is coming around to you."

He moved cautiously forward, weapon poised, and confirmed the man was dead as several more rounds of gunfire erupted. Conor stood motionless in the tense silence that followed until Bishan gave the all-clear signal, then he took a shaking breath and bent to search the man's pockets. When he'd found what he was looking for he worked his way up to the black sedan, gun forward, confirming no other passengers were inside or lurking nearby, and then joined the others. He found Bishan engaged in a similar pocket-picking exercise while Sedgwick, bleeding steadily from a shoulder wound, sat in the doorway of the van. The still-handcuffed Costino was sitting next to him.

"Lucky night for you after all, Tony." Conor tossed the Russian passport at his chest. "If we hadn't come along, Dragonov's hitmen would have killed you by now. Looks like Pawan Kotwal's protection isn't what it used to be."

30

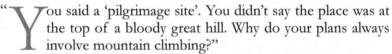

"You said a 'pilgrimage site'. You didn't say the place was at the top of a bloody great hill. Why do your plans always involve mountain climbing?"

"You sound like we're scaling the Khumbu Glacier. It's not that high, and there's a staircase."

"Which we can only climb after taking our shoes off."

Sedgwick glared back over his shoulder at Conor. "Who's going to know if we don't?"

"I will."

He bent to untie his boots before shifting to do the same for their shackled prisoner, while Sedgwick set about picking another gate lock to get them into the grounds of the shrine. At close to three in the morning they'd reached the shuttered, sleeping hamlet of Shravanabelagola, fifty miles from Mysore and far more modest than its elaborate name suggested. The town was squeezed between two dome-shaped hills, the tallest topped by one of the Jain religion's most important centers of pilgrimage. Seeking distraction while Bishan parked the van in a less conspicuous location, Conor read the Tourist Board's sign posted at the front entrance, by the light of a still-glowing full moon. In addition to a complex of ancient temples spread over the hillside above them, the site held India's largest megalithic monument—an enormous tenth-century statue carved from a single piece of granite, depicting the enlightenment of a prince called Bahubali. As he took in the historical details he kept one eye on Costino, but it was hardly necessary. The captive had slumped into a plastic chair in front of the gate and was gazing at the worn, uneven staircase carved into the barren hillside. Conor couldn't deny a quiver of fellowship with his glum resignation.

They were all exhausted at this point, and Sedgwick—without fooling anyone—was irritably pretending his shoulder wasn't a source of constant, throbbing pain. He hadn't suffered a bullet injury, as Conor at first assumed, but a knife wound, accidentally inflicted by the young carjacker as Conor yanked him to the ground. Miraculously missing the agent's jugular, the knife had carved a deep, ugly laceration along his shoulder. This required a quick rearrangement of roles and priorities as they hurried to escape the scene, leaving two dead Russians and a collection of stunned villagers in their wake. Bishan took the wheel, Costino the passenger seat, and Sedgwick joined Conor in the rear of the van. To Conor's relief a well-stocked first aid kit proved as ubiquitous an item for Curtis Sedgwick as the Stanley thermos was for Frank Murdoch. He washed the wound as best he could, and when the bleeding had slowed, Bishan switched on the light in the cargo area and pulled into a small grove of palm trees off the main road. Conor snapped on a pair of latex gloves and picked up a package containing a pre-threaded surgical needle, while Sedgwick smoked and watched with nervous attention.

"Your training included this?"

"Yeah, of course." Conor tore open another package he'd lifted from the kit. "Here's an injectable dose of codeine, which you're going to need. Hike down your trousers a bit. I'll stick the needle in above your hip."

"No shots. Get on with it, I'll be fine."

"Look, the only thing I ever stitched was a pig's foot, so leave off the heroics and let me—"

"This isn't about heroics, it's about survival."

Conor reflexively jerked his hand back, startled by his vehemence. Sedgwick relaxed, and with a shrug of apology took the syringe and tossed it into the kit. "More than that, it's about a promise. Codeine is an opium alkaloid, Conor. I can't risk the stuff."

"Damn. I wasn't thinking. I'm sorry." Conor removed the curved needle from its packaging. "Really sorry, because I think this will hurt like hell."

"Yeah, thanks. Impressive bedside manner, dude." Sedgwick put on a game smile. "Pig's foot, huh?"

"An embalmed one, and I wouldn't even say I paid much attention. The first-aid teacher was my weapons instructor, and at the time I was trying to get her into bed with me."

Sedgwick's smile widened. "And?"

"Didn't go quite the way I expected. Just as well, really. We weren't suited." Conor took a firm grip on the shaft of the needle and added quietly, "First time I've understood what that means."

After the procedure and by unspoken agreement, they deferred the interrogation of Costino and completed the drive in silence, giving Sedgwick a chance to rest and allowing their combined tension and adrenalin to dissipate. From the agent's movements now, Conor could tell the shoulder was stiffening, but the stitches were holding. Sedgwick slowly straightened from the lock and the entrance gate swung open with a low, rusty groan.

When Bishan reappeared Sedgwick asked him to remain below and stand guard. Costino had not left his seat, but now shifted to rest his head in his hands, long hair falling forward to obscure his face. "If this is all so you can shoot me and drop me off a cliff, I'd rather skip the death march and take the bullet right here."

"Well heck, why didn't I think of that?" As though released from a spring, Sedgwick flew over to him and planted the muzzle of his Glock against Costino's exposed neck.

The younger man stiffened, but made no sound. He stared straight ahead at Conor, his water-blue eyes expressionless. After a few seconds Sedgwick removed the gun, speaking more gently as he bent to pull at the laces of his own boots. "You're at a holy site, Tony. Have a little faith. After all, we already saved your ass once tonight."

Sedgwick distributed penlights for navigating the staircase, afraid anything brighter might draw attention. They didn't need them, anyway. The moon continued to guide their footsteps, tracking their progress while gradually withdrawing to the horizon. They spared no energy for conversation, which gave Conor a little too much time to be alone with his thoughts.

He'd not been able to avoid looking into the face of the man he'd shot, or—why not the blunt truth? —the man he'd killed. The latest man he'd killed. An image of the Russian's staring, lifeless eyes took hold, growing larger as though rising through water. He tightened his jaw and caught at the railing along the staircase, the chilly iron steadying him as he squeezed the vision from his mind.

"You all right?" Sedgwick asked, from behind.

"Fine. You?"

The agent spat a short-tempered affirmative, panting with exertion. Near the summit, a rough-hewn, columned passage served as the entrance to the walled complex. Moving through the humid, mineral odor of its interior, they continued up the diminishing staircase until it sank into the hillside, and walked onto an expanse of rock that looked like the pockmarked surface of an alien planet. In front of them, the first Jain temple sat loftily atop a terrace supported on all sides by stone buttresses. To their right, a second flagstone terrace with a small shrine formed a lookout point, providing a view of the sister hillside and the town nestled in between. A temple tank dominated the vista below, a massive square acre of water standing out from the darkness like a polished, moss-green jewel. When they reached the shrine, Sedgwick sank against the side of its covered portico and Costino flopped on the stairs next to him, chest heaving.

It made a change for Conor, realizing for once he'd come through in better shape than his companions. While waiting for them to catch their breath, he ducked into the shrine's tiny sanctuary and turned his penlight on the object of worship. The dark, tombstone-shaped slab featured haloed figures carved in relief, resembling a blend of pagan and Christian symbolism. As his gaze lingered over the image, he sensed the approach of something ancient and transcendent, the response to a subconscious summons. A current pulsed at the surface of his skin, but Conor's muscles contracted in resistance. He felt its heat pull away from him like a wave subsiding, leaving a sharp, forlorn chill hanging in the air. He took in a quick, shivering breath and stepped outside.

With his socks catching on rough bits of stone he walked further up the terrace, peering at the summit. The serene head and shoulders of the colossus Bahubali gazed out above the walls of the central temple. There was no noise of birdsong or other night sounds—the air was wrapped in deep, primordial silence, which made a sudden stirring in the trees seem much louder. A spectral procession of figures emerged, crawling over the ground in spasmodic rhythm, a halfhearted imitation of human movement. The unearthly tableau made the hair on his neck stand at attention, until one of the figures paused and turned a flat, silver-bearded black face toward him. A gray langur monkey, out for a pre-dawn excursion with his troop. Conor expelled a half-groaning gust of air, and gave a start as a voice shattered the silence even more dramatically.

"McBride, what the hell? Are you taking a leak or something?"

Conor returned to the shrine, an aura of heightened awareness still tingling through him. He descended a few steps and took a seat next to Sedgwick, who sensed his mood and flicked the penlight in his face.

"What's wrong?"

"Nothing's wrong." He chewed his lip while studying Costino, struck once again by the change in the man. Not a trace remained of the boyish, cherubic innocence he'd affected. The pretense had been dropped, and something in the attitude of his hanging head and rounded shoulders suggested a bone-deep weariness Conor wanted to understand. "Earlier, you said you were tired of it all. Tired of what?"

After a slight hesitation, Costino replied without raising his head. "Of the game. Of never being able to tell the truth, never getting to go home. Tired of feeling shitty about myself. You're told you're one of the good guys. You keep convincing yourself it's true. When you have to admit it's not, you tell yourself there are no good guys. That's what I'm tired of; aren't you?"

A startled pause followed before Sedgwick shifted uncomfortably on the step and exploded. "Who gives a fuck what he's tired of? We need to get back on track with this."

"Look, there's something important here and we're missing it." Conor turned again to Costino, who seemed to be regretting his confessional moment. He'd twisted himself around on the stairs to stare up at them, nervous and alert.

"Never mind. Doesn't matter, anyway."

"Yeah, well I think it probably does. Time to come clean. Tell us what we don't know." The aggressive approach getting no response at all, Conor tried a different one, angling his head in sympathy. "You're tired, Tony. You just said so and you sure as hell look it. Why not say what we're missing? Where's the right place to start?"

He said nothing more; he could see it was coming. Costino's resistance crumbled like a landslide in slow motion. Conor gripped Sedgwick's good shoulder, holding his impatience in check while their captive inched toward surrender. It was worth the wait.

"The right place is with Robert Ryan Fitzpatrick, alias Michael Fitzpatrick, alias Robert Durgan. I supplied the passport for that last one. I was his CIA case officer. My first assignment." Costino scratched at his unkempt beard and dropped his head again. "I never worked for the DEA during the Dragonov operation. The CIA embedded me in your team and my job was to keep them briefed. My second assignment, and the last."

The silence around them became absolute. Conor couldn't tell if something had happened to his ears or if everything in the universe had been struck dumb, incapable of speech or sound. He and Sedgwick eventually emerged from the void with different but simultaneous objections.

"You expect us to believe Robert Durgan is a CIA agent?"

"Langley would never have the balls to embed a covert operative in a federal agency."

"The DEA knew," Costino replied quietly. "They just didn't tell your boss. Walker never knew a thing." He looked at Conor. "I wouldn't call Durgan an agent, no. He's a psychopathic criminal, but the Agency thought he could be useful."

"This is a load of crap," Sedgwick said.

Costino shrugged. "Tell yourself that, if you need to. I don't blame you. The truth is pretty pathetic. Conor got sent to India to convince his brother to help MI6 catch a guy they didn't even realize was the same paramilitary informant they gave a passport to twelve years ago. A passport they got from the CIA, who then used him and his Indian mafia connections for their own operation. When the DEA stumbled into it, they decided playing ball and covering their ass was more important than taking out a

Russian arms dealer. Seems like the definition of an inter-agency cluster-fuck. What do you think?"

Next to him, Conor detected the rank odor of sweat soaking through Sedgwick's shirt, mingling with what had dried earlier. He sensed his partner's intense fury winding up, getting close to a point of no return. The Glock pistols had been stowed in the backpack on the platform behind them. Conor turned quickly with the intention of securing the bag, but Sedgwick shot out a hand, fastening on his wrist.

"Don't," he said hoarsely. "Just ... don't. We need to hear this from the beginning."

"You feckin' thought it was *me* going to shoot him?!" Conor pulled his hand free.

His rage punctured, Sedgwick blinked at him. "You thought I was?"

"Oh merciful hour, what are we like?" Conor rubbed his eyes and waved at Costino. "From the beginning. Go on, for fuck's sake. We're all ears, and apparently neither of us is going to shoot you."

Pulling at his beard, Costino rose and began a restless circuit back and forth in front of them. "It started seven years ago. The CIA wanted to assess the Mumbai mafia—their reach and potential for serving as a financial conduit for extremists. They assigned me to collect intel on Pawan Kotwal and infiltrate his inner circle. So, I get started. I find out the FBI had targeted his New York restaurants for money-laundering as part of an investigation on a guy named Michael Fitzpatrick. Along with being tight with Kotwal, he's washing money for a bunch of other restaurants, and has a reputation for being a scary bastard who works alone and might have killed at least three clients who got on his bad side. I throw the name into the CIA database and out came the story: MI6 had struck a deal with the IRA, if you can believe that. The IRA was going to dismember the IPLO, and they wanted a US passport and safe passage for their informant, Robert Ryan Fitzpatrick. The passport got issued in the name of Michael Fitzpatrick. I do more research, find out where Fitzpatrick works, where he lives, that he's landed himself a rich wife descended from a royal family. Bavarian or something—"

Costino whirled at the sound of a loud rustling. Conor squinted at the adjacent Jain temple, and caught a glimpse of the shadowy line of figures moving amongst the trees.

"Only monkeys," he said, stretching his 'talent for repose' to its limit. "Keep going."

Costino released his breath. "Eventually, I barge in on the FBI operation spouting a lot of national security bullshit and tell them Fitzpatrick is ours. We get a team together and scoop him up at his office one evening, throw him into a van, and drag him and all his files off to a safe house. The stuff we pull off his computer shows he clearly did kill those three restaurant clients, and he's got an elaborate scheme for getting rid of his wife after—"

He angled his head at Conor, appearing curious. "After she'd turned thirty and inherited a fortune. You said something about that earlier. Do you know her?" Not trusting his voice, Conor met the question with silence and let Sedgwick vent a little steam before his indignation smothered him.

"Stop pacing and twisting and pausing," he roared. "If you can't stand still then sit the fuck down. We haven't got much time before dawn."

Costino sat at the foot of the steps, but otherwise ignored the outburst. "The bastard made me sick. I suggested throwing him back to the FBI, but the word came down that we wanted him. So I tell him he can cooperate on our Kotwal operation, or end up extradited to a prison in Northern Ireland where some loyal republican would probably stick a shiv between his ribs. I also tell him that life under his current alias has to end and he can never go back to that name. Michael Fitzpatrick is finished."

He spread his hands in a hopeless gesture. "I was trying to protect the wife, inoculate her. If we killed off Michael Fitzpatrick, he couldn't inherit her fortune. He might think of some other way to get at it, but maybe not involving murder. It was the only part of the scenario he didn't like, and of course he couldn't tell me why. I tell him to sleep on it and lock him down for the night, but two hours later he asks to see me, and says he'll play ball. He's got another alias he'd started using with Pawan Kotwal—Robert Durgan. Even better, he's already got a plan for working with him in Mumbai—an Irish bar that will be the central hub for processing all Kotwal's money. He just needs a couple more months to secure the capital that he'd agreed to bring to the deal. Instant infiltration. It was like a gift, and I grabbed it."

"The capital was the grant money," Sedgwick mused. "He was waiting for the application Thomas submitted to be awarded."

Costino nodded. "Although, I didn't know anything about Thomas at the time. The exit strategy was pretty simple. The wife's family has a place on Long Island Sound. He was supposed to take one of their boats out, make a production out of swamping it and falling overboard in case any witnesses saw him. I'd be in a boat nearby with a few other staffers. We'd discreetly haul him out, stow him below, and then call the Coast Guard. We set a date for the end of August, but on the day, he shows up in the Sound with the wife and some other guy on board. Freaked us out, but it didn't matter. The whole thing actually appeared more convincing with the other guy sailing because he clearly didn't know what the hell he was doing. I guess that was Thomas. Obviously, he and I never discussed it."

"Sorry. I need a break." Conor abruptly got to his feet. Keeping his voice steady he added, "Don't stop. I'll catch up in a minute."

He headed away from them, walking up the steps and around

to the rear of the shrine. Bracing his back against the cool stone he slid to the ground, acknowledging an emotion he'd avoided until now. His brother never told him of his involvement in the macabre business of "killing off" Michael Fitzpatrick. On the first day of their reunion in Mumbai Thomas had confessed everything else about his entanglement with Robert Durgan, but had kept this episode entirely hidden. Because of his shame? Undoubtedly. He'd played along in a reckless plan involving an innocent woman, a scheme that inflicted lasting trauma and nearly resulted in her death. Of course he was ashamed. Conor was ashamed of him as well, and felt guilty for it, and heartbroken that he'd never be able to confront his brother and clear the air.

"He saved her, though," Conor said aloud, as if advocating for his brother's soul. "He saved her, and stayed with her." He remembered Kate's words as she described her harrowing experience and its aftermath.

He let me rage at him—hit him even—and then he held me while I cried. He never left my side that day, but he hardly ever said a word.

31

After a few minutes Conor returned and got an update on what he'd missed. Following the escapade in Long Island Sound, Costino left New York on a flight to Mumbai with the newly christened Robert Durgan in a seat six rows in front of him. They met once a week in clandestine locations while Thomas and a team of carpenters worked on the pub. Costino knew of Thomas by then, but the two of them remained strangers, and he was certain Thomas never had an inkling of Durgan's involvement with the CIA. When the pub opened and the money—and intelligence—began flowing, Costino returned home, and discovered on a return trip in October that Durgan had vanished. He was no longer in Mumbai, but had left a note behind assuring his continued cooperation.

"I should have reported he'd disappeared, but I didn't. I thought it would wreck my career," Costino said. "I didn't want to admit I'd screwed up my first assignment, especially since the intelligence kept coming. In the note, Durgan said Thomas would send the reports on the business to him, and he'd continue to forward everything using the channel we'd established. Which is exactly what happened, and he sent decent stuff—all the transactions, all the players involved—so I decided to ignore the fact I had no idea where he'd gone. The next time I had any contact with him was when we set up the Geneva meeting to try and recruit him for the Dragonov operation. When Walker and

I first met with Kotwal, he handed over Durgan's email address without even blinking. That was a little embarrassing."

"Yeah, the Dragonov operation. About that." Sedgwick dropped a cigarette butt on the growing pile at his feet.

"Right. About that." Costino got up to pace, then apparently remembering it had been an irritant, sat down again.

The temple complex still lay shrouded in darkness, but far below they heard the distant sound of an occasional horn, and the tractor-like growl of auto rickshaws as the town rose from sleep. Obviously uncomfortable from the shoulder wound, and perhaps anticipating further torment, Sedgwick began picking at his bandages. Conor pulled his arm away.

"Leave off. You'll pull it to pieces and the kit's at the bottom of the hill. Go on," he added to Costino, rubbing his eyes wearily. "Let's have part two, and we need to hurry. It's nearly five o'clock."

"Right after Walker presented his plan for the Dragonov operation to the DEA, Langley got briefed," Costino said. "Through a leak or official channels, I'm not sure which. In theory, the CIA had no problem with the idea of capturing Dragonov, but like most other agencies they'd been using him as an informant so they had conditions. First, they wanted their own man on the inside to keep them briefed—they picked me, since Walker's plan involved recruiting Pawan Kotwal to buy guns from Dragonov—and second, they wanted veto authority on any capture strategy."

He broke off with a hollow laugh, face twisted in disgust. "Ironic, right? We'd been spying on Kotwal for a year and turned up squat, but now the DEA wanted to turn him into an extremist, and I was pumped for it. My first cover assignment overseas. Get a taste of field experience. The only fear was getting myself blown in a face-to-face meeting with Durgan, but the danger went away when Walker came back from Geneva saying we couldn't work with him. Turned out to be the beginning of the end of Durgan's relationship with Kotwal. Pawan-bhai was pissed, thought the whole thing made him look bad. He followed up with Durgan, chewed him out and halved his commission, and gradually cut him off completely. Since we had Thomas, none of us needed Durgan. I didn't even need him for the CIA piece anymore. I could get the intel from Thomas by pretending I was collecting for the DEA operation. So I was home free, and totally up for it." Costino peered up at them, as though inviting comment on his naiveté. "I didn't get how shitty it would be, lying to people you respect, every day for five years. Making sure they think you're a ladder-climbing idiot so they'll forget to be careful around you. Knowing you're good at what you do even while you hate what you're becoming."

In mid-drag, Sedgwick sucked in a whoop of air and cigarette smoke and choked. He fumbled behind him, reaching for the backpack with a sardonic glance at Conor. "Water. I'm just going for the water."

"Can I have some?" Costino asked without looking, as though expecting a refusal.

"Come on up." Conor accepted the bottle from Sedgwick and took a swallow. "I won't waterboard you."

They passed the water around like a peace pipe, Costino now sitting on the step below them. "You started out with the CIA, too." He offered the bottle to Sedgwick. "They said you did an undercover gig in St. Petersburg that really fucked you up."

"Yeah, but I was lying to a bunch of heroin addicts, not my own colleagues." Sedgwick snatched the bottle and threw it into the backpack. "We're not here to talk about me. Get to the part that matters."

"The Gulmarg meeting." Costino nodded. "Walker didn't have clearance, Sedgwick. Remember, we went to DC a few months before the meeting so he could present the capture strategy. When he'd finished, I stayed behind with some excuse about paperwork, and went into another room full of senior officers from both agencies. The CIA vetoed his plan. Not the right time. Walker got the news the same night, but when I asked, he said he hadn't. We went back to Mumbai, and a day later, as you recall, he gathered us together and said we were 'go' on the capture strategy. He was off the reservation. I didn't know what to do, because I *liked* Walker, I admired him, and I'd wanted the fucking thing to be a 'go', as much as anyone. If I reported him, his career would be finished, but I worked for the CIA, and the CIA wanted Dragonov free. So, I tried to come up with a way to save face for everyone."

"You tipped off Dragonov," Sedgwick said.

"Not him personally, an anonymous tip to his middlemen. I thought I'd been clever, but Dragonov plays informant for every intelligence agency in the world. He's got a lot of resources at his disposal. Nothing happened for a while. No word from his people to cancel the meeting, no sign Walker would reconsider. We did one more trip to DC before the meeting, his last attempt to get the DEA behind him, and when we came back the two of you were on the train to Rishikesh with Thomas. The next day, I got an email with a zip file attached. Looked like spam, but I'm on a secured network so ..."

Costino's face suddenly crumpled. "They were pictures of my family. All of them. My parents on their back deck, my sister with her kids at the grocery store. Her husband. My younger brother—they had a picture of him taken right inside his office. I didn't even get it, at first. I'd only seen them about three times in the last five years and I was happy—ah, shit." He rubbed at his face. "It was just so fucking good to see them."

Sedgwick released a long, whistling sigh and pulled the water out again. He placed the bottle on the step next to Costino and gave Conor a nudge. "Let's take a walk."

They strolled over to the wall and looked out at the bulky, rounded hillside across from them, watching its shrubs and boulders come into focus under the gradually brightening sky.

"Stupid bastard," Sedgwick breathed. "He did everything wrong."

"Would you have taken a mission like his?" Conor asked. "If you'd stayed with the CIA?"

"Probably. Crap assignment, but yeah, I probably would have."

"What would you have done about Walker?"

"Turned him in," Sedgwick said, without hesitation. "I admired him too, but Jesus, you've got to understand when you can color outside the lines and when you can't. He was obsessed with Dragonov. Killed his judgment, and Costino was in over his head from the beginning. What are you going to do once the enemy is holding your family hostage?"

"Whatever he tells you to," Conor said.

They stayed at the wall until the rhythmic, sonorous tolling of a temple bell sounded, followed by the higher pitched jingle of hand bells. The morning puja ritual began with the dawn; they would need to be on the road soon.

"Sorry," Costino mumbled, when they rejoined him on the steps. He'd regained his composure, but the water bottle had been twisted into an unrecognizable lump of plastic.

Whether from exhaustion or compassion, Conor couldn't muster any fury against him. "Look, we can figure out most of the rest from here—Dragonov forced you to sabotage the capture strategy and set the trap in a way that allowed him to still get his twenty million dollars."

Costino nodded. "I didn't expect them to attack us. They told me they'd send someone expendable to the meeting who would pretend to be Dragonov. We'd transfer the money and arrest him and find out later we had the wrong guy. Not too bad, I told myself. I never questioned the idea they'd give up one of their own so easily. I guess I didn't want to. I was scared stupid."

"Stupid," Sedgwick echoed, "and now they're on your ass because they think you kept the money."

"The funny thing is, they actually do believe me," Costino said. "Tonight wasn't the first time I'd seen those two Russians. They tracked me down fast in Mumbai. I hadn't even been hiding from them; I figured I'd done my part. I just wanted to find some way to spin the whole mess into something I could tell my bosses. Walker was dead and I thought you were too, so nobody to contradict me, and I assumed if Thomas was still alive he and Conor were probably already back in Ireland. Then Dragonov's guys show up saying the transfer didn't go through. They had me at gunpoint, telling me to try again. I got into the account, and when I saw the transfer had gone to an undisclosed location I had a full-blown meltdown—pretty obviously authentic. They believe I don't have it, but told me to be quick about finding it for them. I've been hiding from them ever since, throwing myself under the protection of Kotwal while I tried to locate Thomas, or at least Conor. Now here you are ... at last, and if the two of you don't know where that twenty million is, I'm out of ideas."

"We said we didn't take the money. We never said we don't know where it is. It's in a bank account in Porto Allegre, Brazil." Sedgwick gave Conor a friendly thump on the back. "McBride has the password."

Conor whirled to stare at him, mouth hanging.

"Give it up, buddy." The agent smiled. "You're pretty good with a lie—almost perfect—but I've been doing this longer than you. Everybody's got a 'tell'."

"What's mine?"

"When I'm sure you'll never lie to me again, I'll let you know." Sedgwick began rifling through the backpack and briskly addressed Costino. "Okay, this part of my plan is pretty much shot to shit. We were going to get Durgan's contact info and a few other tasks out of you by whatever means necessary, before shackling you up next to Bahubali for the tour guides to find in the morning."

"What's the plan now?" Costino asked nervously.

"You're coming with us. You're going home."

"How can I do that? I've been AWOL for months. They'll debrief me about Gulmarg and I'll be arrested."

"You were never in Gulmarg," Sedgwick said smoothly. "You broke cover and told Walker you'd report him to his DEA superiors if he went ahead with the Dragonov capture, and he had you thrown into the Arthur Road jail in Mumbai. I just found you there. So, like I said, you're going home."

He pulled out a contraption all-too familiar to Conor—a laptop with an attachment for establishing an internet link via satellite. "However, first we're giving Vasily Dragonov his twenty million dollars, because I don't much feel like giving it back to the DEA, and saving the lives of you and your family seems a little more important—but someday, Tony, since no agency in the world has the guts for the job, you and I are going to track down that sorry-assed Russian, and kill him."

32

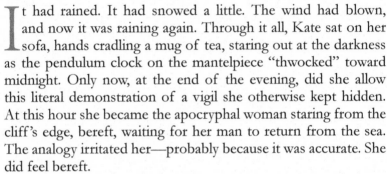

It had rained. It had snowed a little. The wind had blown, and now it was raining again. Through it all, Kate sat on her sofa, hands cradling a mug of tea, staring out at the darkness as the pendulum clock on the mantelpiece "thwocked" toward midnight. Only now, at the end of the evening, did she allow this literal demonstration of a vigil she otherwise kept hidden. At this hour she became the apocryphal woman staring from the cliff's edge, bereft, waiting for her man to return from the sea. The analogy irritated her—probably because it was accurate. She did feel bereft.

He'd been gone for three days, four if she counted the day he left, and why wouldn't she? She'd given him a kiss in the morning, then he was off to WalMart, and that was the last she'd seen of him. Four days, and no word. Was that normal? What was the protocol on undercover agents phoning home? She couldn't decide whether to be frightened, or pissed.

"I have no idea what I'm doing," she said aloud to the empty room. "I don't know what this is."

She gave up for the night a half-hour later, and had crawled into bed when she heard what sounded like an avalanche of boxes tumbling around somewhere below her. She yanked on her dressing gown and flew down to the lobby, and found Conor scanning the inn's register

Next to him, Sedgwick was being pulled from the floor by a man she'd never seen before. The scene hardly registered while she was focused on immediate business, but once Kate surfaced from a long and satisfying kiss, she gave the two of them greater attention.

"What's wrong with him now?"

Holding her in a tight embrace, Conor tore his eyes from hers to glance at Sedgwick. "Infected knife wound, although it's the duty-free Jack Daniels that's got him legless. We stopped at the hospital on the way home for some antibiotics. He won't swallow a Percocet, but he seems to think the drink's no bother to him."

"Knife wound. Okay." Kate decided further questions could wait until everyone looked a little less comatose, but as Conor was still staring at her, arms locked around her waist, she discreetly tilted her head in the stranger's direction.

"Oh, sorry. This is Tony Costino. Another holy terror from your federal government."

She extended her hand uncertainly to the longhaired, bearded man who appeared ready to pass out himself. He took her hand, his red-rimmed eyes widening in apology.

"I'm sorry we woke you." He was struggling to keep Sedgwick upright. "I told them we ought to go to a hotel."

"You didn't wake me, and this is a hotel. You're ... very welcome here." Kate frowned at Sedgwick, who had managed only a few unintelligible words, and reluctantly removed herself from Conor's arms. "I suppose we should get him upstairs, he's pulled half the bandage off."

"Yeah, he's like a little, feckin' drunk two-year-old," Conor said tiredly. "I was trying to figure out what's available. Where do you want them?"

"Everyone on the third floor. Let's not mess up the guest rooms. Tony can have the spare room, and we'll put Sedgwick in your room."

"My room? Well, but where am I going to—oh," He gave her a bleary grin. "Right. Good plan."

While she settled Tony with fresh towels and the usual innkeeper's speech, Conor managed to get Sedgwick down to his underwear and under the covers. Kate sent him to bed and went for first aid tape to fix the agent's bandage.

"Here she is, the natural redhead," Sedgwick sang out as she entered his room. He lolled back and forth against the headboard, as if trying to find his balance. "Hey there, Red. Did you miss us?"

"One of you, anyway. Sit still." She snapped off a length of tape. He stayed quiet as she tidied up the bandage, but when she pressed the tape down across his shoulder he bolted up, hurling obscenities.

"Oh God, I'm so sorry." She jumped back, startled.

"No, it's all right. I'm okay." Sedgwick clumsily reached out to catch her by the hand. "Sorry. I'm sorry. You're really something, you know?" He pulled her closer, his voice thick. "You're so beautiful. I mean ... Whoah. I'm not trying to make a play here. Hey. No way. That's not it. I'm just saying that you're beautiful and good, and I'm always an asshole. And, I'm sorry. That's all I mean. I'm sorry I'm an asshole."

"You're forgiven." Kate tucked his hand gently under the covers. "Go to sleep now." She settled him against the pillows, careful not to hurt him again, and slipped out of the room.

She didn't find Conor in her bed where he was supposed to be, but sitting straight upright in a chair in the living room, fast asleep.

"Oh, honestly," Kate sighed, worried if she woke him he'd take a leap at the ceiling. She considered leaving him alone, but decided to risk a different strategy. Giving herself plenty of room to spring clear of an adverse reaction, she leaned over and kissed him tenderly on the lips. Conor's body jerked, but only slightly as he hitched in his breath and opened his eyes just wide enough to see her.

"Aha. Magic button," she whispered. "Welcome home."

He pulled her into his lap and continued kissing her for a

while, but he was still half-asleep. "Why didn't you go to bed?" she asked, running a finger over the thick stubble on his cheek.

"I was going to, then I realized I've never put so much as a toe inside your bedroom. Seemed like I should wait for you."

"Carry me over the threshold?"

"Maybe not tonight. I need the energy for something else." He gave a particular spot near the base of her throat a nuzzle, raising a shiver in her stomach.

"Hmm. You're very stubbly." She drew in a breath as his mouth caressed the tip of her ear.

"Want me to shave?"

"No. I can't wait that long."

Allowing for his nervous warning that he'd slept for no more than eight of the last ninety-six hours, Kate kept her expectations low, but Conor seemed to gather a second wind from the novelty of his "inaugural" visit to her room. Not only did he have the stamina to accomplish what she had in mind, he also stayed awake long enough afterwards for an account of the past several days. Cocooned together under her down comforter and with her head on his chest, it was the most eccentric brand of pillow talk she'd ever heard, but she hung on every detail.

"So, now we know what happened after he went overboard," she said when he'd finished, amazed by how quickly she'd learned to speak about her no-longer-dead husband with such detachment. "But, I still don't understand why Tony thought faking his death was necessary." Conor's hand tightened on her back before moving up to stroke her hair. "There's something you're not telling me. What?"

"Leave it there for now, love. The rest is better told in daylight."

Seconds later he was asleep, still cradling her in a protective embrace.

At ten o'clock the next morning, Kate was sitting at a table in the corner of her dining room with her state senator, eight local business leaders, and the Vermont Commissioner of Tourism and Marketing. She'd offered to host them months earlier, but was now struggling to contribute any thoughts on regional branding while her mind clattered along a different track altogether. She'd been more or less managing, but halfway through the meeting, when her MI6 lover and his undercover colleagues turned up in the doorway, she had to bite back a hysterical laugh. Without so much as a glance at her, Conor directed them to a table on the opposite side of the room and briefly disappeared into the kitchen. Sitting next to her and watching it all, Yvette aimed a poker-faced gaze at Kate but remained silent.

"I'm not sure when I'll be able to explain this to you," Kate whispered to her, after the meeting had mercifully ended and she was walking everyone to the door. "Or if I'll be allowed to."

"Explanations are over-rated. I just want you to be okay." Yvette gave her a long, close hug, nearly reducing her to tears. "Come see me when you can."

Back in the dining room, Abigail was removing a litter of empty dishes from the covert operatives' table, making space for more bacon and a platter of maple walnut scones still warm from the oven, icing melting down their sides. With a group of ravenous men to feed, she was in her element.

"Plenty of bacon if you want more, and I'll get that lunch started." Offering Kate a happy smile, she swung back through the kitchen door with a bang.

Kate joined them, taking the empty seat at the table. They were all clean-shaven and much improved after ten hours of sleep. "So? What's next?"

Conor licked a bit of icing from his thumb. "We may sit here and eat for a few more hours. I think Tony plans to finish off a hog."

"I haven't had bacon for two and a half years." Tony looked surprised by his own revelation. His face appeared much younger without the beard, and he still seemed dazed by the sudden change in his circumstances. Kate turned to Sedgwick, who had been avoiding eye contact.

"How's your shoulder?"

"Better. Yeah, it's better. Thanks." He reached for a scone. "Listen, I'm sorry if I was rude last night."

Conor thumped his mug down on the table. "What does that mean?" He looked at Kate. "What did he do?"

"Nothing."

"He said he was rude."

"He was just drunk-talking."

With a nervous glance at the three of them, Tony rapidly collected the remaining bacon into a napkin and excused himself, saying he needed some fresh air.

"Well? What did you 'drunk-talking' say?" Conor swiveled back to Sedgwick, whose hands shot up in surrender.

"Jesus, McBride, chill. I don't even remember. Trying to cover my bases, here."

"You were exactly yourself, only more so," Kate said, an observation that satisfied neither of them but which she thought quite clever. "Apology accepted. Next item."

After a lingering glare at Sedgwick, Conor let it drop. "Next item is to drive to Burlington Airport, return the car we rented at Logan, and put Tony on a flight to DC. Abigail's packing him a lunch. We'll pick up the truck I left in the parking garage earlier this week, and come back home."

"Tony's leaving? Didn't you tell me last night we need his help? Don't we need to make a plan?"

"We did already. We talked upstairs before we came down to eat."

"Of course," Kate said, feeling once again sidelined and

powerless. "I should have known you'd decide everything without me."

"Kate, it wasn't like that," Conor protested.

"We just couldn't wait for your little Chamber of Commerce meeting to wrap up," Sedgwick added, flashing his customary sarcasm. Kate gave him a flat, heavy stare and he folded immediately, extending his third apology in the last twelve hours.

"You may wish I was no more than the caretaker of your 'safe house'," she said coldly. "But I'm a participant in this, and I expect to be treated as an equal partner."

"You are. You will be," Conor assured her. Abigail appeared with a large, insulated lunch bag and he got to his feet. "We'd better go, but I promise we'll brief you on the whole thing when we get back."

He went upstairs for his jacket while Sedgwick stepped outside for a cigarette. Kate joined him on the front porch. He angled his head, blowing a stream of smoke away from her, and eyed her uneasily.

"How bad was it?"

Kate thought she'd probably tormented him enough. "I honestly don't have much. You said something rude, and swore at me pretty dramatically when I was clumsy with the tape, but only because I'd hurt you. Then you apologized for everything and got very sweet."

"Sweet?" He looked skeptical.

"Trust me." Kate grinned. "Look, you and I got off on the wrong foot, straight from the beginning, but there's a way for us to be friends, if you agree to my terms."

"What are they?"

"Under any condition, drunk, sober or delirious, don't you ever call me 'Red' again."

"Oh, God." His mouth tightened in a mortified grimace, but resolved into the warm, genuine smile that completely transformed his face. "Deal."

The most important part of their plan, as they described it to her later in the evening, was to impress upon their enemy the extent of his dilemma. To convince him the leverage he thought he had was gone, that he had no cards left to play. Which was nothing less than the truth.

"We've been thinking of him as Frank's 'wizard', this great mastermind, but that's giving him too much credit," Conor reasoned. "The eejit's been canting the ball out of play from the beginning. He was sloppy enough with his New York business to get tagged by the FBI before Tony showed up to save him. He destroyed his relationship with Kotwal by botching the meeting with Walker in Geneva, and he took it out on Frank's brother Desmond. Murdered one of the few associates he had who might have helped him right now."

Full of nervous energy, and seemingly anxious to be implementing the plan rather than describing it to her, Conor was pacing in front of the living room window. Following this matter-of-fact reference to her husband's depravity, he abruptly stopped and swung around to her, looking apprehensive.

By now he'd given her the missing pieces from the previous evening's story. Kate understood her husband had murdered at least three other people in addition to Frank's brother, and if Tony Costino had not come along her most recent birthday might well have been her last. The revelations terrified her—for the danger she'd been in, of course, but also for the fact that she could attach herself to a man so evil and suspect nothing. If her life hadn't been saved by an accident of fate she might have known the truth only at the last minute. Or, maybe not even then. She sensed a reckoning was on the way. A time when she'd need to give room to a growing deluge of self-doubt about her own instincts, and whether she could ever trust them again, but this was not that time.

"It's all right," she said, attempting a smile to reassure him. "Go on."

Conor gazed at her—eyes bright with something she couldn't help but believe in—and finally turned away to resume pacing. "His kidnapping plan was a disaster. The only partner he had left is in jail, spilling details about that as well as the grant fraud business. Frank had all his bank accounts frozen. Even if he's got the price of a ticket, he can't get out of Ireland under his current alias, and the only criminals in the country sophisticated enough to help him are plugged right in to the republican network. Somebody might recognize him for a traitor the minute he showed his face. He's stuck on an island with enemies closing in, and only one person in the world can help him."

Kate had been—very carefully—changing the dressing on Sedgwick's shoulder. At this second dramatic pause she dropped her hands, exasperated.

"You're going to make me ask? Who, for heaven's sake? Who is the only person in the world that can help him?"

"His CIA case officer," Sedgwick said, through gritted teeth. "His case officer can show up with a plane ticket, a passport and a fresh identity, and get him set up in a brand new life."

"And why shouldn't he expect that?" Conor added, retreating from the window to the couch. "It's what happened the last time. Costino swooped in, saved him from the feds and sent him off to India. Makes things a lot simpler for us. Before we understood Tony's history with Durgan, the plan included all this desperate shite about getting him to force Durgan to lure me somewhere on some pretense I couldn't refuse—"

"That wasn't desperate shite," Sedgwick objected. "It was a decent strategy."

"Well, anyway, we don't need your plan." Conor indicated the laptop sitting on the coffee table. "Tony's been communicating with Durgan through the chat function of an online service. The site is ehm—"

"Wait a second." Fresh bandage secured, Sedgwick slithered from Kate's grasp and bounced from his chair, landing next to Conor on the couch.

"It's a porn site," Conor resumed, cautiously. "The messages are coded into the photographs."

"Naturally." Kate dropped into the empty chair. Men were nothing if not predictable. She pitched the roll of tape at them, which Conor successfully dodged while continuing the narrative.

"Durgan is waiting for a response to the offer he made a week ago: information about me in exchange for a passport and a lot of cash and a plane ticket to his destination of choice. He'll be getting an answer tonight, but not the one he expected. We're flipping this relationship back to the beginning, when Costino had the upper hand. Sedgwick speaks CIA, so he'll get onto the site using Tony's user name and password—"

"Jennifer24/7," Sedgwick chimed in.

"—And send the message."

"And what will you be telling him, Jennifer?" Kate asked.

"That he's finished. Over. Robert Durgan is toast. His name, picture and arrest warrant are all logged with Interpol for conspiracy to kidnap an heiress and possible terrorist connections, and he's in every immigration and enforcement database in the world. My supervisors want to throw him under the bus, but I've convinced them he might still be useful. They've agreed to an extraction, with zero negotiation. If he wants a fresh start, he should be at the bar in Kerry Airport a week from tomorrow. An agent carrying a copy of *A Brief History of Time* will be there to bring him in. If he's not there, game over."

Kate nodded, fascinated by the cinematic quality of the scene he described. "Why that book, in particular?"

"Skinny, easy to recognize, and guaranteed to be the only one in the room because nobody ever fucking reads it. I'll be the agent waiting for him in the bar. We'll have tickets for Dulles, connecting through London, but when we get off the plane at Gatwick, Frank Murdoch will be at the gate with MI6, 5 and whoever else, greeting him with a set of handcuffs. Durgan might be extradited back to the States, but it seems fair to give the Brits first crack since the CIA owns the blame for this whole cock-up. So ..." The agent trailed off and gave Conor an inquisitive glance, as if inviting him to jump in, but Conor stared down at his folded hands, thumbs tapping together. "So, yeah." Sedgwick suppressed a smile and turned back to Kate. "That's the plan. What do you think?"

"I'm certainly no judge, but it seems solid to me. Will he show up?"

"He's got no choice, and he'll have plenty of time to travel from wherever he's been hiding. Probably Dublin. Easier to stay invisible in a bigger city."

The thumb tapping picked up speed. He was clearly anticipating Kate's next question, and she felt a little sorry for Conor, because she was already several steps ahead of him. "Are you going to do this alone?" she asked Sedgwick.

"Um, well ..."

"No." Conor pulled his hands apart and sat forward, taking the plunge in a rush. "He can't. He needs backup. I'll be perfectly safe though, Kate. Durgan will never even see me. I'll be way off stage, practically in the bushes, monitoring everything on the radio."

"In case something goes wrong," Kate said, stating the obvious.

"But nothing will go wrong. It'll be fine."

"Because it's all gone so well up to this point?"

"Well, no."

She let him grope for a more credible argument for a few seconds before smiling. "Relax. I understand."

"You do?"

"Of course. I never imagined you wouldn't go with him."

"Oh. Good. Brilliant." Conor released his breath and exchanged a glance of surprised relief with Sedgwick. "We were afraid you might not agree."

"I can see that, but after everything that's happened, after all you've been through, how could I not let you have this closure? How could I try to make you stay home?"

Kate beamed bright, sympathetic understanding at both of them. Had they caught on, yet? No. No, they hadn't, and that was probably just as well. It was getting late, and she didn't want to start an argument right before bedtime.

33

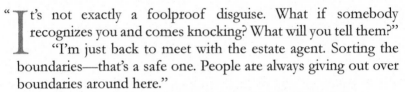

"It's not exactly a foolproof disguise. What if somebody recognizes you and comes knocking? What will you tell them?"

"I'm just back to meet with the estate agent. Sorting the boundaries—that's a safe one. People are always giving out over boundaries around here."

"But I thought you sold everything before you left."

"The sale wasn't posted." Conor rubbed at his forehead and pulled the bill of his cap a little lower. "I signed a load of papers and sent them back to Frank. I don't know whose name is on the bloody deed, but the farm belongs to MI6. He said they've kept the house habitable."

"I can't wait." Kate wriggled in her seat and Conor shot a sour glance at her over his sunglasses. "What's wrong?" she asked.

"You look like Jigger, bouncing around over there. We've flown half the night and we're nearly three hours in the car, now. Aren't you tired?"

"I think I'm overtired. Makes me spastic. Anyway, lighten up." Kate gave his knee a slap, and let her hand remain on his thigh. "You've had enough time to be tense and surly about this. You're past the expiration date."

Eyes still on the road, Conor smiled a little. "These are not the circumstances under which I thought I'd be introducing you to my birthplace."

"Believe me, I do sympathize."

Sure she does. Conor brought her hand to his lips. *But not enough to stay home.*

He should have seen it coming, and he'd berated himself for yet again underestimating her, thereby making the success of her campaign a foregone conclusion. At first, he'd been patient, solicitous even, indulging every argument until she'd talked herself hoarse, and then refuting all of them with solid logic. He fought gently and—he thought—shrewdly, but as the battle continued and he realized he was losing, his panic ignited a pompous rage which he used as his last remaining weapon. He unleashed it on her two days before departure while they emptied the trash, the fumes from that evening's seafood entree hanging in the air.

"Your arguments are all ridiculous, Kate. You wouldn't be making me or anyone else safer. Exactly the opposite, in fact. You've no experience and you're not trained for it. You're an unacceptable risk and you'd be a liability to the entire operation."

"I don't care." She remained maddeningly calm, refusing to face him as she tossed the final bag into the dumpster. "You've had liabilities before; you'll deal with this one."

"We shouldn't have to fucking deal with it." He brought the lid down with a crash and slammed his fist on top for good measure. "You're being completely unreasonable and selfish."

"Selfish?" Kate's quiet, controlled emotion extinguished his anger in the space of a heartbeat. Conor had already surrendered before she said another word. "He took everything from me—family possessions, my art, trust in my own judgment. My courage. Don't I deserve to at least get a look at him, even if only from the bushes? Is that selfish?"

"Of course not. No." He slipped an arm around her shoulders, conceding defeat. "A load of rubbish, you know." He kissed her forehead. "That bit about courage. You've more than anyone I've ever met. That's what scares me so much."

He dithered over how to break the news to his partner, and delayed for as long as he could. Sedgwick was already in London, immersed in meetings with Frank and his colleagues, and would arrive at Kerry Airport the day before the meeting with Durgan. Frank had suggested using the farmhouse in Ventry as their safe house, and as the venue for an early morning briefing with the special Garda units called in to assist. The former McBride farm was within an hour's drive of the small, regional airport, and isolated enough to ensure privacy. Conor would fly to Ireland earlier to open up the house before picking up Sedgwick. Only when he and Kate were sitting at the JFK departure gate did he finally call to present the operational wrinkle. Sedgwick picked up on the second ring.

"How are things going?" Conor asked.

"Fine. The food's as bad as I remember, except for the curry."

"Did Frank book you at the Lanesborough?"

"The Lanesborough? Hell, no. He's got me in a dive over the Bayswater tube station. How about you? Everything on schedule?"

"Yeah, sure. Right on time." Conor decided he should come to the point. "I need to warn you of a small complication I've failed to avert. There will be two of us picking you up at the airport tomorrow night. Kate's with me." He waited for the agent to explode, but after a long pause Sedgwick startled him by laughing instead.

"I suppose we're just lucky she plays for our side."

The agent's composure had done nothing to relieve his own concerns, but despite his sullen mood Conor took reluctant pleasure in Kate's introduction to Ireland. Her enthusiasm for the experience was apparent as soon as they'd stepped out of Shannon Airport into a cool morning of misting rain. While he loaded their bags into the rental car she stood with her nose turned up, water collecting on her face, mist clinging to her dark green sweater in twinkling droplets.

"I'm getting the smell of it," she explained. "Every place has its own fragrance. New York has vented subway air and pretzels. Right now, home smells like snow, even though there isn't any yet. Here, I'm getting something like a campfire after you've thrown water on it. Also, a little like wool."

"That would be your sweater, don't you think?" Conor brushed some of the moisture from her shoulders. "Did you not bring a rain jacket? You're taking optimism to the limit. We'll stop in Tralee for breakfast and buy one for you." He bobbed his head at the car. "Right, so. In you get. Nope. This side."

The rain had stopped as they left Tralee after a late breakfast, and now the skies cleared as they started for the farmhouse, which lay several miles past the town of Dingle. A pang of nostalgia hit Conor as they crossed the bridge over the River Lee, and he saw the rolling, emerald outline of the Slieve Mish mountains running up the spine of the peninsula. He decided he should obey Kate's command to lighten up. The emotional sledgehammer she faced—with a courage she wouldn't allow herself to acknowledge—was heavier than anything he had in front of him. He'd shared a deep bond of friendship and more than a few pints with the man he'd known as Phillip Ryan, but they hadn't joined their lives together. If she could sit beside him, cheerful, wide-awake and absorbed by every sight and "fragrance" around her, who the hell was he to be sulking? When he came to a fork in the road, he abandoned the N86 route and stayed to the right, following the narrow R560 toward the Conor Pass.

"I know I don't speak Irish, but wasn't that a sign for Dingle?" Kate twisted around to look behind them.

"*An Daingean*," Conor confirmed, feeling a warm fellowship with the ancestors who had invoked its name before him. He tossed his sunglasses into the center console and winked at her. "I'm taking the scenic route."

They coasted along the northern side of the peninsula where the North Atlantic sparkled under a brightening sky, and then turned inland, climbing bit by bit until the road suddenly shrank to a narrow track, carved out of the rock of the most spectacular mountain pass in the country. The route rolled forward in a winding, vertiginous loop, clinging to the side of moss-covered cliffs rising on their left. To the right, a majestic, glaciated landscape stretched into the distance, dotted everywhere with corrie lakes—dark, mirror-flat basins of icy water, reflecting the clouds above them with photographic intensity.

At the highest point on the pass, Conor pulled the car into a lay-by. Next to them, a slender waterfall spilled out over a tabletop arrangement of boulders, and in front the panoramic view spread out before them like a living postcard. As they stared together through the windshield he could sense Kate's speechless wonder, but when she slipped out for a closer look Conor didn't follow right away. He switched off the engine and sat back as she crossed to stand at the low rock wall lining the road. This moment was all he wanted—simply to watch her, to experience this place for the first time through her eyes. Eventually, he got out of the car and went to stand behind her, circling his arms around her waist. They were alone on the road, and the only sound came from the rain shower melody of the waterfall behind them.

"I'm not going to describe this very well." She took his arms and drew him closer. "The little bit of cloud out there above the lake seems alive, and I'm floating with it, even while I'm planted here, holding on to you and feeling the gravel under my shoes. I'm out there, and right here, part of everything. Such an odd sensation. I guess it must be jet-lag."

"It's not," he whispered. "It's Ireland."

The house offered another opportunity for his heart to stumble and shake inside him, and Conor wondered why he hadn't prepared more carefully for the sentiment this homecoming would evoke. After passing through Dingle and the small village of Ventry—essentially an intersection with a post office and two pubs—he turned the car from the main road onto a smaller one, no more than a paved path. They climbed uphill, past acres of empty fields, then turned again to bump through a gate and along a short, muddy driveway to the farm itself. He parked behind the tractor shed, ensuring the car was hidden from sight, and on their way to the house they paused to gaze across the pasture at the view of Ventry Bay.

"So?" Conor asked. "Did I give an accurate description?"

Kate smiled. "Just like Lake Rembrandt, but with the ocean at one end. It's perfect."

He led her down a flight of stairs to the flagstone terrace at the back of the farmhouse, and with the key he'd used all his life, opened the Dutch-style door and let it swing inward. They stepped into the tiny kitchen, too small for a dining table but large enough for the enormous antique dish cupboard squeezed against one wall. Happy and surprised it was still there, Conor absently brushed his fingers over the shelf before the shock of realization floored him: everything was still there, looking exactly as it had on the day he'd left. *Fully habitable*, Frank had told him, and now he understood. MI6 wasn't using the place at all. They hadn't touched a thing.

Conor sniffed the air—cool and damp, but not as stale as he'd expected. They went through into the large, sunlit space where the McBride family had lived out its life—its eating and drinking and visits with friends, its naps by the soot-stained fireplace. Its fiddling and songs.

Receiving his vague nod and directions, Kate went upstairs to use the bathroom while he remained in place, lost in memories. When she returned, he noticed her spastic energy had run its course, and she was cold. She stood by the fireplace hugging herself, and gave a wide, shivering yawn.

"The central heating's turned off; I should probably get the boiler running again. Or, I could get a fire going if you like," Conor suggested.

"Wouldn't we be warmer in bed?" she asked sleepily.

"Without a doubt. Good idea. My room's up on the right."

The worn springs and faded patchwork quilt of his bed provided a sharp contrast to Kate's pillow-topped luxury, but she stripped and tumbled in as though she'd been waiting for it all her life. Conor wasted no time in following. Within a few minutes they had warmth enough to spare, and before long drifted off to sleep.

He woke later with a violent start—breathless, nerves sizzling, his head a jumble of spiking, incoherent static. He didn't know where he was, and for a paralyzing instant he didn't know who he was. After several deep breaths, Conor faced the more ordinary mystery of what time it was. He sat up, getting reacquainted with the room and its homely furnishings, while next to him Kate slept on, flat on her stomach. Her breathing was so light that he perched over her on one elbow, holding his own breath until he'd tracked a few cycles of her inaudible intake and release. He'd expected it to be surreal and maybe a little awkward having her here—in his home, in this bed—but he felt only a boneless sense of relief, as if something painfully wrenched out of joint had clicked back in place.

He found his watch resting on the pile of clothes on the floor. Three o'clock. They would leave in another hour to pick up Sedgwick. Pulling on his jeans, he left Kate to sleep a while longer and went to the bathroom. Out of habit, he twisted both faucets, but was astonished a minute later when the water got hot. Had he never turned off the bloody boiler, after all? Yes, he definitely had. His memories about everything on that last day were as vivid as a picture book.

Conor shut the water off and studied his reflection in the mirror, the old unmistakable tingle traveling up his spine. He stepped to the second floor landing and stopped, listening, then trotted down the stairs to survey the living room, this time with an eye for something other than nostalgia. He walked into the kitchen and heard what he hadn't earlier—the faint, gremlin buzz of the refrigerator. A natural, well-remembered sound that he shouldn't be hearing at all. He remembered unplugging it. He pulled the door open. A package of sausages sat on the top shelf, and a liter of milk on the door. He picked up the milk, confirmed it was fresh and closed the door, his gaze wandering along the counter to see what else he'd missed. Tucked into a corner by the stove he saw a small loaf of bread next to a red-capped jar of Bovril.

Bovril's your only man for puttin' the life back into you.

"Oh my God, are you joking me?" His hushed disbelief vanished in a shout as Conor wheeled away from the refrigerator. "Kate, wake up! We need to get out of here!"

As he raced through the doorway, headed for the stairs, a shape loomed on his left. Before he could react, he both heard and felt the excruciating crack on the back of his head, and then nothing more.

34

There was no electric jolt propelling him awake this time; there was only a slow, relapsing climb from darkness into more darkness. His effort to interpret the ghostly light illuminating it finally brought him around. He lay on his side on the floor of the living room, with his hands tied behind his back. Slowly, Conor registered the pale blue gleam he'd taken for moonlight as the glow from a laptop sitting on the large oak dining table. The last moments of a fading daylight remained visible beyond the drawn curtains. Fighting a stomach-churning pain, he lifted his head and saw Kate, tied with a length of orange electrical cord into a straight-backed chair, arms pinned to her side. Beside her, relaxing against the table, her husband stared down at him, his face hidden in shadows.

Thinner but otherwise unchanged, he still looked like the broad-shouldered, rusty-haired man Conor had once considered more steadfast than his own flesh and blood. He thought he'd grown used to the idea that the nemesis he'd loathed as a stranger wore the face of a friend, but confronting it now filled him with helpless grief—until the figure bent toward him, and his mocking eyes became visible in the computer glow. There was no friend called Phillip Ryan in the room now, or any loving husband named Michael Fitzpatrick. There was only this murderer, Robert Durgan—the man who had played with all of their lives like a maniacal *púca,* the shapeshifting goblin of Irish folklore.

"Welcome back, Conor." His accent—expressed in the same bell-like tenor Conor remembered—had always been a bit of a muddle. "Like chickens home to roost aren't we, the pair of us?"

"Are you here since ... ?" Conor fumbled for words, forcing his ability for speech to catch up with his thoughts. "Have you been living here all along, for fuck's sake?"

Durgan smirked at him. "What a hoot that would have been, right? But no, sure I only turned up early this morning. I've been floating around in a cabin cruiser on the Shannon River Estuary for the past month. I thought it would be nice to spend my last night in Ireland on—well, actual land. I got the motorbike out of storage, rode up to check the place out and leave some groceries, and went back to the harbor to collect a few things off the boat. Imagine my surprise when I came back—Jaysus, here's Conor McBride in his old bed, fast asleep with his legs wrapped around my beautiful wife." Turning to Kate, he bent to her ear and began singing softly.

"As I went home on Thursday night as drunk as drunk could be
I saw two boots beneath the bed where my old boots should be.
Well, I called me wife and I said to her: Will you kindly tell to me ..."

He stroked the back of one finger along her cheek, and Kate squirmed in her chair, trying to avoid his touch.

"Stop. Shut up."

"Ah go on, darlin'. That's not how it goes." He pouted and caught her face in his hand, giving her chin a playful pinch.

"Get your hands off her." Trying to sit up, Conor strained against the cord wound around his wrists.

Durgan lifted himself from the table and casually laid a boot on his shoulder, pressing him back down to the floor. "Why? I've had me hands all over her from the minute I put the mallet to your head. Conjugal rights, mate. She didn't' complain."

With a quick jerk, Conor rolled away from the boot and swung his feet forward, bringing one of them up to land a hard kick on Durgan's thigh. Kate cried out as he stumbled back and tripped over one of the straight-backed chairs.

"Conor, don't. He's got a gun. And he's lying, anyway."

This time Conor managed to struggle up to a sitting position and then to his knees, examining her more closely. One cheek seemed red and swollen, and bruises had begun forming on her arms.

"I'm all right," she said, tears streaming down her face.

"Tell me," he begged. "Are you saying he—"

"I'm saying he didn't. He's still more interested in my money than anything else. We've been looking at bank accounts for the past hour. He's changed the passwords."

"Lucky break, her turning up here, since my own hard-earned money is unavailable. Lucky, but probably not a coincidence, no matter how much Kate wants me to think so. I'm hoping you can explain it all to me, Conor." Durgan righted the chair he'd toppled over, and with exaggerated care took Conor by the arm and lifted him into the seat before returning to lean against the table. "Did my friend Tony track you down on his own? Has the CIA decided they like you better than me? Nothing to say? Well, maybe this will help my wife chime in with something more sensible." Durgan strolled forward and struck Conor across the face, and then went on hitting him.

The blows themselves were endurable, but they rocked Conor from side to side and heightened the sickening pain at the back of his head. Closing his eyes only made the dizziness worse, and though he fought the growing nausea, breathing in shallow spurts, he eventually lost the battle. He twisted from the chair and heaved everything in his stomach onto his grandmother's hand-loomed rug.

He heard Kate screaming surrender and tried to tell her not to talk, but couldn't blame her when she didn't listen to him. He imagined he looked a pretty sorry sight, doubled over on the floor next to his own mess. She was terrified for him.

"She's not trained for this," he reminded himself, sorrowfully. "I never should have brought her." This was before Conor began paying attention to what Kate was saying—before he realized he had underestimated her again.

"Untie me first."

"Nice try. You're hardly in a position to make demands."

"It's not a demand." Kate sighed. "This cord is hurting me. You have a gun, and you've made sure he's not going to get up anytime soon." With effort, she kept her eyes on her captor and away from Conor, who lay motionless, his face to the floor. "You're not afraid of me, so why do you have to keep hurting me?"

"Oh, Michael, if you ever loved me ..." He affected a whining falsetto that cracked into an unpleasant laugh. But then, he untied her.

Despite his pointed reference, she had not addressed him as Michael. She hadn't addressed him as anything. She didn't know what to call the monster that had appeared at the foot of Conor's bed like a ghost in a nightmare. The man she'd once loved now seemed a familiar stranger, but as she'd been reminded earlier, some things hadn't changed. There had always been a certain expression—one of tense, fearful hunger—that he'd never been able to hide when he needed something from her. A similar sort of tension stiffened his face now, an awareness of his vulnerability. He knew nothing, and his ignorance offered the only advantage she had.

If she told the story carefully, she and Conor might live long enough for help to arrive. Either the Garda would discover them on their evening rounds between the farmhouse and Durgan's house in Dingle, or Sedgwick would arrive. His flight had been scheduled to land a few minutes earlier, and it wouldn't take him long to suspect something.

Her instincts told her not to get tripped up in lies, but few were needed. The first was simply to pretend they had come to the house with the intention of being alone for the night. The second was more complicated. The only way to keep this villain from slipping the noose was to make him believe he should walk right into it. Kate rubbed her hands against her arms, tingling now as the sensation returned to them.

On the floor, his face still turned away from them, Conor shifted a little and groaned. She allowed herself a brief glance, hoping he'd understand what she was trying to do, and started her confession. "The CIA isn't sending anyone to help you. This whole thing is a plan hatched by the DEA when Conor and one of their agents went to India and found Tony Costino—"

Waving a hand at her impatiently, he dragged another chair forward and sat down. "I don't give a damn who hatched the plan. Skip the acronyms, and the history and all your bleedin' midnight strategy meetings. Just tell me what's supposed to go down tomorrow at the airport. I was told to meet a guy in the bar at ten o'clock. Who's he got coming with him?"

"That's the problem. Nobody is coming with him. He's a DEA agent and he doesn't even know the two of us are here. We—well, Conor, but I insisted on coming—we were planning to sit in a van outside, to see for ourselves when you showed up, to make sure you didn't get away again." Kate covered her face. "It's all so ridiculous. This was never going to work. Nothing was going to go down at the airport."

"Just me and him sharing a pint and a laugh? Not bloody likely. You're having me on."

Kate braced herself for the lie that mattered most. "We thought the idea was stupid too, but he didn't ask our opinion. No arrest was planned until the plane landed in Washington. The agent meeting you was just supposed to keep this fiction going that the CIA is bringing you in for something new. He's even got your new identity with an authentic passport, and the plane tickets." She paused before adding an apparent afterthought. "You were supposed to fly to Gatwick first."

"And what happens at Gatwick?"

He was listening with greater interest, just as she'd hoped. Kate shrugged. "Nothing. You wait for your next flight. Sit in the bar, hit the duty free store, they didn't care. It's completely hands-off until you arrive at Dulles. They'd let you wander around wherever you want rather than have you suspect anything. You could walk out the door and hop a bus if you wanted, which is the point I tried to make to everyone."

"Or catch another flight." He gave a soft laugh, rocking his chair back.

"I suppose," Kate said in a small voice.

He was quiet for several minutes, then threw a speculative gaze at the laptop and got to his feet. "The details for the new identity. What are they?"

"I don't understand. Why would you need—"

He gave her face a sharp slap. "You don't need to understand. Answer the question."

"I don't know the details, but Conor helped the agent create the identity. He has everything in a folder in his bag upstairs."

In his eagerness, he didn't bother to tie her up again. He took the gun from the table and bolted up the stairs while Kate threw herself on to the floor next to Conor. She gently rolled him on his back and he grinned up at her, eyes shining in admiration.

"In the name of God, woman. Where did you ever learn to do that?"

At first, it looked like her plan would work. Almost immediately,

Durgan jogged downstairs with the folder in his hand and smirked at Conor, who still lay prostrate on the floor.

"Right, mate. Soak up a little tenderness while I start spending her money. The first item I'm going to buy is a plane ticket out of Gatwick."

He sat facing them with his back to the wall, waving the gun as a stern reminder, and then focused on the laptop. He was too preoccupied to pay either of them any attention, but readily agreed when Kate asked permission to help Conor.

"The smell coming off him is desperate." Durgan didn't take his eyes from the screen. "Clean him up but leave him tied and don't turn on the lights, and make us a cup of tea."

The kitchen, of course, was full of potential weapons. Kate went so far as to pull an impressive-looking meat cleaver from the drawer, but acknowledging the lunacy of thinking she'd be able to overpower a muscular armed man, she put the knife back and took out the teaspoons instead.

The darkness outside was now complete, and she had only the glow from the laptop guiding her steps when she returned to the living room. With a basin of soap and hot water and several towels, she cleaned up Conor and the floor around him, then got him across the room and onto the couch. She sat beside him, feeding him small sips of tea while they whispered together.

"Are you all right?"

"I think so. It's like being drunk. As soon as you've puked, you feel a lot better." His smile was brief. "Don't let on, though. Let him think he's pummeled me witless." His face darkened as he looked at the bruises on her cheek. "Kate, what did he do to you?"

"I'm okay. Don't worry about me." She took Conor's arm and held tight, desperate to keep him from flying at Durgan in a suicidal rage. "Let's focus on getting through this. Sedgwick will find us. He just needs time to get here."

"Well, you've bought that for us. I hope it's enough." He regarded her sadly. "But if not, Kate—"

"Right. Done and dusted." Durgan snapped the laptop shut and got to his feet. Kate was almost happy for the interruption. She hadn't liked the enigmatic expression in Conor's eyes.

"Come on, and get him up, too." Durgan yanked her from the couch, aiming his gun at Conor. "We're getting out of here."

Kate stared at him. "You're leaving? Now? And taking us with you?"

He'd clearly made a more elaborate plan than she'd intended. She didn't know whether to argue or not, since the alternative to going with him might be even more dangerous, as Durgan confirmed with his next command.

"Get him up. If he can't manage, I'll shoot him right now. He doesn't matter that much."

Conor had fallen back on the sofa with his mouth hanging open, playing possum. At least, she hoped he was. She scrambled to lift him, suggesting under her breath he might give her a little help. They were leaving before the cavalry arrived. They were out of time.

35

Conor stopped at the last bend in the steep, M-shaped promenade and braced his hands on the wall to peer down at the deserted Dunquin jetty. Under a blanket of starlight the water lapped against the concrete ramp, and he heard the lazy, slopping rhythm as each wave rolled forward.

"Are you mental? It's a tricky run even in daylight, but in the dark? You'll have all three of us killed before you're done."

"I can do this run with my eyes shut." Durgan met Conor's incredulity with a smug grin. "You're forgetting I worked the ferry all summer, once I'd lost my old job, and I've still got the keys." He jangled them in front of Conor's eyes. "Plus, my wife can tell you what a dab hand I am with a boat, right, darlin'?" He sent Kate ahead of him with a push, and gave Conor a sharp poke with the gun. "Keep walking."

The directive was easier to obey now that his hands were untied. Conor had been pressed into driving the rental car with Durgan next to him and the gun firmly planted against his ribs, while Kate sat in the back seat. He'd been surprised when they'd turned away from town to head west, but he soon understood at least part of Durgan's strategy when he threw a pen and paper into the back, ordering Kate to provide phone numbers for her father and grandmother.

"Your father may not think you're worth the price. Cheap little caffler would light a smoke in his pocket before he'd share one. Your old hag of a grandmother is a different story, I'll bet. She'll open every bank box in Zurich for you."

It was an eerie journey along the dark winding road with the wide expanse of Dingle Bay on their left. The wind picked up as they continued west, roaring at full gale when they rounded the bend at Slea Head at the tip of the peninsula. By the time they reached the remote, isolated harbor at Dunquin and parked the car near the ferry's ticket kiosk, Conor had guessed the rest of the plan. Stalling, he'd continued to play up his head-injured condition, stumbling and falling at every opportunity until Durgan crouched down to growl a threat into his ear.

"Do you think I have any use for you at all, Conor? The only reason you're still alive is because I know she'll lose her rag as soon as I shoot you. I'd rather not deal with hysterics just now, but I will if you make me. So, you can get down this ramp and help her put the inflatable into the water, or I can send you on to kingdom come. Your choice."

The "inflatable" was a twenty-foot boat with a small outboard motor, used for transporting passengers out to the ferry, which sat anchored in deeper water a hundred yards from shore. Conor and Kate began hauling the boat from the corner of the jetty while Durgan kept the gun trained on them, smoking a cigarette at the water's edge near the end of the ramp.

"Do you know what's going on?" Kate whispered.

"Kidnapping the heiress, take two," Conor quipped, hoping to dampen some of their edgy fear. "See the outline in the distance? *An Blascaod Mor*, the Great Blasket. Still has a few broken down houses, but the people living in them got evacuated in the early fifties. The island is uninhabited now, except for day-trippers and sheep during the summer. The tourist ferry stops in October, and they usually take the last of the sheep off by the end of the month, so I imagine it's well and truly deserted by now."

"And he's going to dump us out there," Kate said. "Leave us

and demand a ransom for telling my family where we are."

"Seems to be the general idea." Conor got a tighter grip on the ropes of the inflatable, deciding it would be unwise to shatter the illusion about the "we" part of her theory. "He figures if he ties us up and throws us into one of the houses, nobody will find us for a good while."

"What are we going to do?"

"I'm working on it."

"We need to get the gun away from him."

Conor wiped the sweat from his forehead and glanced at her, eyebrows raised.

"Okay, I know. Easier said than done." Kate gave the boat a half-hearted shove. "At least my story worked. He's still planning to go to the meeting tomorrow. Sedgwick will have to be at the airport, hoping he'll show, and I'm sure he'll find a way to make Durgan confess where he's put us. Worst-case scenario is we get locked away on an island for a day."

This was far from the worst-case scenario, but Conor said nothing to spoil her brave composure. He was keeping a watchful eye on Durgan, looking for any chance to disarm him, but the man was alert to every twitch of muscle, and eager for an excuse to pull the trigger. There didn't seem to be a move he could make that wasn't suicidal.

The inflatable carried them to the ferry, and once onboard Durgan made Kate tie up Conor again, then brought her into the wheelhouse while they got underway. When the ferry had moved far from shore, he allowed her to return to the back deck, locking the wheelhouse door behind her as she exited.

"He said our only escape would be to jump overboard and drown." Wearily, she fell onto the bench next to Conor and began working at the knotted cord around his wrists. "How long does it take?"

"Drowning?"

"The ride to the island," Kate clarified patiently.

"Usually about twenty minutes. He'll go a bit slower in the dark."

She looked out at the inflatable boat, secured to the rear and trailing along in their wake. "What if we leap out onto the dinghy, start the motor and cut the rope?"

Conor smiled. "It's at least twenty feet back. Can you leap that far?"

"I'm not sure," Kate admitted. She rubbed at his chafed wrists, bending her head to kiss them, and her shoulders began to shake. "I guess I'm not too good at this."

"*Whisht*, Kate. You're talking rubbish again. You're the only one who's done anything useful at all, so far." Conor cupped her face in his hands. She was not crying but shaking badly, which worried him. "Are you all right, love? Are you cold?" He opened his jacket and wrapped her up against him with his cheek on her head, protecting her from the sea spray irregularly showering them, rocking her slowly until the tremors stopped.

"You'd be able to tell me, wouldn't you?" Conor thought carefully before continuing, knowing he needed to ask, afraid of saying it wrong. He hadn't the slightest idea how to address something like this. "If he'd done anything to you. You could talk to me? If he did, I mean. I'm not trying to make you if you can't, or if you haven't anything to tell ..."

Kate put her fingers to his lips. "He wanted to, but he couldn't."

The comment was not at all what he'd expected. Conor pulled back to squint at her, which made his head pound even harder. "What do you mean, he couldn't?"

"Exactly what you think I mean. I heard you yelling for me, but I was barely awake when he got to the bedroom, and he was on top of me before I could move. He groped and pawed, but that was all he could do." She turned to gaze behind them at the mainland, which grew ever more shapeless and indistinct as it retreated. "He had issues, even when we were together. I guess he still does. Sometimes—a lot of the time—he needed me to help him, and I would. This time, I didn't. He was embarrassed, so he started hitting me. The first few were pretty hard, but they were better than the alternative. I expected him to go on until he'd knocked me out, but he didn't. He wanted to get at my bank accounts." She shivered, huddling against him. "If anything else had happened, I *would* be able to tell you, I promise. Do you believe me?"

"I do. Of course, but I'm ... a little surprised." Gobsmacked, to be strictly accurate. Holding her close, Conor chewed on his lip and looked through the dripping window of the wheelhouse door, trying to channel his helpless rage into something more effective. Inside, Durgan stood tall and confident, making small adjustments to the steering. Conor began to sketch the outline of a strategy of last resort.

"Kate, I don't know how you'll feel about it but I think I can use this. In fact, I think I might need to."

Her muscles tensed, but then she looked up at him, eyes narrowed. "Good."

The next break they got was the discovery of six signal flares, hidden by a pile of life preservers under the bench. Conor waited until they'd drawn closer to where Durgan would anchor the ferry off-shore, and then sent all six blasting up into the night—a beautifully choreographed maneuver with Kate serving as assistant gunner, ready to lob him a new shell as soon as he called for one. They ran through all of them in fifteen seconds while Durgan was still fumbling to unlock the wheelhouse door.

Once out, he charged across the deck, chambering a round and pointing the gun at Conor's chest. With the six beacons trailing fire and hanging overhead like bright red stars, Conor dropped the last empty shell and raised his hands in surrender, maintaining the glacial calm that always centered him at such moments.

"Blood all over the ferry, boss? Is that what you want? Now you've a bit less time than you thought, it's maybe not the smartest move—to start improvising. Also, you may want to go sort the steering. We're headed for quite a big rock, there."

Spewing obscenities and rage, Durgan ran back inside to correct course, and ten minutes later he dropped anchor near a sheltered cove—the landing spot for generations of Blasket Islanders. Once on shore, Conor and Kate started up the path while Durgan followed behind with a flashlight in one hand and his gun in the other.

Even steeper than the ramp at Dunquin, the path was an assortment of slick stones with tufts of wet grass growing around their edges. Conor knew the way. He'd walked this route with his mother many times, at all ages, in sun and rain. When they reached the top of the bluff, he turned automatically to the right, toward the sad, deserted village. The oldest of the stone houses were in an advanced state of ruin, their roofs long since torn off by North Atlantic storms. A collection of newer houses farther up the hill survived in better condition. Built to face the mainland, their whitewashed walls were just visible in the darkness. Conor thought Durgan probably had one of those houses in mind for Kate.

Far ahead and below them, he heard the muffled crash of waves on the White Strand, a long wide beach he'd often seen crowded with sunbathing seals, the lowest and flattest spot on the entire island. The rest was steeply pitched on all sides, every direction leading to the surrounding bluffs and a precipitous plunge down to the ocean. You didn't want to lose your footing on the paths of the Blasket. You would roll straight through the furze and heather like a bead of rainwater running down a windshield, until you dropped off the edge of the world. Conor thought Durgan probably had one of those bluffs in mind for him.

Caol ait. Thin places. Those spots where the barrier between the physical "here" and spiritual "there" becomes translucent. The Great Blasket maybe hadn't started out as one, but the lonely spirits murmuring through the crumbling walls had made it "thin". Their sorrows and the weight of inevitability pressed down on Conor, closing in around him. He'd play his hand to the end, but it wouldn't change the outcome. He could already see himself rolling.

Kate felt more frightened now than at any point during the night, a night that already seemed as long as a week. The stark, silent desolation of the island unnerved her. Her skin prickled, and a coldness at the back of her neck surged and receded like the waves in the distance. She couldn't fight the constant temptation to check behind her but each time saw only Durgan, several yards back, urging her forward. Lit by the glow of his flashlight, his face appeared wary and uncomfortable as well.

Next to her, his hand warm in hers, Conor had grown quiet, head tilted as though listening to the sounds of the ocean far below. After a few more steps, he whispered "Right," and stopped walking an instant before Durgan called out the order. He turned to her, lifting her face, and gave her a long, slow kiss.

"I love you." He breathed the words into her mouth, her ears, her hair. "I love you." And then, "Do you trust me?"

"Of course. You know I do." She held him tight, noticing Durgan had also stopped walking and seemed to be waiting for something. "What's going on? You're scaring me."

Incredibly, Conor grinned and gave her nose a light pinch.

"I'm going to poke the bear. Trust me, and stay right here. Whatever happens, don't move. I don't know how this will work, but it won't work at all if you get in the middle, so stay right where you are. Promise?"

She didn't want to, but she nodded. He caressed her cheek, drew a calloused fingertip over her lips, and walked back toward Durgan.

"Here, I suppose?" Conor veered off to stand on a rounded hump of land several yards from Durgan. "This is what you had in mind? The angle is about right?"

"Cooperation. Unexpected, but appreciated." Durgan's smile flashed in the darkness.

"Is that what you think this is? It isn't." Conor took another step forward and spat on the ground. "This is me, standing here, dying like a man and I'm looking straight into the face of something else. A coward. A limp, fucking traitor."

"Careful, Conor. I can make things worse than they need to be."

A scream rose in Kate's throat as Durgan raised his gun. Without looking at her, Conor signaled her to stop, palm forward as though slamming it against a wall.

"Worse, how? You'll shoot off little bits of me? Send me over the cliff piece by piece because you're too bloody useless to take me down with your own hands?" Conor's voice rasped with a contemptuous, mocking sarcasm. "I suppose it must feel good to have a gun in your hands, right, Robert? To be able to fire off something and know it's going to work for a change. You can take down a man like Desi Moore with a couple of shots, and mutilate him when he can't fight back. You can ruin what other people have—love, decency, honor—and pretend it compensates for what you can't do on your own."

"Shut the fuck up." In his fury, Durgan began to shake like a man with a fever, but he seemed transfixed and Kate had also frozen in place, each of them immobilized by Conor's litany of abuse.

"You couldn't keep faith with your Irish brothers, you couldn't be a criminal without getting caught. You thought you had my brother by the balls, but in the end Thomas ran circles around you and you didn't even know. How's that make you feel, Robert? Inadequate? That's the root of your problem, right? You think I don't know? You can't start anything, or keep it going, or finish it off without having the whole lot melt into a soft pile of shite."

Durgan lunged forward with a grating sob, and Conor was ready. He turned and dropped down to meet the charge, driving his shoulder into Durgan's mid-section. The gun flew from his hand as they went down together, but Conor couldn't maintain the advantage. Durgan suddenly twisted and flipped him onto his back, cracking his head against the ground.

Kate heard his cry of pain and could not keep her promise to stand still. She ran forward and picked up the gun while Conor, eyes squeezed shut, grappled his opponent into a clinch hold. He opened his eyes, and seeing her with the gun pointed at Durgan's back his face stretched in horror.

"Kate, no. For God's sake, don't do it."

Arms still locked around Durgan, he gave a mighty heave and rolled away from her, but then they kept rolling, and Kate saw the consequence of her broken promise. As she numbly watched, they tumbled together down the steep island hillside, and over the cliff.

Years earlier, Kate had seen the man she loved fall away from her, and without a second thought—really, without any thought at all—she'd plunged into the water after him. This time, she didn't. Because she was older, wiser? More afraid? Because taking a dive from a boat into deep water was not the same assurance of death as taking one off a cliff? It wasn't for any of these reasons. She resisted running down the hill and over the edge, not because she was afraid to die, but because she was already dead—incapable of any decision, any emotion or sensation, or action. Dropping the gun, Kate fell slowly to the ground and remained there, cold as stone and just as insensible, until Sedgwick found her.

When it arrived, as she would learn later, the only place the Coast Guard helicopter could have possibly landed was on the beach, but that was useless because the strand was too far away from her. Instead, the aircraft hovered overhead, several hundred feet away from Kate. Sedgwick was lowered on a hoist, and sprinted to her side just as she began to register the deafening roar of the rotors. He cradled her head with his ear to her mouth, straining to catch the mumbled details amidst her gibberish. As soon as he learned the most important fact, he raced to the edge of the cliff, scanning the area below. After that he became frantic to go, but worked carefully and patiently to connect Kate to the harness. Once they'd been lifted up into the helicopter, she looked at Sedgwick's stricken face, and something shattered inside her.

"We'll find him, Kate." He put his arms around her, holding her tight as she sobbed. "We won't leave until we do. He's down there somewhere and we'll find him, and bring him home."

The first body proved easy to find. Robert Durgan had fallen about thirty feet onto a jagged outcrop and still lay balanced on the edge like a rag doll, his back quite obviously broken, his neck cocked at a gruesome angle.

Sedgwick shouted at the Coast Guard crew as they began preparing the hoist. "He's dead, for Christ's sake. We can all see it. Keep looking and go back for him later."

The helicopter's spotlight worked itself away from Durgan, traveling to his left and right and down the cliff, and Kate followed the beam as though hypnotized, unable to look away even while Sedgwick gently tried coaxing her from the window. There was no need. He wasn't there. The spotlight dug into every crevice, and began working itself out in a sweeping movement across the water.

"I've got something." One of the crew with night vision binoculars shot a hand into the air, signaling the helicopter to move in closer. "In the tidal pool, right below. Yeah, definitely a ... man." His glance hit Kate and quickly swiveled away. "Have we got a swimmer ready?"

"I'll get him," Sedgwick said quietly.

"You need a suit."

"No, I don't. Hurry up."

He was wrapped in Sedgwick's arms as the hoist slowly reeled them back from the sea. The agent bowed his head as they eased him inside, unable to meet Kate's eyes. She slipped from her seat and sank to the floor, taking Conor's hand as the medic scrambled into action. She thought he looked beautiful. His skin was the color of marble, perfectly smooth, his dark lashes wet and glistening. Miraculously, there wasn't a mark on him. A minute later, more miraculous still, Conor began to cough.

36

The water came out of him in prodigious foaming gouts, and before long Conor was trying to talk while still fighting for air. "Jaysus ... the both of ye ... crying?" He looked at Sedgwick in tender bemusement, and then at Kate with fierce, operational urgency. "Where is he?"

Sedgwick answered for her, wiping his eyes. "Bent double over a chunk of cliff. Backwards. They're mobilizing another chopper from Dublin to pick him up."

"No. Get him now."

"Easy, Conor. He's dead. Somehow, you're not. The hospital's not far. We're already over the mainland."

"Go back. Get him now." Conor became so agitated his vital signs began swinging wildly, alarming the young, redheaded medic.

"I'm trying to stabilize him, for fuck's sake. If that's what he wants, go back and get him."

The pilot turned to Kate, and then all of them did, ceding the decision to her.

"Yes. Go back."

She understood the source of this superstitious compulsion. She'd already seen the grisly sight of her husband, tangled on the rocks. He might haunt her dreams for a while but he wasn't coming back this time. He couldn't hurt them anymore, and Conor deserved to see it for himself. He'd paid for the privilege.

The county seat of Tralee was a busy market town, but as the Coast Guard helicopter touched down in a field next to the local hospital Kate guessed the residents probably didn't often experience such sights. This was her second emergency air transport in as many months, and as before, Conor got whisked from sight with only vague explanations. The concussion was a concern, and given the amount of water he'd aspirated, his temperamental lungs were also a priority.

She took her customary spot on a padded plastic chair in the waiting room. They looked the same all over the world. This time she had Sedgwick for company—when he wasn't chain-smoking in the parking lot—along with some dark-suited phantoms who by now were entirely recognizable.

"Frank's working his network." Sedgwick nodded at one of the suits positioned at the emergency room door. "No news is getting out of this place tonight if he can help it." He bit a cheese and tomato sandwich in half, and swallowed the remainder in the next bite. "Unbelievable how much better the food is here, and I got that out of the vending machine. Do you want one?"

"Actually, I do. I'm starving."

Between the two of them, they made a healthy dent in the vending machine inventory before Sedgwick sat back and gave Kate one of his better smiles.

"So. How do you like me now?"

"You're my hero. Forever," she said, without sarcasm.

"Don't get carried away." He laughed. "You don't know me that well."

"I think I know all I need to." She passed him a bag of M&Ms. "Tell me how you found us."

"Of course I figured something had gone wrong, just wasn't sure how bad it was. Always safer to assume the worst, so I didn't risk the phone call." Sedgwick drained his can of soda and reached for another from the three lined up on the low table in front of them. "I got a taxi to take me all the way to the house. I go inside and it's empty, smells like puke. Your bags are there. Weird, cut up cord on the living room floor. I get back in the taxi, trying to figure out what to do next when the guy's radio starts going crazy about all these flares that just went up off the coast near Slea Head. Didn't take a genius. I mean, how much goes on in freakin' Dingle on an average night? I called Frank and he got busy, and about thirty minutes later the Coast Guard picked me up off the beach in Ventry Bay. So, that's me. How was your day?" He gave her an apologetic shrug. "I don't mean to pressure you, but I've got to leave soon and catch a military transport back to Andrews."

After she'd told the other half of the story, Sedgwick went to the nurse's station to demand a visit with Conor before leaving. He returned with encouraging news. "I think he's all right. Wouldn't stay awake for me, though. Some kind of gratitude, right? I told the staff to put a cot in his room, should be ready for you in a few minutes. You look exhausted, Kate."

"So do you. Don't leave," she pleaded. "Can't they give you a few days off?"

"Not likely. The DEA had me on administrative leave for months. They started sending alerts a week ago to report to the mother ship for active duty, but I've been ignoring them. I called in an hour ago to some dickhead who said if I don't show by noon tomorrow they'd start an investigation. Fine by me. I've got things I'd love to get off my chest, but I imagine we'll all be a lot happier with my resignation."

"You're going to quit the DEA?" Kate's eyes widened.

"Yeah. I think I'm better off on my own."

"What will you do instead?"

He gave her a sly wink and a bashful peck on the cheek before heading for the door. "Don't worry about me. I've got a bucket list."

When she came into his room Conor was sleeping soundly, with a merciful absence of high-tech tubes and wires to worry her, but he was still very pale. She curled up on the cot against the wall and focused on every breath, listening for the faintest wheeze. Before long, her concentration put her to sleep. When she opened her eyes again he was sitting on the cot beside her, dressed and shaved, all trace of pallor gone.

"Sorry, but it's ten o'clock in the morning and they're kicking us out." He smiled, running a hand along her arm. "My brain didn't swell and my lungs didn't fill. I'm a right disappointment and they're bored rigid with me. Sounds like you've caught cold, though. How do you feel?"

Not terribly well, she had to admit. Her ears and nose were blocked solid, and her head felt three times its normal size. "Stay away from me," she croaked.

He laughed and scooped her into his arms. "No."

For the next several days, Kate was rarely out his arms. He'd paid no attention to her, thank God, because she couldn't have endured him staying away. She needed the constant reminder of his presence—that he hadn't gone from her, that he wasn't dead or missing or floating someplace where she couldn't find him. She never had to search for him. Intuitively, Conor seemed to understand what she needed, and was never far away.

In addition to being grounded by her miserable head cold, he'd been strongly advised to stay off airplanes for the next seven to ten days. They returned to the house in Ventry, and she became the compliant invalid for a change while he heated up bowl after bowl of the most delicious vegetable soup she'd ever tasted—a national recipe, he assured her. One evening, she sat on the couch, wrapped in a quilt and drowsing on his shoulder, while he peeled an orange and chivalrously ignored her stuffy red nose and the reek of Vapo-Rub. In the background, the RTE's Lyric station was featuring a program of Sinatra music.

"Now I have an idea of how your violin feels," Kate said. "I've always admired how beautifully you take care of her."

"Have you?" He slipped a slice of the orange into her mouth. "Well, you're quite like the Pressenda. Rare. Beautiful. Full of old-world character, and not nearly as fragile as some might think."

"I wish you had it here to play for me. I feel as though I need ... something." She closed her eyes for a minute, listening to the music, and opened them to face the fire dancing in the open hearth—observing the shades of red, slivers of green, and a line of flickering blue along the bottom. What was it? That particular color? Smalt-blue. Yes. The earliest of the cobalt pigments.

"Conor?"

"Hmm?" He'd been about to feed her another piece of orange, but pulled his hand back.

"I need paint."

37

He was the wonder of the modern age. The stuff of legend. The man who'd plunged from the Blasket cliffs and lived to tell the tale. Conor just thanked his lucky stars and Frank Emmons Murdoch that nobody in the world knew it was him. He heard the story at Eileen Graham's tiny grocer's shop in Ventry village, and at the pub where he got the soup Kate couldn't get enough of, and on the sidewalk outside the Dingle art supply store where she sent him on a regular basis, with a list.

Sometimes, the story was romantic tragedy—it was a couple of lads from Ballyferriter, in a fight to the death over a girl. Other times, it was tragicomic—two drunk American eejits on a lark, stole the Dunquin ferry and brought out the Coast Guard and who was going to pay for that, now? Whatever the version, everyone was delighted to see him and fill him in on the news, too full of their own local wonders to question his vague report of his whereabouts over the past year.

After a week at the house in Ventry, he and Kate had agreed to stay for another before heading back to Vermont. Conor estimated they were stretching to the limit what Abigail was willing to endure before catching a flight for Shannon and turning up on the doorstep. He'd needed all his persuasive charm to talk her out of doing exactly that when he'd called at the beginning of the week. Over the course of an hour-long conversation, he'd provided a general account—somewhat sanitized—of what had been happening, while she gave extensive instructions for the care of Kate, further advice on the treatment of concussion, and a recipe for her chicken soup, which he'd pretended to write down.

"It's lonesome here without the two of you." Abigail's gruff emotion made him realize how much he missed her, too, along with everything else to do with the new life he'd begun in that spectacular country setting.

"We'll be home soon, Abigail," he promised. "Keep the kettle on for me."

Frank arrived at the beginning of their second week, unannounced and unexpected as always, presenting the deed to the house as he walked in the door.

"With my gratitude, Conor," he said simply.

They sat in the living room, in the same two chairs they'd occupied on the first day of their acquaintance, but this time Conor brought out the Jameson's instead of tea.

"Where is our Kate?" Frank's expressive eyebrow lifted in concern. "I hope she's not unwell?"

"She was pretty unwell last week, but better now. She's upstairs working in Thomas's old room." Conor handed Frank his drink. "She's started painting again."

"Ah, marvelous."

"I've been at the art store in Dingle half a dozen times now, collecting little aluminum tubes, canvases, brushes. I'd no notion how many different kinds of brush you need to paint anything."

"I'd love to view some of her canvases." Frank smiled at Conor's dubious frown. "Won't she let me?"

"I don't think she's ready to bring them out for general display."

"But you've seen them."

"I have.

"And?" Frank asked.

"Stunning, and I mean that literally. She's got incredible talent Frank, but Jaysus, these are pretty dark."

"Does that worry you?"

Conor considered the question. "No. I suppose not, actually. Better on a canvas than boiling away inside her. I think that's why she couldn't paint at all for so long. She must have had an idea it would come out like this—why wouldn't it? Kate doesn't trade much in darkness. She had to give herself permission."

Frank took an appreciative sip from his glass, regarding Conor fondly. "The two of you are well suited."

"Well suited," Conor repeated with a private smile. "I hope so. Feels that way to me, anyway. I hope you're planning to stay, Frank. I can't promise much for supper, we're neither of us any use in the kitchen, but you're very welcome. She'll be sore with us both if I interrupt her, but she'll be gutted if she doesn't get to see you."

"I'd be delighted. I'll cook, I'm rather good at it."

"I'm not surprised." Conor grinned, and then sighed. "So, let's have the rest, now. You didn't come all this way to cook for us. Please God, it won't give me a headache. Took me all of a week getting rid of the last one."

"I've not come to test or torment you, but hopefully to tempt you." Frank removed a thick manila folder from his ubiquitous leather briefcase and laid it on the table. Just looking at the buff-colored card stock turned Conor's stomach. Frank covered the folder with his hand, recognizing his distress. "I beg your pardon, my boy. Thoughtless of me. It's nothing explosive, nothing at all to do with you. Only a few documents I'd like to leave for you to read at your leisure."

"About what?"

"Read them later. A matter of some interest to us in Eastern Europe. You've been to that region, I believe?"

Conor gave him a jaded look. "You know I have. You're

my biggest groupie. I did a recording session with the Prague Philharmonic Orchestra."

"Prague. Indeed." Frank beamed. "As it happens, Eckhard will be conducting in Prague next spring. He's in the market for a soloist. I am in the market for a cover agent. We've discussed this rather extensively, as a collaborative opportunity." He placed his glass on the table and straightened in his chair, discarding the light, bantering tone. "We want to work with you, Conor, both of us, obviously for different reasons. You are talented, magnificently so. Your combination of skills comes once in a generation in the intelligence community, if we're lucky. You needn't answer now, but will you at least consider the idea?"

A devil's bargain. Sign on for undercover work and do things he probably wouldn't like, in exchange for the opportunity to do what he'd always wanted. Conor wasn't sure if he was tempted or not, but it wasn't a decision he'd make alone.

"I'll think about it if you want me to, but I won't keep this from Kate. I won't ever keep anything from her again, so you should consider that before leaving your folder with me."

"Fair enough." Frank tapped the manila folder. "Show her the file."

"Seriously? I didn't think these things worked that way. Suppose she wants to come along? I couldn't keep her home this time."

"We'll train her," Frank responded immediately.

Conor stared, horrified. "The hell you will. That's not what I meant and certainly not what I want."

"Well. Rather up to her, don't you think?"

Conor bit his lip, smiling. After all this time, he was still so naive. "You thought this all the way through before you came, didn't you? You've got some fairly impressive skills yourself, boss."

"I do like to think so."

On a cold, sunlit afternoon the day before they left, Conor dug a full-length oilskin coat out of the closet for Kate and drove them out along Dingle Bay, back around the hairpin turn at Slea Head, and brought them down to a spot on the shoreline where they could look out at the Great Blasket, lush and serene now under a cloudless sky.

"I wanted you to see it in daylight," Conor explained. "It's where my mother was born. I took her over for the last time a year ago this July, when she was still feeling good. She still remembered everything. Seems like they had a name for every rock and gully on the whole island, and she knew them all."

"We'll take it back," Kate said, giving his hand a squeeze. "We'll go out again someday and take it back for her."

"Smudge sticks?" Conor smiled.

"Definitely. We'll need a lot of them." After a moment she added, "What happened to you out there? Do you remember anything? We never talked about it."

He'd asked himself the same question every day for two weeks, and still had no answer. "To be honest, I don't have a clue. We went over together. I remember crashing onto a ledge on top of him and then falling, and hearing a voice. I've thought about this a lot, because it went on way too long to make any sense. I should have hit the side of the cliff, or the rocks at the bottom. I should have hit something. But, there was only space, and the voice, and then nothing. Next thing, I opened my eyes and there was Sedgwick, blubbering over me."

"What did the voice say?"

"*Muinín dom.*" Conor swallowed. "Trust me."

He didn't need to ask. Kate gave him a quick kiss and left him alone. Walking down the sloping field to a large smooth boulder, she sat down facing the island. After a few minutes of wandering inside his own head he noticed her again. The dark copper gleam of her hair lifted in the breeze above the black oilskin, irrepressible, reminding him of how Kate seemed to be her own form of light—a new, undiscovered element illuminating the universe around her. Illuminating him.

She slipped an arm around his as he joined her on the boulder. "I would have pulled the trigger," she said quietly. "You knew that, and didn't want me to. I've wondered why, and thought maybe you were trying to protect me. You didn't want me to have that on my conscience, his blood on my hands."

"Oh." Conor scratched at his chin. "Ehm ..."

"That's not it?" She turned to him, surprised. "Well, tell me why, then."

"It was point blank range, Kate. You'd have sent the bullet through him and straight into me. I thought I had a better chance with the cliff."

She stared at him, at first appalled, but then gave a snuffling gurgle. He snickered, choked while trying to stop, and before long they had tumbled from the boulder together, paralyzed by laughter.

"Oh dear," she groaned, wiping her eyes. "I have a lot to learn if I'm going to keep hanging around with you."

Conor pulled her from the cold ground and rolled her up on top of him. "Ditto." He looked out again at the Great Blasket, thinking of everything he'd lost and gained, and about Frank's proposal for the future.

A devil's bargain? Probably. So, what else was new?

Acknowledgments

I would like to thank the following people for their assistance in making possible this latest installment in the adventures of Conor McBride: Margaret Candelori, Holly Gathright, Christopher Gibbs, Coleen Kearon, Janet Krol, Susan Z. Ritz and Shelagh Shapiro, for their ears and eyes and insightful feedback; Richard Lawhern, PhD, not only for insightful feedback but for his expertise on sailing technique, holster clips and everything in between; Michael Murphy, Chief of Police in Boxford, MA, and FBI Special Agent Robert G. Ross (ret.), for advice on making an irregular scenario more plausible; and of course my mother, Claire Guare, for always believing I could do it, and for getting all her friends to read my book. ♥